HARPER BLISS

Two Hearts TRILOGY

ladylit publishing

Other Harper Bliss Books

Next in Line for Love
A Lesson in Love
Life in Bits (with T.B. Markinson)
A Swing at Love (with Caroline Bliss)
No Greater Love than Mine
Once Upon a Princess (with Clare Lydon)
In the Distance There Is Light
The Road to You
Seasons of Love
Release the Stars
Once in a Lifetime
At the Water's Edge
The French Kissing Series
High Rise (The Complete Collection)

the Pink Bean Series

More Than Words
Crazy for You
Love Without Limits
No Other Love
Water Under Bridges
This Foreign Affair
Everything Between Us
Beneath the Surface
No Strings Attached

Published by Ladylit Publishing – a division of Q.P.S. Projects Limited - Hong Kong
ISBN-13 978-988-74415-3-3

To my wife, the Zoe to my Anna

The Two Hearts Trilogy
BOOK ONE

Two Hearts ALONE

1

ANNA

HEMINGWAY DOESN'T CARE that it's snowing outside. He sits by the front door, waiting for me. I've tried ignoring him for ten minutes, but even when I don't see him, I can still sort of see him. That sad, disappointed face with the dramatically droopy eyes, which he only ever puts on when I don't snap on his leash at 10 a.m. sharp.

But the mid-January cold seems to have seeped into my bones and the prospect of going outside fills me with more dread than usual.

"Remind me again why I got you?" I ask Hemingway.

He turns his face toward me and turns up the drama in his eyes, his snout pointing wistfully toward the door.

As soon as I grab my coat, Hemingway perks up. He wags his tail in anticipation.

"You and I," I mumble, "we're not the same. I wonder how we can even live together." I'm reminded of a podcast I listened to the other week, in which someone claimed that dogs used to walk themselves. But walking Hemingway is one of the reasons I got him in the first place. If I didn't have to take him out twice daily, I'd never leave my house most days. He's my connection to the outside world.

Hemingway gives an excited bark as I put on his leash. I find my warmest hat and gloves, and head into the snow.

The cold hits me hard in the face, but Hemingway is pulling on his leash, and I don't have time to feel sorry for myself. He tugs me forward along our usual route. I half-walk half-jog behind him, keeping my face down. Because Donovan Grove is the kind of town where people keep their driveways clear, it's not that hard to make my way along the sidewalk, but I do have to ask Hemingway to moderate his tempo for fear of slipping on the snow. It wouldn't be the first time. When I got him two years ago, in the middle of winter, I let his enthusiasm get the best of me a few times and paid for it by ending up face-down in the snow.

What I like most about Hemingway is that he's so utterly predictable. Every single day, he does his business on the same street corner—and I dispose of it in the doggy waste bin that was put there especially for Hemingway's needs by the Donovan Grove council. I would never have requested a waste bin myself, but for some reason my mother felt it necessary. So, there it is.

"Good boy, Hem." I give him a scratch behind the ear and, in return, he gives me a look filled with such love it almost makes me forget about the cold.

We continue our walk. The streets are quiet, even Main Street where usually a few shoppers dwell. I follow Hemingway's paw prints on the thin layer of snow that has fallen since the sidewalk was last shoveled. Then I slowly get used to the cold and I lift my head up a little higher. This is how it goes every single day in winter. Getting out of the house is the hardest part, but once I'm out, I try to enjoy the walk as much as Hemingway does.

The familiarity of my surroundings soothes me. The

window displays in the stores change as we cycle through every season, but that's about it. When we reach the end of Main Street, I do notice something different. Bookends, the bookstore that's been empty for months, has a light on inside.

And not just that, but a big heart's been spray-painted onto the window.

"Oh no," I mumble, making Hemingway stop in his tracks. "Don't tell me the old bookstore will be turning into some cheesy gift shop."

I peer through the window and I can hardly believe my eyes. Granted, it's been a while since I actually looked through the window, since the place has been boarded up for months, but still, the transformation from derelict bookstore to whatever this is, is impressive.

The old, dark bookshelves have been painted with bright colors and stacks of books are waiting to find their place. My heart does a little jump at the prospect of the bookstore reopening, but then my gaze is drawn to the big heart on the window again. Inside it, also spray-painted, someone—presumably the new owner—has written: *Valentine's Day is coming!*

I only got rid of my Christmas tree last week—always a bit of a sad event. Not only because I love the coziness of Christmas, but also because soon enough, and the evidence is already glaring straight at me, I'll be reminded of how society believes it's awful and pitiful that I'm single. It's bad enough already that my mother thinks so, although she has gotten a bit better at hiding her dismay.

"Can you believe this?" I mutter under my breath, my words visible in the small cloud that emanates from my mouth. But Hemingway doesn't care. He just wants to get on with his walk.

"We'll go in a second," I reassure him, not that he understands. I look past the ridiculous drawing and words on the window and try to see more of the store inside. Mrs. Fincher, who ran the bookstore until she retired last summer, always had a recommendation for me whenever I came in—and I did often. The closing of the old Bookends left a gaping hole in my schedule for a long time. But Mrs. Fincher, especially after Mr. Fincher passed away, hated Valentine's Day as much as I do, and she would never have disgraced her store window with a ludicrous drawing of a heart. In fact, I'd wager, if she were to walk past right now and notice it, she might have a heart attack, just like her husband did.

"This is basically a health hazard," I say, but Hemingway still doesn't care. He has calmed down now and sits quietly by my side, glancing around.

I see some movement in the shop. A young woman—she can't be older than Jaden, my nephew—is hauling a big box.

The sight of another human is enough to make me back away from the window and continue my walk swiftly.

2

ZOE

"SOMEONE WEIRD WAS JUST LOOKING INSIDE," Brooklyn says. "They hurried off as soon as they saw me though."

"A future satisfied customer, no doubt." I have to keep my own spirits up as well as my daughter's.

"There isn't much else in this town, so sure, Mom." At least Brooklyn's trying today, as opposed to yesterday, when I could barely get her out of bed. The move from Queens to upstate New York is much harder on her, especially because it's happening in the middle of the school year. Things have not gone down the way either of us had planned.

"It will take some time, sweetie," I repeat. It seems to have become my mantra. Things will change for you as soon as you start school again, I add in my head. If I were to say it out loud, it wouldn't go down well. The changing of schools is still a very sore subject—which I do understand.

Brooklyn looks around the store, which is a mess. We only removed the shutters last night. The first thing I did this morning was paint an obnoxiously big heart on the window. I refuse to let my lonely heart make me cynical—or I can at least pretend that it doesn't.

"That you gave up your cushy Amazon job for this," Brooklyn says on a sigh.

"Come here, *mija*." I hold out my hand to her. She just stares at it. I bridge the distance between us and take her hand in mine. "I know this is hard. It's the middle of winter, Mama just left, and we're in this brand-new town where we don't know anyone, but…" I pull her a little closer. "You have me. Your mom. And we're going to make the best of it; that's what we Perez women do. And you know what? In the end, it will be amazing."

"If you say so." She hugs me back a little, which is the most I can expect from my fifteen-year-old under the circumstances.

"Once the store is open, we'll meet lots of people." Which is why I want to get it ready for opening as quickly as possible. I had hoped to be able to open for business in a few days, but with how things are looking right now, it might actually take a couple of weeks.

"God knows what they'll be like." Brooklyn grumbles it more than she says it.

Her hand is still in mine as I lead her to the window. "Look at it," I say. "Isn't it picture-perfect?"

Brooklyn just shrugs. Maybe I did ask too much of her. Maybe I should have stuck it out in Queens, and everything it came to stand for, until she finished high school.

I look out the window, taking in Donovan Grove's Main Street. There's the diner across the street, where we will go for lunch later, after we've unpacked a few more boxes. There's the hardware store and the mini-mart and the bakery, all filled with people we've yet to meet. A happy mother will always make for a happier child, I repeat in my head.

A man and a woman walk past the window and briefly stop. The woman gives a quick wave, then they're back on their way through the snow that keeps on falling. Bernard, who owns the candy store next door, was quick to tell me that not clearing the sidewalk in front of your dwelling could result in grumbling neighbors, of which, I got the impression he surely would be one if I didn't get my shovel out quickly. So I've tasked Brooklyn with keeping the sidewalk as clear as possible. If this snow keeps up, she'll have to go out again soon.

"Do you want to call Marsha and Juan?" I ask, referring to our friends back in Queens, the ones that were hardest to leave behind.

Brooklyn's body releases some tension. "That's okay, Mom," she says. "We have shit to get done." She wriggles her hand loose from my grasp and opens a box. She sighs the sort of sigh only a teenager can get away with. "Where do you want these?" She holds up a pack of bright-red Valentine's Day cards.

"We need to put the rack together first. I'm not sure it's a job for two women on their own." I hold my smile.

"Oh yes, it is. There's not a job in this place the two of us can't get done." The sullenness in her voice has been replaced by feistiness. "Where is it?"

I point at a box close to the door. As my gaze sweeps around the store, I am briefly reminded of what Brooklyn called 'my cushy Amazon job'. It might have paid well, but it was far from cushy or comfortable. This store might be a mess, but as Brooklyn just said, it's nothing we can't handle. It will take some elbow grease and a lot of energy, but this is the beginning of our new life together, in a brand-new town—Donovan Grove, where there happened to be a bookstore for sale just as I started looking for one. Just as I started to gently contemplate a different life for us. So here we are.

Brooklyn's tearing open the box. "Just because I'm putting together this rack," she says, "doesn't mean I approve of you selling this sappy, capitalist crap."

"We give people what they want," I counter. "So we can make a living."

"This is not what people want, Mom. Maybe when you were young they did, but Valentine's Day is simply not woke."

"Ouch, girl."

"I bet you that no one of my age will buy one of those cards."

"Oh really?"

"Just retired people. And men who have something to make up for with their wives," she says.

"So young, yet so cynical." I flatten the cardboard box she just tore open.

"I guess that's what happens when your other mother decides to no longer give a f—" She stops herself before I can chastise her for swearing. "To not care about you any longer."

"Eve does care, baby. She loves you." I have to say these things, even though I could have strangled Eve when she told us that she was moving abroad months earlier than planned. The moving abroad alone was enough of a punch in the gut for Brooklyn, but making her change her plans—making her move out here with me much earlier than anticipated—was like pulling the rug from underneath her feet entirely.

Brooklyn rolls her eyes. "Let's not do this again. If she really cared, she wouldn't be where she is right now."

"I know, baby. I know." I look at the rack we're trying to assemble, hoping to distract her.

"It's just for a year," Eve said, when she first told us she was moving to Shanghai.

"A year is still twelve months of your daughter's life that you'll miss," I said.

Because Eve was going to be away for a year, we agreed that Brooklyn would stay with her in the city, while I got settled in Donovan Grove. That way, Brooklyn could make the move in the summer and she'd get to spend some extra quality time with her other parent. Now, she's had to move out here with hardly any notice, while her other mother lives the high life in Asia. It's hardly fair on Brooklyn, but it's how it is.

"I can do this on my own." Brooklyn squats down.

"But you don't have to." I crouch down next to her and give her a hand.

3

ANNA

"I've seen them around," Sean says, when I inform him of Bookends' imminent reopening. "A foxy lady and her teenage daughter."

I raise an eyebrow at the word 'foxy'. If any other man had uttered it, I might be offended, but not when Sean does.

"You know what I mean." Sean shrugs. "And for your information, I used the exact same word when I described the new woman to Cathy." He bends to pet Hemingway, who is sitting next to him, waiting for the treat Sean always gives him.

"Anything I need to know about?" I bring the topic of conversation back to business.

"I really don't know, Anna. I've just seen them walking around town. I really don't know if she's—"

"What are you talking about?"

"The new Bookends owner. What are *you* talking about?"

Hemingway puts his head on Sean's knee.

"I was talking about business, of course."

"Ah," he says pointedly. "You pulled an Anna. You moved on without telling me."

"Don't call it that. People do that all the time."

"Sure." He looks at his screen. "Nothing new. The Lindsay Hare cover is due tomorrow, but..." He narrows his eyes as he focuses on his screen. "You've sent it to me already."

"If it's not early, it's late." I repeat what I always say.

"Hm," is all Sean replies. "Nothing new. Things are usually a bit slow in January."

"At least we didn't get any Valentine's Day related orders this year." I shake my head. "I think the new Bookends is betting big on V-Day this year."

"Really? I'll have to hop in then. Surprise my lady."

"It's not open yet," I say dryly.

"It's not Valentine's Day yet."

"Thank goodness for that."

"Hey, when the day comes, you should spend it here. There's always a free desk for you here, Anna. You know that."

"What are you saying? That I shouldn't be left alone on the most stupid, over-commercialized holiday—if you can even call it that—ever?"

"Um, no, that's not what I mean at all," Sean says.

"Well, you know I only work from home, so..." Sean should consider himself lucky that I pop in a few times a week to have a quick chat.

"Hm." He's an expert in giving monosyllabic replies. He finally reaches for the drawer where he keeps the dog treats. Hemingway's ears perk up immediately.

"We'll be off then," I say, after Hemingway has devoured a few dog biscuits.

"Bye, handsome boy," Sean says, then looks at me. "I was talking to Hemingway."

"Give my love to your better half." I close the door behind me and brace for the cold again.

A few years ago, Sean expanded the office he rents into a co-working space. I'm not sure where he got the idea that I wanted to share an office with anyone, even him, but I made quick work of telling him that he'd better rent out the desk he was saving for me as well.

At first, it was mainly just him in the office, but these days, even Donovan Grove has more and more people working from home who just want to get out of the house a few days a week. To show my support, I gave him a few paintings to hang on the walls, and offered a couple of other interior design tips, which he sorely needed, but that's as far as my physical co-working with anyone will go. Sean and I co-own a graphic and web design business, and that's more than enough collaboration for me to handle.

Ideally, I'd work alone, but I need someone like Sean to deal with the people side of the business, not that his people skills are so stellar, but at least he doesn't mind doing it. Sometimes, I swear he believes he's good at it. He must have some expertise because we haven't gone out of business yet, even though we both realize our small company won't ever make us rich—or even well-off. I'm fine with that. I make a mental note to check in with Sean if he still is—it's been a while since I've done that.

Sean's a good guy that I've known all my life, whom I consider my best friend. I can trust him and we have a good set-up going.

I snicker at the memory of Sean calling the new Bookends owner 'foxy'. Personally, I haven't had the pleasure of running into any new townsfolk that could be considered foxy. What else did he say? A mother and daughter? It must've been the daughter I caught a glimpse of when I looked into the store window. Usually, it's families with two point four kids who are sick of city life that move to Donovan Grove and the surrounding towns. Usually, they don't take over bookstores either. Mrs. Fincher might have been ready to retire, but she didn't exactly leave a thriving business behind.

As I make my way home from Sean's office, I keep my eyes peeled for any unfamiliar faces. Donovan Grove isn't that small a town and there are thousands of people who live here that I don't know, yet someone new is always easy to spot. There's the sense of unfamiliarity in their gaze. And sometimes, oh horror, they're so keen to make eye contact because they want to meet the locals—and walking around with Hemingway makes me an easy target. If I had my way, I'd go on my daily walk without talking to anyone, but, except for the year I thought I'd try to make it in the big city and failed miserably, I've lived here all my life and that automatically makes me acquainted with too many people eager for a chat.

"How's Hemingway?" they ask.

"He doesn't reply when I ask him," I always think, but never say out loud.

I'm almost home and it doesn't seem as though I'll need my voice anymore today. Despite the too early display of Valentine's Day eagerness, I'm happy that Bookends is reopening. I believe in supporting local businesses—being co-owner of one myself, even though ninety-five percent of our business is conducted on the internet—and having to shop online for books hasn't been the same.

I do wonder if the 'foxy lady' will have any recommendations at the ready. She must be a reader. Otherwise, taking over a bookstore in a mid-size town wouldn't make any sense at all.

I can see my house now, with its bright red front door. Every single time I approach my home, something inside me flutters. I've spent years and all the money I've ever earned on making it just right for Hemingway and me. Most days, I don't need anything but the coziness of my house and the company of my dog.

4

ZOE

An older woman I've seen walk by a few times stops in front of the store window. She taps the glass with a fingertip. I wave to beckon her in, which is clearly what she wants.

The door is unlocked and she breezes inside, bringing in a gust of icy wind. Somehow, the air feels colder here than it did in Queens.

"Hi." Her lips are stretched into a wide smile. "I'm Sherry Gunn. I just wanted to introduce myself. I'm so excited this store is reopening. For the longest time, it looked like it would be empty forever." She offers me her hand.

"Hi Sherry. I'm Zoe Perez. Thanks so much for stopping by." I'm just glad for the opportunity to strike up a conversation with another adult. "I've seen you walk by a couple of times."

Sherry nods. "I didn't want to disturb you before, but it looks like you're almost ready to open." She glances around the shop. "I love what you've done to the place."

"Thank you." Our days of unpacking and redecorating are finally paying off. "The store will open this weekend. I'm very excited. Just waiting on a few last-minute deliveries."

"My daughter's going to be thrilled that Bookends is back," Sherry says. "She always has her nose in a book. She was crushed when Mrs. Fincher retired. I told her. 'Anna,' I said, 'maybe this is a sign. This is your chance to own your very own bookstore.' But she just likes to read books, not sell them."

"In that case, I can't wait to meet her."

"I'm sure you will soon enough. How are you settling in? You're new to town, aren't you?"

"My daughter and I moved here from Queens a few weeks ago. It's quite the change. Brooklyn's starting at Donovan Grove High on Monday. She's a bit nervous, as you can imagine."

"How old is she?" Sherry asks.

"Just turned fifteen."

"Same age as my grandson Jaden. Tell you what. I'll try to pop into the store with him when you open on Saturday... Maybe Brooklyn would like to meet someone who goes to DG High before she starts?"

"That would be so lovely, Mrs. Gunn. I'm sure she would appreciate that."

"Oh, please, call me Sherry. Mrs. Gunn makes me feel so ancient." She cocks her head. "It's a personal point of pride for me that Donovan Grove is a welcoming town. Have you seen the noticeboard in the grocery store? Every few months, we try to get people who are new to town together at Lenny's, the local bar, which is just down the street from here."

"Wow." I haven't seen the sign. I've been far too occupied with getting accustomed to a new store—where you still pay an actual cashier at the checkout. "That's so lovely. Do a lot of people turn up to these things?"

"It depends. We don't get that much new blood into Donovan Grove anymore these days. The odd family escaping the rat race, perhaps, but they tend to keep more to themselves. Parents with young children in a new town are usually quite busy. But if and when we do have someone move to our lovely town, we treat them well. Most people who leave the city prefer the more picturesque towns, or somewhere smaller than here. Somehow, the Grove is always somewhat overlooked. But we do our best."

Sherry is a well of information. And an excellent first point of contact in Donovan Grove, it would appear. "I'll see you at the next meet-up then."

"You'll see me before that. On Saturday. For the grand opening." Sherry looks around with what I think is approval.

"Of course. I hope Jaden will make it. Is he your daughter Anna's son?"

"Oh, no. Anna doesn't have any children. Jaden is my son Jamie's child. He has a younger boy named Jeremy as well. His wife's name's Janet. They like the letter J in that family, as you can tell. They even have a cat named Jazz." She shakes her head briefly.

I smile at her. "I can't wait to meet them all."

"Anna's not going to be fond of that big heart on your window, though. Every single year, the same speech. Even when she was still with Cynthia, she would rail against it. It's kind of her thing. She simply cannot stand Valentine's Day and being who she is, she can't just let it slide." Sherry straightens her posture. "But they're my children and I must accept them, quirks and all." Sherry gives me the kind of smile that implies she would accept anything from her children. The kind of smile that radiates motherly love—and that seems to extend to new people in her town as well.

I decide on the spot that I like Sherry and her very forward but welcoming way.

"I'll let you get on with things. Unless you need a hand?"

"That's very kind of you, Sherry. But as you can see, we're as good as ready to go. But thank you so much for stopping by. I really appreciate it."

"I think you'll do well here," she says. "In fact, I know it." With that, she turns and is out of the door, stepping into the freezing cold without hesitation.

It's only when Sherry has been gone a few minutes and I've had the chance to mull over our conversation in my head that I realize she just outed her daughter to me. Anna has an ex-girlfriend named Cynthia. No children. Sherry basically gave me the lowdown on her entire family in the span of five minutes—and from what I understand, her daughter isn't straight. Things are looking up already—and I haven't even opened the store yet.

With a spring in my step, I start stacking the books in the Self-Help section.

5

ANNA

"OH, ANNA," Mom says, then stops. It's as if she can only stop herself from saying something when the words are already coming out of her mouth.

I know what she was about to say, however. It's only recently that she has stopped expressing utter despair over how I choose to dress and style—or rather not style—my hair. She cuts her gaze away from me and I ignore her unsaid comment. I'm nervous enough as it is. I'm not sure why my mother insisted I join her at the opening of Bookends—it's not as though I received a formal invitation or anything. And a gathering of more than two people I don't know will always agitate me. But she insisted and, over the years, I've learned to compromise—to give her what little I have to offer as a daughter. Showing up to Bookends is, in many other ways, easy enough. I walk past here every day and I love bookshops. So much so that my curiosity almost wins over my anxiety.

Until I spot, in the corner opposite me, perusing the Young Adult section, the last person I want to see.

"Oh shit. Cynthia's here."

"You two still get along, don't you?" Mom says. I'm

surprised she's even listening—surprised that she hasn't yet wandered off to mingle because, unlike me, she must know every single person here.

"I wouldn't call it that."

"It's been two years since you guys broke up, Anna," Mom says. "You should be able to deal with bumping into her unexpectedly."

I just nod, even though I disagree. Cynthia is quite possibly the kindest and most patient person I've ever met, yet I managed to drive her away. I will never be able to deal with my failure as a partner and seeing her will always remind me of that.

"That woman over there." Mom points at a woman balancing a tray of cupcakes on her hand while smiling widely at everyone she turns to. She looks very glossy—dark, bouncy hair like she's just stepped out of a shampoo commercial and perfect, light brown skin—in a long, flowy dress. Much too glam for Donovan Grove. Or maybe her appearance makes me feel extra frumpy. "She's the new owner. Her name's Zoe. I met her the other the day."

"Of course you did." If anything, I admire my mother's ability to strike up a conversation with anyone. It's just a pity that none of that ever rubbed off on me.

"She's lovely. I must introduce you. I imagine you'll become one of her best customers."

"Sure." I always cringe when my mother wants to introduce me to someone. And I haven't forgotten my first glimpse of the new Bookends. The big sappy heart painted onto the window way too soon—and too inappropriately. I wonder if a woman so fond of something as inauthentic as Valentine's Day can ever recommend a book I will enjoy reading.

Just then, I see Cynthia is making her way toward us.

"Stick around," I whisper to my mother. I know it makes me

sound like an insecure teenager, but that's actually pretty much how I feel. "Cynthia's coming over."

"Sherry." Cynthia greets my mother first—something I can hardly blame her for. "How lovely to see you. It's been too long."

They hug as though they are long lost friends. Cynthia and I were together for the better part of six years, so in a way, they are.

"Anna. Hi," Cynthia says. "How are you?"

"Hi." I'm not one for exuberant greetings. Luckily, Cynthia knows this about me and she keeps her distance. "I'm fine. You?"

"I'm elated Bookends is reopening. Have you met Zoe?" Cynthia asks.

"Can't say that I have."

Cynthia narrows her eyes and gives me a look I can't decipher. "We should get together some time, Anna. It's been too long. We should catch up."

"What an excellent idea," Mom chimes in, making me regret asking her to stay. She still clings to the idle hope that Cynthia and I will get back together, even though it's been two years since we broke up.

"Sure. We'll set something up." I don't mean it, but I know that's what I'm supposed to say. Why would I open old wounds by meeting up with my ex?

"I'd like to talk to you about something," Cynthia says. "Something I'd like you to hear directly from me." She looks at her watch. "Want to go for a drink after this?"

"Hm, I don't think I can. Hemingway needs—"

My mother clears her throat. "I can take Hemingway for a walk."

"Why don't we walk Hemingway together?" Cynthia asks.

"Hi. Welcome to Bookends." The woman my mother pointed out to me earlier has appeared next to us, a huge smile plastered on her face. "Welcome back, Sherry," she says, instantly endearing herself to my mother.

Mom introduces us, and for a minute it's an awkward jumble of limply exchanged handshakes. Then, somehow, both Cynthia and Mom have their backs to us—someone they both know must have just walked in—and I find myself standing in front of Zoe on my own.

"Your mother promised me you'd be one of my best customers," Zoe says. Even her lips are shiny. Everything about her is so sparkly, I fear I might be blinded.

"I used to come here all the time." I know I should at least try a hint of eye contact, so I make the effort. Zoe's eyes are dark, but that's all I get from the first glimpse, before I feel compelled to look away.

"Then I hope to see you again soon," Zoe says.

"Are dogs welcome?" I ask.

For some reason, Zoe thinks this is a funny question. "Sure. Of course. I'm more of a cat person myself, but do bring your dog. Does he like to read?" She chuckles.

I chuckle along while suppressing an urgent question of my own: *What's with the obnoxious heart in your window display?*

"I'll stop by soon," I promise and watch as Zoe continues her lap through the crowd that has gathered in her new shop.

I'm still recovering from the brightness of her smile, and all of her appearance, when my mother turns back toward me.

"Even the mayor's here," she says. "Quite the turn-out."

"I think I'm going to go now."

"Already?" She gives me that concerned look I know so well.

"I've been here long enough. And I'll be back."

"Jamie isn't here yet with the kids," she says, followed by, "All right, sweetie. See you tomorrow." She kisses me very lightly on the cheek. "Enjoy your chat with Cynthia."

Surely she must know there will be nothing at all enjoyable about that chat for me. I wish it was over already, although I am curious as to what Cynthia has to tell me. It must be quite something if it's not suitable for an email, which is how we mainly dealt with each other after the break-up.

I cast one last glance into Bookends. Zoe stands out as though a spotlight is following her around, making sure all attention is focused on her. She's talking to the mayor now, engrossed in conversation with her as if she has known her forever. She's one of those, I think, as I walk home, my fists dug deep in my more shabby-than-chic pants pockets. One of those people that are the absolute opposite of me.

6

ZOE

"THAT WENT WELL." I turn to Brooklyn, who's collecting paper cups and plates.

"Not that many books sold."

I put her in charge of the register so I could focus on building a rapport with the people who stopped by today.

"Today wasn't about selling books. It was about networking." I kick off my heels because my feet are killing me. "Speaking of… you seemed to get along well with that boy." I waggle my eyebrows at her while I sit down on the bottom step of the stairs that lead to our apartment.

"Who?" Brooklyn tries to sound nonchalant, but I know the inflections in my daughter's voice like the back of my hand.

"That cute blond guy who kept hovering around the cash register. Did he at least buy something?"

"Oh, Jaden. He bought a card for his grandpa's birthday."

"Jaden?" The name sounds familiar. "Is he Sherry's grandson?"

Brooklyn shrugs. "I didn't really inquire about his family tree, Mom."

"Does he go to DG High?"

"Yeah." She drops the garbage bag she's been filling. "He said I'd see him there on Monday."

My lips draw into a smile. I pat the space next to me. "Come sit with your old Mom for a bit."

The look on her face is reluctant, but the way she leans into me after she sits is the opposite.

"Thank you for moving here with me. Doing this with you from the get-go makes it extra special."

"I suppose it'll be all right."

She has certainly changed her tune. She must really like Jaden. I throw my arm around her. "How about we clean this up tomorrow? Go for a walk through our new town and pick up a pizza?"

"Why don't you just say you don't feel like cooking me a nutritious meal." Brooklyn leans her head on my shoulder. It's been a long time since she has done that so I enjoy the moment —it might be the very last one ever. She's growing up so quickly now. Back in Queens, when Eve and I would share custody, she would come home after a few days and I could swear she didn't look the same as when she'd left for Eve's. That she had grown an inch. That something undefinable about her face had changed. Three more years and she'll be going to college—that's what's hardest to believe of all.

"I very much don't."

"Pizza it is then." Brooklyn doesn't make to get up and we sit in silence like that for a while, overlooking the store that will be a big part of our new life.

It's Saturday evening and even though it's cold, the weather has cleared up, and I find myself nodding at quite a few people on our impromptu walk. Brooklyn might be on the way to making a friend and I have started breathing new life into Bookends. What a difference a day can make.

As we walk in silence, Brooklyn's arm hooked through mine, I wonder what Eve is doing now. If she regrets leaving early—leaving her daughter in the lurch like that. I also wonder how someone you've known forever can suddenly change on you like that. Or was it not that suddenly and perhaps I just missed all the signs? Eve and I divorced when Brooklyn was only ten, but for her sake, we always tried to get along. We had Thanksgiving and Christmas dinners together. We even went on a trip to Mexico once, although that soon proved to be an unrepeatable experience.

As Brooklyn aged, she needed us less, and we spent less time together, but I never once got the feeling that Eve just wanted to up and leave.

"You're leaving too," she told me during a heated argument.

"To a town not even a two-hour drive from the city," I countered. "As opposed to a fifteen-hour flight to China."

Brooklyn was always going to spend her weekends here with me—

"Weren't they at the store earlier as well?" Brooklyn pulls me from my reverie. "They're so obviously lesbians. They didn't strike me as being a couple."

Coming toward us are Anna and Cynthia, flanked by a golden-brown dog with fluffy fur that curls at the edges.

"I don't think they're together." I remember what Sherry told me about her daughter and her ex, Cynthia. "They used to be."

"This might be as good as it gets for you, Mom." Even though I'm not looking at her, I can imagine the grin on Brooklyn's face perfectly. "This town can't exactly be crawling with lesbians."

I laugh and shake my head. "Don't you worry about that, baby."

"But I do. Moving to a place like this as a single lesbian... what are the odds you'll ever find someone again?"

"That's very dramatic, even for a hormonal teenager." Anna and Cynthia are approaching. It feels different than seeing any of the other guests again. I shake off the thought. Just because they're lesbians, shouldn't make it different at all. But I don't think it's just that. Even though we only exchanged a few phrases at the party, I sensed an unusual energy coming from Anna that made me curious to get to know her better.

They seem to be wrapped up in conversation. They might not see Brooklyn and me at all.

"Don't tell me you've never considered it, Mom."

What I am considering at this very moment is that my daughter is not the one I should be having this conversation with. I need to make some friends in this town, people I can lament the possible lack of lesbians with over a glass of white wine. For that reason alone, I'd like to say hello to Anna and Cynthia. They're obviously still on friendly terms. Maybe we can form our own little lesbian gang of three.

"It was not my prime concern when moving here." I hold onto Brooklyn a little closer.

We're about to walk past them.

"Hi," Brooklyn shouts, and stops walking so abruptly I nearly bump right into her.

"Oh, hey," Cynthia says.

Anna just smiles stiffly.

"Is this the cutie you want to bring to the store?" I ask. Brooklyn has already crouched down to pet the dog.

"This is Hemingway," Anna says.

"Very suitable dog for a bookstore," Cynthia adds.

We all chuckle. I look down and see that Brooklyn and Hemingway might have fallen head over heels in love already. He has his front paws on her knees and his tail is wagging out of control.

"He's always welcome," I say to Anna, who smiles shyly. Under the feeble light of the streetlamp, her eyes gleam an odd kind of blue with hints of gray and green.

"Has he fathered any puppies that need a home?" Brooklyn has managed to stand back up.

Hemingway looks up at her longingly.

"His procreation days are long behind him, I'm afraid," Anna says. "But if you're looking to adopt a dog, I can point you in the right direction. There are—"

"Oh," I interrupt her. "We're really not. We're just settling in."

"And you're more of a cat person," Anna says.

"Right." I'd forgotten I'd said that. Although, in the handsome company of Hemingway, I might be easily swayed into a more canine-loving direction.

Then Hemingway starts pulling on his leash. "Dogs can be as much in charge as cats," Anna says.

We say our goodbyes and they continue their walk.

"So?" Brooklyn asks. "If you had to choose between the two of them, who would you pick?"

"What kind of a question is that?" I loop my arm through hers.

"A logical one," Brooklyn counters.

"One I won't dignify with an answer."

"Oh, come on, Mom. Humor me. It's the least you can do after dragging me out here to the middle of nowhere."

"First of all, Donovan Grove is hardly the middle of nowhere. More than fifteen thousand people live here." When I say it, I realize it's a far cry from Queens. "And maybe you feel like I dragged you here, but even so, that doesn't give you the right to ask me inappropriate questions."

"I still don't see what's so inappropriate about my question," Brooklyn protests. "But fine, don't tell me."

For a brief moment, I do consider humoring my daughter,

who did follow me out here for the only reason that she is my child and I wanted to start over. While Cynthia might be considered more conventionally attractive, in a wholesome, girl-next-door way, my instinctive answer to Brooklyn's question would be Anna. There is nothing conventional about her appearance: shortish, dark hair that looks self-cut and finger-combed, a slightly crooked mouth that doesn't seem to smile much, and a definite preference for comfort clothing. But it's this unconventionality that makes Anna more interesting to me. "They both look very lovely," I say, to not be too much of a spoilsport.

"I'd go for the one with the dog. He's so adorable." I love the lightness in Brooklyn's voice. An unexpected sense of warmth fills me at her statement, as if I was somehow waiting for her approval of my choice between Anna and Cynthia.

"He sure is. But don't go getting any ideas into your head about adopting a dog."

"Isn't that supposed to be a perk of living in the countryside? Having pets?"

"This is hardly the countryside."

"Could have fooled me." Brooklyn sticks her nose up and sniffs. "I believe I smell pizza."

7

ANNA

"ARE you getting any vibes off her?" Cynthia asks.

"Off Zoe?" I have my eyes on Hemingway, who has caught the scent of something. "No. I really don't."

"I'm not sure," Cynthia says. "I'm getting some."

"I'm sure we'll find out soon enough. I couldn't help but notice how Tom Granger kept invading her personal space at the opening earlier. It's only a matter of time before he asks her out."

"And who can resist Tom Granger?" Cynthia scoffs.

Hemingway halts to stick his nose in a bunch of leaves, so we stop as well.

"Do you know he asked me out a few months after we broke up?" she says.

"Oh, the ignorance of some people."

"He said, and I quote, 'that I might want to try a man, now that I was single again'." She snickers, then her snicker changes into something I can't quite define. "Turns out," Cynthia continues, "he wasn't too far off the mark."

"What do you mean?" Hemingway has finished his intense sniffing session and is guiding us forward again.

"I mean that I've met someone, Anna. Someone unexpected. A man."

I'm the one who stops in my tracks now. "You what? Who?" I'm not sure I'm understanding this correctly.

"It just happened. I suddenly found myself attracted to him." Cynthia sounds as though she needs to convince herself of this astonishing fact as much as me. "It surprised me as well, but you know... It happens."

I start walking again. My brain is frantically trying to process the information Cynthia has just given me. "I didn't know you were bi," I say, because I don't know what else to say. My muscles have tensed up and I find myself falling out of step.

"I didn't really know either, but here we are. It's never too late to find out something new about yourself." When I look at her, she has a big smile on her face.

"Is it someone I know?"

She nods. "Before I tell you, I need you to promise me you won't freak out."

"Why? You're not having an affair with my brother, are you? Or with Sean? Or, heaven forbid, Tom Granger?"

"No, silly." She inhales deeply, as though calming her nerves, yet there's something very serene about her face as well. "It's John Macklehorn."

"Why would I freak out over that?"

"Because we've both known him basically all our lives and... it's all a bit weird, I guess."

"It is a bit weird. I mean, were you ever attracted to him when we were still together?"

"No, of course not. This has nothing to do with us, Anna. We've been over for so long now."

"Is it the shortage of lesbians in this town?" It's only a half-joke.

Cynthia chuckles. "No."

"Sean just made a new website for John's business. Online store and the whole shebang."

"I know."

"Thanks for telling me." I still don't know what to say. Perhaps I should express that I'm happy for her, except that I'm not entirely sure that I am. I should still say it, though. "How long have you been seeing each other?"

"A couple of months. We wanted to go to the Bookends opening together this afternoon, but I figured you'd be there, and I wanted to tell you first. You might see us around town together from now on."

"I'm really happy for you, Cyn."

"Thanks." She bumps her shoulder lightly against mine.

"Mom's not going to be very pleased. You were always the ideal daughter-in-law for her."

"She has Janet."

"That's what I keep telling her, but the woman will not rest until I'm married, I'm afraid. She believes it's vital to my happiness that I'm with someone."

"Is it?"

It's strange—and hard—being asked that question by my ex-partner. "No, I think we both know it's not what I want. I sabotaged our relationship toward the end."

"You were going through a lot of stuff, Anna."

"Aren't we all?"

Cynthia is the one who stops now. She comes to stand right in front of me. "No. Not like you. I can see that now."

"I never wanted any special treatment." We're skirting dangerous conversation territory. Soon, the connection between my brain and my mouth will short-circuit again. The only thing I can think of doing is to start walking again.

When Cynthia catches up with me, I say, "This isn't about me, anyway."

"Maybe you and I and John can get together some time?" she asks.

"Maybe," I say, already dismissing the idea in my head.

"He's just such a sweet guy, Anna."

"I know he is." Sometimes I forget how sweet Cynthia is herself.

"I just want to make sure that you don't see me being with John as some kind of reflection on you," she says. We seem to have stepped up the pace somewhat.

"What? No, of course I don't. Why would I?"

"I don't know. I've had trouble before figuring out how your mind works."

So have I, I want to say, but I bite back the comment—and the self-pity of it. "I don't feel less of a lesbian because my ex is with a man now."

"Can we please stop for a minute." Cynthia doesn't wait to do as she has requested and I find myself having to turn back.

"I'm sorry. It's just… I'm having a little trouble picturing you with John, that's all. It's unexpected. Of course I knew you wouldn't be alone for too long. Someone as lovely and warm and wonderful as you. Maybe that's what I'm having an issue with right now." Maybe I'm just plain old jealous because my ex has firmly moved on.

"But, Anna," she says, "you weren't hoping that you and I might—"

"No, no, don't be silly," I interrupt her. "Of course not."

"You're not as hard to love as you think you are, you know," Cynthia says. "I sincerely hope you realize that."

"I'm really not looking for a relationship, Cyn. And I am genuinely happy for you. Even though, yes, I'm a little jealous. I guess it's normal. I did love you for a long time. I still have very warm feelings for you and you still mean a great deal to me."

"Same here. That's why I needed you to hear this from me."

"Okay." I shuffle my weight from one foot to the other. It's too cold to just stand around like this. "I think I'll go home now. I need to process."

"All right, but promise me that when I invite you to spend some time with us, you will at least consider it."

Cynthia knows me all too well. "I promise." I do mean it this time because when she looks at me like that, I have no choice but to mean what I say. And I only have to consider it. I don't have to promise to actually be witness to Cynthia's new-found romance.

"Thank you." She takes a step toward me and draws me into a clumsy hug, the thickness of our winter coats a heavy barrier between us.

"Have a good night," I say.

She crouches down and gives Hemingway a quick cuddle. Then, my dog and I watch her walk off—probably on her way to meet John.

8

ZOE

Bookends is closed on Mondays, which meant I could devote all my attention to accompanying Brooklyn on her first day at her new school, including having freshly baked cookies ready for when she got back, as though it was her first day in elementary school.

Today, Tuesday, is the first real day the store is open for business. Brooklyn's no longer around to distract me. All the shelves have been stacked. For the first time since moving to Donovan Grove, it all feels very real—and I have time to consider if I made the right choice, uprooting our lives like this.

A few people stop by the window display, but don't come in. I can't judge the future of the store on what happens during the first day, but still, every time a shadow darkens the window, my heart skips a beat.

I pour myself cup after cup of coffee, which doesn't promote calmness of mind. As I putter around the shop, moving things around because I can't help it, I wonder what my day would have been like if I had stayed in New York. It would have been an ordinary late-January day. And I know for a fact that, even though it's only Tuesday, I would have been looking forward to Friday already. About a year ago, there came a day when I realized I just couldn't do it anymore. Go to that office day after day. So I consider myself lucky to be here, even though everything about my future is insecure. It's much better than the rat race I found myself in.

When Amazon eventually decided against opening headquarters in New York, I didn't see it as a defeat. It simply accelerated my decision to leave because every day that went by, I felt like I belonged there less.

Do I belong here? I ask my empty shop. What folly to take over a brick-and-mortar bookstore in this age of e-commerce. Ninety-nine percent of the people I told my plans to, gave me the same kind of warning. I'm not here to prove them wrong, although it would make me feel good if I could do it. If I could make this place work.

There's a shadow by the window again. I send whoever is looking in a big smile, even though I'm not sure they'll actually be able to see it.

And then, as if my worrying has conjured him, the door opens, and in walks my first potential customer of the day.

"Welcome to Bookends," I say, trying to curb the enthusiasm in my voice. "Let me know if you need any help." I don't recognize the man who has just walked in.

"I heard you have your Valentine's Day stuff out already. I figured I'd get a head start."

"Excellent idea." I walk over to him. "I'm Zoe, by the way. Nice to meet you."

He has a slightly startled look on his face. He's probably not used to such an enthusiastic greeting when going into a store. It's hard for me to hold myself back at the best of times, but today of all days, I have energy in abundance—and all that coffee isn't helping.

Then he extends his hand. "Sean Denton. Pleasure to meet you, Zoe." His face breaks into a smile as I shake his hand.

"What's your significant other into?" I ask, not wanting to presume anything about the gender of his partner.

"Cathy's pretty traditional. A card and some chocolates should do. My work wife"—he curls his fingers into air quotes —"on the other hand, despises Valentine's Day with a vengeance, so I just want to get her something to tick her off. Just for my own amusement, really."

I chuckle. "They're both very lucky ladies, then."

"Anna won't speak to me for days, but that will just add to my glee."

"Anna?" I ask. "Short black hair? The most adorable dog called Hemingway?"

"That's the one. We co-own a business. Last week, when you'd just painted that heart on the window, she was already fuming about it."

"Oh." I guess I shouldn't expect Anna at the store until Valentine's Day is over. "Well." I quickly regroup, because what do I care that one of Donovan Grove's lesbians hates Valentine's Day? It's completely according to expectations. Lesbians aren't usually very big on consumer-driven, hetero-normative holidays. They prefer to recycle their garbage instead of giving their partners flowers. "It will be easy to find something for your wife. I'm going to have to think about what you can get Anna."

"You mean you're going to help me get on Anna's nerves?" Sean looks as though he can hardly believe it.

"Of course."

"All I ever got from Mrs. Fincher was a speech to 'leave that poor girl alone'," he says, while glancing around. "She didn't have such a vast array of possible gifts on display either. In fact, she hardly had any."

When he says it like that, the overall mood of the store does suddenly strike me as rather red and sappy. But I don't mind. And I'm the one who has to spend my days here.

"It's a bit of an experiment. In New York everyone's so incredibly jaded when it comes to Valentine's Day, you know? I get that you want to rail against the capitalist angle, but in the end, it's still a celebration of love."

"That's right. You and I are on the same page, Zoe."

"So what business are you and Anna in?"

"I do web design. She does graphic design."

"How cool."

Sean shrugs. "We get by. We're just a couple of nerds sitting in front of our computers all day." He gives an unexpected shy smile, as though he's embarrassed by what he has just said.

"Anna designs a lot of book covers. She used to spend hours in here looking for inspiration. Mrs. Fincher didn't mind. She liked having Anna and Hemingway around."

Mrs. Fincher's name keeps popping up. I'm surprised she hasn't turned up yet. "Does Mrs. Fincher still live around here?"

"Oh, yes. But she's on a cruise. One of those long ones with forty-something stops in Europe."

"Making the most of her retirement." And the amount I paid her to take over her bookstore.

"Who can blame her?" Sean shuffles his feet. "I'm just going to have a look around."

"Of course. Shout if you need me."

"Thanks." He heads to the Memoir section.

I go stand by the cash register and wait. It feels a little uncomfortable because, despite working for the biggest online bookseller on the planet, I have very little experience hand-selling. I need to get used to the different dynamic. But I did enjoy that little chat with Sean a lot. And I can take the time to think about what he can get Anna to rile her up for Valentine's Day.

9

ANNA

I OPEN the door to the store and am met with a wave of very welcome heat. Before heading in, I look for Zoe. She's right by the cash register.

"Are you sure Hemingway can come in? He's not very good at wiping his paws on a mat."

"Of course," Zoe says. "I'll mop up after him."

"Is he the first dog to enter the premises under their new owner?" Relieved, I usher Hemingway into the warmth.

"I believe he is." Like most people, Zoe seems naturally drawn to Hemingway. His soft fur is so inviting. He gives her a short enthusiastic bark when she pets his head. "Does he want some water?"

"He's fine. He's hardly been on a long hike on a hot summer's day." I pet Hemingway on the head as well. "Sit, Hem," I say, hoping he will obey. He does, making me proud. "How's business?" I ask, because it seems like the polite thing to say.

"A bit too early to say." Zoe chuckles.

I nod and make my way farther into the store. I didn't come

here to make small talk. I want to explore what the revived Bookends has on offer.

"Are you looking for anything in particular?" Zoe asks.

"Just having a browse. Can I leave him here?" I point at Hemingway.

"Of course."

"He won't bother anyone," I assure her. "Hemingway. Stay." I quickly give him a treat before taking in the bookstore. It looks very different now that there aren't dozens of people drinking from paper cups and shooting the breeze. Right now, the store is very red with Valentine's Day decorations, but if I look past that, the new warm decor gives me an instant sensation of calmness, which is not something that happens very often. Then again, I've spent hours in this store in its previous iteration. It's been spruced up, but its soul remains the same. If I ignore the rack with Valentine's Day cards and skirt the table with stuffed animals holding hearts, and just focus on the books, it feels a bit like stepping back in time.

Walking around the store with Zoe there is different than when Mrs. Fincher was behind the cash register. I had gotten so used to having her there, and she was so unobtrusive with me, sometimes it felt like I was all alone in the store. It's going to take a few visits before I'm used to the new owner's energy, which seems much more palpable and present.

Mrs. Fincher used to have little handwritten notes sticking out of the books she recommended—suggestions I used to take her up on often. Zoe hasn't taken up that tradition yet. In fact, it's hard to determine what she would recommend. But this is my first visit, I'm just doing recon. I'm not here to criticize. Just to observe.

I walk to the Romance section, not because it's my favorite genre, but because I work a lot on romance book covers. When I'm stuck, I usually come here to have a look around and to feel inspired. I could go online and surf Amazon, and I do, but there's something different, something more elemental, about holding the books, about seeing their covers in real life, about skating a finger over the indented texture of the titles and author names.

All of a sudden, Hemingway appears by my side. He shouldn't be walking around the store like that.

"I'm sorry." I look at Zoe but she's smiling.

"He's been there a few minutes, but you didn't notice," she says. "You were so absorbed in studying that book. A romance fan?" She quirks up one eyebrow.

"Oh, no. I'm really not. I'm more into literary fiction."

Zoe waits to comment until I've escorted Hemingway back to the entrance.

"What's your favorite?" she asks.

I chuckle. "That's actually a pretty intimate question."

"Is it?"

I shrug. I don't really know. And I always have my answer at the ready for occasions like this, although, surprisingly, very few people actually ask me what my favorite book is. "*A Little Life* by Hanya Yanagihara" I say.

"Wow. That's heavy stuff."

"I haven't come across anything more impressive since I read it."

"Oh, it's exquisitely written, but the subject matter is... hard to digest."

I nod. "I can't reread some parts. But eighty percent of it, I can, and I do regularly, because it's just so beautiful."

"I've met Hanya Yanagihara," Zoe says, a grin on her face.

"Really?" Unlike most other people on this planet, I've never had any desire to meet the makers of my favorite works of art.

"She lives in New York and I used to work for Amazon. We had an event one day where she did a reading. She signed my copy of *A Little Life*."

"That's amazing." I'm pretty sure my facial expression doesn't match my words. "You used to work for Amazon?"

Zoe nods. "I was part of the team that tried to get the Queens Headquarters off the ground. That didn't turn out too well."

"Oh yes, I read about that. The people of Queens were not happy."

"I lived in Queens all my life. I was very happy at first, until I actually started listening to the arguments against it. In the end, I couldn't even stay at Amazon anymore."

"How remarkable. I bet it's not often that an Amazon employee ends up opening an independent bookstore in a small town." I'm looking at the new Bookends owner in an entirely different light. What she did took guts more than anything.

"You could also call it a midlife crisis, I guess." Zoe still has that ever-present smile on her face. "The Big 5-0 is looming."

I do a double take. "No way. I just figured you had your daughter really young."

"I wish." Zoe leans her elbows on the counter. "I hope I'm not being too forward, Anna, but, um, would you like to go for a coffee some time?"

"Erm." How did we go from discussing *A Little Life* and Amazon to coffee? "Yeah, sure." What? Why didn't I say no. It's my go-to answer to most other social invitations.

"Great. How does tomorrow after closing time sound?"

"T—tomorrow?" Why so soon? I won't have time to come up with an excuse by tomorrow. What is my body language saying right now? Zoe can't possibly get the impression that I'm the best person to have coffee with in this town. There are far better people to invest time in if you want to discover the ins and outs of Donovan Grove.

"Does that work for you?"

In theory, it does. I don't have any plans on Wednesday evening. "It will have to be decaf, though."

"Decaf it is."

Hemingway finds this an opportune time to bark, as though he has understood and is very much looking forward to it already.

"Okay." Without further ado, and without buying any books, which was the prime reason I had come here, I stumble out of Bookends, an impromptu coffee date on my schedule.

10

ZOE

"It's not a date," I say, as I apply lipstick.

Brooklyn, who hangs out with me at the store after school until it closes, doesn't believe me. "Of course it's a date."

"She doesn't even know that I'm a lesbian, so how can it be a date?"

"Hm, newsflash, Mom. These days, you don't actually have to tell people you're a lesbian anymore. If you ask them out, it's implied. *Duh.*" She says this as if it's the most obvious thing ever. Oh, to be part of my daughter's generation. No more coming outs required, apparently.

"We got talking about books and I just suggested we go for coffee. That's all."

"Just to be sure, I'll make my own dinner tonight," Brooklyn says.

"Fine." I'm not going to argue over this anymore, but Brooklyn's skepticism does make me wonder. Anna did react a little oddly when I asked her. Maybe she sees it as a date and that's why she ran off so quickly after we set it up. And have I really just outed myself by asking her? I suppose I'll soon find out. "How do I look?"

"Like you're going to a cocktail party on the Upper East Side, not for coffee in Donovan Grove."

"Good. Exactly the look I was going for."

"Is there even a coffee place that's open after six?" Brooklyn asks.

"I'll be sure to let you know, Smartass." I kiss Brooklyn on the cheek, making sure to leave a bright red lipstick mark.

Then the door opens and Anna walks in. I can't see beneath her coat, but she's wearing the exact same pair of jeans and boots as yesterday. I do feel a little overdressed now, even though, by my standards, I'm not dressed up at all.

"Oh." Anna does a double-take. "Hi."

"Hi, Anna." Brooklyn gets up. "I'll leave you to it." On her way upstairs, she shoots me a big fat wink. I hope Anna didn't see it.

"I—I thought we were just going next door," Anna says. "We could go to Lenny's, I guess."

"Lenny's?" I slip into my coat.

"The bar near the church."

"What do you prefer?"

"Yeah, that would be good. It's too late for me to have coffee now, anyway," Anna says. She looks like she could do with a drink.

"Lenny's it is." I turn off the light and lock up the shop. "Is that where the newcomers gathering takes place?" I ask as we stand outside.

"The what?" Anna just starts walking.

"Your mother told me about it. Drinks for the new people in town once every few months."

"I really couldn't tell you." She looks at me. "I also didn't know Donovan Grove had that many newcomers that needed welcoming."

"I don't think it does." I have to quicken my stride to keep up with Anna, who marches resolutely through the snow.

Luckily, the bar isn't very far and we're there in no time. Once inside, despite it not being a coffee house, I still feel overdressed in comparison to everyone else present, but it doesn't bother me. It's a good way to stand out. I've never minded turning heads.

"Anna, what a surprise." As soon as we've sat down, a woman walks up to us. "It's not Friday, is it?"

Anna shakes her head. "I wish, Lisa, but alas."

"What can I get you ladies?" Lisa gives me a thorough once-over.

"I'll have my usual," Anna says, then looks at me.

"What's your usual?"

"Beer," is all Anna says.

"I'm not much of a beer drinker." I try to look past Lisa at the bottles behind the bar. "White wine?"

"One beer and one white wine," Lisa repeats.

"I come here every Friday after work with my brother and Sean," Anna says.

"Your business partner?"

Anna nods.

"He came into the store yesterday."

"Yeah. I know."

I look around the bar. There are a few people drinking at the counter, but that's about it.

"Probably a bit different than what you're used to in New York," Anna says.

"Not that much. Queens has changed a lot the past ten years, and places like this are harder and harder to find, but gentrification isn't complete just yet. In fact, Lenny's reminds me of a bar in my neighborhood that I used to go to."

"Do you miss Queens?" Anna asks.

Before I have a chance to reply, Lisa brings our drinks.

"Cheers." I hold up my glass. "Thanks for bringing me to Lenny's."

Anna holds up her glass briefly as well. I sip from the wine. It could be better, but it's not as bad as I had expected—as the look of the place suggested.

"I miss my family and friends. And my routine. But it was time for a change, I could feel that in my bones. It's hard to explain. The city suddenly felt so… stifling."

"And your daughter?"

"She doesn't feel the same way at all. It was a big ask. If I wanted her to grow up in the country, I should have moved out here ten years ago, of course. She was meant to stay in New York for the remainder of the school year, but it didn't work out that way. Some bullshit with my ex."

"Brooklyn's dad?"

I chuckle. So much for Brooklyn's prediction that asking Anna for coffee would equal coming out. "Not quite." I find her eyes, but as soon as our gazes meet, she looks away. "Her other mother."

"Oh. Sorry. I—I didn't realize that…"

"That's fine. It's not exactly written on my forehead."

Anna shuffles in her seat, then takes a large sip of beer. "Is that… why you asked me for coffee? Because it might as well be written on my forehead that I'm a lesbian?"

I try a smile, which often works like magic to soften people up, but Anna seems a harder nut to crack. "Full disclosure, your mother might have mentioned that you had an ex called Cynthia."

"Oh Christ. My mother wouldn't know discretion if it bit her in the ass." A tiny grin appears on her lips. "Sometimes I wonder if she's actually my mother, but the physical resemblance is too uncanny."

"She does like a chat. But so do I. She was very sweet to me."

"That's my mom." Anna peers into her beer glass. "You can't have told her that you're into women, otherwise I would surely have known about it already. Heck, she would have set us up already." An actual grin appears now. "She's my mom and I love her, but she's a bit much sometimes, even for me."

We chuckle together, which is a nice feeling. Even though it's at the expense of another person. But it was only a gentle jibe, the kind a family member can easily get away with.

"I asked you for a drink because you're clearly into books and I run a bookstore. And, well, I'm new to town. I have to meet some people."

"I'm surprised Mom hasn't taken you around the town yet, introducing you like a debutante." Anna drinks from her beer again. She seems suddenly very thirsty. I knew she was a lesbian when I asked her to meet me, but she didn't know it of me. She probably has some recalibrating to do in her head.

I take a sip of my wine and Brooklyn's inappropriate question from last weekend pops into my head: *Which one of the two would you choose?*

"I didn't mean to make you uncomfortable, Anna. I'm just looking for a friend, that's all." My instincts tell me this is what Anna needs to hear. If that changes during the course of the evening, and she suddenly starts flirting with me, then I might go about things differently as well.

But not quite yet.

11

ANNA

How did I not see this? I keep taking sips from my beer to get my bearings, but I can't. I don't know why I'm making such a big deal of this. But everything suddenly seems different now that I know that Zoe's a lesbian.

While I find her very attractive—who wouldn't, with her glossy lips and smooth skin and energizing smile?—I'm not interested in anything more than this drink. Not that I believe that the likes of Zoe would be interested in someone like me, but I guess beggars can't be choosers.

"Are you okay?" she asks.

"Yeah. Sorry. Just processing. I should be glad that another lesbian has arrived in DG. Now that Cynthia has taken up with a man."

"Has she?" Zoe quirks up her eyebrows. I probably shouldn't be telling her this. I don't know if Cynthia's telling people—but she told me, and I'm a person.

"She told me the other day, when we ran into you and your daughter."

"How does that make you feel?"

I shrug. "I just want her to be happy."

"Is that why things ended between you? Because she had feelings for men?" Zoe surely doesn't mince her words. I'm used to my mother telling it like it is—I look forward to hearing what she has to say about Cynthia and John—but Zoe is something else. There's a directness about her that I'm not used to, and don't necessarily know how to deal with.

"God, no. That was all down to me." This would be a good time to deflect attention from myself. I don't want to talk about why Cynthia and I broke up—I don't want to revisit my failures in front of, as far as I know, the only other lesbian in town. "How about you and your ex?"

Zoe chuckles, as though I've just asked her whether she wants another drink instead of a probing question into her personal life.

"Is she the reason you moved out here?"

Zoe shakes her head. "No, Eve moved away from New York herself. She's in Shanghai now. Literally the other side of the world to where her daughter is." She knocks back a large gulp of wine, leaving me to conclude this is a sore subject still. "She was only supposed to leave in the summer, so Brooklyn could stay with her while I set up everything here. So Brooklyn wouldn't have to change schools in the middle of the school year. But then Eve suddenly decided she didn't care about any of that anymore and fucked off to her new life in Asia early." Zoe finds my gaze for an instant, but I can't hold it. "But Eve and I were over long before all of that. Let's just say it didn't take her long after we broke up to find herself a younger and no doubt better model."

"No way." It's so cliché, I don't really know how to respond. Also, if you're married to someone like Zoe, how can you possibly find yourself someone better-looking? She's certainly the hottest inhabitant this town has seen in a very long time. Oh shit. I should be saying something comforting, not getting lost in my head, concluding how hot Zoe is.

"Oh, yes. Eve's ten years younger than me and I guess I was getting too old for her." She throws in a small chuckle, for which I'm grateful. It's hard for me to know whether Zoe's being serious or not.

"That must have been hard."

"Breaking up is always hard, especially when there's a child involved."

I hold up my glass. "Well, fuck Eve," I say. "She clearly had no clue what she was doing when she left you."

Zoe holds up her glass as well. "I'm not completely blameless, of course."

"None of us are," I say, and clink the rim of my glass against hers, suddenly feeling as if I'm sharing something intimate with someone else—a sensation I haven't experienced in a very long time.

"Thanks, Anna," Zoe says. "With the way you changed the topic of conversation from yourself to me, I guess I shouldn't ask why you and Cynthia broke up."

"That would be very nice of you." I manage to hold Zoe's dark-brown gaze now. I haven't come across someone so easy to talk to in a very long time. I know it's all down to her, because I'm well aware—too aware, most times—of my own clunky abilities to keep a conversation going. But I do have to give her something. "I lived in New York for a few months," I say. "And I hated every single second of it."

For some reason, Zoe bursts out laughing. "I can sort of see how the Big Apple wouldn't agree with you."

I have no idea what that means. Is it an insult? The smile on her face says otherwise. "I got into Columbia. The arts program. I was going to do an MFA in Visual Arts, but that didn't really work out as planned."

"Really?"

"Neither the college experience, nor life in Manhattan, held any appeal for me. So I just came home without a degree." And without any of the confidence I'd mustered up from some unknown source before I left, I think.

"Why was it so hard for you?" Zoe looks genuinely interested—concerned even.

"I have… a hard time being away from home. Always have. But I went, because going to college is what you're supposed to do. And because I'm a lesbian and I've always believed that lesbians were supposed to move to the city. How else could we ever find love?" I shake my head. "I had a lot of misconceptions in my head about how life was supposed to be. Maybe it's supposed to be like that for most people, but I'm not most people, so… it wasn't like that for me."

"So you came back and started your own business?"

"Did my mother tell you my entire life story?"

"No." That smile again. It could instantly melt all the snow that has fallen over the past four weeks. "Sean came into the store the other day. He told me about your joint venture."

"You seem to know much more about me than I know about you." It's a bit of a disconcerting feeling. I make a mental note to quiz Sean some more first thing tomorrow.

"People in this town really like to divulge personal information." Zoe leans over the table a little. "And I don't even know half of what I'd like to know about you."

Instinctively, I shift back a little, so that the distance between us remains the same as before. I take a breath. This is fine, I tell myself. Whatever vibe I think I'm getting, it's all in my head—as usual. "Well," I say. "I came back to Donovan Grove. Moved back into my old room in my parents' house for a bit. That was fun." I attempt a smile myself. The wattage is nowhere near what Zoe can produce when she curls up her lips, but I have to work with what I've got.

"I bet." Zoe finishes her wine. "Shall we get another?"

"Sure." I signal Lisa behind the bar to bring us the same again. She nods at me and I find some much-needed comfort in her gesture. It anchors me as I try to tell Zoe about my life. "I lived with my parents for a few years while I took a bunch of online courses, during which I started to pick up some graphic design work here and there. Then Sean graduated from college and started his web design business. He needed someone with an eye for graphics and we've worked together ever since."

"And you no longer live with your parents?" Zoe asks, a grin on her lips.

I chuckle. "Thank goodness, no. I rented for a while, but then the economy tanked, and I was able to buy a house way below market price." Ah, my house. No matter how physically attractive and easy to talk to Zoe is, a part of me always just wants to return to my house. "I have a good life here. A life I like." Talking about myself always exhausts me, so I need to be quick to ask the next question. But being smart in conversation is not my forte. It's no wonder Zoe's much better at it than me.

"What sort of things do you design?" she asks, before I'm able to come up with a question of my own.

"I used to mock up a lot of the websites Sean made, but his work has changed a lot over the years. There are so many free website packages on the internet now, he has taken the last couple of years to really specialize in jobs that need a lot of bespoke coding."

"Ahem." Zoe clears her throat.

I look at her.

"I was asking about *your* work, Anna," she says in a way that makes me feel quite inadequate. My cheeks flush a hot pink.

"I—I do a lot of cover design for books, actually." Thankfully, Lisa brings over our drinks. I can't even begin to explain to Zoe why this is so hard for me. I hope she doesn't interpret my blush the wrong way.

We thank Lisa and as soon as she's gone, Zoe says, "That's why you missed having a bookstore in town."

"It's one of the reasons." I quickly take a few sips from my beer. It does calm me down a little, even though I've learned not to rely on alcohol to enhance my conversation skills.

"Have you designed anything that would be for sale at Bookends right now?"

"I used to work a lot for traditional publishers, but most of my work has shifted to indie publishers in the past few years, and you don't find a lot of those books in brick-and-mortar stores."

"Are you happy with that shift?" Zoe asks.

"Oh, yes. Indies are far less demanding than trads. When I was designing for a big publisher, it wasn't unusual to go through at least ten rounds of back-and-forth, if I was lucky. And I understand that, because a lot more money was at stake for them. With my indie clients, especially when I've worked with them a while, I only have to do the back-and-forth a few times. It's much more time-efficient."

"Well, there you go. One thing to thank Amazon for."

"Oh yes, your previous employer." I tilt my head— buoyed by the drink, I realize. "Thank you, Amazon, for making my life easier. That must have been a big leap for you, from a corporate behemoth to being self-employed."

"It's a bit scary, I must admit."

"Do you have plans for an online store?"

"Plans, maybe… but very long-term plans. I strongly believe that a store like Bookends can thrive in a town like this. I did my research. I didn't just come here with a suitcase full of vain hope that if I tried, I could perhaps make it work. I believe in Bookends."

"I believe in it too. I was just saying that if you needed an online store done, I could help you with that."

"Are you about to launch into a sales pitch?" The skin around Zoe's eyes crinkles as she smiles.

"No. God, no. Please don't think that." My cheeks must be

the color of very ripe cherries now. "I was just offering my help. For free. Really. I—I didn't mean to imply anything else."

"Anna." Zoe brings her hand forward and, before I can pull back, puts it on mine. "It's fine. I was only teasing you."

Her inadvertent touch makes me want to flee the bar there and then. But all I do is clumsily pull my hand out of her grasp.

"Oh, I'm sorry. I'm such a touchy-feely person. I forget not everyone is." She sends me an apologetic smile.

I drink from my beer until it's half-empty, then get up. "Sorry, uh, I just forgot. I need to go. I was supposed to meet my dad for something."

Zoe leans back in her seat. "You're leaving?" She narrows her eyes. "Why? What did I do? Or say? I genuinely don't know what I did wrong, Anna." There's no longer a smile on her face.

It's not you, I want to assure her, but the words don't come. "Nothing. It's my dad. He's expecting me. I promised I'd help him with something. I—" I what? I didn't expect us to be here this long? I didn't expect you to put your hand on mine? I didn't expect to enjoy your company so much? I may as well nip any kind of expectation, no matter how flimsy, in the bud right now, and save both of us any possible disappointment along the way. "I'm sorry. I'll see you around." I quickly stop at the counter and tell Lisa I'll pay for the drinks on Friday. Then, face burning, head pounding, heart in tatters, I get out of there.

12

ZOE

"How was your date?" Brooklyn asks as soon as I arrive home.

"Trust me when I tell you that was not a date." I sink into the nearest chair. I'm not sure why I feel so deflated. I'm puzzled more than anything. While I finished my glass of wine, Anna's half-empty beer glass standing in front me as a glaring reminder of her abrupt departure, I tried to figure out what made Anna up and leave like that. One minute, we were having a pleasant conversation; the next, she just left.

It can only have been my tactile nature. I'm a hugger. I'm always touching other people, putting a hand on someone's arm, literally patting them on the back. Clearly, Anna is the opposite. But still. We're both adults. She could have just said something. Or just pulled her hand away, as she did, and make it clear she didn't like that, and moved on.

Anna moved on all right, but in a way that I find hard to stomach. She just ran away from me as if, instead of putting a reassuring hand on hers, I'd tried to kiss her against her will.

"Oh," Brooklyn says. My statement that it was most certainly not a date seems to quell her enthusiasm about it.

"Well, there's still the other one." She keeps her face turned to the TV.

"What other one?" I get up from the chair and sit next to her in the couch.

She pauses whatever she's watching. "We ran into two lesbians the other day, didn't we? You tried one. Clearly, things didn't go your way. On to the next one."

"Jesus, Brook. Sometimes I wonder if you are truly my flesh and blood."

"Why?"

"The things you say." I kick off my shoes and draw my legs under me. At least I have my daughter to come home to, no matter how blunt she can be.

"What about them?"

"On to the next one? What are you trying to imply?"

"I just… want you to find someone, Mom. I want you to be happy."

"Aren't we happy, just the two of us? In our cozy little apartment above our awesome bookstore in Donovan Grove?" I nudge her thigh with my toe.

"Sure, Mom," she says in the way only a teenage girl can—voice dripping with sarcasm, eyes nearly rolling out of her head.

"Tell me about school today. How was it?"

"I already told you. I'm also not six years old. You don't have to ask me multiple times every single day."

"Of course I do. It's your first week at DG High."

"I was actually watching this. I wasn't expecting you home so early."

"Excuse me for wanting to spend some quality time with my only child."

"All we do is spend quality time together, Mom."

"Turn your show back on. We'll watch it together."

She looks at me, her face pulled into an 'as-if' expression. "I'm watching *Riverdale*."

"That's fine with me, baby." I watch my daughter as she presses *play* on the remote and focuses her attention back on the TV. I don't care what we're watching. Brooklyn loves *Riverdale* with a passion I've rarely seen in her. A passion that, apparently, makes her prefer watching it on her own—maybe she can better focus on whatever dramatic plot the teens on screen are going through. I might have also made fun of it a few times too many for her to let me watch it with her. But tonight, she indulges me. Maybe she senses that I need the comfort of sitting next to her in the couch.

I wonder what Anna's doing right now. Clearly the thing she supposedly had to do with her dad was made up. Or maybe she did go and see him. I don't even know if he and Sherry are still together. I know from experience that you can't just assume.

We've only been watching a few minutes when the episode ends and the countdown to the next one appears on the screen.

"Have you eaten?" I ask, suddenly keenly aware of my own hunger.

"Only Cheetos and string cheese," Brooklyn says.

I shake my head because it's my job to do so as a mother. "I'll make us something. TV dinner?"

Brooklyn nods. I only let her eat in front of the TV on very rare occasions.

"We can watch something else," she says. "I've seen this before."

That's the understatement of the year, I think, and smile at her. "Whatever you want, baby."

"What made it not be a date?" she asks as I get up, picking up my shoes in the process.

I huff out some air. "It was never a date in the first place, although we did end up at the local bar instead of the coffee shop, for which, I think I was a touch overdressed." I glance down at my dress. Before I make dinner, I need to get out of it. "We were actually having a nice time, until, very suddenly, we didn't. She just… ran off. It was all a bit weird."

"I told you from the start she was weird."

"Did you?"

Brooklyn just shrugs, then gets up. "I'll help you."

"Thanks, sweetie." Automatically, I curl an arm around her shoulders. "Have you been hanging out with Jaden?" I ask, as we head into the kitchen.

"A bit," she says, not looking me in the eye.

"Tell me more." I open the fridge to see what I can rustle up. I take out a carton of eggs and some lettuce.

"There's not much to tell." For the past year, I've been amazed at how quickly Brooklyn can go from being the very open, talkative girl she's always been to a secretive teenager. I have learned not to take it personally.

"Tell me anyway," I insist.

"He's a bit of a weird one as well. He's cool, but also such a nerd at the same time."

"Must run in the family then."

"Or in this town." Brooklyn chuckles.

"Invite him over whenever you want." I crack a few eggs into a bowl and start whisking. Without being prompted, Brooklyn puts the lettuce in a bowl and makes a dressing. "Not without supervision, of course."

"When would I be unsupervised?" Brooklyn asks. "When you go on a non-date with the other one?" She grins at me.

Fat chance of that, I think. The other one is no longer available.

13

ANNA

EVEN THOUGH I don't much feel like returning to the scene of my latest crime against general social rules, I go to Lenny's with Sean and Jamie after work on Friday anyway. More because it's what I do every single Friday—and I need to get my weekly dose of social interaction—than because I want to hang out with my brother and my colleague slash friend.

I try to discreetly settle last Wednesday's bill with Lisa, but of course she asks me how Zoe is, and of course Sean hears her.

"Did you come here with the foxy lady?" he asks.

"What foxy lady?" Jamie asks.

"Zoe, the new owner of Bookends," Sean tells Jamie, then he fixes his gaze back on me. "Wait... is she one of yours?" He purses his lips into a very quizzical pout.

Now I do wish I had gone home instead of coming here. I wish I was in my studio, working on the painting I started when I got home on Wednesday, after my faux pas with Zoe. I'm so ashamed about it, I even changed Hemingway's walking route, much to my chagrin, so that I didn't have to go past Bookends.

"As a matter of fact," I proclaim, as if it's my proclamation to make, "she is." Lisa saw us together. Word will be out soon enough.

"I met her at Bookends' opening." Jamie whistles thought his teeth. "Zoe's way out of Anna's league."

"Guys, we just had a drink." Speaking of, I eagerly sip from the beer Lisa just planted in front of me. "She's looking to make friends in town. That's all."

"And she chose to befriend you of all people?" Jamie's my brother and has always gotten away with saying whatever he wants about me. He also knows me better than most—and likes to test my boundaries regardless. "Bad luck for Zoe." He shoots me a playful wink. Because of the circumstance, us having an after-work drink on a Friday night, and the atmosphere of casual banter, which I do enjoy, I let his remark slide. "Actually," Jamie says. "Jaden said something about the new girl at school being the daughter of the new bookstore owner. I think he might have taken a shine to the city girl."

"Punching above his weight, just like his dad, then," I say.

"Maybe it runs in the family," Sean says. "Why didn't you tell me you went out with Zoe, Anna?"

"Like I always give you a detailed report of my previous evening." I drink some more. Sean has already emptied his glass. He likes to drink hard and fast on a Friday.

"Usually, there's not much to report. This was something special. I thought we were best buds, Anna." He pulls what's supposed to be a sad face, I guess.

"I was at Bookends. We got talking. I design book covers. She runs a bookstore and used to work for Amazon. She probably thought we had some common ground, so she asked if we could go for a coffee. We ended up here instead. End of story." I remember—vividly—the bright-red dress Zoe had chosen for the occasion.

"That sounds like the mere beginning of the story to me, Sis," Jamie says. "How did it go?"

I shrug. "We talked. It was nice. Then the night was over."

"Will you be seeing her again?" Sean asks.

"Probably around town." Inside me, dual forces are at war: instant embarrassment when I think of how I abandoned her here, versus the desire to see her again because, before I panic-bolted, I was actually having a lovely time with a lovely woman.

"What is wrong with you, Anna?" Sean says. "She's hot. She's new to town. And interested in you. Were you waiting for the many other eligible lesbian bachelorettes of Donovan Grove to ask you out first?"

I shake my head. "You know I'm not looking for anything. For a relationship, I mean. I'm off the market."

"I thought that was just out of necessity. Or scarcity." Sean won't let it go. He might be my best friend, but I don't often allow myself or my relationship status to be the subject of conversation between us. We mostly talk about work or, when we're out with Jamie, about superficial stuff that's going on around the town, making our interactions a source of comfort and easy friendship for me.

"Is it because Valentine's Day's coming up that you're so cranky, Anna?" Jamie asks.

"Tell me about Jaden and Brooklyn," I say, trying to steer the conversation into another direction.

"Seeing as they only just met, I'd say it's early days," Jamie says.

I give him a look—a look he must recognize very well. It's the get-Sean-off-my-back-please look.

"Just don't mention Brooklyn at Sunday lunch, Anna," Jamie says. "You won't be Jaden's favorite aunt any longer if you do."

"She's his only aunt," Sean butts in. He's being particularly antagonizing today. Maybe he's really upset that I didn't tell him about Zoe. But there really wasn't anything to tell.

These guys may be the people I'm closest to, but that doesn't mean I can give them the full story about running out on Zoe. They'll only tease me more—and they won't understand, anyway.

"Why did Zoe move to Donovan Grove?" Sean asks, his tone milder.

"She wanted a change. A different kind of life."

He nods, as though he fully understands the compulsion, then sends me his warmest smile.

I fight the impulse to leave the bar—I can paint all weekend long—and stick around a while longer, if only as practice for possible future encounters with foxy ladies.

14

ZOE

I SPOT HEMINGWAY FIRST. He rounds the corner, then sits and waits for his mistress patiently. I feel something twitch in my belly while I, just like the dog, wait for Anna to appear in my field of vision. It takes a while so I just keep walking. I approach Hemingway with caution, because I'm not sure he will recognize me.

"Hello, buddy," I say, because I can't help myself. He's such a ridiculously handsome dog and his fur always looks so soft and eager to be ruffled.

"Oh." Anna finally turns up. My presence has clearly startled her.

"I spotted this cute thing." I give Hemingway a scratch behind his perked-up ear.

"Zoe, um, I—I owe you an apology, but, well, they're just another thing I'm really bad at."

Hemingway gives himself a full-body shake and a few flakes of snow fly off him.

"It's okay. You don't have to apologize." This is my standard reply when someone wants to say sorry to me. While her running off was confusing, even rather irritating at the time, I'm sure she had a good reason for it.

"Are you busy?" Anna asks. "My house is right there. I can make us that cup of coffee we never had."

I'm surprised by her sudden forwardness. Maybe this is her way of apologizing. "I would love that." It's Sunday afternoon and Brooklyn's out with Jaden, doing who-knows-what teenagers do on a Sunday afternoon in a town like this. "It's not just us," my daughter assured me. "We're hanging out with a bunch of kids from school." I didn't feel I had any other choice but to accept that.

Anna's carrying two Tupperware containers in her hand, making it difficult for her to find her key and open the front door.

"Even though I'm in my forties, my mother still thinks she needs to feed me half the time. Sunday lunch leftovers, made especially for me. Could you?" She hands me the containers while she digs her front door key out of her jacket pocket.

"Hem. Wait," she says. "He's probably so over-excited by having a visitor, he thinks he doesn't need his paws wiped."

She invites me in and while I stand in the hallway, still holding the food containers, I watch how she gently cleans her dog's paws with a cloth.

"Good boy," she says, and gives him the go-ahead to enter the house.

My gaze is immediately drawn to a painting of Hemingway on the hallway wall. "You had him painted?" The painting is so lifelike, it almost looks like a photograph.

"I painted that myself." Anna holds out her hand and I give her back the containers. She puts them on the cabinet beneath the painting of Hemingway and shrugs off her coat.

"You painted that?" I half-exclaim.

She does this funny thing that's halfway between a nod and a shrug.

"That's amazing. Wow. You're so talented."

"Mwah," she groans, as though it's physically hurting her to accept my compliment. "Can I take your coat?"

"Sure." While I take off my coat, I keep my eye on the painting. It's only now that I'm starting to discern little details in it that I hadn't noticed before. The wallpaper behind him, consisting of the most delicate little flowers, painted in such a way that they appear out of focus. I take a step closer. "I'm by no means an art buff, but this is a truly exceptional painting."

"I'm just a crazy dog lady painting pictures of her dog," Anna says, and leads me into the living room. It's not what I had expected from someone who is, as far as I can tell, always dressed in the least fashionable clothes. Her living room looks like it could be in a home design catalogue. The couch is dark-green velvet. The wallpaper behind it has a subtle pattern of shiny brown leaves, matching the color of the couch's legs.

One wall is entirely covered by frames of all shapes, sizes, and colors, some of which contain paintings that she surely must have painted herself.

"I should have asked you to help me with the decor of the shop," I say, once I've been able to match the preconceived idea I had of her and how things actually are. "Your home is absolutely gorgeous."

"It's where I spend ninety percent of my time, so," she says matter-of-factly.

Hemingway has jumped onto a very soft-looking maroon ottoman. Lying there like that, he looks part of the plush, opulent decor.

"I can see how it would be hard to leave here."

"Please sit. Make yourself comfortable. I'll be right back with the coffee."

"Do you mind if I follow you into the kitchen? I'm just really dying to see it." I feel as though I can be a little bit forward with her—and after seeing the living room, I am really curious to see more.

"Oh." She always sounds so surprised, but in quite a demure way. "Of course."

She leads me to the room adjoining the living room. Light pours from the doorway, even though it's not particularly bright outside.

"Jesus, Mary and Joseph," I stammer, as I walk into Anna's kitchen. The entire back wall is made of glass, letting in all the light from outside. "You were going to keep this from me?"

"Not deliberately," she says. "I just get really clumsy when someone watches me make coffee."

"I only have eyes for your kitchen. I promise." Hemingway has turned up as well. He's standing next to his food tray, looking at us with big, sad eyes.

"Hemingway's favorite hobby is pretending he never gets fed. Don't let him persuade you that he gets anything less than two healthy meals a day."

Standing in Anna's beautiful kitchen with her dog, I suddenly get such a sense of the kind of person she is. A fierce animal lover. A very talented artist. Someone who struggles to let the humor and kindness she has inside her come out. I also get the feeling she doesn't invite that many people into the privacy of her home.

"Espresso? Cappuccino? Latte?" she asks, making me feel like I'm in some sort of home-version of Starbucks.

Just black coffee, I want to say, but since that wasn't on offer, I decide not to confuse her. "Espresso, please."

"I read this article the other day," Anna says, as she turns away from me. As promised, I don't watch her prepare the coffee. I can't keep my eyes off the rest of her kitchen, anyway. Every single surface is spotless. All the counters and cupboards are in the brightest, cleanest, sparkliest white, reflecting the light streaming in. The kitchen is completely different from the lovely and cozy living room, but its starkness is broken up by a myriad of trinkets on the built-in shelves on the wall across from the stove. There's even a reading corner by the window. If this were my house, I'd never leave the kitchen.

"Sorry." I have no idea what Anna has been saying. "How rude of me. I'm just in awe of your kitchen. Of everything I've seen so far. Are you sure you're not some highly sought-after interior decorator?"

Anna doesn't seem to mind that I didn't listen to what she was going to say about coffee. "I have considered it, but I can only ever do this for myself. Not for anyone else."

There's a mustard-yellow armchair by the window that I'm drawn to. A navy ottoman and a small side table containing an impressive stack of books stand next to it. A large soft-pink dog bed is placed next to the chair. I can just see Anna sitting in her chair, her feet up, Hemingway sleeping next to her.

Through the window, I see a wooden deck with a couple of red Adirondack chairs. At the end of the garden, there's nothing but trees. I feel like I'd like to sag into that armchair, grab one of those books, and just sit there for an hour or two.

Behind me, I hear the coffee machine hiss. I wait until silence has returned, to say, "You don't happen to be looking for a couple of roommates are you?"

"God no," Anna is quick to say. She hands me my espresso, presented in a tiny, bright-yellow cup. "I hope it's not too strong." She's holding one of those tiny cups herself. "We can stay here. Please, take the armchair."

"Oh, no. That's fine. It's your chair."

"Take the chair, Zoe." Anna pulls back a kitchen chair and sits in it. That was suddenly very forceful.

I turn the armchair away from the window and sit down. It's so soft and comforting, I forget where I am for a moment. Then I remember why I'm here. Anna wanted to apologize to me—even though, as far as I'm concerned, inviting me into her home is more than enough to make up for running out on me last week.

"Look, um, Zoe. I'm not very good at… chat. I like to use the front-end/back-end metaphor when trying to explain it to someone. I've actually stolen it from Sean, because he's a web developer. What goes on in the back end, in my head, is not always what you see in the front end, as in what comes out of my mouth." She taps a fingertip on the table. "There are a few bugs in my system." She chuckles. "And customer service isn't always what it should be either."

"Okay." I'm not entirely sure what she means by that—or what to do with it.

"I'm sorry for storming out of Lenny's. It was totally uncalled for. You must think I'm some sort of whack job. But please don't think it was anything you said or did. You're so lovely and warm and kind and, I don't know, I… I didn't want you to get the wrong idea, just because we were two lesbian having drinks."

"What do you mean?"

"You know, that just because we're both gay, we need to at least go on a date together."

I burst into a chuckle. "That's not what I think at all, Anna. Is that why you ran off?"

"No. Yes. Partly, I mean." She pauses to drink from her coffee. I do the same. It's delicious. All floral and chocolaty notes with not a hint of bitterness, but strong nonetheless. "It's really hard to explain. Something in my brain short-circuited, I guess. The situation suddenly got too intense for me."

"Did I make you uncomfortable?"

"Not really. It wasn't anything you did. It's all me. It's why I don't date anymore. I'm just so sick of all that pretending. It just takes too much energy."

"What are you pretending to be?"

"Normal," she says.

"Am I normal?" I'm not sure what I've walked into here, nor what Anna is trying to tell me.

"I don't know you very well, so I can't answer that."

"What would make me 'normal' in your eyes?"

"That it's effortless for you to make conversation with people—even people you like spending time with."

"That's not something you feel you're very good at?" Yet you're doing it now, I think, although it's impossible for me to know how much sitting here with me is taking out of her.

"Forty-three years of living have given me more than enough evidence that I royally suck at it."

"I don't think you do, Anna." Maybe she's being a bit hard on herself.

She doesn't respond, just digs her fingers into Hemingway's fur.

"So you're an introvert? There's nothing wrong with that. In fact, I dare say it's all the rage these days."

She huffs out a chuckle. "I am most definitely an introvert, but it's not just that." Again, she doesn't say anything else.

I don't get the impression we'll spend the rest of the afternoon hanging out at her house and making conversation. In fact, I suddenly get the distinct impression I'm already about to overstay my welcome.

I sit up a bit straighter, indicating that I'll go if she wants me to. "Tell me this, Anna. Would you like to go for another drink with me some time?"

Her cheeks flush the same hot pink as they did a few times when we were at the bar. "I—I'm not sure that's a good idea."

"Okay." I believe I've let her know my intentions. All I can do is ask. "If that's how you feel."

"Yes, but Zoe, please know this is not a reflection on you. You seem perfectly lovely…"

"And *normal*?" I push myself out of the chair, which is hard, because it's low and plushy and built so that all you want to do is fall straight back into its warm embrace.

"I'm not like you. And I'm not looking for anything," Anna says.

"Not even a friend?"

"I'm… not much of a friend."

"Look, Anna, I'm not sure why you feel compelled to say these things about yourself, but—"

Anna rises, making me lose my train of thought. She takes a deep breath. "Will you please stay a little longer?"

"I'm not sure if I'm welcome to." As if he's trained to remove the tension from these kind of situations for his owner, Hemingway walks toward me, as though he, too, is asking me to stay.

"You are. I just got in my head again. Running into you earlier was already a surprise—"

"Because you've been avoiding your usual dog-walking route past the shop?" I sit back down.

"Yes. And I also hadn't exactly planned beforehand to invite you over. It's a big day for me." She manages a smile. It looks real enough. "Would you like another coffee?"

"Do you have anything stronger?" I ask.

"Of course." Anna stays standing. "I'll be right back." She doesn't ask me what I want. I guess she is full of surprises then.

While she's out of the kitchen, my eye is drawn to the stack of books next to the armchair. I don't recognize them as anything I would sell at Bookends. When I look closer, I notice that all four of the books are lesbian romance novels. Didn't Anna explicitly tell me that she was a hard-core literary fiction lover? And that *A Little Life* is her favorite book ever? A smile spreads on my lips.

15

ANNA

One-two. One-two. While I stand in front of the liquor cabinet, I count my breaths. I need to do something to stem the swirl of emotions inside that threatens to spiral out of control. Did Zoe just try to ask me out? For the life of me, I can't fathom why she would do that. It must really be a case of me being the only lesbian in town, although I'm probably not. In a town of nearly twenty thousand inhabitants, Zoe and I can't be the only ones. I start counting my breaths out loud to stop my thoughts from spinning out of control even more, even though it doesn't appear to be working very well. I focus my attention on the bottle of booze in front of me. I didn't even ask her what she wanted to drink. I'm in no state to be mixing elaborate cocktails, so it will have to be something extremely simple. I reach for a bottle of vodka. Then I remember she drank white wine at Lenny's the other day.

"I have some white wine open in the fridge, actually," I say, trying to sound casual, when I walk back into the kitchen.

To my surprise, Zoe has her nose buried in the book I was reading. It's called *Nights of Passion* and it totally lives up to its title. *Damn.* What must she think of me now?

"This is… *very* interesting, Anna," she says. Her eyes are different when she pins her gaze on me next.

"Isn't it?" I say, stupidly. "Is wine okay?"

She nods while a massive grin appears on her face.

I turn away from her to get the wine and a couple of glasses. I just hope she didn't open it on the page I had bookmarked, but chances are that she has. That's the problem with almost never inviting anyone into your house—your vices are often on full display.

"You didn't get these from Mrs. Fincher, I take it," Zoe says when I give her the glass of wine.

"No, she didn't have much of an LGBT section. And most of those wouldn't be on display in a bookstore anyway. I sometimes ordered them through her, but even that was often difficult. I usually buy them direct from the publisher or author." I try to say this with a straight face, as if we're discussing an important piece of business.

"Is *Nights of Passion* any good?" She's still holding the book.

"Not bad." I quickly take a sip of wine.

"Have you read other books by…"—she studies the cover, her eyes narrowing—"Lizzie Harris. Christ, I could barely make out the author's name."

"She's one of my favorites, actually."

"Would you recommend this book to me?"

"I don't know, because I don't know your taste in books."

"I thought you were a literary snob, what with you raving about *A Little Life* like that, although I do feel like I've learned an important tidbit about you." Zoe is having way too much fun at my expense.

"I can like both. I like all sorts of books."

"So I see."

"And yes, if you like an engrossing lesbian romance, then yes, I would recommend it."

"From what I've just read, it's not exactly a slow-burn." She actually snickers.

"These books always have lots of sex scenes. It comes with the genre." I realize I sound a little defensive.

"Oh really? All lesbian romance books have lots of sex scenes? Well, I guess I'd better take your word for it, Anna. You sound as though you know what you're talking about."

"The ones you'll find on that table do, anyway." I briefly look into Zoe's eyes. At least the earlier tension has been defused and it no longer looks as though I've chased her out of my house. In fact, she looks as though she may stay a good while longer.

"Let's see what else we have here." She puts down her wine and goes through the other books. "*Indira's Lover.*" She purses her lips and nods. "*Daylight Fading.* That sounds quite tame, actually."

"It's not," I say dryly.

"Oh right, because the daylight has faded." Zoe nods again. "I get it, I think."

"Don't you read lesbian romance?"

"Not really. Especially not these days. Because I don't sell these books at Bookends and I feel like I should try to at least read some of the books I sell, to make recommendations. And something tells me that these wouldn't exactly fly off the shelves if I stocked them."

"They wouldn't. Not just because the market isn't there, but have you seen the covers? *Nights of Passion* is such a great book. So well written and so engaging. And I really mean that. And then they put on a cover like that? Some horribly pasted together botched-up Photoshop job." I shake my head. "It's such a shame."

"So when you say well written and engaging." Zoe picks up the book again and opens it. "Do you mean: she opened her legs and—"

"I was trying to have a serious conversation about my work," I half-shout, realizing too late that I have unnecessarily raised my voice.

"All right." Zoe takes it in jest and she drops the book. Thank goodness. "I won't be asking you to read from this any time soon."

"This is causing you way too much glee."

"Can you blame me?" She drinks from her wine again and when I sneak a glance at her face, I see how her eyes sparkle.

"Take a look at the one at the bottom," I ask.

Zoe slips *Alive in Your Eyes* from underneath the other books. "This cover is gorgeous. I'd put this in the store window in a heartbeat."

"Next to your Valentine's Day display, no doubt." I can't help myself—she set the tone.

"Seriously. Just the color on this is so alluring. Not a hint of poor Photoshop skills on this one."

"That's because—" I find it hard to say. I don't know why. "I designed that cover."

Zoe nods, as though it all makes perfect sense to her now. "Wow. Yeah, I can see it now. The details that are in your Hemingway painting are in here as well. Subtle, but they're there. This looks exactly like a mainstream romance cover."

"It's hardly mainstream, but yeah, that's what I was going for. Trying to change lesbian fiction covers one design at a time."

Zoe opens the book to the first page. "It's signed. To you."

"Sometimes authors like to send me a signed copy as a token of appreciation. Not very often, though."

"How lovely. 'For Anna, for making my vision come alive.' Aw, that must have made you feel good."

"It did. It's always nice to be appreciated."

"I can try to sell this at Bookends, you know? By way of experiment. If you can get me the details of the publisher, I'll contact them. And I would put it in the Valentine's Day display. It's perfect for it."

"You can try, but it won't work. It's just wishful thinking."

"Oh, okay. Way to kill the vibe."

"But it's true. I've corresponded with Dinah, the author, a lot. She has tried everything to both sell and advertise this book to a more mainstream audience. We even put a cover on it that would appeal to a broader spectrum of readers but the readers just aren't there. That's not to say that lesbian romance isn't a lucrative genre. It can be. Most lesbian romance readers are just as voracious as straight romance readers, there just aren't as many of them, which makes perfect sense, really. So why would the book buyers in Donovan Grove be any different?"

"Sounds like you have given this some serious thought, Anna."

"Well, yes, because I work with more and more lesbian fiction authors, because I'm so passionate about the genre, but a lot of them believe that they don't need to pay a few hundred dollars for a pro cover. Readers buy their books no matter what the cover looks like. Many publishing rules are different in lesbian romance because the readership is, by definition, very different. Look at me. Look at my house. I love something well designed. Nothing makes me happier than good color composition. Look at the cover for *Nights of Passion*. It doesn't appeal to my design aesthetic at all, yet I bought it. I loved it. And when the next Lizzie Harris comes out, I'll buy it again, regardless of the cover design. Because to me, it's of far lesser importance than the experience I know I'll get from reading the book." I hope I haven't gone off on too much of a tangent.

"So the number of hot scenes in the book eclipses the need for a good cover." Zoe looks pretty pleased with herself again after that statement.

"No. That was really not what I was trying to say." Her easy jokes do make her a delight to talk to, which is not an experience I have with many people. The first fifteen minutes she was here, I felt very ill at ease, now I want her to stay for the entire afternoon.

"I do get what you're saying, Anna. You're always starved for a good lesbian romance and there isn't the plethora of choice that other genres have, so a cover is not what makes you buy a book."

"Which doesn't mean that I don't wish the covers were better. Then I wouldn't have to hide them away in the basement after reading."

"Have you contacted Lizzie Harris? Asked her if she'd consider you as her cover designer?"

"I don't do cold calls like that. I actually don't have much direct contact with most of our clients. Sean's in charge of that."

"Really?" Zoe arches up her eyebrows.

Another one of my flaws revealed. They're coming out at breakneck speed. "I—I'm not very good at it."

"And Sean is?"

"Maybe not stellar, but better than me. And most importantly, he doesn't mind it. An unexpected email from a client doesn't throw off the rest of his day like it would mine."

Zoe nods as though she understands although I suspect it's extra hard for her to understand because she comes across as ultra-sociable.

"So you hate Valentine's Day, but you love romance. Phew."

"One doesn't exclude the other, you know."

"Hm. I beg to differ."

"Valentine's Day has nothing whatsoever to do with romance. It's all about making money from unsuspecting people's romantic feelings."

"And a romance novel isn't?"

I knot my eyebrows together. "Of course not. Reading a

book is an experience. In the case of romance novels, it's a means of escape. Of being transported into an impossible dreamworld for a few hours. That's very different from being goaded into buying the person you love all year round a tacky gift on one specific day just because the calendar of capitalism tells you to."

"The *calendar of capitalism*?"

"You know what I mean."

"Maybe, but I refuse to be cynical about love, and for me personally, that includes peddling Valentine's Day gifts. I've never objected to getting a present on the day. Not ever. I always loved it."

"Good for you."

"Your ex never got you anything for Valentine's?"

"She tried. Once." Because it's Zoe sitting across from me, I can't suppress a smile. "She never did again."

Zoe snickers. "What did she get you?"

"Flowers." I roll my eyes.

"You don't like flowers?" Zoe asks.

"I love flowers, but—" Zoe's phone starts ringing and I'm glad for the interruption. I've made my point and I hate repeating myself, even though I know I do so much more often than I would like.

"It's Brooklyn," Zoe says before she picks up.

I get up and pretend to do something in the living room to give her privacy.

"Brooklyn forgot her keys. Again," Zoe says on a sigh. "I've threatened to make her wear them on a collar wherever she goes, but to no avail."

I nod. I guess this means she has to go. Inside of me, a sense of deflation wars with relief. Because she's so easy to talk to, I want her to stay, but her being here, in my personal space where hardly anyone ever sets foot, has also drained my energy.

"No key under the mat?" I joke.

Zoe looks at me as though I'm being serious. "Do people leave keys under the mat here? Is that something you can actually do?"

"My parents used to do it when Jamie and I were little, but that was quite some time ago."

"I have to go, Anna. I'm sorry, because I was having such a lovely time." She sends me one of her super-radiant smiles—the kind that could melt all the lingering snow from yesterday's snowstorm.

"Me too," I say. I walk her to the front door. Hemingway follows on our heels. He probably thinks he'll be treated to an extra walk. He has that special bounce in his step.

"See you soon." Zoe turns to me, that smile still on her face. Then she lunges forward and tries to kiss me on the cheek. I should have expected it, but I didn't. It's not how I greet or say goodbye to the people in my life. Instinctively, I pull away. Her lips barely graze my cheek.

She takes a step back and looks at me, her eyes quizzical under knotted eyebrows.

"I'll pop into the store soon," I say, because I have no idea what else to say, to erase the uncomfortable moment I created. It reminds me of a T-shirt I bought and only wear in the dead of winter, when I can hide it under layers of other clothes. It says: *I came. I saw. I made it awkward.* It could be my life motto.

Zoe grins at me, then nods, and goes. Hemingway and I watch for a while as she walks away. Even from the back, she's gorgeous. Even if you didn't know Zoe, if you saw her from behind, you'd know that her face would be utterly captivating.

"Oh shit," I mutter to Hemingway, "I think I have found the subject for my next painting—and we both know what that means."

16

ZOE

On Tuesday, my first customer of the day is Sherry. Anna was right. While they have the same bright-blue eyes, high cheekbones, and set of their jaw, their demeanor couldn't be more different. Sherry looks as though she wants to give me a hug and doesn't seem to have much knowledge of the concept of personal space.

"How are you settling in?" she asks.

"Very well. Thanks for asking, Sherry."

"Good. And how's business?"

"The Valentine's stuff is flying off the shelves, although I fear all the Donovan Grove wives might get the same heart-shaped candle this year. They've been selling like hotcakes."

"I'll have to get my own, as usual, although Jamie might get me one. No such luck with my husband. Suffice to say that Anna doesn't get her aversion of all things Valentine's Day from a stranger."

I have to chuckle. I'm also happy that Sherry has already started talking about Anna. I wonder if she knows that Anna and I went for a drink. Anna doesn't strike me as the type to tell her mother these things, while Sherry is very much the kind of woman who would know every little thing going on in this town.

"Has she been in yet? Don't let her linger too long without buying anything." Sherry smiles broadly at me. "She can stare at book covers for hours."

"She's allowed to. She's so talented." I'm not entirely sure how I feel about Anna. She blows so hot and cold, it's kind of exhausting.

Sherry quirks up one eyebrow. "Have you seen her work?"

"I went to her house on Sunday. She showed me—"

"Hold on." Sherry leans farther over the counter. "Anna invited you into her house?"

"Yes."

"Okay. Sorry, that's just quite unusual. Even I hardly ever go there. She prefers to come to our house. And woe is me if I ever dare turn up at her door unexpectedly. Sometimes she doesn't even open the door to her own mother."

While I'm very interested in hearing more about Anna, I wonder how she would feel about her mother divulging all this information about her to me. It's as though Sherry feels she somehow has to make up for all the things Anna doesn't say out loud.

"The painting of Hemingway hanging in her hallway is so beautiful. So lifelike, yet also special in a way that a photograph could never convey."

"She's a very good painter."

An idea takes root in my brain. "Has she ever exhibited her work? Or sold any?" I can already see the Hemingway painting on the wall above the door.

"Anna?" Sherry says as though I would suddenly be referring to another person. "No, she would never ask money for her paintings. She only ever paints people or objects or, mostly in her case, animals that she really likes. Then she gives the paintings away. It's her hobby. Why do you ask?"

"In New York, every coffee shop is basically also a gallery with the work of a local artist. Often, bookstores will promote local artists as well. I have a shop; she's an extremely talented painter..."

"She must have invited you into her house for a reason, Zoe," Sherry says. "But, as her mother, and the person who has known her the longest, I would bet Anna would have zero interest in that kind of attention. She likes to keep herself to herself. But you can always ask. She might make an exception for you." She narrows her eyes. "You aren't..." she starts, then waves off her own words.

"I'm not what?" I'm almost fifty and over the decades I've developed a sixth sense for the question I'm about to be asked.

"I don't mean to pry into your personal life, Zoe, although my grandson couldn't be excused from Sunday lunch early enough to hang out with your daughter." She throws in a wink.

Here it comes, I think.

"Are you a lesbian?"

It's actually quite refreshing that Sherry just comes out and asks it, that she can be much more direct about it than most people. "Yes, I am."

"You don't look it," she blurts out.

I can't help but chuckle. "What does that mean?"

"When I think of the word lesbian, I can't help but picture my own daughter. Or Cynthia. But not someone like you."

Sounds to me as though Anna should have a word with her mother about stereotypical, narrow-minded thinking. "Well, Sherry"—I can't keep a hint of condescension from creeping into my tone—"just like any other group of people, lesbians come in all shapes and sizes."

"Not in Donovan Grove, they don't." Sherry has a comeback for everything.

"I guess they do now."

Sherry's smile has faded from her face. Have I offended her

while she was actually in the process of offending me? It wouldn't be the first time that has happened while I was in conversation with a white cisgender person, even though she's the mother of a lesbian. "Are you and Anna... involved?" she asks. Contrary to what Anna told me about her mother, Sherry doesn't sound very enthusiastic about the prospect.

"No. We're just friends." I'm not even sure we've known each other long enough for that, but I have to qualify it somehow.

"More than anything, I want my daughter to be happy. I spend a good part of every day worrying about Anna's happiness. She's not like most people. She's not like you and me. She —" For the first time, she catches herself while speaking. "She needs certain things in a relationship that not every person is capable of giving."

"Don't we all?" God, this family. I should ask Brooklyn to introduce me to Jaden, just to see what he's like.

"Yeah," she says wistfully. "All I'm asking is that you're... kind to her." Did Sherry's voice just break a little.

"Of course." I'm not sure what gave her the impression that I would ever be anything else.

The door of the store opens and that seems to snap Sherry out of whatever she was thinking of saying to me next. "I'll let you get on with things. I'll come by later to buy my Valentine's Day gift."

I wave Sherry off and greet the woman who just walked in. She goes straight to the Kids' Books section, which has proven to be the most popular so far. There must be a lot of parents of young children in Donovan Grove.

As I walk over to her to see if she needs any help, I ponder what Sherry just revealed to me about Anna. I hadn't expected her to give me what was basically a warning. Either way, both mother and daughter are quite the characters.

17

ANNA

At least now I can walk my usual route along Main Street and past Bookends again, but it takes me until the next Thursday to gather the courage to go inside the store. It's closed on Mondays, and on Tuesday and Wednesday, when I walked past, there were people inside, and I wasn't in much of a people mood. I also didn't know what to say to Zoe. But today, I'm in actual need of a book. I just finished the one I was reading last night and I won't be able to go to sleep if I don't have another one ready. Obviously, I have quite a few books at home that I haven't read yet, but this is what I've told myself so that I can make it over the Bookends threshold.

Something in my belly does a funny spasm as I open the door. I truly don't know why I'm so nervous. Or yes, I do. I like Zoe and whereas for most people that would make them more inclined to seek out her company, in my case, it's the opposite, because the many voices of anxiety in my head have already laid out to me in great detail how this is going to play out—not well.

But, I told myself—and those relentless voices—maybe we can be friends.

"Hi." Thankfully Zoe doesn't greet me with a kiss on the cheek, although I had mentally prepared myself for the possibility. "Lovely to see you," she says.

"I'm looking for some litfic." I actually know which book I want to buy, if she has it in stock, but I'm curious what she might recommend.

"No lesfic?" Zoe asks.

"Do you have any?"

"No," she says dryly, and does something with her face that really appeals to me. She's trying to be serious while all she really wants to do is smile.

"Do you have any recommendations?"

"I do, but let me say hello to this handsome guy first." She walks from behind the counter and crouches down to pet Hemingway elaborately. If she keeps this up, I'll become jealous of my dog. But no, that's not what I want. *Friends.* It's good to have friends. To make a new one once in a while. It will only add points to my normality score—to be able to make friends with the new woman in town.

Next thing I know, she's standing beside me. Her soft-pink sweater clings to her skin in a—in my opinion—very inappropriate way.

"Hi," she says again, as though she has only just realized I walked into her store.

"Hemingway really likes you too," I say. He likes everyone, I think, unlike me.

Zoe grins at me, then cocks her head. "Are you free for lunch?"

"Sorry? What?" She keeps throwing these curveballs at me. And it's only eleven thirty.

"I'm closing in half an hour. Would you like to stay for lunch? Nothing fancy. Just a quick bite upstairs."

I want to say yes and I want to say no. This never-ending indecisiveness inside my brain is what trips me up the most. I take a breath. This is Zoe, whom I have just identified as a possible new friend. Moreover, Zoe needs friends in Donovan Grove, not that she'll get far with me as a starting point—I doubt she'll want to go to Lenny's with Sean and Jamie on a Friday night.

"Depends," I say, surprising myself. "Which book you recommend. It will tell me a lot about your preferences and thus your personality."

She sinks her teeth into her bottom lip. "You're putting my bookseller skills to the test?"

"I feel like I should. Have your personal book recommendation skills been tested at all?"

"A little." She chuckles and the sound of her soft laughter soothes me in a way I hadn't expected. I want to hear that chuckle again as soon as possible. "I could do with the practice, though. But, I have to disappoint you, Anna, my stock's a bit low on smut." She puts a hand on her side.

"Cheap shot." I'm actually quite curious to see Zoe's apartment, although I don't expect to find any steamy lesbian fiction lying around, what with her sharing the house with a teenager.

"Oh, come on." She softly elbows me in the bicep. I hardly feel it because I'm still wrapped in my thick winter coat, but still.

"Do you need time to prepare your recommendation?" I zip open my jacket because I'm starting to get really hot.

"Not at all. The new Xandra Melani came out on Tuesday and I've been waiting to sell you a copy."

I can't suppress a smile. "That's actually the book I came to buy. I've been looking forward to it for a long time. Have you read it?"

"Halfway through."

"Does it live up to your expectations?"

"I wouldn't be recommending it if I thought it was bad, but everyone is different. Still, I think you'll enjoy it."

"Sold."

"Did I pass the test?"

"You did, but it was quite easy. Harder tests will follow. But for today, I'll give you a break."

"Well, then, if you would be so kind as to browse the Valentine's Day merchandise until the clock hits twelve." Zoe beams me a wide smile—one that I know will get me into trouble with my intentions of trying to be her friend.

"I won't do that, but I can pack it all in a box for you so you can just pretend the whole travesty doesn't exist."

"How about I ring up your book and you browse the rest of the store. Or if you want, you can go upstairs already."

"Really?" I'm amazed she would let someone into her home like that, unsupervised. "What about Hemingway?"

"Both you and Hemingway are very welcome." Zoe has a way of saying things that adds extra meaning to the message. She makes it impossible for me to misinterpret her invitation—and I'm the queen of misinterpretation. What I realize, as I stand here before her, is that being around her just makes me feel really good—almost normal, even.

"I'll give his paws a thorough clean, of course."

"Thanks." Zoe heads behind the counter. I see how she takes a copy of the book she recommended from a shelf behind the counter, as though she kept one back for me especially—maybe she did.

"I'll wait for you," I say, and head to the Young Adult section. Sean got an email from a YA author this morning who is looking to rebrand a trilogy. "I have some research to do."

"Bookends should get a percentage for all the inspiration it provides you," Zoe says.

"But instead, you're offering *me* lunch." It's hard to focus on book covers when it's just me and Zoe in the store.

"I have something to discuss with you," Zoe says.

Now my ability to focus on anything else but Zoe has completely deserted me. “What’s that?”

“Have you spoken to your mother recently?”

“Yes. Just this morning, actually.” I did notice that Mom sounded a bit less buoyant than usual, but I figured that even the hurricane that is my mother has slower days.

“Did she happen to mention that I came out to her? Or more accurately, that she asked me if I was a lesbian?”

“What?” I put the book I’m holding back on the shelf and walk over to Zoe. “Oh God, I’m sorry. She can be so obnoxiously direct.”

“It’s fine. It’s not a secret. And she only asked because I told her I’d been to your house.”

I’m trying to figure out why my mother didn’t call me the minute she learned that Zoe is gay—and that she’d been at my house. Both facts must have delighted her beyond reason.

“Ah,” is all I can think of to say. “I do hope she didn’t ask anything else inappropriate.”

Zoe purses her lips, but doesn’t say anything. But I know my mother and I know that once she gets going in a conversation, she doesn’t know when to stop. It’s highly unlikely that asking Zoe if she’s a lesbian is the only untoward thing she said.

“She’s… very concerned for you. It was quite touching, actually.”

For crying out loud. As if I need my mother expressing her concern for me—her very grown-up daughter—all over town. “She means well, but it’s kind of infuriating. I hope she didn’t overstep any boundaries. She does that. A lot.”

“It’s really fine, Anna. I just wanted you to know. And I was curious if she’d said anything to you about it.”

“She might be keeping so quiet because she’s planning our imminent, inevitable wedding already,” I joke.

Zoe now gives a loud cackle of a laugh. It's a true delight to see her face light up like that. "She's a piece of work."

"You have no idea." I shake my head as I think of my mom, who I'm a hundred percent certain means well. For that reason, I can easily forgive her for her lack of boundaries, which is good, because, in my world, forgiveness is a million times easier than confrontation.

18

ZOE

"YOU SHOULD DO 'blind dates with a book'," Anna says, holding a spoonful of soup in front of her face. "I've seen it on Instagram. The book is completely wrapped so you don't know which one it is, and it only comes with a very short, but intriguing description. If you put that in the window display, instead of those heart-shaped candles, people won't be able to stop themselves from coming in."

There's a lot to unpack in what she has just said. Anna's on Instagram? I should look her up. But I start with, "Those heart-shaped candles have been my best-selling item since the store opened."

Anna just groans. Most of all, she amuses me. I don't think she realizes that she's really fun to be around. I'm also quite fond of teasing her, which is rather easy.

"You have an Instagram account?"

"For business. It only shows the covers I make. As adorable as my dog is, I'm not one of those people who post pictures of their pet every day. Or their child. Or how picture-perfect their life is."

Oops, sounds like I hit another nerve.

"Have you heard of the grump lit genre?" I ask.

"Yes. I love it," she says so matter-of-factly, that I burst out laughing.

"Are you sure you're not secretly writing some under a pen name?"

"Oh, absolutely certain, because female writers aren't allowed to create such grumpy characters."

"You could use a male pen name."

She shakes her head. "I'm not a writer. I prefer to express myself visually."

I'm reminded of what Sherry said about Anna only painting people or things she really likes.

She spoons some more soup into her mouth and a drop lands on her sweater. When she notices, her cheeks pink up, making her look utterly adorable.

"This is why you'll never see me in expensive clothes," she mumbles.

"Really? That's the reason?"

She just shrugs and when she fills her spoon now, she takes extra care when she brings it to her mouth.

"I really like your blind-date-with-a-book idea. I might try it out this afternoon."

"Then I'll have to stop by tomorrow and try to guess which book's inside."

Something in me lights up at the prospect of her coming into the store again tomorrow—or even just walking by the window. Even though I'm getting very mixed signals from Anna, I can't help but think she quite likes the idea of seeing me again tomorrow as well.

"Are you on Instagram?" she asks.

I nod. "Just to see what Brooklyn's up to, mostly."

"She hasn't blocked you?"

"She's not allowed to. I'm her mother."

"Jamie's always complaining that Jaden blocks him on social

media. These teenagers don't want their parents knowing what they're up to all the time."

"Then they shouldn't post it on Instagram."

"Jaden hasn't blocked his Aunt Anna, though. Maybe because he knows I won't tell Jamie."

"You don't tell your brother what his son is up to when he asks you?"

"Of course not. It's not my job to tell him that."

When she puts it like that, it sounds really convincing. "Do you have a good relationship with your nephew? Because Brooklyn sure seems to like him."

"He's a good kid. A bit of a geek. I'm surprised your hip city girl of a daughter likes to hang out with him so much."

"Why?" Perhaps it also surprises Anna how much I like hanging out with her.

"I don't know. The balance seems somehow off. Don't get me wrong. I think it's great, for both of them. That Brooklyn has made a good friend so quickly, and that Jaden is coming out of his shell a bit more."

"I'm thinking of having him over for dinner, just to get to know him a bit."

"Probably a good idea."

"Would you... like to join us?"

"Me?" It amazes me how Anna can sometimes have no clue of where a conversation is going. "Why?"

"Because he's your nephew and I don't think I'm quite ready to invite his parents yet." And it would be a good opportunity for you to get to know the most important person in my life, I catch myself thinking.

"Okay. Sure," Anna says curtly.

"I'll wait a little while, though. See if they still like each other in a few weeks."

"And if we still like each other in a few weeks," Anna says.

I can immediately tell she hadn't intended on saying that at all. She drops her spoon and looks away.

"Why wouldn't we?" I'm not one to let a comment like that slide.

"Many reasons." She sounds very determined.

"It's not the first time you've put yourself down like that. Why do you insist on doing that?"

"Because I'm… more of an acquired taste."

"I don't think you are at all. In fact, I think you see yourself very different than how you actually come across."

"You haven't known me for very long yet."

"But I'd like to." I lock my gaze on her even though I can tell it makes her very uncomfortable.

"You really…" she begins to say, then pushes her chair back.

"Please, don't do that. Don't run away again."

She nods and then just sits there with her chair pushed away from the table.

"Why do you do that? We're just having lunch. We were having a perfectly nice conversation. What did I say that made you suddenly feel so threatened you wanted to escape?"

"Zoe, I… it's not you. It's—"

"You could have fooled me, Anna."

"I'm not very good at expressing what I feel. Not in words. I mean, you must have guessed that I quite like you, but I don't really know how to deal with that. I just want to avoid disappointment all around. For both of us."

"So you keep saying, but what does that mean?"

"That's not a conversation I can have right now." Are her eyes getting misty? What on earth did I say to provoke tears in Anna?

"When do you think you *could* have it?"

"I don't know. When I've prepared for it, maybe."

"Okay. How much time do you need to prepare?"

"You're being very forward." Anna stares at me with a defiance I haven't seen in her before.

"Is that a problem?"

"I don't know yet." She pulls her chair closer to the table again.

"There's so much either one of us doesn't know yet, Anna."

"I know," she says, and smiles. "Are you free tonight?"

My social calendar hasn't exactly filled up yet—I should really make some more effort.

"Ideally, I'd have you over tomorrow, but I always go to Lenny's with Sean and Jamie on Fridays after work, so."

"Tonight's fine."

"All right. I'd better go and prepare then." As she gets up, so does Hemingway.

19

ANNA

By the time Zoe arrives, I have a good idea of what I want to say to her, but no clue, as always, where to find the words. The very prospect of having sentence after sentence of what I'm trying to articulate coming out all garbled and not making sense has prompted me to reach for my phone multiple times and call Bookends to cancel tonight.

Something stopped me, however. The thought of Zoe in my house again, I presume. It can really only be that. When she rings the bell and stands in my doorway in all her glory—all dolled up and overdressed again—I know for certain that, despite my nerves, and despite only seeing her a few hours ago, I've been dying to feast my eyes on her again.

We settle in the living room and I see how her gaze is drawn to a small painting of the shelf against the opposite wall that I've framed and put on said shelf.

"Is that the same..."

"It is. I call it 'shelf within shelf.'" It sounds so ridiculous when I say it out loud. I don't think I ever have. Apart from my family, I haven't had many people over since Cynthia and I broke up.

"There's something about it. I mean, it looks exactly the same. What happens when you change something in the actual shelf?"

"Then I make a new painting."

"Of course." Zoe purses her lips and nods. I'm not sure if she's mocking me or if she truly agrees with my logic. "You must really love painting."

"I need it," I say. "Painting is how I… deal with a lot of my emotions." It's the only way I've ever learned how to do so.

Zoe drinks from the white wine I've poured her. She slings one nylon-clad leg over the other. How can she be wearing a dress in this weather? And how did she even walk here in those high heels? Some things I will always fail to understand.

I tried to make an effort in the sartorial department, because I had a sneaky suspicion Zoe would pull a stunt like this on me again, but, unlike Zoe, I have opted for comfort over bling, as I always do. I did iron my shirt and that's saying something, if only to me.

After we've made the obligatory small talk about the store and the weather and Hemingway, who has nestled at her feet, a silence falls. I know it's up to me to fill it, which makes it even harder to do.

"The very nature of what I'd like to explain, makes it almost impossible to do," I say.

"If there was a prize for being cryptic, Anna, you'd have won it a dozen times since we've met." Zoe smiles at me and the effortless brightness of it reminds me of how easy I have found it from the get-go to connect with her on a certain level, not deeply, but still satisfyingly, for me.

I try to remember what I rehearsed in my head earlier, after abandoning work for the afternoon, which caused an extra bout of stress. The reason I never miss a deadline isn't because I pride myself on it, it's because when I come too close to any deadline the time pressure kills the very creativity I need the most in that moment.

"In *A Little Life*, do you remember when the character Willem thinks about the three things you can have in a relationship? The three things you can hope for and nothing more?"

Zoe quirks up her eyebrows. "You're going to have to refresh my memory."

"He claims that you can only expect your partner to have three qualities you admire, at the most. For instance, being loyal, being a good listener, and being kind. That's it. You should never expect more than three, because that would be very unrealistic."

"Okay. That's not one of the things I remember from the book, but sure." She holds the bottom of her wine glass in the palm of her hand.

"I've learned, from the demise of my relationship with Cynthia, that I don't even have three qualities to offer. For that reason, it would be very unfair to make anyone believe that I'm open, um, to... that."

"Honestly, Anna, I don't believe that for a second. Nor do I agree with Willem's conclusion that one person can only stand for three things in a relationship. It's fiction, you know. *That* I do remember thinking when I read that book: thank God, this is fiction."

"Yes, well, you haven't been in a relationship with me."

"No, but I'm getting to know you and I can already tell you more than three things that I admire about you."

I shake my head. "You may think so, but you'd only be guessing."

I realize I went about this the wrong way, which is no surprise. I believed that if I talked about a book we both love, we'd be on common ground, that we could connect over that, but it was wrong of me to assume that would happen.

I'm just going to have to come out and say it, otherwise, I'll never be able to make myself clear. But it's hard because it's not something I go around telling people and it's the very issue that drove Cynthia and me apart.

"While I was with Cynthia, I was diagnosed with Autism Spectrum Disorder," I mumble. I'm not sure Zoe has understood but this is no time for me to be making eye contact. I'm also scared of what I might see in her glance, even if I could find the nerve to meet her eyes.

"Really?" she says, after a few seconds of silence. "Did Cynthia leave you because of that?"

"No. No, of course not. Cynthia is kindness personified. She would never have left me *because* of it. I drove her away because I couldn't deal with it."

Zoe nods.

"It wasn't just that," I say. "Life is, by definition, unpredictable. And it's in my very nature to always try to control everything. That drove her quite nuts in the end as well, but... yeah."

"So things were going badly before you were diagnosed?" Zoe asks.

"No, not really. There was tension at times, but she was always very supportive. I think, in the end, subconsciously, I wanted to be alone with it. I needed time and space to figure out what this meant for the rest of my life."

"And? Have you figured it out?"

"No, not even close. Because what the diagnosis basically confirmed is that my brain doesn't operate the way most people's does. That I'm impaired in some way. The society we live in is not geared toward people like me, yet I have to live in it. All of that. Being 'normal' is really all I've ever wanted to be, probably because I never fit in anywhere and I was always the weird one." I pause and take a deep breath.

"I really wanted for it not to be true," I continue. "That the suspicions I had about myself were incorrect. But they weren't. And then I felt like I had to constantly reassess myself and the life I've had so far. If only I had been able to say all these things to Cynthia, but I just couldn't at the time." I'm surprised I can do it now, even though I've had years to think about it. Zoe's inviting nature must have something to do with it.

"I'm sorry you had to go through that, Anna. That you're still going through this. That society isn't more accommodating or understanding toward people with an impairment."

"But that's the thing. I don't want to be seen as disabled in any way. Not by myself and not by anyone else. I was quite fine just being the weird lesbian of Donovan Grove, you know? And if I was able to be with someone as well-adjusted and lovely as Cynthia, surely I wasn't that bad. But then I went and fucked that up and now she's like this big, living symbol of my failure. Another strike against normality."

Oh, to have a peek inside Zoe's mind now, to be able to see her thoughts without the filter of her turning them into acceptable words.

"Do you have people to talk to about this?" There's concern in her voice.

"I have my family," I mumble. "My mom's a terrible busybody but she's been such a gem through all this. Because of my dad. I'm a lot like him. It's often genetic and it's obvious I got it from him. Except, until a few years ago, no one ever knew because ASD presents very different in women than it does in men."

"Are you getting professional help?"

"Like a shrink? Do you mean something like talk therapy?"

Zoe nods. The smile has been wiped from her face.

"No. I... Honestly, the mere thought of seeing a therapist makes me so incredibly nervous, it immediately defeats the purpose. Seeing someone to help me curb my anxiety gives me such anxiety, that I just can't get myself to do it. I can't rise above the initial anxiety. It's a bit of a vicious circle, I do realize that."

"Wow. That's a lot."

"I know. I'm sorry. I know this is a lot to take in, Zoe. I don't expect you to stay. I—"

"Not for me, Anna. For you. That's a lot to deal with all on your own."

"I have my family."

"But still," she says.

I'm again surprised by her kindness, and her willingness to remain on that couch.

"I'm afraid I'm going to need a bit of an education about this." Zoe's tone is soft, a little guarded. "I don't want to presume what ASD entails just from what I've seen on TV or have accidentally come across over the course of my life."

"Are you serious?" Even though most of my energy reserves have been depleted just from disclosing this at all, something inside me is still lit up, still wants her to stay. "You want to know more?"

"I want to know more about you, so yes, I do."

"I can recommend a very comprehensive book about it. About ASD in women specifically."

"That should be right up my wheelhouse then," Zoe says.

Part of me can't help but wonder if she isn't just being polite. Whether Zoe feels she can't blow me off right now and have that come back to bite her in the ass, as the newcomer in town, later.

"I'm really glad you told me, Anna. That must have been really hard."

"I'm glad I told you, but…" I'm also very surprised that I was able to. "I never wanted for this to define me, or to elicit any special treatment from anyone. Yet, it is something you need to know about me… Or not. Half the time, I don't even know what I'm doing, just blundering through life. And then…" For the first time in a while, I look Zoe in the eye. "Then you came to town."

"This doesn't change anything for me. I just know you a little better now."

How I wish I could just go along with Zoe's fantasy. I might have told her, but that doesn't mean she understands what it actually entails.

"You must realize that, because of what I've just confided in you, I'm absolutely not looking to date. It would be so unfair."

"Unfair on whom? On me? Because I think I get to decide that."

"I'm hard to love, Zoe. I'm stuck in my routines and my anxiety cycles and half the time, I'm completely wrapped up in some drama in my head."

"Not when you're with me. This person you're describing, I don't know her much at all. I haven't met her often, Anna. That's not who I think of when I think of you."

"That's very kind of you to say, but..." Either I have too many arguments against this and they all fail to come to me just because of their sheer number. Or, when faced with Zoe, with her patience and warmth and that delightful smile that can break through at any moment—it's as though every nerve ending is poised, waiting for it to appear—I have no arguments at all. Maybe that's what she does.

The point is I know very well that I can't trust whatever's going through my brain right now. Whatever momentum of sensation, of feeling a tiny bit more like other people, must be ignored because I know it's treacherous. I know from years and years of experience. From over and over again being convinced that this time will be different, this time, I will be able to forge a true connection to another human being—and time and time again, I've been let down. Sometimes by others—whom I've never blamed for one second, because how could I? —but mostly by myself.

"We all make mistakes, Anna," Zoe says. "Then, we learn from them. I screwed up a bazillion times with my ex-wife and so did she. That doesn't mean I won't ever make the same mistakes again, but at least I have the experience and perhaps even the wisdom that came with making them the first time around. Which gives me hope that things can always be different. Better. Even if it's only a fraction."

I grin at Zoe. "I'm just so amazed at how… patient you are with me. How hopeful." I don't really understand why, but that's a question I can't push out of my mouth right now.

"Maybe I like you," she says, and drinks from her wine again.

Why? A voice in my head screams. *Why would you like me?*

When I don't say anything, Zoe clears her throat. "At the beginning of this conversation, you claimed that you're not very good at expressing emotions and at articulating what you want to say, but you just did exactly that. You told me something that was extremely difficult for you to verbalize."

"What I told you is just the tip of a mammoth iceberg."

"So? Isn't that what getting to know someone else is all about?"

"Wow. You're such an optimist."

"What will it take for you to absorb a tiny fraction of my optimism?"

"I don't know. I mean…" I wring my hands. "I like you too, Zoe, but…"

"'Buts' don't fit into my optimistic theory, so my suggestion is that you just drop the buts and see what happens."

"If only it were that easy."

"Anna." She moves to the edge of the couch and puts her glass down. "Stop it. Just simply stop it. Right now, the only thing that really matters is that I like you and you like me. All the rest is of no importance." She holds up a finger to preemptively silence me. "It's not."

"Okay." I obey because there's that smile I've been waiting for. It's not because I'm convinced that I'm utter crap at being in a relationship that I don't feel the longing for Zoe course through my every cell right now. The longing to sit with her for hours, the desire to trace a fingertip over the soft-looking skin of her cheek, the need to see her again tomorrow and the day after, and the week after.

"Maybe we should go on a proper date, then," she says. "Not drinks at Lenny's or an impromptu lunch or anything like that."

"What do you suggest?" I ask. "I'd cook for you, but that would really not make for a great first date."

"How about I cook for you?" Zoe offers. "Here, in your house. Unless you want my fifteen-year-old daughter hanging around."

"That sounds good. Very good, actually."

"Wonderful. When?"

"Hm." I pretend to think, although my social calendar always looks the same. At least it did until Zoe came to town. "Saturday?" Or is that too soon?

"Saturday it is." Her face lights up even more. "You do know what date Saturday is?"

"Oh, God no." I shake my head in genuine despair.

Zoe sits there nodding triumphantly. "Valentine's Day."

"You'll be exhausted from selling all that last-minute Valentine's Day crap. I can't possibly expect you to cook for me after that."

"I'm a single mother to a teenager. I'm used to much more than that, Anna. Don't worry about me."

"Let me at least do the shopping. Send me a list of what you need and I'll go to the store."

"Deal." She finishes her wine. "Do you want me to stay?"

"No, that's all right." The truth is that I'm mentally completely drained, although a surprisingly large part of me would like Zoe to stay, but she very much looks like she needs to be somewhere.

"I promised Brooklyn I'd help her with something for school and it's getting late."

"Of course. I'll see you on Saturday."

"On Valentine's Day." Zoe gets up, a huge smile plastered across her face.

20

ZOE

The next day, as soon as I'm in the shop, I place an order for the book Anna recommended to me about women with Autism Spectrum Disorder. When prompted for the number of copies I'd like to order, I order five, because if Anna says it's 'very comprehensive', it must be. I completely trust her on that. And I figure that at least a few people in Donovan Grove would think it important to find a book about Autism in women in their local bookstore.

Or maybe I'm ordering five copies because I want to show Anna that I care, that I'm not scared off because of what she confided in me.

After Brooklyn went to bed, I spent the better part of the evening and night scouring the internet for information, because I want to know more. I want to know all the things Anna didn't tell me about ASD—about her.

I've only just turned around the shop's Open sign, when the door opens, and a familiar face walks in.

"Hi," Cynthia greets me warmly. "Thank goodness you're open already."

"How can I help you?" I ask.

"Years of not being allowed to celebrate Valentine's Day nearly made me forget that the big day is tomorrow. I need to get something for... John." There's definite hesitation in her voice when she pronounces her new partner's name.

"What does he like?" I give her my warmest smile—the one that Eve always said would make me the most natural sales person in the world, after which she would kiss me profusely, and keep me smiling until my cheeks hurt.

"The man sure loves to bake a cake." She pats her hips. "I've gained quite a few pounds since we've started dating."

"They look good on you," I say.

Cynthia waves me off. Now that she's here, I'd like to take the opportunity to extract a little information about Anna.

"When you weren't 'allowed' to celebrate Valentine's, was that because you were with Anna?" I try to make my voice sound light and innocent—as though my question doesn't have an ulterior motive.

She rolls her eyes. "Oh, of course she's told you about that. I can just picture her storming in here and giving you the sermon about love being the last thing that should fall victim to capitalism. It just got her so incensed. I could barely believe it. Like she held a very personal grudge against it." She shrugs. "Maybe she did."

I step from behind the counter to close the distance between us, while hoping that no one else will come into the store.

"Anna has, um, told me some of the reasons you and she broke up."

"She has?" She quirks up her eyebrows.

I nod. "We've been... getting to know each other better."

"Oh, right. I see." She narrows her eyes and studies my face. "Oh... Okay." She chuckles nervously. "She told you about her diagnosis?"

"Yes."

"Wow. In that case, she must really be very fond of you."

Something inside me glows. "I'm quite fond of her as well," I hear myself saying, even though Cynthia is the last person I should be saying that to.

She inhales quickly, then exhales slowly. "Look, Zoe, Anna and I are friendly now, but our break-up was… gruesome, in many ways. She can be her own worst enemy, but, maybe the fact that she has told you already means she's changed. That she's become more accepting of herself."

"I don't really have anything to compare it to, but yeah… we're going on a date tomorrow."

"No way! Not on Valentine's Day," Cynthia blurts out. "She would never."

"I think she might have forgotten it was the 14th of February when we agreed to meet up tomorrow." I snicker inwardly at the memory of the look of horror on Anna's face.

"She must really, *really* like you then." Cynthia's shoulders relax. "I loved her. I thought we were going to grow old together. That was something we would have long, lazy conversations about. What we'd do when we were both old and gray." She pauses. "When we eventually split, it was long overdue. I finally walked away from her, but I was still devastated. I was tired and angry and so sad about it all, because it didn't work out, and it really felt like *she* didn't want it to work anymore. As if she was actively fighting me on everything and trying to prove that she was now, suddenly, somehow defective. That despite all the evidence to the contrary—because we'd been happily together for years by the time she received her diagnosis—she was no longer cut out to be in a relationship." She stops abruptly, as though she has said too much.

"I'm sorry. I didn't mean to upset you, Cynthia."

She shakes her head. "I promised her I wouldn't tell anyone about her diagnosis and it's a promise I kept. Anna doesn't disclose her ASD easily, which was also a problem between us, because she only ever had me to discuss it with, and what did I know? I'm not a mental health professional. So, in a way, I'm glad she told you, Zoe, but… Yeah, I don't know."

"I'm sorry it ended badly."

"Me too." She straightens her shoulders. "Anyway, I believe I came here to get a present for my boyfriend."

"That you did." Eve always told me I had the innate ability to make anyone open up to me without even trying. It worked with Anna and now with her ex as well. "Come with me." I lead her to the Cookbook section, which has proven very popular so far. "How about some Paul Hollywood?"

She nods, then rolls her eyes. "I suspect John's secretly a huge fan, so yes, please." She smiles a little sheepishly. "They do have the same kind of piercing blue eyes and John's much nicer, so it's all good." She gives a sudden nervous giggle when I hand her the book. "Look, Zoe, I didn't mean to speak out of turn. Anna hurt me but that doesn't mean I don't still care about her. I worry about her sometimes still. I don't mean to question your intentions, but please don't see her as a 'cause' or anything less than any other human. She may not be neurotypical, but, in essence, she's just like the rest of us, even though she likes to claim otherwise."

"I won't," I say, although that's hardly a promise I can make. I'm not one to overthink this kind of thing. All I really want is to spend some more time with Anna. "I have no inclination to fix her or to take her on as some sort of challenge or anything like that."

"You know what?" Cynthia holds the book I gave her close to her chest. "I believe you, Zoe. And I'm glad Anna has found someone she can confide in. I'm not entirely sure she'll be happy with the conversation we've just had, so break that to her gently, will you?"

"I will." I ring up her purchase and wrap the book in hot pink wrapping paper. "If John's interested in baking, why did you come to a bookstore instead of getting him some baking supplies?" I ask, when I hand her the wrapped present.

"It's your window display," Cynthia says. "It's simply irresistible." She puts the book in her bag. "I have to run."

My first thought is that I can't wait to tell Anna what her ex said about my exuberantly red window display. I can't keep the fact that Cynthia and I talked about her and her diagnosis from her, anyway. I just hope she won't run away again when I tell her. Although that might prove hard, since I invited myself to her house.

21

ANNA

WHILE I GET the blank canvas and paints ready, I need to tell myself over and over that this is not a Valentine's Day present. I'm painting this because I have no choice. I need to get this image out of my head. I need to spend time with it and process it in the only way I know how. I can also choose not to give it to Zoe. She may actually think it's weird.

I've put my painting song, "This Is Me", on repeat. I must have heard it a million times by now and the message of the lyrics may as well be part of me. It's coming up to the jubilant chorus and I want to have my first brush stroke on the canvas by the time the music swells to a high. So I begin.

By the time the songs starts winding down and I pause, as I always do, to let the words "And I know that I deserve your love" sink in, the first sketch has been made.

I can't explain where the ability to do this comes from, or how my brain can make it happen, but I've always been able to see a painting in my head and replicate it on the canvas. The colors. The shapes. The details. It's all there. All I have to do, I used to joke when Cynthia asked me about it, is turn up with a brush in my hand. She could never understand that, for me, it was that simple.

But I can't just paint any picture at any given time. I can't come into the painting studio off my kitchen, which has the same kind of light streaming in, and tell myself to paint the landscape in front of me or something my mother has asked me to paint. I've tried many times but it doesn't work that way. I guess, when I really think about it, which I do often, I can only paint what's on my mind—or in my heart. And today, that's Zoe.

There's so much to unpack, so much to unravel, so much I can't communicate or express in any other way. While I paint this picture of her, while I try to catch the warmth in her gaze in a blend of various shades of brown, the easiness of her smile with a few flicks of my wrist as I drag my brush across the canvas, I can only think of her. But the thoughts don't come to me in words or sentences. They're just feelings, sensations, a wave of awareness coursing through me. And trying to make Zoe's essence come to life in my painting, or at least what I think is her essence to me in this moment—her kindness and her patience and the way she has of drawing me out—is also my way of preparing for this date, of not trying to screw it up before it happens by being in my head too much and overthinking it to death.

Because that's how I screwed up my relationship with Cynthia. I can see that now, after more than two years apart. I convinced myself of the fact that she didn't want to be with me anymore after she found out who I really was, and then I made it come true. Meanwhile, I forgot to ask her what she really wanted. Because I was scared of the answer, perhaps. Or because I was so full of stubborn self-hatred that I couldn't possibly conceive that she might think of things otherwise.

I have many paintings of Cynthia in the basement, many versions of her in all sorts of colors. But today, I'm painting

Zoe. In my head, she's wearing white, and it contrasts so deliciously with the darker color of her skin. The song repeats itself and I paint and paint, and it feels so good, so utterly glorious, to feel close to Zoe in this way—my way. To just feel my way through it as her face becomes more and more detailed on the canvas. And then the light starts to go and Hemingway appears in the doorway and looks at me in that way he has, his eyes so full of adoration, because he's not human and he can look at me like that, and I know it's time to stop.

I look at my work of the past few hours and I'm pleased with what I see. And for a brief moment, I can fully enjoy what it's like to be me. I may not be able to connect to other people very well, but I connect with this. This makes me come alive and, most of the time, that's all I need.

Then it's time to scrub the paint off my hands and switch off the music, because I'm late to meet Sean and Jamie at Lenny's and I always get nosey questions from them when I dare to turn up only five minutes late.

"Jaden's going on a proper date with Brooklyn tomorrow," Jamie says. "This can only mean one thing: his old man is getting truly old."

"You may be older, but you're also wiser," Sean says. "And, well, looking on the bright side, if they do get serious, Jaden will have a very foxy mother-in-law."

"He's only fifteen," I blurt out.

"Oh, she speaks," Jamie says. "What's with you tonight, Anna? Is it because tomorrow's Valentine's Day and you don't have a date?"

I roll my eyes, because that's the only reaction a comment like that deserves.

"Or is it because Cynthia's with John now?" He doesn't let up.

"I have absolutely no problem with that. I'm glad she's with someone. And John's a nice guy."

"In all seriousness," Sean says. "Were you surprised when you found out Cynthia was dating a man now?" I can so tell he's been sitting on that question all week, waiting for the time when we all had a beer in our hand to ask it.

"Surprised? Yes. A bit. I hadn't expected it."

"You didn't know she was bisexual?" Sean asks.

"She never told me. So no, I guess I didn't know."

"But it doesn't bother you?" Jamie asks.

"No, of course not. Why would it?"

He shrugs. "I don't know. No reason, I guess." He looks at me quizzically.

"John is a good guy," Sean adds. "They both deserve a happy ending."

I quirk up my eyebrows. "What does that mean?"

"You deserve a happy ending as well, of course, Anna. I just never really know if you're already living your happy ending or whether you're still looking for someone else to be happy with…" He shakes his head. "That came out kind of wrong."

"It's fine," I say. Sean's my best friend and Jamie's my brother, which, in theory, makes them ideal confidantes, but I can't tell even them about having dinner with Zoe tomorrow. Not even when things were going south with Cynthia did I open up to them in that way.

It's not how the three of us are together—it's not something I've ever thought I needed. I don't believe I need it now, but part of me does want to blurt out that, somehow—I still don't really know how or why—I've scored a date with that 'foxy lady'.

"You know I'm not looking for anything," I say. "I'm perfectly happy hanging out with you guys every Friday night."

I hold up my bottle of beer. "And I can even find it in my heart to wish you both a lovely Valentine's Day, if you must succumb to the pressure of that particularly cynical side of capitalism." I throw in a smile. "If you're willing to part with your hard-earned cash to tell the women in your life on that specific day of the year that you love them, that's also fine with me. I wish you lots of fun doing it."

"Okay." Jamie sits up. "Now I know that something's going on with you, Sis. First you say nothing for half an hour, you just sit there brooding, and now you wish us a happy Valentine's Day." He shakes his head. "Something's not adding up here."

"You're seeing things that aren't there, Jamie," I assure him. Another reason why I can't tell them about the date is that, when you're me, there's always a distinct possibility that things will go south. My anxiety about messing up the date has started to flare up already, and not even trying to paint it off me has helped. I must be showing my anxiety, especially to the people who know me best. "I was painting before I came over. It just took a while for my brain to catch up."

"What were you painting?" Sean asks. He's been begging me for a painting of his wife for years, and while I have nothing against Cathy whatsoever, I haven't been able to reproduce her features on a canvas.

"A self-portrait," I blurt out.

"Really?" Jamie says. "Because you don't appear to be big on self-love today."

"I'm my own Valentine, every day of the year," I say. "So I decided to paint myself. That's all."

"Before the new girl came to town," Jamie says, "Jaden wanted to take drawing lessons, but now he's suddenly become way too busy for them."

"The kid's smitten," Sean says. "I know you're old, Jamie, but don't you remember what it was like back in the day? The first girl that, for the life of you, you couldn't get out of your head." He sighs. "Those were the days."

"I don't have to remember. I just have to take a good look at my eldest and I'm instantly reminded." Jamie grins. "It's Brooklyn this, Brooklyn that. If he deigns us worthy enough to share with, of course. But even if he doesn't, it's written all over his face. He just can't help himself."

Their conversation makes me think of how my own expressions are never that readable. If they were, surely these two would have figured me out by now. They would have worked out that it isn't just Brooklyn capturing hearts in Donovan Grove. Her mother's doing a good job of that as well. Maybe the fact that both Sean and Jamie picked up on something means that I must be showing some signs of outward infatuation. Am I infatuated with Zoe? It's hard not to be. But for me, there's only ever been a very thin line between opportunity and the feeling of being overwhelmed.

"Anna?" Sean's voice interrupts my train of thought. "You were miles away. Again."

"Sorry. Yes, Jaden's in love. How lovely," I mumble.

"If I didn't know any better," my brother says, "I'd think you were hung up on some lovely lady as well."

I shake my head to dismiss him.

"Anna, come on," Jamie insists. "Jaden might be in the throes of puberty, but do you really think he doesn't tell me anything? I know you're having Zoe over for dinner tomorrow night."

"W—what?"

"I wanted to let you tell me yourself, but you really weren't catching my drift."

"Wait a minute," Sean butts in. "You're going on a date with Zoe? On Valentine's Day." His eyes are the size of saucers.

"It has nothing to do with Valentine's Day," I protest. I curse myself for letting the obvious escape me again. Of course, Zoe would have told her daughter, and if Brooklyn is as smitten with Jaden as he is with her, the subject of her mother dating his aunt must have come up. "And it's just dinner."

"Just dinner?" Jamie says. "The last time you cooked an elaborate meal, we came this close to calling the fire brigade." He holds his thumb and index finger very close together—exaggerating gravely, as usual.

"Zoe's cooking," I say matter-of-factly, while I rack my brain for the missed signs of Jamie giving me the opportunity to tell them about Zoe. But my mind is whirring around way too frantically for me to retrieve anything from my short-term memory.

"Hallelujah." Jamie gives me a thumbs-up. He knows me well enough to not ask why I didn't spontaneously volunteer any information about the date. "Let me know if you need help with anything, Sis. Some DIY around the house to make it look extra nice." Jamie hung all the frames in my house—and there are many. In fact, he and Sean did most of the painting and hung the wallpaper—and all the other practical things I'm too clumsy to handle myself.

"You're going out with the foxy lady," Sean says, then nods, as though something is only just now sinking in. It probably is.

"Can we stop calling Zoe the foxy lady from now on, please?" I can't help a smile from spreading on my lips regardless.

"It won't be easy," Sean says, "but I'll try."

22

ZOE

"I KNOW you don't do Valentine's Day," I say, once Anna has ushered me into her kitchen, where all the ingredients I asked her to pick up at the store are laid out on the table, arranged in little groups.

I've been racking my brain about this all day—in between tending to the store on the busiest day it's had so far—and I concluded it would be best to just give Anna her present as quickly as possible. If I risk her going on another anti-Valentine's rant, which I think is highly likely considering the date, I might lose the courage to give it to her at all. And I really want her to have it, but I also don't want to make too big a deal out of it in order to not make her too uncomfortable.

"But I got you this." I take a package out of my bag. Before I give it to her, I say, "It's actually quite a funny story." I'm still getting used to Anna's glam outfit—her kind of glam, anyway. Instead of blue jeans, she's wearing a pair of shinier, black jeans, with a shirt on top that actually looks like she tried to iron it. She made an effort—and she looks mighty good in the shirt, regardless of the creases. "Your colleague, Sean, asked me for something silly he could give you for Valentine's Day, just to annoy you, really." Her face isn't giving much away. "And it did get me thinking… and I suppose I could have waited until your birthday, but I have no idea when your birthday is, Anna. And fuck it, I just really wanted to give this to you today."

"Wait." Anna scratches her cheek. "What does Sean have to do with this?"

"Him asking me for a silly gift for you somehow sparked the idea in my head for what I'm about to give you now. That's all. I wasn't going to let him give you this." This gift is by no means silly, I think. I might be feeling a little too pleased with myself about it. But I'm utterly convinced Anna will love it, which is another reason why I can't wait to give it to her.

"You got me a Valentine's Day gift?" There's slight panic in her voice now.

"How about we consider it simply 'a gift'?" I step a little closer. "Here you go." I hand her the hefty, rectangular package, which I have wrapped in gaudy pink-with-red-hearts wrapping paper—because I couldn't help myself.

"Okay." Anna smiles now. She turns the package around in her hand. "The shape looks quite familiar." She gives it another once-over and then, gently, peels off the wrapping paper.

"Look inside," I urge her.

She opens the front cover of the hardback copy of *A Little Life* I gave her. Then she stills, as she reads what the author has written inside it, especially for her.

"Damn." She keeps staring at the book. "That is so very nice." She looks up now. "I'm a bit lost for words."

"I still have quite a few connections in New York." I can't suppress the smile on my face. "It was a pleasure to use them to this end." I take another step closer and, very slowly and very briefly, bring my hand to her shoulder.

"Thank you so much." Anna sounds as though something is stuck in her throat. "I appreciate this so much."

Because I don't want to ruin the moment, I keep myself from wishing her a Happy Valentine's Day.

"What you got Hanya Yanagihara to write is so... beautiful."

"It's my absolute pleasure, Anna. Truly."

I can almost see the cogs in her brain whirring as she tries to place being on the receiving end of, even if I do say so myself, such a thoughtful gift.

"I wasn't sure about this." Anna walks over to her reading chair and carefully places the book I gave her on top of the stack she keeps next to it. "But, um, follow me, will you?"

"Of course." I follow her out of the kitchen into an adjacent room. She switches on the light. A spotlight is trained on a large canvas on a wooden easel close to the window. Wait. I recognize that face.

"Oh my God," I half-shout. "That's me."

"Yeah." Anna's tone is so dry, so matter-of-fact, as if it's the most logical thing in the universe for her to have painted me and to show it to me today, on Valentine's Day.

"Oh my God, Anna." I stand closer to the picture of myself. It's so incredibly lifelike. Did she paint this from memory? The brush strokes are so fine. In the background, there's even a stack of books of which I can make out the titles. I look closer. One of the books is *Nights of Passion*. I burst into a chuckle. What I really want to do is turn to her, take her face in my hands, and kiss her. But from the research I have done since our last chat, I'm pretty sure that's not a good idea. "You are so talented. You do know that, don't you?" I can't tear my eyes away from the painting of myself. I don't care if it makes me come across as self-absorbed, perhaps even a little bit in love with myself.

After the win of being able to give her that signed book and finding out that Anna painted me—especially after what her mother told me about the subjects she paints—I feel like a million bucks.

Anna just shrugs. "It's what I do."

"Where are you going to hang it?" I do look at her now.

"Oh... it's for you. If you want it, of course."

"*If* I want it? I think I want to marry it." I look into her clear blue eyes. Her black hair is all over the place again, because she can never stop running her hand through it. "When did you paint this?"

"I started yesterday. Finished it this morning because I was meeting Sean and Jamie at Lenny's last night so—"

"You did this in twenty-four hours?"

"Well, no, I slept. And I had a bit of work to catch up on this morning."

"I'm truly touched that you painted this for me, Anna." And then, I can't stop myself. I reach for her hand and take it in mine.

"You're cooking me dinner, so it's the least I could do, really." Her voice is but a whisper.

"I want to be understanding and gentle and all the things you need me to be." I look her in the eye and she doesn't look away. "But I would also really like to kiss you right now."

She nods. "Yes, please," she says, and brings her face closer to mine. "I would like that too." She's the one who bridges the last of the distance between us, and my heart leaps all the way into my throat. The kiss is unexpected but it's also not. Like so many things with Anna, I never really know what to expect. Her lips open and she lets me in. I bring my hands to her cheeks and draw her nearer, closer to me.

When we break from the kiss, which I immediately want to resume, she smiles at me, and says, "How does it feel to have yourself looking over you when you're kissing another woman?"

"I quite like it." I'm already pulling her closer again. "In fact, I like it so much, I think I'll do it again." Our lips meet again and, this time, Anna curls her arms around my back and presses herself against me. My hands find their way to her hair, which feels soft and satiny, and then it's not just her kisses I want anymore.

"All of this on Valentine's Day," she says, when we break from the kiss next. "How did you make this happen?"

"I didn't do anything." Our faces are so close, I can feel her breath on me when she speaks.

"Oh, but you did, Zoe. You really did." Her hands are on the back of my neck and she pulls me toward her and as she does, I realize that toward Anna is the only direction I want to keep going.

23

ANNA

Zoe's kissing me. I'm kissing Zoe. Her hands are all over my hair. She's pulling me to her and I let her. As our lips meet again and again, I keep thinking of the words she had Hanya Yanagihara write in the book she gave me—for Valentine's Day, of all things.

To Anna,

It's our differences that make us unique and beautiful.

I'm still at a loss for words because of it, so kissing Zoe some more seems like the best option right now. So I do. Because I really, really want to. One of the first things I noticed about her, were her shiny, glossy lips—and I can't believe I'm kissing them now. That I get to press mine against them is more than a treat, more than something I perhaps dreamed of happening someday far away: it's a revelation. That's the only possible word for it. I revel in her kiss. It makes me forget myself, and all the usual hang-ups that go around and around in my mind, never letting up.

She tastes so good. Fruity and minty and earthy all at the

same time. And then there's the scent coming off her and the way her breasts press into mine. It's a sensation overload and as much as I'm enjoying this very moment, I know that, pretty soon, it will be too much for my brain to process. I'm not wired for big, overwhelming sensations like this. And I certainly hadn't expected to be kissing Zoe in my studio today.

Zoe grins at me when we break from the kiss next. Her lipstick is lightly smeared around her lips and she looks as though all she wants to do is smear it about her face some more.

"That's not usually the reaction I get when I've painted someone," I joke.

"I guess it depends on who you paint." She comes for me again, but I pull away slightly.

"Can we, um, take a breather?"

"Oh." Her limbs stiffen a bit. "Yes, of course." She straightens her blouse. "I almost forgot I'm on cooking duty." She sinks her teeth into her bottom lip. "Are you okay?" She lightly touches a finger against my hand.

"Oh, yes," I say, decidedly. "Very, but… I need to take things slow."

"Come on." As if she's the one who lives here, and she's the one who asked for a break, she takes my hand, and guides me back into the kitchen. "It's going to be a huge pleasure for me to cook in this kitchen. It's so gorgeous."

"I'm glad it's being used." I head to the refrigerator and take out a bottle of white wine. "For once."

"You never cook?" Zoe asks, while she eyes the ingredients I've laid out on the table.

"I can make soup. And eggs. And smoothies. And nachos. Anything more complicated than that"—I point at my head—"and the old brain goes into overdrive." I pour us both a glass of wine.

"Well, I love to cook and I've never had a kitchen like this at my disposal." Despite what she has just said, she just stands there looking at the table, as though she's wishing the ingredients would magically arrange themselves into an edible dish—which is often my state of mind when walking through the grocery store.

"You don't have to cook if you don't feel like it. I can order us a pizza." I can't help but snicker.

"I swear to you that I came here raring to go, but, um, well, I've been somewhat distracted, and I seem to have lost my drive for it… My momentum has veered into a distinctly different direction." She sends me one of her big, seductive smiles. "And it's been quite a day."

"Come." I'm now the one who takes her hand in mine. I lead her into the living room and command her to sit. "Take off your shoes. Put your feet up. And relax."

"I think I met at least half the population of Donovan Grove in the store today. You can feel what you want about it, Anna, but I'm learning that Valentine's Day is a really big thing in these parts. People have not gotten the memo that it's a put-upon overly commercial non-holiday."

I chuckle as I sit next to her. "That's all right. As long as they also buy a book at Bookends once in a while."

"That's the beauty of running a diversified bookstore. People come in to buy a Valentine's Day gift and end up leaving with the new James Patterson."

"Is that what you call it? A diversified bookstore?"

Zoe nods. "Yes. Selling only books is not a viable business plan anymore. I knew that when I came here."

"You're probably right."

"If I'm not making my projected turnover by the third quarter, I can always add a coffee machine and sell coffee on the side. It's all the rage these days."

"In hindsight, it wasn't a bad move to open the store a few weeks before Valentine's Day."

"Nor was it a bad idea to give you that book." Zoe smiles again. Her cheeks must hurt after a day of smiling like that—or maybe she's been reserving this particular kind of smile for me.

"Did you think I was going to swat it out of your hands?" I draw up my legs and sit cross-legged next to her, looking at her. I can't get enough of looking at her.

"No, I wasn't expecting that." Her gaze is soft on me—and very easy to return. "But I also hadn't expected the painting."

"It's just something I do."

"Sure, but you have to understand that, to me, it's kind of a big deal."

I nod my understanding.

"Did you just paint my face from memory? It's so accurate and detailed."

"Yes." I tap a finger against my temple. "It's all stored in here."

"That's really amazing. So you just paint the image that's in your head?"

"Pretty much. Although unexpected things pop up while I'm actually painting. Once I get started, I just go with the flow."

"How about the book covers? How does that work?"

"Hm." I need some time to align the different steps of my process in my head. "Once I get a feel for what the book is about, I like to immerse myself in the genre. Going to Bookends and just being around books has always helped a lot with that. I do that until I have the image and the colors, the entire concept basically, in my head, and then I just make it." I pull up my shoulders. "It's no big deal."

Zoe chuckles. "Do you really believe that the incredibly creative things you do are no big deal?"

"They're no big deal to me," I say. Because I need them to function, I think, they've become an ingrained part of my routine. If I haven't painted in a week, I get so antsy, I feel like climbing up the walls.

"Is that why you've never considered selling your paintings?"

"My paintings are personal. I sell covers and other graphic designs, that's it."

"Okay." She sips from her wine and a silence falls between us.

"I—" she says.

"Jaden—" I start at the same time.

"You go first," Zoe says.

Because I've always had trouble knowing when to speak in a conversation, I gladly take the opportunity Zoe has given me to continue my sentence.

"I hear Brooklyn and Jaden are on their own Valentine's Day date tonight."

"Oh, yes. My baby's getting big. She's been on sort-of dates before, but this seems different somehow. She's really into Jaden. Like, really, *really*." She narrows her eyes and looks intently at me again.

"Jamie tells me that Jaden feels very much the same way about her." I shift in my chair. "Jamie also knew about you coming to dinner here tonight. From Jaden."

"Oh, yes, I told Brooklyn. And she must have told Jaden. And he told Jamie. Is that a problem?"

"I'm not, um, really used to my brother knowing these things about me. I love him dearly and we get along just fine, but we don't have that kind of relationship." I pause. "I would sincerely appreciate it if he didn't tell my entire family at lunch tomorrow that you and I kissed."

"Don't worry. I'm not going to tell Brooklyn about that." Zoe smiles broadly at me again.

"Thanks." I reach for her hand and run a finger over Zoe's palm. "Look, I don't know what your expectations are, but I meant what I said earlier. I need to go really slow. I can't... open myself up to someone just like that."

"Don't worry, Anna. I'm not going anywhere."

"I sure hope not."

"I promise."

"What were you going to say earlier? When I interrupted you?" I ask.

Zoe clasps her fingers around my hand. "I was going to say that I ordered the book you recommended. It should arrive on Monday."

"Thanks for, um, making the effort."

"Of course." She holds on to my hand a little tighter. "Can I ask you a very personal question?"

I nod.

"Is this… sitting here with me, talking like this… Is that hard for you?"

"No." I lift up her hand. "It's a true delight, because I really, *really* like you as well." And I was crazy to believe I would never want this again, I think. I lightly kiss her knuckle.

"Do you like me enough to change your mind about certain things?" Zoe sits up a bit.

"We're on a date right now, so the answer can only be yes." Even though I mean what I say—and I'm so smitten with Zoe that I most certainly want to try—I can't tell her how afraid I am of doing this, even though I want it so much. I'm afraid of screwing things up again. Of not being the kind of person I believe Zoe should be with. Of setting a standard for myself that I can't possibly reach.

Zoe smiles and I mellow even more. She's impossible to resist, even for my anxious heart.

"I truly didn't come here tonight with the intention of kissing you instead of cooking for you," she says.

"Could have fooled me." I bring a finger to her chin and turn her face toward me. Then I kiss her again.

The Two Hearts Trilogy
BOOK TWO

Two Hearts TOGETHER

1

ZOE

I CAN'T HELP MYSELF. I leave a few bright-red candles in the window display. Not for the benefit of anyone who might have forgotten Valentine's Day and wants to surprise their loved one a few days too late, but for my own pleasure. And perhaps also to rile up Anna a bit. I grin at my reflection in the window while I think of her. Every time I do, and I do so often, my mind wanders to the stack of books that arrived this morning. Five copies of *The Complete Guide To Autism Spectrum Disorder In Women*.

When I found myself alone in the store, I started reading immediately, even though just glancing over the table of contents made my head spin. Terms I've never heard of like *time agnosia, alexithymia,* and *demand avoidance* wouldn't usually draw me into a book, but I want to know more about Anna, so my interest is piqued regardless. It's not a book I will read in a matter of days—it's a bit too dry for that, despite my special interest in the subject—and I have a store to run.

I never expected the Tuesday after Valentine's Day to be very busy, and it's not, but I have already sold two of the wrapped blind-dates-with-a-book that I put on display only this morning to replace most of the Valentine's Day stock. Maybe Anna was onto something with that idea.

I watch the wall clock above the counter, which I've noticed myself doing much more since the previous weekend—since Anna and I kissed. She should have set off on her daily walk by now, which means she and Hemingway will walk past the store in a few minutes—and hopefully come in.

But it's not Anna who opens the door next. It's a man I vaguely recognize from Bookends' opening party, but whose name, for the life of me, I can't recall.

"How can I help you?" I put on my best smile.

"Hi, Zoe. Can I call you Zoe?" He runs a hand through what's left of his hair.

"Of course. It's my name."

"Hi, I'm Tom Granger. I just ran into my buddy Joe, who bought a book date or something?"

"Blind-dates-with-a-book. Yes." I nod, remembering Joe from earlier today.

"It made me think…" He shifts his weight onto the balls of his feet. "About going on an actual date, albeit not a blind one."

"Is that so?" I keep a neutral expression on my face as snippets of memory of the previous interaction I had with this man come back to me. The memories aren't overly pleasant.

"Yeah." He beams me a smile. "What do you think, Zoe? You and me? A few drinks at Lenny's?"

"It's very kind of you to ask, Tom." I make my way behind the counter. "But I'm not looking to date."

"Oh. But you're a single mom, right?"

As if this fact would automatically make me want to go on a date. "I am, but… I'm a lesbian. I don't date men. Never have. Never will." Sometimes, you just really need to spell it out and Tom Granger looks like someone who needs the reason for him being rejected thoroughly explained to him.

"What? *You?*" He shakes his head. "No." He follows up with an even more vigorous shake of the head. "No, I don't buy that."

"That's very offensive, actually." I haven't been in retail for that long and I do hope I can keep my cool, because Tom is starting to get on my nerves. Then again, Anna's mother had the exact same initial reaction when I told her. Maybe this reaction will be fairly universal in a town like this, where my appearance doesn't fit in with the general idea of a lesbian.

He taps a fingertip to his chin. "Are you an *L Word* lesbian? Because, frankly, I never believed those really existed."

"Look, Tom, I'm not going on a date with you." I ignore his stupid comment because it's not deserving of a reply.

Just then, the door opens, and this time, it is Anna who walks in, Hemingway hot on her heels.

"Oh, hi Anna," Tom says, as though he hasn't just made the biggest ass of himself in front of me.

"Tom." Anna gives him a curt nod.

"Tom was just leaving," I say, to make sure he's catching my drift. I have half a mind to walk up to Anna and kiss her fully on the lips in front of him, but I don't want to use Anna in that way. Besides, seeing her, and her face that always has a slight hint of bemusement, I've already forgotten about Tom Granger's inappropriate comments.

"Have a lovely day, ladies." He manages a grin before turning around and walking out the door.

As soon as he's gone, I roll my eyes.

"What's wrong?" Anna asks.

"We'll talk about it later." I hurry from behind the counter and drag her toward me. "Give me a proper hello first."

Anna opens her arms wide and curls them around me. "Hello," she whispers in my ear. "Is that proper enough?" She plants a kiss on the side of my neck.

"It will do. For now." I kiss her right back. "I've missed you." Hemingway gives a quick bark, as though he's the one replying to what I just said. “What are you doing tonight?” I ask, as we step out of our embrace.

“Nothing in particular. Although I’ve been thinking about bringing over your painting. If you’re free.”

“I’m free.”

“I’ll bring it after closing time then.” Anna smiles at me.

“Want to stay for dinner?”

Anna hesitates, then wrings her hands together. “I would, but I don’t want to encroach on your time with your daughter.”

I nod my understanding. I guess I can see how that would be awkward. “How about I come over to yours after I’ve given Brooklyn all the mommy time she can stand. I’ll just take the painting home myself.”

Anna looks at my arms as though they’re not capable of carrying one of her paintings.

“You should see me haul boxes of books into here,” I say.

“I would love to see that, actually.” Anna hasn’t stopped smiling since Tom Granger left.

“If seeing my guns is what you’re after, it’ll be a while before it’s short-sleeve season.” I take a step closer to her again.

“Spring will be upon us before you know it.” Anna takes my hand in hers.

“I can’t wait for that snow to melt.” A shadow glides by the shop window and, as though by instinct, Anna takes a step back and drops my hand.

“I—I suppose we should go on another date,” Anna says.

“Are you asking me out?” I say coyly.

“Does you coming by tonight qualify as a date?”

“Sure.”

“We can’t be standing around in Bookends like this every day. People will start talking.” She says it with a grin on her face.

“Your mother will find out in no time.”

Anna rolls her eyes. "Tonight, then."

"Should I bring you leftovers?" I joke.

Anna shakes her head. "I can take care of myself perfectly."

2

ANNA

WITH A SPRING IN MY STEP, I walk from Bookends to Sean's office. As I approach, my jauntiness fades, because I know that he will inevitably ask me about my date with Zoe. Miraculously, Jamie managed to keep his mouth shut at lunch on Sunday. He must have given Jaden a talking-to as well, because my nephew barely mentioned Brooklyn. All throughout lunch, however, I could sense that my mother was on to something. I can't explain how I knew—maybe it was in a glance that lingered a bit too long, or in the twitch of her lips as she bit back a comment—but I did. The question will come sooner rather than later and because it's not something I can control, it's stressing me out already, before anything has even happened. So I consider practicing talking about Zoe to Sean. The fact that I'm not related to him should make it easier, yet I have my doubts.

Once he's done showering Hemingway with affection, he pours us each a cup of coffee.

"Do you want to talk?" he asks.

"About?"

"Come on, Anna. It's me. You know you can talk to me."

The thing is that I can't. Conversation has never been how I have expressed myself. I can do banter and I can crack the odd joke, but I can't possibly put my feelings into words in front of another human, not even a friend. Sean should know this by now.

"There's nothing to say."

"You're not going to give me even a little bit? A tiny sliver of dating goodness?" He pushes his glasses up the bridge of his nose.

"How was your Valentine's Day?" I ask, changing the subject. "Did Cathy get you something?"

"Not a material gift." He waggles his eyebrows.

"Oh, Sean," I groan.

He shakes his head and rummages in his desk drawer. "For you," he says.

"What's this?"

"You're my best friend, so I wanted to give you something for Valentine's Day."

I roll my eyes. "You got me a Valentine's gift?"

"Anyone else would just say thank you." He sits there smirking.

"I'm not anyone else." I shake my head in utter dismay.

"Tell me about it." He just continues to sit there, inappropriately grinning at me. "Go on. Aren't you going to open it?"

I tear at the wrapping. It reminds me of last Saturday, when Zoe gave me that unexpected gift. It seems to be the year for it. I recognize the white box with garish red hearts printed on it as one that lined the counter at Bookends when it first opened. At least he got me something from Zoe's store. That does perk me up. Inside the box is an envelope. I open it and find a gift card for Bookends.

"A gift card?" I try not to sound too ungrateful.

"Yes, well, Zoe let me down, so that's the best I could do."

"What do you mean?"

"She offered to help me find you the perfect Valentine's gift. Something that would rile you up. But in the end, she chickened out of helping me, for obvious reasons. So I went for the gift card, instead." He shrugs. "Happy belated Valentine's Day, my friend."

"Yeah. Thanks," I mumble.

"I should have thought of something better than a gift card, I know." He narrows his eyes and regards me intently.

"Why are you looking at me like that?"

"Zoe was extremely apologetic about letting me down. Then, she told me why."

"Why?"

"Because she was too preoccupied getting you the perfect gift herself."

"What?"

Sean widens his eyes. "Oh, damn. She didn't give it to you?"

"She—she did. But I didn't know she'd told you about it."

"I think she likes you, Anna."

"I can't believe she told you. What else did you discuss about me?"

"Nothing. Come on. It was all well-intentioned."

Zoe seems to be the opposite of discreet. "Oh, I'm sure you all meant well while you were talking about me behind my back."

"Of course, we did." He tilts his head. "And this to a guy who just gave you a present."

"A Valentine's Day present, Sean. You know how I feel about that."

"Is this how you reacted when Zoe gave you her present?"

I can't keep a small smile from widening my lips. "Of course not."

"Is that because she's a million times hotter than I am?"

I shrug. "You're more of an acquired taste. I'm sure Cathy thinks you're superhot," I joke.

"I was just goofing around, Anna. In friendship. To show you that, you know, I appreciate you."

"You don't have to give me gifts to show me. I know you care."

"But still." He sips from his coffee.

"Have you… told Cathy about me going on a date with Zoe?"

"She's my wife."

"I'll take that as a yes," I say on a sigh. "I just don't want this to spread around town just yet. Yes, we like each other, and we had a good date, but that doesn't mean anything. So much could still happen."

"Hey, there could be worse things being said about you than that you're dating Zoe from Bookends, believe me," Sean says.

"I do believe you."

"So the date was good?" Sean tries again.

I nod. How can I not?

"What did she get you?"

"Oh, she didn't tell you that, did she?" I smirk at Sean.

He shakes his head.

"A signed copy of a book that means a lot to me," I say, my heart warming as I speak.

"Hey, I'm happy for you, Anna."

"She is really, *really* foxy."

Sean chuckles. "No doubt." He rests his gaze on me for a few seconds. "Do you have any business to discuss or is it all Valentine's Day chatter with you today?"

3

ZOE

I STAND in front of Anna's bright red front door. It's later than I would have wanted it to be. Being on my feet all day is very different than being stuck behind a desk for eight hours a day. On top of that, Brooklyn kept on chattering away about a Skype call she'd had with Eve. It wasn't the kind of conversation I could easily walk away from. She's made friends quickly and she might not dislike Donovan Grove too much, but she has just gone through a massive upheaval at a very tender age.

When Anna opens the door, her hair is pointing in all directions and she looks quite frazzled. She's wearing a pair of pajamas.

"Did I wake you?" A large smile sneaks across my lips.

"It's after ten." She holds the door open. I detect a smidge of utterly adorable just-woken-up crankiness in her voice.

"I'm sorry." I hurry inside, not just because it's freezing cold outside, but because I can't wait to be engulfed by the warmth of Anna's home. "Brooklyn needed me. I know it's late, but I wanted to see you." I reach for her hand. The instant our skin touches, she pulls me close.

"I'm glad you're here." Anna embraces me and pushes her body against mine. I'm fairly certain she's not wearing a bra.

"I'm glad you dressed up for me," I joke.

"You can't arrive at someone's house after ten and expect them to be wearing a tux."

I chuckle as I run a hand across her back. Definitely no bra.

In the living room, Hemingway's spread all over a cushion on the floor.

"There's not much life in him after ten," Anna says.

"Did he have an exhausting day?" I ask.

"Every day's a full-on party when you're my dog," Anna says. "Can I get you anything?"

I shake my head. "Let's just sit." She has prepared the painting for me to take home. It's leaning against the wall, covered in Bubble Wrap. She has also fashioned a handle with some rope around it so it's easy for me to carry. "How was the rest of your day?" What I really want to ask is if I can kiss her, but I figure that if that's what she also wants, she'll make that clear to me in due course.

She rubs her palms on her pajama bottoms, giving me the impression that something's bothering her. Or perhaps she's having trouble articulating what she wants to say.

"I talked to Sean," she says. "You told him you got me a Valentine's Day present?"

I purse my lips. "That might have slipped out." I try to look Anna in the eye. "I was supposed to help him find a funny present for you, but I got too caught up finding you a genuine gift myself." I try a smile.

"I—I really don't like it when everyone's all up in my private business."

"I thought he was your best friend." Maybe Anna's definition of a best friend is very different from mine.

Anna shrugs. "He's my friend, but that doesn't mean I want him to know everything about me."

I wish I had asked for a glass of wine now. "Anna... Does Sean know about your diagnosis?"

"What does that have to do with anything?"

"I'm just curious."

She shakes her head. "Only my family knows. And Cynthia. And now you. And I'd prefer to keep it that way."

"But why wouldn't you tell Sean?"

"Because... it's not something that I want people to know about me. It's my private business."

"But Sean is not just 'people'..."

"You may have had your *Sex and the City* girlfriend gang when you were living in New York, but that's not something I relate to. I don't tell my friends everything about myself. I have no need to share every tiny little thing that happens to me."

"I kind of did, yeah." Anna's reminded me of Marsha, my neighbor in Queens, and I'm suddenly aware of how much I've missed her. I've been too busy getting Bookends off the ground to invite her up here—and too preoccupied with getting to know Anna. "Although it was all far less glamorous than on TV."

"You must miss them," Anna says, her voice small.

"Yeah," I nod. "But I've been keeping myself busy. And I know I'll make friends here eventually. Which reminds me..." I push Marsha from my mind. She's only a few hours' drive away. I'll go into the city soon enough to catch up with everyone from my old life. "This weekend there's the newcomers' welcome drinks at Lenny's."

"Oh yeah. Mom will be there with bells on."

"I was thinking of going. Would you like to go with me?"

"I'm not new to town. I was born here."

I chuckle. "As my date?"

"I don't think it's the sort of event you take a date to," Anna says. "You should go with Brooklyn."

"I somehow doubt I'll convince my teenage daughter to come with me."

"Look, I'm sorry, but that's too soon for me. I would like our next date to not be in a public place. Besides, my mother will be there, and she'll want us to apply for a marriage license if she sees us together."

"So you won't come with me?" I give her an exaggerated look of sadness.

"It's not my thing, Zoe." She puts a hand on my knee. "But that doesn't mean I don't want to see you this weekend."

"Date night on Friday?" I put my hand over hers.

"Oh… no, I can't. I go to Lenny's with Jamie and Sean every Friday night."

"Every single Friday night of your life?" I drag my fingertip around one of her knuckles.

"Well, um, yeah. It's what we do."

"And… is it completely unfathomable to give up your weekly booze night to spend time with me?"

"Um, no, I suppose not." Anna doesn't sound too convinced.

"I need to check when the newcomers thing is." I need to lighten the mood. "I'm not sure if it's on Friday or Saturday, actually."

"Whichever night you're free, I'll be free." Anna smiles now. She shuffles a little closer.

"Thank you," I whisper, then lean in so close our lips almost touch.

"Your lips are so…" Anna pauses, then, instead of saying anything else, kisses me. I kiss her back, because I don't need to hear her say what she thinks of my lips. What she's doing with them right now is making it abundantly clear how she feels about them.

Our tongues dance, and her hands move to my hair and she pulls me closer still. I lose myself in this kiss. I seem to have been waiting for it for a very long time.

"You'd rather drink beer with Sean and Jamie than do this?" I ask, jokingly, when we break, gasping for breath.

Anna just shakes her head and pulls me closer again.

4

ANNA

"What's going on?" Jamie asks. "You seem even more uptight than usual."

"Mom's going to be walking in here any minute now." I roll my eyes.

"Ah, that time of the year," Sean says. "When Mrs. G. likes to introduce herself to the very few people in Donovan Grove who haven't yet had the pleasure of meeting her." He squints at me. "Sometimes it's so hard to believe you're related to her, Anna."

"I struggle with the notion every single day," I say.

"Oh, come on, it's fun when Mom's here," Jamie says. "She's always the life of the party, whether there's a party or not." He chuckles.

"It's just that... Zoe's coming as well," I say.

"I see," Jamie says. "Don't worry. I'll keep Mom distracted."

As if we summoned her by talking about her, the door opens and my mother walks into Lenny's. She looks around the place and fixes her gaze on us, then heads straight over.

"My darling children," she says, already in full performance mode. "My two beauties. Come here." She makes a show of kissing us on both cheeks. "And Sean." He isn't spared her affection, although he looks as though he doesn't mind in the slightest.

"Expecting a big turnout tonight, Sherry?" Sean asks.

Mom scrunches up her face. "Not really. The holiday season isn't peak move-to-Donovan Grove time. But that's all right." She looks around again. "I don't think anyone new has arrived yet, which gives me time to buy you guys a drink."

She goes through the motions and soon we all find ourselves with fresh beers in our hands. I can't keep my eyes from the door. When Zoe told me that the newcomers' event was on Friday night, I was of half a mind to cancel my weekly standing date with my brother and Sean. But I didn't—because I would never hear the end of it—leaving me to face my mother's unpredictable nature when she's among people.

"I haven't seen you all week, Anna." Mom gives my shoulder a gentle squeeze. "A lot of work?"

"Yeah." I smile at her and wonder, again, whether she knows about Zoe and me. But if she did, she wouldn't keep it to herself. At least I don't think she would. That's the thing with my mother—she can still end up surprising me. Even after all these years of being her daughter, I still can't always read her.

I've asked Zoe not to engage in any public displays of affection, because that's not how I want my mother to find out we're dating. Ideally, I wouldn't have to tell her anything yet. It's way too soon to be telling anyone anything—which is one of the reasons it annoyed me so much that Zoe told Sean she got me a Valentine's gift. I don't want to jinx this by prematurely informing people—I have too many odds stacked against me already.

"She made a great cover this week, Sherry," Sean says, surprising me. We're not the type of colleagues to shower each other with compliments. We appreciate each other's work in what I thought was a mutually agreed upon silence. "Were you feeling particularly inspired, Anna?" *Oh.* He's egging me on. This is going to be a long night—and Zoe hasn't even arrived yet.

"I had a good week," I say drily, hoping my mother will hijack the conversation soon, as she tends to do. Instead, she looks at me funnily. *Oh shit.* She does know. How, though? How do people pick up on these things? I know she's my mother but that doesn't mean she has direct access to how I feel inside—far from it.

I realize I'm stuck in another anxiety thought loop, when the door opens, and someone I've never seen before walks in. This is my mother's cue to tear herself away from us and greet the newcomer with an abundance of cackles and smiles.

"You gotta love Mom," Jamie says.

"She should be the real mayor of DG," Jamie says.

Jamie and I burst out laughing. I look at him, and he shakes his head. "That would be the worst idea ever."

"Why?" Sean asks. "She'd get the votes."

I stop listening because the door opens again and in walks Zoe. She has dressed up—it seems to be her thing. She's wearing a very tight, cream-colored blouse with a whole lot of cleavage. Jesus Christ. Where did she think she was going? I take a sip of beer to get my bearings.

Sean and Jamie have both stopped weighing up my mother's options as potential mayor of Donovan Grove.

Before Zoe even has the time to see me, she's intercepted by my mother, who opens her arms wide to her, as though Zoe is already an official member of her family.

"I know I'm not allowed to call her 'foxy' any longer," Sean says, "but damn it, Zoe's so damn foxy."

"On the political correctness scale, is swearing worse than calling a foxy lady foxy?" Jamie mumbles to no one in particular.

"Aren't you going to say hi?" Sean asks.

"I will, but I'll let Mom do her thing first." I watch how my mother introduces Zoe to the man who came in just before her.

"Don't you wish you'd ironed your shirt this morning, Sis?" Jamie asks.

"For crying out loud, guys. Can't you keep it together a bit more?" Secretly, I'm a little bit proud they're fawning over Zoe like that. But Jamie's right. Compared to her, I look like the frumpiest woman in town.

Then Zoe spots us and she gives us a wave before heading over.

"Hi." Her smile is wide and warm. "Great to see you guys again." She finds my gaze and I feel myself melt a little when she looks into my eyes like that.

"And you," Sean says.

"My son can't stop talking about your daughter," Jamie says.

I listen to them talk about Jaden and Brooklyn for a bit, but mainly I watch Zoe, as she wraps my brother and Sean around her very elegant finger, just by having a chat with them. How does she do that? It's a sort of superpower. An easiness with other people I've never been able to fathom, even though I've seen it in action with Mom all my life. But with Zoe, it's different. Probably because I'm developing strong romantic feelings for her.

Zoe slides into the booth next to me, her thigh touching mine.

"I wasn't sure you'd be here," she whispers in my ear.

Because Sean and Jamie are watching us, I feel my cheeks grow hot instantly.

"Well, here I am," I manage to say.

No more newcomers must have found their way to Lenny's, because my mother has turned up at our table again.

"Glad to see you're getting along," she says, in a way that

leaves no doubt in my mind that she knows. I have to at least appreciate the courtesy she has given me by not asking me about it the moment she found out—because it goes very much against her nature. "Can I sit?" Mom doesn't wait for a reply, nor does she wait for Zoe to make room for her on the bench. She all but shoves her against me with her hip. At least she's not sitting across from me. But I also can't escape from the booth without explicitly asking both my mom and Zoe to move.

The door of the bar opens again, and I hope it's another newcomer so Mom would have to get up again, but it's only Tom Granger.

"Him," Zoe says, her voice dripping with disdain.

"Wasn't he at Bookends the other day?" I ask.

"Oh, yes. He asked me out, actually," Zoe says.

"What?" Why hasn't she mentioned this before? "Really?"

"Yes and he was pretty insistent about it, even after I turned him down on account of being a lesbian. I couldn't have given him a more explicit reason," Zoe says.

"Guys like Tom," Sean says, shrugging, as if that's supposed to mean something to us. It does mean something to me, perhaps because I grew up in this town.

"He had some trouble accepting I was actually a lesbian," Zoe says. "Can you believe that? In this day and age? That people still have this very fixed idea of what a lesbian should look like." She shakes her head.

"Like Anna you mean?" Jamie grins at me.

Zoe doesn't dignify his stupid remark with a reply and I could kiss her for it. Tom Granger heads straight for the bar and doesn't pay us any attention.

A short silence falls, which is surprising with my mother at the table, but I take the moment to be grateful I'm sitting here with all my favorite people.

"I believe I might have displayed the same kind of ignorance when Zoe told me," Mom says. "I do apologize for that. Let me buy you a drink to make up for it."

"It's fine, Sherry. You weren't asking me out on a date. It's not the same thing," Zoe says, probably endearing herself to my mother even more.

"What are you drinking?" Mom asks.

"White wine, please. Thanks." Zoe's gaze follows my mother as she heads to the bar. Mom doesn't just order drinks; she also goes to have a chat with Tom Granger.

"Another reason why Sherry would make a great mayor," Sean says. "She can't abhor any kind of bigotry."

"Is your mother running for mayor?" Zoe asks. Even though Mom is no longer sharing the bench with us, Zoe hasn't moved an inch away from me. Her thigh is glued to mine and I can feel her body heat radiating onto me.

"No, we were just joking."

"Welcoming new people to town is actually the mayor's job." Sean is unwilling to let this go. "Why isn't she here?"

"She came to the Bookends opening party," Zoe says. "She made me feel very welcome to Donovan Grove."

"But you run a store. Not every newcomer does."

"The mayor knows she doesn't have to be here tonight because Mom's here," Jamie says.

"Mom's not a politician, Sean," I say. "Her heart's too much in the right place for that. She can't play dirty."

"Here you go." Mom has returned. "And you can rest assured that Tom Granger will no longer be bothering you." She hands Zoe her glass of wine.

"Thank you so much, Sherry," Zoe says.

I wish I could see her face right now. And in the grand scheme of things, if things do work out between Zoe and me, it's good to know that she and my mother will get along swimmingly.

"Are you always out and about on your own?" Zoe asks.

"I am," Mom says resolutely.

"Dad's the biggest homebody you'll ever meet. He's probably in his workshop right now," Jamie says. "Turning an old door into a chair or something like that."

"I'd love to meet him some time," Zoe says.

"Why don't you come to Sunday lunch?" Mom asks. "You and your daughter, of course. We always have a big family lunch on Sunday and there's always plenty left over. You and Brooklyn are more than welcome to join us."

"I may need to check with Jaden," Jamie says, chuckling.

Zoe turns to me. "Is that okay with you?"

"Um, yeah, sure," I mumble, because I can hardly say, in front of my mother, that it's way too soon for Zoe to be having lunch with my family. I'll need to talk with my mother beforehand, even though I don't want to, because the instant I confirm to her that something's going on between Zoe and me, she'll take that as a sign to start officially butting in, to ask me about Zoe multiple times a week, and to begin probing for information I don't feel comfortable sharing.

"I'd love to, Sherry," Zoe says.

"Brooklyn's not going to freak out about meeting Jaden's entire family?" Jamie asks.

"You'll be there to find out," Zoe says.

"If you want to invite me and Cathy along." Sean beams a smile at my mother.

"Another time, dear," Mom says, patting him on the arm.

"Speaking of my better half." Sean empties his beer. "I'd better get home." He looks at his watch as though, despite being a grown man, he has a curfew. I actually believe that he has.

"One last beer," Jamie says, just like he does every week. The familiarity of his words is always somehow soothing to me.

Unlike any other Friday, Sean agrees with Jamie.

"Why don't you call Cathy and ask her to join us?" Mom

asks. "The more, the merrier." She looks around. "I don't think any more newcomers will arrive."

Sean shakes his head.

Jamie and I have been forever nagging him about inviting Cathy along, even though we both know she teaches back-to-back Pilates classes on Friday evenings and after-work drinks aren't really her thing.

"Who was the first guy who arrived? Is he new?" I ask.

"Just passing through," Mom says. "Which explains why I'd never seen him before."

"So I'm the only newcomer?" Zoe asks.

"The one and only," Mom says.

5

ZOE

I RUB my temples and emit a little groan. I haven't quite got the hang of working on Saturdays yet. When I woke up this morning, I thought of asking Brooklyn if she wanted to earn some extra pocket money by minding the store for a few hours, but then I remembered she was going into the city for the day to see some of her former classmates.

The white wine they serve at Lenny's must contain some diabolical ingredients, because my head's still sore after taking two ibuprofens. And I didn't even drink that much.

As a distraction, I look at the picture of myself, which now hangs above the front door of Bookends. At first, I wanted to put it in my bedroom, but both Brooklyn and I agreed the painting was too good to not be on display in the store—and it didn't feel quite right to place it above my bed either.

We only hung it last night so Anna hasn't seen it yet. I'm sure she'll come by today. No doubt, she'll need to give me instructions on how to behave at lunch with her family tomorrow. I chuckle at the thought. Even though she asked me quite a few times to not engage in any displays of affection at Lenny's in front of her mother, I took great pleasure in squeezing her knee under the table. At one point, I even let a finger dart higher up her thigh, and I had to keep myself in check, because we're not there yet at all. I was just doing it to rile her up and by the look on her face, it was working.

My first customers of the day are Cynthia and John.

"We've come to check out the cookbook section," John says.

"I can't get him out of the kitchen these days." Cynthia has a goofy smile.

I'm sure I've been wearing an equally goofy smile lately. It was so lovely to spend time with Anna and her family, and Sean at Lenny's. Sherry's so easygoing and if Jaden's anything like his father, then I hope Brooklyn doesn't tire of him too quickly. Most of all, it was helpful to see Anna in a social setting, in a place where she feels comfortable. It assuaged some of the worries that have been developing since I've started reading the book about Autism Spectrum Disorder.

"There are worse places than the kitchen for your significant other to be," I joke.

Cynthia looks around the shop and, as though drawn there, her gaze lands on the painting—it's quite the eye-catching piece. "Wow. Anna painted you." The goofy smile from earlier has turned to a look of disbelief. "Is it getting serious?"

"It's early days." I can't suppress a goofy smile of my own.

"Anna must be very serious about you if she painted you. It's kind of her thing." Cynthia leans over the counter. "After the first two she painted of me, I really didn't know what to do with them any longer."

Warmth blossoms in my chest. "I think I spotted a few paintings with your likeness on them when I was in her studio."

"She doesn't keep all of them. After a while, she just paints over them. It's more of an outlet than an artistic expression for her, I think." Cynthia arches up her eyebrows. "Have you asked her if it's okay to hang that up here in the store, for everyone to see?"

"It's a picture of *me*," I blurt out. "And it was a gift to me. Surely I can do with it what I want?"

Cynthia gives a thoughtful nod. "I'd check with her regardless. She can be funny about these things."

"I found what I was looking for." John joins us at the counter. As if he overheard what we were talking about, his eye is drawn to the painting as well. "Anna's very talented," he says. "Much more than she will ever give herself credit for."

"Do you know Anna?" I ring up the cookbook he has chosen.

"I've known Anna Gunn forever. We were all at high school together. We basically grew up together. She mainly drew back then. The painting came a bit later. Isn't that right?" He turns to Cynthia. I wonder if he knows about her Autism. But if Anna hasn't even told Sean, I can't imagine John knowing, unless Cynthia has told him.

Cynthia nods. Then our conversation is interrupted by the door opening.

"My goodness," the woman who just entered exclaims. "I love what you've done to the place."

It takes me a minute to place her. Then I remember—she's the previous owner of Bookends.

"Mrs. Fincher," Cynthia says. "How was the cruise?"

"Delightful," Mrs. Fincher says, while ostentatiously feasting her eyes on the decor of the store.

"We have to run," John says. "We were supposed to meet my mother ten minutes ago."

"You're the one who wanted to quickly pop in here." Cynthia waves goodbye and before I know it, they're out the door.

"Goodness, it's so strange to be back here. It's the same, but also very different."

"Look around as much you want, Mrs. Fincher."

"I will, dear," she says.

I watch her as she shuffles around the store.

"Are you living in the apartment above?" she asks, from the nonfiction section.

"Yes, it's very convenient."

"How's business?"

"I haven't been open that long, but Valentine's Day was really good. It's all looking quite promising." I have to yell slightly for fear she won't catch what I'm saying.

"Good to hear." She turns to me. "If you ever need a hand." A smile appears on her face. "I don't have much going on now that I'm back from my cruise."

"No other travel plans?"

"Not immediately." She heads to the travel guide section regardless.

And then, it happens again. As with Cynthia and John, as though drawn by some irresistible force, Mrs. Fincher notices the painting.

"Oh dear," she says. "That's bold." She squints and, without taking her eyes off it, approaches the painting. "Anna Gunn?" she asks.

For someone who keeps her paintings pretty much to herself, they do seem instantly recognizable to a lot of Donovan Grove residents.

"Yes. How did you know?"

"I've known Anna since she was this high." Mrs. Fincher holds up a flat hand at knee height. "I know what she's capable of with a brush and some paint." She narrows her eyes further and approaches me. "I like to think I know Anna better than most. She came to the store all the time. After my husband died, those first few months when I had no idea what to do with myself, it was like she instinctively knew to stay a little longer. She wouldn't necessarily chat. Anna's never been one for small talk. But she'd just linger and her quiet, calm presence, soothed me. And it's as if she could somehow sense that, so she kept doing it." A soft smile appears on her face. "When I sold the store, she gave me a painting of it, as a farewell gift. I gave it a prominent spot in my living room and looking at it fills me with joy every single day."

Who knew that hanging up a painting of myself would allow me to find out so much more about Anna?

"That's so nice of her." My chest fills with warmth again.

"Anna's special and, well, she was an excellent customer." Mrs. Fincher folds her features into a more unsentimental expression. "I have to be honest, I never truly believed this place would sell. You're brave to have taken it over in this day and age, Zoe."

"Or insane," I joke. "And foolishly clinging to some romantic ideal of the small-town book store."

"It's a lovely thing for the Donovan Grove community to have. We used to have readings here, mostly from authors of children's books. The place would fill with children, and then I would always be convinced the world would turn out okay." She chuckles softly. "How's that for a foolish romantic notion?" Our conversation is interrupted by a deafening phone chime coming from her purse. "That's probably my daughter wondering where I am." She just looks at the screen but doesn't pick up. "I have to go, dear. Good luck and give my best to Anna." She sends me a quick, unexpected wink before she exits the store.

It's another hour before Anna arrives. She and Hemingway are in the store for a full ten minutes, before she notices the painting. My pulse quickens as I remember Cynthia's words from earlier. I fondle Hemingway's ears, and watch Anna as she stares at the painting.

"That's not for sale, I hope," Anna says, after what must have been a minute of silence.

"Of course not."

"Are you worried people won't realize this is your store?"

"Are you making fun of me?" I ask.

"I wouldn't dare."

"Good, because this is your art."

"You could have chosen to just hang up a mirror if you missed the sight of your own face so much."

"Are you calling me vain now?" I like Anna when she's like this: playful and not overly self-conscious.

"I'm not calling you anything at all, Zoe. I'm just… observing."

"You don't mind that I put it up there without asking you first?"

"I've given it to you, so it's yours to do with as you please. But, truth be told, I thought you'd be the type to hang it in your bedroom, just to catch one last glimpse of yourself before you go to bed." She stands there grinning.

"Very funny." I stop petting Hemingway and grab her hand. "What do you take me for, anyway?"

"An extremely good-looking lady," Anna whispers in my ear. "I've even heard you described as 'foxy'."

"Is that so? By whom?"

"That's a confidence I can't betray." Her body shakes against mine as she laughs.

"You're in a good mood today." I had somehow expected her to be all up in arms about tomorrow's lunch.

"I'm about to make my mother very happy, so… wouldn't you be?"

"Are you spending the afternoon with Sherry?"

"I'm on my way over to give her and Dad the news. About us, I mean. I can't sit through a lunch pretending we're not dating, even though it's still so early."

"Should I have declined her very kind invitation?"

"I know what my mom can be like. She's hard to say no to. If she hadn't invited you for lunch this Sunday, she would have done so for the Sunday after. And as much as I'd like to keep this from her for a while, it's very hard to do so, even more because she already knows. I need to tell her something, otherwise there will be too much tension between her and me, and I don't want that."

"Okay." This reminds me that I should have a conversation of my own with my daughter before we go to lunch at the Gunns tomorrow. "Small towns can really speed things up."

"You don't mind that I'm telling my parents already?" Anna asks.

"It's not like you're bringing a U-Haul to our second date, Anna."

"I don't drive, so I would never do that." She gives me a funny look.

"What?"

"I want to say something, even though, again, it's way too soon to say anything of the kind."

"Doing certain things too soon seems to be the trend between us." Some things, at least, I add in my head.

"I'm not the U-Haul type. At all. I live alone because I need to. I don't, um, cohabitate."

"You and Cynthia never lived together?" The question's out of my mouth before I can stop it—before I can reassure her that I and my fifteen-year-old daughter won't be moving in with her and Hemingway any time soon.

"No. We always had our separate houses. I need a lot of time on my own, to recharge, to just be. I can't be around other people all the time."

"Noted." An amused smile spreads across my lips.

"Are you mocking *me* now?" Anna asks.

I shake my head. "It's just funny that I'm having a meal with your family and we're discussing not moving in together before we've even... *you know*."

Instantly, Anna's cheeks turn bright red. "I—I know, but,

we've only, um, been on one proper date. I mean, it feels like more and we see each other all the time—"

"Anna." I bring my hands to her shoulders. "I was just kidding. I'm sorry. I didn't mean to make you uncomfortable. I really didn't. I blurt things out sometimes. Come here." I curl my arms around her and pull her close. "I wasn't implying anything."

"It's fine." Anna stands rather stiffly in my embrace despite her saying it's all good. "I'd better go. Mom's expecting me."

"I'm about to close for lunch." It strikes me that Anna's the third person who has come into the store today mentioning a family member waiting for them. Family and community seem to be a big thing in Donovan Grove. "Do you want me to come with you?"

The expression on Anna's face couldn't be more surprised. "No. I'll tell them on my own. I'll see you tomorrow."

"Tomorrow? How about tonight?" The disappointment in my voice is very deliberate.

"Um. Yeah. Saturday night is..." Anna doesn't finish her sentence.

"It's okay. I understand if you need to be alone tonight. Brooklyn's in the city all day and I'm sure she'll have a lot of tales to tell when she gets back."

"No," Anna says resolutely. "Come over if you want to. Call me if you do." Her smile is genuine enough, I think.

"I'll let you know." I kiss her on the lips before I watch her go.

6

ANNA

HEMINGWAY SEEMS to have many more lampposts he needs to sniff today, while all I want to do is walk fast from Bookends to my parents' house to expel some nervous energy. Why did I have to say that about the U-Haul? Why did my mother have to invite Zoe to lunch in the first place? I'm aware that I'm mostly nervous about telling mom and dad about Zoe and me. Not about giving them the actual information, but what it implies about us—about our relationship, if you can even already call it that. This is all happening way too fast for me and my slow-processing brain.

Then Zoe threw in the comment about sex—that we have not slept together yet—and now my brain, while it's still processing all of that, is about ready to combust. Because telling my parents and taking things a step further with Zoe are both an act of vulnerability. And in the end, showing vulnerability is my biggest weakness. The mental hurdles I need to overcome to put myself in a position of vulnerability are almost impossible to take—and there are many.

"Come on, Hem," I half-shout, taking my frustration out on

my poor dog. To make it up to him, I give him a thorough scratch once he catches up with me.

Too soon for my liking, I reach the house where I grew up —it really is a theme these days. I could do with another fast walk around the block, but Hemingway sprints onto the driveway, announcing our presence.

"Where's Dad?" I ask Mom, once I'm inside.

"Workshop," Mom says, knowing I don't need any further explanation. "I think he really is turning an old door into a chair this time."

"He probably is."

"Last night was fun, wasn't it?" Mom says.

"Yeah."

"Pity there weren't more new people to welcome, but Zoe was more than enough, wouldn't you agree?"

Great. She's fishing already. I wonder if I should get my dad so I can tell him in person. He won't know what to say, anyway. Still, it feels important to tell them both at the same time. It's not because my mother is much more outgoing and in the know that she has automatically earned the privilege to be told everything first.

"I'm just going to say hi to Dad."

"Do you want to stay for lunch?" Mom asks as I head into the corridor that leads to the garage slash workshop.

"Yes, please." Any meal I don't have to prepare for myself is a win. This reminds me of the meal Zoe never cooked for me.

Dad is hunched over a bench in the workshop. He's wearing a dust mask, as though he's performing surgery on a piece of wood, and a pair of plastic protective glasses.

"Dad. Hi."

He pulls down the mask, takes off the goggles and his eyes light up.

"Hi, sweetheart," he says. Neither one of us is a naturally

tactile greeter and we've learned long ago that a hug hello or goodbye is not required in our relationship.

"Can you come into the kitchen, please? I need to talk to you and Mom."

Behind me, from the doorway, Hemingway gives a pitiful yelp. We taught him from the start that the workshop is not a safe place for him to freely wander.

"Sure. I'll be there in a second." As soon as he's clocked Hemingway, my dad starts putting away his tools.

"What are you making?"

"A birdhouse," he says.

I swallow the words 'another one'. Both mine and Jamie's back yards are full of these things already. They're my father's favorite object to make.

"Why don't you let Anna paint them and I'll sell them," Jamie once offered.

Both Dad and I had many arguments against that plan, because even though we really like to create things, everything changes once you start producing them for money. It would take away an essential part of the joy we feel when engaged in our arts and crafts.

"I could do with another one," I joke, and go back inside to wait for Dad. Hemingway remains seated in the doorway.

Mom looks at me with a very practiced look of patience on her face. But I have to give her some credit, because being my mother hasn't always been a walk in the park—I suppose it still isn't. Dad just sits there, waiting. With him, it's not a matter of patience, I know. He's just giving me the time I need to gather my thoughts, which I should have done on the way over, but I was too busy obsessing over my conversation with Zoe.

"Zoe and I are dating," I blurt out, quickly, as though I'm

telling them I've contracted an embarrassing infection or something.

"Oh, Anna." Mom clasps her hands together.

"Who's Zoe?" Dad asks, and I burst out laughing.

Mom shakes her head, but she does a good job of hiding any disdain she might feel.

"She's the new owner of Bookends, Sam," Mom says. "I told you about her."

"You tell me about so many people. I can't keep up."

From this exchange, I can only conclude that my mother hasn't told my father anything about Zoe in relation to me, because I know he would remember that. I secretly applaud her for that.

"Good for you, darling," Dad says, then turns to Mom. "Do we like Zoe?"

"We do. Very much," Mom says.

"Good." Dad nods. "I'm happy for you then."

"She's the one I invited to Sunday lunch. Zoe and her daughter, Brooklyn," Mom says.

"You invited strangers to Sunday lunch? *Again?*" Dad says.

"They're not strangers. Anna's dating Zoe," Mom tries to defend herself.

"But you didn't know that, because Anna only just told us."

"Don't be so difficult, Sam. I've met Zoe quite a few times and we hit it off last night at Lenny's. And, for your information, Brooklyn's dating your grandson."

"That's right, I helped Jaden make a Valentine's Day present for his girlfriend, actually." Dad scratches the stubble on his chin. "Does this mean I need to dress up for Sunday lunch?"

"You can dress however you like," Mom says, then she looks at me. "I had an inkling of this, you know, Anna," she says. "I couldn't be sure, but I was beginning to have my suspicions."

I just nod. I don't feel like challenging her on this, even though I'm pretty sure she had much more than an inkling.

"I'm happy for you too," Mom says.

"The reason I'm telling you today is because I don't want any fuss made over this tomorrow at lunch. We've only just started seeing each other and we don't need any added pressure from my family."

"Of course not, dear," Mom says. "But I'm glad you told us."

I find my father's gaze. He gives me the slightest nod of the head.

"Neither one of them are vegan or vegetarian, are they?" Mom asks.

"I'll need to check for any dietary restrictions." Once again, it hits me that this is all happening too soon. But this is how it is. This is how the events were set in motion. I would be foolish to stop them now.

7

ZOE

"We hung the painting together, Mom," Brooklyn says. "You don't have to spell everything out for me. I'm not stupid."

"I know, *mija*, but I just wanted to take the pressure off of you. This lunch isn't about you and Jaden. It's Anna's mother's way of getting to know me better, as in the woman dating her daughter."

"I'm not worried about any of that." Brooklyn's had a persistent, sullen look on her face since returning from the city.

"You miss your friends?"

"Not just my friends," Brooklyn says.

"Your other mom?" Eve hasn't entered my thoughts in a while.

"She's just... not in touch as much as I thought she would be. What's that about? She has a new life in Shanghai now and it's convenient to forget about her daughter?"

"I'm sure she hasn't forgotten about you, sweetie. She's very busy with work, and with the time difference..." I don't sound very convincing, even to myself, and make a mental note to email Eve about being more present for her daughter.

Brooklyn shrugs, tugs at her sleeve, then looks me square in the eye. "Jaden told me something about his Aunt Anna."

"What's that?" I called Anna earlier to tell her I wouldn't be coming over. Not only because I wanted to spend time with Brooklyn, but also because I sensed that she needed some time on her own. I've been making my way through the book she recommended and I've learned that quiet, alone time is a big thing for people like Anna.

"She has Autism," Brooklyn says.

I didn't expect that Anna's nephew would know. She told me that her family knows, but I wasn't sure that included the youngest members of the Gunn clan. But I am certain that Anna would not be okay with Jaden sharing this private information about her with Brooklyn. Because if he told her, who else has he told?

"You didn't know?" Brooklyn asks.

"I did know," I say. "Anna told me. But—" I'm not sure if I can admonish my daughter for this, and it isn't my place to tell off her boyfriend, but this is all very uncomfortable. "Why are you telling me this?"

"Because you just told me you're dating her."

"While I appreciate the sentiment, it isn't for you to tell me that, Brooklyn."

"You're my mom. Of course I'm going to tell you."

Fair enough. "Just, please don't tell anyone else, okay? Anna's very discreet about it. Jaden shouldn't have told you."

"I guess he only told me because he likes me."

"The reason doesn't matter, Brooklyn Adriana Perez." I hardly ever use my daughter's name in full—only when I'm upset. And I'm upset for Anna.

"His grandpa has it too," Brooklyn half-whispers. "I thought you'd want to at least know that before we have lunch with him."

"This is all very personal information, sweetie."

"Family's a big thing here," she says. "I'm sure Jaden didn't mean any harm by telling me. His family's not like ours, where one parent just leaves the country and you and I end up in this town, away from everyone we've ever known. He's very close to his family. He didn't say it to gossip." Her voice shoots up.

"Okay." I meet her gaze. "I understand why he told you." I'm so glad Anna found the courage to open up to me because this is not something I would have wanted to learn from my daughter.

"It's, um, not a problem for you that she's autistic?" Brooklyn asks.

"No." Of course, it puzzles me, and I have many questions, a good portion of which I know I can't ask Anna yet.

"Could you tell? I mean, Jaden says his grandpa is a bit weird, but he's also pretty awesome. He taught him to make things like this." She fishes into her jeans pocket and digs out a heart-shaped key ring made out of wood.

"Does that mean you'll never forget your keys again?"

"Mom." Brooklyn rolls her eyes at me. "I'm trying to have a conversation with you about something important to me."

"You're right. I'm sorry, honey. Show me."

She hands me the key ring. "Jaden said his grandpa didn't want to help him make anything heart-shaped at first, but he put his anti-Valentine's Day principles aside just to please his grandson."

"This is beautiful." I run a finger over the smooth surface of the wood. Because I'm now a business owner, the thought that I should stock these for next year's Valentine's Day crosses my mind. But I also know that, if Anna and her dad are so alike—and I sense that they are—there's no way he'll ever agree to make them for commercial purposes. "A handmade gift. He must really like you then."

"I like him too," Brooklyn says, her voice suddenly sugary sweet.

"I hadn't noticed." I smile at her.

"Isn't is a bit weird that you're seeing his aunt?"

"Anna's not his mother. *That* would be weird."

Brooklyn shakes her head. "Ew," is all she says.

"I'm looking forward to spending time with Jaden and his family," I say. "I think it'll be good for us."

The only people who don't appear nervous are Jamie and his wife Janet. Now that I see them all in action side-by-side, it's obvious that Jamie takes after his mother in the personality department. It's hard to read Sam, Anna's dad. Sherry's her usual buoyant self and she's clearly in her matriarchal element today.

The table we're gathered around is large, but having two extra people squished in does make us sit rather cozily close. Brooklyn's on my left side, Jaden on hers. Anna's on my right and it's as though I can sense the nerves that are racing through her body.

This occasion is a breeding ground for awkwardness, I guess, but only if you let it—that's always how I've felt about these things. But I'm not Anna.

Between them, Sherry and Jamie are quite skilled at keeping the conversation flowing. When a short silence falls, Janet jumps in, and asks, "I'm very intrigued, Zoe. You used to work for Amazon, yet you've taken over a struggling bookstore in the sticks?"

"Donovan Grove is hardly the sticks, babe," Jamie says.

"I like to believe that a lot of people still prefer the personal touch of a store as opposed to just clicking for things online," I say, not caring how naive that makes me sound.

"Hear, hear," Sherry says.

"But buying a book on Amazon is almost always cheaper," Janet says.

"Is it really cheaper, though? There's the cost of delivery, not to mention the cost to the planet."

"Yeah, but most people don't care about that," Janet says. "They just care about paying as little as possible."

"I dare to disagree. I think there's a shift happening at the moment, where more and more people are becoming aware of the environmental cost of how we've grown accustomed to live. Visiting an independent bookstore fits into that trend perfectly."

"Did you leave Amazon on good terms?" Janet asks.

"Sure. I just wanted to do something else with my life, you know."

"Oh, maybe this is your second mountain," Janet says.

"My what?" I take in her face, with its wide-open eyes and easy smile.

"She's obsessed with this book, which she got on Amazon, I might add," Jamie says.

"I bought it months ago, before there was any talk of Bookends reopening," Janet says. "But I only recently started reading it. The idea is that the first mountain you climb in life is when you achieve all the conventional, expected stuff, like getting a degree, getting married, having children, paying off your mortgage. Until you reach the top of the first mountain and the only way is down. Then you start falling and falling into the valley between the first and the second mountain."

Janet reminds me so much of Marsha, whom I miss on a daily basis.

"I think you'll find this is also called a midlife crisis," Anna says, casually.

"Well, sure, it can have many names," Janet says, "but the point is that figuring out how you can be helpful to the community, or to other people, or doing something that isn't centered solely around yourself, is the only thing that will allow you to climb your second mountain."

Jaden expels a deep sigh. Jeremy, Jamie's youngest, who has the face of an angel but the most mischievous glance in his eyes, chuckles in response.

"The boys have been hearing about mountains all week," Jamie says.

"It can't always be all about them," Janet says.

"Are you having your midlife crisis, Mom?" Jeremy asks. "Is that why you can't shut up about those mountains?"

"Maybe, sweetie. Maybe." She smiles at her son with a warmth in her glance that I recognize from feeling it myself when I look at Brooklyn, at the person I've created. This person who would never even have existed if it hadn't been for me. "Anyway, Zoe, my point is that opening a bookstore in Donovan Grove might be your way out of the valley."

"Well, if you put it like that—maybe. I hadn't really thought about it in terms of a midlife crisis."

"Muse on it," Janet says. "We can talk about this among ourselves some other time if you like, away from this crowd who don't appreciate our spiritual quest."

"That would be lovely, Janet."

"I'm surprised she hasn't emptied the self-help section yet at the store," Jamie says.

"It's the new religion," Sam suddenly says. It's the first time he has spoken since we've sat down to lunch. "People always need something to believe in. It used to be a higher power. Now they just believe in themselves."

"And they need a lot of help doing so," Anna says. I watch her exchange a glance with her father, and I see Sam's eyes light up.

"So far, the cookbook section and the children's book sections are proving to be the most popular, but self-help isn't far behind," I say. "Although some people might not want to buy a self-help book in a small store in their hometown."

"You should set up a web shop," Jamie says. "I'm surprised Sean hasn't tried to sell you on the idea yet."

"They haven't really spent a lot of time together, Jamie," Anna says, as though she has to defend both me and Sean.

"But that would defeat the whole environmental purpose," Janet says.

"There must be some way to buy anonymously and in an environmentally friendly way," Brooklyn chimes in. She has been very quiet, but I guess that's to be expected at the first meal with her boyfriend's family.

I sneak another peek at Jaden. He's a head taller than Brooklyn and he hasn't grown into his long limbs yet, but he has kind, long-lashed eyes and a pretty dazzling smile.

"That's for your generation to figure out," Sherry adds, while spooning some more potatoes onto my plate, even though I'm already more than full.

Uh-oh, I think. I hope Brooklyn doesn't take the bait. If I were to say something like that to her in a private conversation, I wouldn't hear the end of it. But she seems to be biting her tongue and refrains from offending our host, for which I'm grateful. I raised her well, after all.

8

ANNA

I'M GLAD THAT, after lunch, Brooklyn went home with Jaden to Jamie and Janet's house, so Zoe and I—and Hemingway, of course—get to walk back alone.

"We do this every Sunday," I say. "That's enough of Jamie and Janet together for me. He's always so much more hyper when he's around her."

"I like her," Zoe says. "She's feisty."

"I like her too. I just don't need to see her more than once a week."

Zoe slows her walk and turns to look at me.

"What?" I ask.

"That's a bit harsh," she says.

"I didn't mean for it to be harsh. I just told you that I like her, and I know she and Jamie are very happy together, despite her pending midlife crisis, which, if you ask me, only exists in her imagination. Or because she's read a book about it."

"Hm, *definitely* harsh," Zoe says.

"Really?" I stop in my tracks entirely now.

"You wouldn't say that to her face, would you?" Zoe asks.

"No."

"Or to Jamie?"

"No, because there's really nothing to say. What are you getting at?" I must be missing the point here—again.

"I'm just trying to understand," Zoe says.

"I assure you that I have nothing against my sister-in-law. She's just a bit much for me. I wouldn't seek out her company deliberately. When she just moved here, she asked to go for a drink. I tried to bond with her, I really did. But that's just not something that comes naturally to me."

"I might have drinks with her," Zoe says.

"Okay." I can see how that would make sense.

"Why is it so hard for you?" Zoe asks.

"Because…" How to find the words to explain this. "I'm not that sort of woman. The kind that goes for cocktails with her girlfriends and talks about shades of lipstick or the latest spiritual guide I've read. That's, like, the opposite of me." *I like to be alone,* I add inside my head. I like not to have another person's eyes on me, their expectations of me visible in them.

"I think I've figured out by now you're not much of a lipstick girl." Zoe starts walking again and I follow. Hemingway is waiting for us at the end of the street.

"Excellent powers of deduction." We walk in silence for a while, for which I'm grateful. What I have been able to deduce is that Zoe Perez is not the quiet type, which is, if I'm honest, one of the reasons I'm so attracted to her. Even though I have trouble with it at times, I like her forwardness. I know I can use it to force myself out of my shell more.

When Zoe still hasn't said anything by the time we reach my house, I'm starting to worry, however.

"Something bothering you?" I ask, once we're inside. We seem to have automatically drifted to the kitchen, where Zoe has crashed into my armchair as though it's her private chair.

Zoe finds my gaze. "Brooklyn told me that Jaden told her

that you have Autism. So Brooklyn knows. And she and Jaden have been discussing it."

I don't know why other people knowing causes such a rush of panic inside me every single time, but it does. My stomach seizes up while a number of doomsday scenarios are relentlessly projected in my mind. I don't want to say anything, so I just shut up and sit there, frozen.

"I told Brooklyn it wasn't Jaden's place to tell her, but, you know, they're kids. They talk. Your nephew is dating my daughter and things come up in conversation."

"I just... I don't know. I don't want Brooklyn's opinion of me to be based on me having ASD. I try so hard to not let it define me..."

"Why, though? It's such a big part of you. In a way, it's who you are."

"It's *not* who I am." My voice shoots up of its own accord and I look away.

"You sound as though you're ashamed of who you are when you talk about your Autism, Anna," Zoe says.

I don't know how she's looking at me right now, but I imagine it's with pity, which is not how I want to be looked at by someone I'm dating.

"I'm not ashamed; I just don't want everyone to know."

"Why not?" Zoe asks.

"It's not like coming out as gay, you know. It's coming out as disabled. There's a big difference."

"I've been reading the book you recommended." Zoe does not let up. "And I've been researching online, because I want to understand what it's like for you. But when you say things like that, the way I understand it, is that you believe yourself to be less than... less than neurotypical people, while you're just different from them, but by no means less. Diversity is—"

I hold up my hand to stop Zoe from continuing. "This is going to sound really rude, even though it's not meant to be." I can barely get the words past my throat. "I'm about to go into a meltdown and I don't want to do that in front of you."

I see Zoe get up and then I put my hands in front of my eyes. I hate how a meltdown can still just sneak up on me like this, so completely unexpectedly. I have Sunday lunch with my family every single week. But of course, Zoe and Brooklyn aren't there every week. And I haven't done enough painting to ground me, and I'd barely recovered from Friday night. I can only hope that Zoe has already reached the chapters in the book about sensory overload and meltdowns, because I'm in no state to be doing any explaining right now.

Why isn't she leaving? Why haven't I heard the front door close. Usually Hemingway comes to lie next to me when I'm like this.

"Anna," Zoe whispers. "I'm here for you."

Oh, great. She wants to save me from the meltdown, while my only priority is for her to not witness me having one.

"I *really* need you to go," I plead.

"Call me later. Please." I briefly feel her hand on my shoulder and then I hear the tap-tap of her heels in the hallway and then the front door bangs shut. She's gone and the relief of that washes over me.

"Too much," I whisper to myself. "Too much." And I try not to let myself wonder why anyone would ever want to be with the likes of me, if they have to deal with this. Why draw the short end of the relationship stick if, like Zoe, you could have anyone you wanted? Everything about her—every exquisite little detail—screams that she's a long-end-of-the-stick kind of woman. I wonder how I stack up next to her ex-wife. I bet she's not disabled.

Most of all, I try not to hate myself while I wait for the whirlwind of emotions inside me to die down or at least quieten to a tolerable level, so I can function again.

I wrongly believed my feelings for Zoe would have carried

me through the rest of the weekend. Or maybe it's my very strong feelings for her causing this episode. But there's no point in trying to figure out anything now, while my brain is in the grip of extreme anxiety mixed with self-loathing and—always worst of all—self-pity.

But at least she's gone. She's not seeing me like this. I feel Hemingway's snout against my shin and then I finally remove my hands. The kitchen looks blurry through the mist of tears. My tears aren't just born from frustration and anger for not seeing this coming—again—but also because I so clearly remember that meltdowns like this are one of the main reasons why I had to break up with Cynthia. I felt it was my duty to set her free from experiencing me like this. That it was the very least I could do for her. Even though she told me time and time again that she would be the one to decide which experiences she would have in her life and which ones she wouldn't.

"Hey." I bend over and bury my face in Hemingway's fur. He's not an official emotional support animal, but his support to me is invaluable. And the thing is that, after Cynthia, I had resigned myself to a life with just him. I had decided that I could be perfectly happy like that and it didn't feel like I was compromising at all. My best life might be another person's solitary nightmare, but isn't that the case for so many people? I didn't need for Zoe to come along. Hem and I were just going about our lives and it was all I needed. Do my work. Create my paintings. See my family. Go to Lenny's. That's it. I didn't have to convince myself that was enough because, for me, it was more than plenty.

But now, there's Zoe and her daughter discussing my condition with my nephew. I never even wanted to tell the kids. It was hard enough telling Jamie. I didn't even want to get diagnosed at first, but Cynthia coaxed me into believing that I needed to know. The assessment was grueling enough and then I had to tell people about it? No, thank you. Why can't I just keep myself to myself? It's all I want.

But no, if I'm being completely honest, I do want more. Now that I've gotten to know her, I want Zoe. Even though my life would be so much easier if I didn't. But I do.

An hour later, after I've sufficiently calmed down, I text Zoe to apologize.

No need, she texts back almost immediately, as though she's been waiting, phone in hand, to hear from me since she left. *Can we talk?*

Zoe sure likes to talk, while I'm not too crazy about expressing myself verbally. But I like her, so I have no choice. I can't just invite her to come back over and sit with her in silence. Maybe we can have a brief chat and watch some TV after.

At least my desire to spend time with Zoe is more powerful than the inertia I usually succumb to after a meltdown. After my brain has been so utterly suffused with anxiety, it often leaves me too depleted to do anything at all.

When Zoe appears in my doorway, not even two hours after I've asked her to leave, I can barely believe it. I start to go into overdrive almost immediately, because I feel I need to make it up to her. It's either that or a remorseful, rather pathetic silence.

"Calm down, Anna," Zoe says, while I fuss over her, fluffing a pillow that looks more than sufficiently fluffed already. "Come here." She opens her arms to me. "Come on." It sounds more like an order than anything else and while I'm usually not big on obeying orders, I can't resist hers. Her embrace feels calming for a few seconds, until I get restless again, and I need to do something—anything—to make her forget about what happened before.

"Can I tell you a story?" she says, after we've both sat down. "About a friend of mine back in New York?"

"Sure."

"His name's Ted and he's a brilliant guy. Very funny and warm and kind with everyone but himself. He's gay, but by no means in the closet, yet he's never been able to fully accept his homosexuality. He wouldn't be caught dead in a gay bar, back in the day when those still existed. Any guy who comes on to him gets rebuffed immediately. He tries to adopt this macho sort of walk, but it never works, because it's simply not him. And he gets his rocks off every few months via some anonymous sex, or through Grindr. He has never allowed himself to be loved for who he is. Never. And he tells me he's happy with the way things are, and I want to believe him, because I want him to be happy—because every single person on this planet is equally deserving of happiness. But as long as he can't accept himself, he can't be truly happy. So he settles for this life he has created, always minimizing this vital part of himself. And maybe it's enough for him and I shouldn't judge him, but I do, because it pains me. Because I see all the missed opportunities. And what you told me earlier, reminded me of Ted a little."

Holy hell. I need to take a minute to process Zoe's speech—and to fully comprehend what she's trying to say to me. "You can't compare being gay to being disabled." I feel like I'm repeating myself.

"That's not what I'm doing, Anna. I think you know that."

What was I expecting, anyway? To just be let off the hook again? This is starting to remind me of Cynthia, who somehow believed that, once I had some sort of official document in my hand certifying my impairment, I would be able to deal with it better. That surely backfired.

"Then what are you trying to do?" I ask.

Zoe shrugs. "I don't really know, Anna. I just don't like the way you talk about yourself sometimes. It makes me think you can't really accept yourself for who you are."

"Could you?" I feel tears prick behind my eyes again, but I'm determined to keep them inside. "If you found out that you would never be like anyone else, while that's all you ever wanted to be?"

"But why would you want to be like everyone else? What does that even mean? Everyone's different."

"I mean in general. I don't want the things that society makes you believe you have to want. I don't want to live 'my best life'—God, how I hate the expression—and then post about it on Instagram. I don't want to go out with my girlfriends and drink cosmopolitans while we discuss our sex lives. I didn't even want to join the LGBT alliance when I was at Columbia. I don't want any of that. Most of all, I want to stop pretending that it's what I want." I'm pretty sure I have not gotten my point across and that the examples I've used do not demonstrate what it is I actually want to avoid, but these are all the words I have in this moment. These are the only sentences my brain has allowed me to string together in this conversation. And I know very well that, for this very reason, I can't let Zoe in fully. I can't express myself adequately and if that doesn't drive her nuts, she must be some sort of saint. She surely is the kind of person someone like me doesn't deserve to be with. And whether I accept myself or not has little to do with that.

"But all of that," Zoe says, "is what makes you uniquely you."

"The aspirations that you seem to have for me, I don't have for myself. I've already been very lucky in my life. I have my family. I have a job I can do on my own terms. Many women with my condition have not been so lucky. I function, and half of the time, I'm happy. I don't need more than that. And I certainly don't need woo-woo self-help mumbo jumbo spouted at me, that's been made up by people who have no clue what it's like to be me. I used to want to be a 'better person'. Or a more 'palatable one'. And I've read all these self-improvement websites, and I started journaling and meditating and doing yoga in my living room and getting up at 5AM to fit it all into my day, and it just made me miserable."

"Maybe I should have included a trigger warning," Zoe says. "Because something I've said has obviously triggered you."

"Look, Zoe..." I don't want to ask her this. My stomach is clenched into the tightest ball and I can feel a drop of cold sweat trickle down my spine. "What do you want? What do you want with the likes of me? You can't fix me. Let me just be very clear about that. I'm sure there are plenty of people out there in need of fixing, but I'm not one of them. I know who I am, and whether I accept that is my business. For the record, I accept myself a great deal more already than I ever have—"

Zoe holds up her hand. "Please, Anna, just stop." She shuffles forward to the edge of the sofa. "I don't want to fix you. Cynthia already warned me about that."

"Cynthia?"

"Before you go on a tangent about that, let me just say that everyone I've met who knows you, only wants the best for you." She sighs. "She came into the store and we got talking. It happens. Maybe not to you, but to me, it does."

"What did she say?"

"What I just told you." There's impatience in Zoe's voice.

"I'm sorry." If I want to save today at all, I need to get my mind off Cynthia and Zoe talking about me behind my back. "I can only ever be me and I feel it's my responsibility to not give you any false ideas about who that is, Zoe."

"There's no chance of that." It sounds as though she has gone off me completely in the space of five minutes.

"But I do know that I need to compromise, although I often forget how to do that."

Zoe drinks from the wine I poured her earlier when I was fussing over her—when it looked like this afternoon could still be saved.

"When we met, I felt something," Zoe says. "I was drawn to you. There was something about you. Then I got to know you better, and even though you were sending very mixed signals, I could still so easily see that you were into me. And I liked you. I like your conviction, and your opinions, and your humor, and your obvious intelligence. But I don't like your defensiveness. And I'm not a big fan of your self-pity, either. I'm perfectly willing to acknowledge that life has been, and still is, hard for you, but you know what? It's hard for everyone. My ex-wife left for Shanghai, leaving our daughter to wonder what she might have done wrong to deserve that. I made the decision..." Zoe stops talking mid-sentence. "No, you know what? I'm not going to do that. I'm not going to list a bunch of bad stuff that happened to me, because I don't feel like it. I don't want to focus on the negative. I want to look ahead. And when I was looking ahead earlier, you played a big part in that, Anna. Now, I'm not so sure any more. You don't have to prove anything to me. I just want to spend time with you, but not if it's going to be this difficult every single time."

I swallow hard. My brain's working overtime trying to come up with something to say. But the pressure of finding the one thing I might say to get Zoe to stay is too much, and I already know I'll come up empty.

"I'm sorry, Zoe. I don't want it to be difficult." Panic floods my veins. "And I don't want you to go."

"Then show me that you want me to stay."

"W-what do—" I get the distinct feeling that I shouldn't be asking her what she means by that exactly. Does she want me to kiss her? Is that what this is all about? Are we going too slowly? Does she need to see some signs of obvious progression? Some hope?

She gets up, and it's as though my backside is glued to the couch. I'm frozen in my spot. I can't move, and I can't speak, and I certainly can't show Zoe what it is that she wants to see. Because I don't know what that might be. I've never known. While that seed of connection to another person is all I've ever wanted to locate in myself—it's not there. It has never been there.

"Bye, Anna," she says, and then I feel my heart break to the sound of her receding footsteps.

9

ZOE

Brooklyn should be home by now. I try to focus my thoughts on my beautiful daughter who feels like the one thing in my life that I've done absolutely right. Even though, most of the time, I have no clue what I'm doing while raising my child. But still, the thought of her has gotten me through a lot of dark days.

I don't even know why I'm so sad about things not working out with Anna. I did push her and I hated to see her crumble like that. But clearly it wasn't going to work out. She's too much work.

When I approach Bookends, I see no light on above the store and the curtains are still wide open. Brooklyn must still be at Jaden's. I haven't given her a curfew, and Jamie and Janet must not have kicked her out yet. I decide to go pick her up.

I turn up the collar of my coat, hoping I don't run into anyone who wants to chitchat about books. Then my phone buzzes in my pocket. Being a mother, I can never ignore a text message. But it's not from Brooklyn. It's from Anna.

I'm so sorry. I didn't have the words. But this is not what I want. Can we talk, please?

Anna isn't the only who can lose the capacity to find the right words. Most of all, though, I feel like I'm utterly and completely out of my depth with her. And I've surely also overplayed my hand. But I can, in all honesty, say that all I wanted to do was help. And Anna clearly doesn't want to be helped. So I don't reply, because I can't go back to her house tonight and say the wrong things all over again.

Jamie and Janet live about halfway between Bookends and Sherry's. I didn't even give it that much thought when Brooklyn asked if she could go back to Jaden's house after lunch. I was too preoccupied with spending time with Anna. I suppose I'll have to host Jaden at my apartment soon then, according to the law of reciprocity.

I'm happy that Janet opens the door to me because my brain has already catalogued her as a friendly face. Immediately, as I'm guided into their home, I'm struck by something very specific I've been missing. The feeling—the colors, the atmosphere, even the very smell of it—of domesticity. It reminds me of my best days with Eve, and Brooklyn's first ten years on this earth.

In the living room, Jamie, Jaden, Jeremy, and Brooklyn are hunched over a game of Monopoly.

"I'm just the bank," Janet says.

"As in real life," Jamie jokes. "The keeper of the purse strings."

They act as though my visit was fully expected.

"I'm glad to see you again so soon," Janet says.

"The game's almost finished, Mom," Brooklyn says.

"I'm winning," Jeremy screams.

"You be the bank now," Janet says to Jamie. "Zoe and I are going to have a drink in the kitchen."

Are we? I could certainly do with a drink, so I follow Janet.

"I hope my daughter has behaved," I say. "Thanks for having her over."

Janet holds up a bottle of wine, and I nod.

"Brooklyn's an amazing girl and, quite honestly, I'm glad to have some female energy in the house," Janet says. "So you're very welcome." Janet sits at one end of the kitchen island and deposits my glass very close to hers. "I was going to get your number off Brooklyn and call you this week to go out for a drink."

"That would be lovely." I perch on a high stool and take a long drag of cool wine. After I swallow, I exhale deeply—perhaps a bit too dramatically.

"Are you okay? Your energy's very different than earlier," Janet says.

I'm not sure if I can talk to her. Anna's her sister-in-law—and Anna would probably hate me for it. But I'm desperate for a friend in this town, for a deeper connection with someone who's not Anna. "My afternoon didn't really go as planned."

"Something with Anna?" Janet asks.

"How did you guess?"

"I've been a member of the Gunn clan for almost two decades," Janet says matter-of-factly.

"I don't feel comfortable talking about Anna behind her back, but, um, well, I think we might not be seeing each other anymore." Sadness coils into a ball in my stomach. I drink some more wine, hoping it will dissolve the anguish lodged deep inside me.

"Oh, God, no. I'm so sorry to hear that," Janet says, then briefly puts her hand on my arm. "What happened?"

"I said some things. She said some things. You know."

"Despite having been with her brother for more than twenty years, I don't really know Anna that well. I've tried to, but to some people, she's just completely impenetrable. I've never been able to find a way in with her, even though we get along on a superficial level. Is it something like that?"

Pretty much, I think. "I feel like I've tried my best. More

than my best. But it's like she deliberately misinterprets certain things I say just so she can hold them against me later. I don't want things to be difficult between us like that. Not at this stage of our relationship." The words come easily now. I haven't been able to truly talk about Anna with anyone.

Janet regards me intently and an uncomfortable silence falls between us.

"She has told me about having ASD," I say. "We've talked about it and I'm educating myself about it. I'm trying to learn as much about it as I can, and I feel like a real asshole for holding it against her, because I know it's not fair, but… I just don't know what to do. This is completely unknown territory for me."

"I lost all our money to our children." Jamie walks into the kitchen. "Oh, sorry. Am I interrupting something?"

I take a deep breath.

"Look, Zoe," Janet says. "Seeing as it involves Anna, do you mind telling Jamie?"

"Tell me what?" Jamie asks. "What's going on with Anna?"

I give Janet a nod because I'm worried about Anna too. I don't know how she deals with situations like this. Whether she needs someone to be with her or if she just wants to be alone—I suspect the latter, but I can't be sure and Jamie might know.

"They broke up," Janet says.

"What? When?" Jamie asks.

"Just now, before I came here," I say.

"How was she?" Clearly, Jamie's first concern is for his sister. "What state was she in? Agitated or the opposite?"

"I would say the opposite." I haven't been able to erase the image of a completely frozen and shut-off Anna from my mind.

"I'll call her," Jamie says.

"Don't, um, tell her that you know. That I told you," I say.

"I know how to deal with my sister," Jamie says, while he fishes for his phone in his pocket and walks toward the hallway.

"It's good that you came here, Zoe," Janet says. "Anna has told Jamie, in her own way, how much she likes you. If it's ended, she'll be so upset, but she's not the type to just call up her brother and ask for help."

I'm suddenly deflated, as though it only now dawns on me that it's over. Once again, it feels like it hadn't even really yet begun.

"I'm here if you need to talk," Janet says. "Jamie will always be worried about Anna first, but I'm here if you need me, okay?"

"That's very sweet of you." I glance into the living room. "I should take Brooklyn home." I try to listen in on what Jamie's saying, but I only hear some muffled noises. "You know, um, Jaden told Brooklyn about Anna's Autism and Anna wasn't too pleased about that."

Janet nods as if she instantly understands. "I'll talk to him." She looks at me. "Can I ask you a really personal question?"

I chuckle. "You might as well."

"Are you in love with Anna?"

I huff out some air. "I don't know. I think she's very special. And a part of me believes that being with her could be the experience of a lifetime, but, honestly, I barely got past the threshold with her because she sees herself as someone defective and I'm not sure I can deal with that."

"Wow. That's very honest."

"Is it?"

"If you said something like that to Anna, I can imagine she didn't take it well. Her family, they love her and they mean well, but they're not always a very direct bunch, if you know what I mean."

"I don't see any point in not telling it like it is."

"And good for you, Zoe." Janet looks me in the eye. "You're under no obligation, just because you moved to Donovan Grove, to do anything else other than what's best for you and your daughter."

"Whatever happened to climbing the second mountain, though?" It's about time to lighten the mood, even though my heart feels very heavy.

"It's a very long process," Janet says, on a sigh.

Jamie barges into the kitchen, scratching his head. "She's fine, I think. I didn't get that much out of her, but if I go over there now, she'll only get suspicious."

"I'm sorry, Jamie," I say.

"What happened?" he asks.

If only it was that easy to explain.

"Zoe came here to pick up Brooklyn," Janet says. "Not to talk about Anna."

Jamie exhales deeply. "She said she was going to do some painting."

"She'll be fine, honey." Janet pulls her husband toward her.

"Are *you* okay, Zoe?" he finally asks.

I give a quick nod. A silence falls. There's not that much left to be said—not with Jamie in the kitchen, trying to find out more about his sister.

"I'd better get going." I slide off the stool. "Thanks." I look into Janet's eyes for an instant.

"I'll call you," she says. "Soon." And I believe her.

10

ANNA

WHY DID JAMIE CALL ME? He only just saw me at lunch. But he does do that sometimes. It's not out of the ordinary enough for me to become paranoid. And I have other avenues down which to let my anxiety run free. In fact, for a brief instant, when I heard my brother's familiar voice, I considered telling him about Zoe and how we left things. Jamie's like a light version of Mom, less pushy, but still very easy to talk to. But what would I even say to him? *I fucked it up*. I haven't fully figured out how I managed to screw things up so finally between Zoe and me, but I know—I feel it in the pit of my stomach—that there's no coming back from this. It was as though, when she was here earlier, I could feel a screen come down, a wall being built between us at high-speed.

I shouldn't have let her come over again after my meltdown. First that, followed by my… what did she call it? *Defensiveness and self-pity.* Especially the last one was like a dagger being bored straight into my heart. Because I truly believed I was steering clear of self-pity at least. I guess I was wrong. I've been known to be wrong about many things.

When Jamie called, I was still sitting in the same spot as

when Zoe left. As though, if I stayed there, time would realize its cruel mistake, and would spool itself backward to give me another chance to say the thing that Zoe so desperately wanted to hear. Although I know, deep down in my bones, that I would never have been able to say it. And I also know that I have to let this go now, this thing between us, whatever it was—and the hope it sparked in me. The sooner I can get past it, the better. But that's just theory and doesn't take into account how I feel inside. How I can still smell Zoe's perfume in my house. How all I want to do is go into my studio and paint her face over and over again. How all I really wanted to do was kiss her again, and I should have just done that, instead of being defensive and full of self-pity.

"Hem, come here." I need to feel the comfort of my dog's soft fur. He obeys immediately, as though he knows how sad I am. He probably does. "It's just you and me again, buddy," I whisper to him. "And you'll see, we'll be just fine."

That night, I don't sleep much, because I keep racking my brain for ways to be less defensive. But the thought of people talking about me, discussing my condition behind my back, causes such tension inside of me that yes, I do automatically go on the defensive. Because of all the unknown factors and all the speculation I get to do about it. But why did Zoe have to be so confrontational with me? And why did she tell me that story about her gay friend Ted? Being gay is not a disability so what the hell point was she trying to make?

In the morning, sleep-deprived and none the wiser, I conclude that it's not going to be so easy to forget about Zoe Perez, because of the effortless lightness she brought into my life. Because of the memory of her glossy lips which tasted, somehow, exactly as they looked. I can barely even remember when and how I ever even earned the privilege to kiss the likes of Zoe. She obviously had some issues with me, while I didn't really have any with her. She might be a bit direct for me, but she has always only been understanding and willing to meet me halfway—even to learn about my disorder. That's already much more than I can expect from anyone who isn't related to me.

In the darkest hours of the night, when the sleeplessness messed with my head so much, the only way out was for me to go online and read about other autistic people's experiences. I came across an article written by someone claiming that the problem is not people who have Autism, but society in general that has a huge problem accepting us. And maybe Zoe's right, maybe I see myself as a problem that I need to solve. Maybe I want to make myself more palatable for others, which, in the end, is almost always too much effort, so I no longer bother. Because if you've already spent forty-three years of your life trying to fit into a world that's always confusing and always demanding something you're not capable of giving, despite your best intentions, then it just becomes so much easier to give up. To have zero expectations and ask for nothing. Just be quiet and grateful for what you have, which, in my case, is a lot.

So now, I revert back to that position, and I try not to chastise myself for allowing myself to want someone like Zoe, to get so carried away with my feelings for her, to the extent that I actually believed it could work. I was hoping for a miracle, but it was just another fool's errand. From now on, I'll be more vigilant. I'll stay in my lane. I'll do my work and fall back into my routine and, ultimately, I'll be all the happier for it.

As I boot up my computer, a small part of me wonders if I shouldn't try to get some sort of closure. Or just let Zoe know that this is not her fault. But I did text her last night. I said I was sorry. And, frankly, today I don't have the energy to try and explain. So I make no attempt to contact her again. But then Hemingway nudges my leg because it's time for his walk and then I have a decision to make.

Even though Bookends is closed on Mondays, Hemingway and I take the alternative walking route I created after my first embarrassing moment with Zoe, when I walked out on her at Lenny's. And I conclude, because that's the kind of mood I'm in today, that our so-called relationship is purely a string of embarrassing moments, caused by me, once again, confirming what I've known all along: that I'm not cut out for a relationship. I can just about handle friendship—and only with someone like Sean, who doesn't ask for much in the way of deep conversation.

I don't go by Sean's office today because I don't feel like answering any nosy questions, although I do know I will have to tell him sooner rather than later. I only wish the social aspect of my fling with Zoe hadn't progressed so quickly. Now it feels as though everyone knows—she's had lunch with my family, for crying out loud—and I have to make sure they know it's already over, thus opening myself up to a bunch of questions I don't want to answer.

Jamie will probably hear it from Jaden, although he will also want to hear it from me. I stop at a bench and sit down for a minute so I can text him, assuring him that I'm fine and that he shouldn't call me. I know he'll respect my wishes as long as he's at work.

I should walk to my parents' house and just tell them, but I can't face that particular ordeal yet. I know they won't bombard me with questions but I also know Mom will be disappointed. She'll again start thinking I'll never be truly happy until I find someone to share my life with. I've told her time and time again that one is not a direct consequence of the other and that there are, in fact, so many people in relationships who would be much happier alone. Case in point, I was doing just fine before Zoe came to town. And that's the real kicker, of course. I can stay inside my house and devise new walking routes for Hemingway all I want, but at some point, I will run into her, because she lives in Donovan Grove now.

Jamie texts me back to say he'll stop by tonight and I continue my walk. I wasn't hungry this morning so I skipped breakfast but now my stomach growls as I approach the Starbucks near Donovan Grove High. It's the one I always try to avoid because there are too many youths hanging around, but the lack of sleep combined with the hunger is making me feel a little dizzy so I decide to make a quick stop regardless of my apprehension.

When I'm inside, I immediately regret my decision, because Brooklyn is sitting alone at a table by the window, hunched over her phone. My hope that she won't see me is in vain because there's only one other customer in the shop and of course she looks up when Hemingway and I enter.

"Hey," I say, and I give her a curt nod and hurry to the counter, where I order a bagel so quickly, the young man behind the counter has to ask me to repeat it.

Then I curse myself for ordering a food item that needs to be toasted, because I'm left standing there, on full display for Brooklyn, who's probably texting her mom that her weird ex-girlfriend, if I can even call myself that, has been spotted out and about.

I keep my gaze on Hemingway, who is being such a good dog I can barely believe it. It's as if he knows I'm upset and he's trying to help me by being on his best behavior.

While I was dating Zoe, I never really took into account the consequences of dating someone with a child. I certainly never contemplated having children myself and although Brooklyn is Zoe's child, it's hard to see her as such, because she's a teenager and I've never known her as anything else. We've also never really had a conversation.

"Can I say hello to Hemingway?" Brooklyn asks from her table by the window.

"Sure." I glance behind me to check on the status of my bagel and walk over to her table.

"Mom told me, um, you're no longer dating," Brooklyn says as she ruffles the fur on top of Hemingway's head. "I'm sorry."

"Thanks." What else can I say?

"Are you okay?" I can feel her gaze on me. Oh Christ, she's just like her mother, it would appear. She's not much for leaving people in peace.

"I'm fine." I briefly meet her eyes. They're the exact same brown as Zoe's. "Is, um, your mom okay?" I have to ask, not only out of politeness, which I usually wouldn't care that much about, but mainly because I really want to know the answer.

"She's sad, I think. I mean, she didn't, like, give me the details or anything."

Brooklyn is such a sweet kid. I didn't even know teenagers like this existed, even though I have a nephew of the same age. She's just like her mother in more ways than one, I think. The pit of my stomach fills with dread again, and I know I won't be able to eat the bagel I came in here to buy.

"Tell her that I'm really sorry." This is probably highly inappropriate but it's all I can think of to say.

"Bagel for Anna," the guy behind the counter yells way too loudly.

"I will." Brooklyn looks at me as if she knows something and then I remember that she does. Jaden told her about me.

"I've got to go. Bye." I hurry outside, vowing to never set foot inside there again. I clench my fist around the paper bag with the bagel inside. It's going to take a while before I'm able to erase Zoe from my mind.

11

ZOE

Because the store's closed, I've had ample time to take the painting down from above the door, but it's big and heavy and I'm unable to get it off its hook and carry it down the ladder without the risk of injuring myself—and I already feel sore enough. But it needs to go. If I'm going to be in here all day tomorrow, I don't want to be staring at a painting that Anna made for me and be reminded of what could have been—and the feelings that inspired it.

As soon as Brooklyn gets home from school, I ask her to help me.

"What are you going to do with it?" she asks. "Give it back?"

"I'll put it in the garage for now," I say.

"Can I have it?" she asks, taking me by surprise.

"Don't tell me you want a picture of your mother in your bedroom?" I almost manage a chuckle.

"Not for now, but, you know, for later. I just don't want you to throw it away or anything."

"I won't." I curl an arm around her shoulders.

"She *is* very talented." She bends over and studies the painting. "It's almost like a photo. How does she do that?"

"I have no idea, *mija*."

Brooklyn turns to me and says, "I actually ran into Anna today. I was waiting for Jaden at Starbucks and she walked in with Hemingway. She said to tell you that she's very sorry."

"Anna said that to you?" I swallow something out of my throat.

"Yeah. Are you going to tell me what happened? What's she so sorry for?"

"I'm afraid that's really none of your business, my darling."

"Does that mean it's well and truly over? Like for reals?" Brooklyn asks.

"I think so." Having to confirm this to my daughter also reconfirms to myself how sad I am about this.

"Jaden thinks it must be because of her Autism. He's only known Anna to be with Cynthia and that ended after she was diagnosed."

"Don't you and Jaden have anything else to talk about?" I'm surprised by Brooklyn's forwardness about this.

"It's not like you've had a thriving dating life since the divorce," Brooklyn says, surprising me further. "I don't know. I guess I'm not opposed to you finding someone to be with and Jaden's family is so..." She gives a brief shake of the head. "They're so nice, Mom. I didn't even know that kind of thing existed."

"What do you mean? We had a 'nice' family."

"It's been a long time since you, me, and Mama were a family. I was just a kid back then."

It's the first time Brooklyn has referred to herself as no longer being a kid, which, in my eyes, she definitely still is. But she has a boyfriend now. And I can hardly argue with the cozy Gunn family dynamic I got to witness myself last night.

"I'm sorry about that, darling." I pull her close to me, which has always been my first instinct with my daughter—trying to hug the bad vibes out of her. "But I don't need to be with someone to be happy. Besides, I have you."

"I'll be sixteen soon, Mom. I'm not going to be here forever. At least when we were back in New York, I was pretty confident that you'd find someone when you were ready. And I was glad when you started dating Anna, because it meant you were, finally, ready."

"Are you trying to marry me off before you go to college? Because that's still a while away, and either way, I'll be just fine." And here I was thinking teenagers were the most self-absorbed creatures on the planet.

Brooklyn does shrug now. "Maybe, um, I want you to like it here, because I really like Jaden. I don't want you to fall out with Anna and decide to up and leave again."

"Oh, sweetie. We've only just arrived."

"Mama left. Then we left Queens to come here. It's not that crazy a thought, you know."

"I'm not saying that it is, but you must know that you're my number one priority. I want you to be happy and I'm so glad that you've settled in here. We're not going to leave because things didn't work out with me and Anna. That has no bearing on our life here at all." It's easy enough to say, of course. But I need to reassure Brooklyn.

"Okay." She finally wriggles free from my hug. "When you see Jaden's mom later, can the two of you not talk about me and Jaden the entire time, please?"

"I promise, sweetheart." We have plenty of other things to talk about, I think.

"Do you think they're having sex?" Janet asks me off the bat. I've barely had time to take a sip of wine. Maybe this is the real reason she wanted to meet with me in private, to find out what our teenagers are up to.

"If they are, it's certainly not happening at my apartment." And I'd like to think that Brooklyn would at least give me an indication of that big step in her life.

"They haven't been seeing each other that long yet. It's only been what? Two months or so, but they are at that age and I just..." Janet shakes her head. "Jaden's not going to tell me or ask any questions about sex if he has any. I've asked Jamie to feel him out, but you know, *men*..."

"Not really," I say.

"Oh, yeah, that's right." She chuckles and I gladly chuckle with her, grateful for the release of tension.

"Do you have any specific reason to believe that Jaden and Brooklyn might be..." I find myself unable to say the words, that's how hard a time I'm having even thinking about this.

"Nothing specific, just that they're getting closer... We tried to raise Jaden to have respect for girls, but you just never know, do you?"

"I can try to broach the subject with Brooklyn, but I can't promise that will go down well."

"Jeremy's twelve, which is only three years younger than Jaden, yet it feels like a lifetime of difference."

"Yeah," I say wistfully. "It's such a cliché, but, in hindsight, they grow up so fast. Only in hindsight, though. Those years between my divorce and coming here sometimes felt like they would last forever."

"Hey, how are you holding up, by the way? I didn't mean to inject all my anxiety about what our kids might be getting up to into the conversation from the get-go." She giggles nervously. "Are you coping?"

"Anna and I had only been seeing each other a short while, even though some things happened so fast," I muse. "I do wonder if I wasn't too harsh on her, but I don't really have anything to measure it against. If it had been anyone else, I wouldn't think that I had been too hard on her, but Anna's not anyone else. Yet I know she would resent me for thinking that, for believing she needs special consideration when I'm speaking my mind." I shake my head. "Still, I can't shake the feeling that I gave up on her too quickly. She did text me only minutes after I walked out. And today, Brooklyn ran into her and Anna apparently asked her to tell me that she was very sorry. But sorry for what? For being who she is? No one should ever be made to feel sorry for that." I've obviously been waiting for someone to ask me how I'm feeling. "Sorry, I'm rambling."

"Sometimes, when things are too complicated at the start, it could just be a sign that they're not destined to work out," Janet says.

"Nah, I don't believe that. My ex-wife, Eve, and I nearly didn't get together because things were very complicated back then, and we went on to get married and have a daughter." I shrug. "We did end up divorced, though, but so many people do." I look at Janet. "What's your secret?"

"There's no secret. That's the secret." She chuckles. "I truly don't know. Maybe Jamie and I just got lucky. Maybe that's all it is, in the end, when two people stick together. Dumb luck."

"Wow, that's actually quite cynical."

"It's not meant to be. Jamie and I have had our ups and downs, but it's never been that hard to get through them. Our children have never caused us any major difficulties." She taps a knuckle against the tabletop. "Knock on wood. We haven't had to deal with any grueling losses. What else is all of that but pure luck? Oh, and, let's not forget that when I look at Jamie, I still think he's the most gorgeous man I've ever seen." A smile breaks on her face. "I read somewhere, quite possibly on some self-help blog, that each person in a relationship should secretly believe they got the better end of the deal. And I do believe that about me and Jamie."

"That's really sweet."

"And just so you know, Zoe, there's always plenty more fish in the sea."

"Yeah, sure…"

"Jeremy's piano teacher is a lesbian and she and her partner broke up last year. I know her quite well. I can always hook you up," Janet says.

"It's very nice of you to offer, but really not necessary."

"I know it's too soon now, but I just want you to know there are always options. Just let me know when you're ready and I'll make it happen."

"Sure." I try to sound as dismissive as I can.

"Unless you want to pull a Cynthia," Janet says. "And fall in love with a man after breaking up with Anna."

"I don't think that's going to happen." I squint, hoping to read Janet's face better. I'm suddenly not so sure of her good intentions any longer. Or maybe I'm reading too much into her comment.

"You've never been in a relationship with a man?" Janet asks.

"Not really. Never anything serious." I could tell her the story of the boy I dated in my senior year of high school, but I suddenly don't feel like sharing too much with Janet any longer. "I'm sorry, but trying to set me up with your son's teacher a day after Anna and I broke up is very disrespectful of your own sister-in-law. Am I missing something here?"

"What?" She leans backward. "No, of course not. I would have loved for you and Anna to still be together."

"I didn't really get that impression."

"Well, no, because you're not together." She tilts her head. "I was just trying to help—trying to say the right thing."

"Oh damn, I'm sorry. I'm just a little sensitive today. I just hate this. Feeling like this. I wish I could fast-forward to a few weeks from now, when I'll feel better."

"Look, in an alternate universe, I'd be sitting here with Anna while she drowns her sorrows about losing you, but Anna and I don't have that kind of relationship. I'm glad I'm here with you, instead. But it's not a matter of allegiance or anything like that. Besides, Jamie said he'd stop by her house tonight to see how she was doing."

"Do you think I should at least accept her apology?" I'm glad to hear that Anna will have her brother's company tonight.

"Depends what she's apologizing for, I guess."

"I'm not really sure, to be honest."

Janet drinks the last of her glass of wine. "Are you… thinking about trying to make amends?" she asks.

"I really don't know, but I think I should see her."

"Don't you think you should give it some time, for your sake as well as Anna's?"

"I have no clue, and it's driving me crazy." Maybe this is how Anna feels most of the time when she's trying to control her environment, when she's trying to quiet that nagging voice of insecurity inside her head.

"I can't tell you what to do, Zoe."

"I know. I'll sleep on it."

"How about we change the subject and have another glass of wine?" Janet asks. "There's a spot opening up in the DG High PTA and you'd be the perfect candidate to fill it."

12

ANNA

When the bell rings, I hope it's Zoe, but I know it will be Jamie. Although I can't be sure, and a tiny part of me clings to the hope of seeing Zoe's beguiling face instead of my brother's familiar features when I open to door.

"Paint delivery," Jamie says. "I figured you'd be running low."

I thank him and usher him into the living room. "Is the invoice in the bag? I'll pay you back first thing tomorrow."

"Whenever's fine." Hemingway sniffs Jamie's jeans with a lot of purpose, probably because there's cat hair on the fabric.

While I have plenty of paint supplies in my studio, I appreciate Jamie's small act of subterfuge. But then we sit in silence, and when even Jamie doesn't have a clue what to say, I know it's time to address the elephant in the room.

"Did Jaden tell you?" I ask.

"Zoe did, actually. When she came to pick up Brooklyn last night."

"Ah, that's why you called."

Jamie nods. "I didn't want you to feel too alone."

"I very rarely feel alone, certainly not 'too alone'," I say.

"I know, but still…"

I get up and fetch us both a beer from the kitchen.

"Did Zoe say anything?"

"Not to me, but she and Janet had a long chat. In fact, they're out for drinks together right now."

"That's good. That she has someone to talk to about this. I mean, not about me, but, about her feelings, I guess."

"Do *you* want to talk about it?"

I fill my cheeks with air, then blow it out slowly. "I'd just told Mom and Dad we were dating. Now I have to tell them it's over already."

"I can tell them if you like."

"I don't want Mom fussing over me as though I've just had major surgery and suddenly can't take care of myself any longer." I sigh. "I shouldn't have told them in the first place."

"So you don't want to talk about it?" He takes a sip of his beer.

"It just didn't work out. There's not that much to say. I wish there was. I wish I could tell you exactly how and why I drove Zoe away, but it's all a bit vague, even to me."

He takes another sip. "How are you feeling?"

"Like crap." Something wells in the back of my throat. "Like I should have known how to do this, even though I'm not completely sure I wanted to be with someone. But I wanted to be with her. I wanted to be with Zoe. I really did. And I somehow screwed it up, and that just royally sucks." That's about as eloquent as I'm going to get.

"Do you want to try and find out what you're supposed to have done wrong?"

"It doesn't really matter anymore." I don't want to feel the way I did last night, when I couldn't move, and couldn't find the words that I needed to get Zoe to stay. All I had in me, and that was after she left, was a stupid text message, to which she never replied—for which I don't blame her, because what was she supposed to say? "It's done and, in the grand scheme of things, it's for the best."

"I saw you with her, Anna. I saw how you were together. How she made you smile and go all soft around the edges. I saw how you looked at Zoe, and I saw how Zoe looked at you, and that's not nothing. It's not something to just walk away from."

"I didn't do the walking away."

"Then do the walking back toward her."

"What's with all the talk of walking? You're going to get Hemingway all excited if you keep that up."

"Anna, come on."

"I know you mean well, Jamie, but sometimes you're a bit too much like Mom. You believe that I will only be happy when I find someone to spend my life with, because that's your reality. It's not mine. I'm perfectly fine on my own. Sure, I'm sad now, because, well, Zoe's just… so amazing and beautiful and warm. But she's also way too direct for me, and too demanding, and she really is rather fond of the sound of her own voice."

"Why is she too demanding?" Of course Jamie would focus on that.

"Because… she wants things I can't give her."

"Oh. Right." He practically hides his face behind his bottle now.

"Not like that." Although, of course, *that* would have turned into an issue down the line as well, I'm sure. "She just… thinks she can waltz into my life and tell me that I don't accept myself and basically ask me what I'm going to do about that, while, quite frankly, I think I've done a pretty good job of accepting myself already."

"She doesn't know you that well yet. She's still operating under neurotypical assumptions. You've got to give her some time to adjust. I know it sucks, but you can't expect people who are not like you to understand you just like that."

"But I don't need her to understand me. I don't need any of this. I don't need to prove to anyone, least of all myself, that I'm capable of being in a relationship. And I don't need Zoe to go to any special trouble to try and prove she can be with me. Besides, she's better off without me."

Jamie shakes his head. "If you said something along those lines to her, I don't blame her for walking away."

"Don't you start with the tough love as well, Jamie. I can't take it right now."

"Can't you see you're burying your head in the sand?" Jamie says.

"My head's right here and I can see very clearly."

"You're the one who always says you want to be treated like everyone else, Anna. That you don't want anyone to go out of their way to accommodate your needs and, worst of all, to pity you. That your diagnosis didn't change your relationships in any way; it only changed your awareness of yourself. But your relationship with Cynthia *did* end and now you're doing the same to Zoe, because you're so keen to prove God knows what..."

It's very unlike Jamie to speak to me like this. "You've lost me. I have no idea what you're talking about any longer."

"I'm talking about you and how utterly infuriating you can be." He holds up his hands. "I say this with love, Anna, and I hope you know that. But you're so full of contradictions and you want everything on your own, very narrow terms. It must be hard for you, but it's difficult for me as well, to see you like this. To see you suffer because another human is trying to find a way in with you, and you're doing everything you can to sabotage it. You're even using the one thing you claim to hate the most: self-pity."

I don't need my brother to tell me that this is no way to live, even though I believed that I could manage. Zoe came and started to tear down my walls and ask annoying questions, and now I have my brother on my back as well.

Sensing that I'm upset, Hemingway puts his head in my lap. I pet him and the soft touch of his fur soothes me a little, but nowhere near enough to calm myself after Jamie's little speech. I've already forgotten half of it, although the sting it caused in my heart only seems to amplify. The words always go, but the pain always stays.

"I'm not expecting you to say anything right now, Anna," Jamie says. "I know that's probably impossible for you. But I'm going to stay here a while longer with you, because I don't want you to be alone and I want you to know that I'm here for you." He puts his empty beer bottle on the coffee table. I haven't even touched mine yet. "Can I switch on the TV?"

I nod and let myself fall back against the couch. I'm glad Jamie's staying, not because I need the company—I could very much do with being alone right now—but because the act of him walking away from me as well would hurt too much. It would reinforce some truths about myself that I've avoided for too long.

He flicks through the channels until he lands on an old episode of *Who's the Boss,* which we used to watch together when we were kids. Then I'm not just glad he has stayed, but I'm grateful for the brother he has been to me, before and after my diagnosis. For the brother he was after Cynthia and I broke up, and I pretended I was perfectly fine. When I pretended that us breaking up was in fact what I wanted, while it tore me apart inside. Because I knew I was at war with myself at the time, and I took it out on Cynthia over and over again.

That's why I'm not angry with Jamie for saying what he just said. I'm thankful that he found the courage to tell me, because no one else ever would—although I have a feeling that Zoe might have done so at some point, if we had made it. Which is probably one of the reasons we didn't.

"Maybe," I begin to say.

Jamie lowers the volume, because we don't need a laugh track in the background right now.

"Maybe I should see someone. Talk to a therapist. Just to sort out some of this mess in my head."

"I'll help you look," Jamie says, then increases the volume again.

"Thanks," I whisper.

"It's no bother, coz I'm your brother," he says, and looks at me out of the side of his eye.

13

ZOE

THE NEXT DAY in the store, I can't help myself. I keep looking out for Anna. I keep listening for the excited bark of a dog. I keep hoping that she won't have changed her route, although I know her well enough by now to know with absolute certainty that she will have. I told Janet I would sleep on it, hoping that the night would bring me some much-needed guidance on what to do about this.

I walked away from her. I said goodbye to Anna. And I believe I did so with good reason, but still. Something gnaws at me and every time I close my eyes, I see Anna's face on the back of my eyelids. The goofy grin that makes her look adorable but also the anguish in her eyes when she doesn't know what to say or do. All of this would be so much easier if she hadn't gotten under my skin already, but she has.

She may be convinced that she's not an easy person to get to know, but I've caught enough glimpses of the real her, the person lurking behind that vast, thick wall of defensiveness she likes to hide behind, to see her for who she really is—or who she could be, if she would allow herself to be. But this isn't all about Anna. This is about me, as well. It's about my reaction to her, to her sensitive nature and the way her face would change when she looked at me—really looked at me. It's about how it pains me that she would think of herself, even for a second, as less valuable than anyone else. It's simply heartbreaking to witness and I need to decide if it's something I can live with, or not.

But I'm not like Anna. I'm not someone who likes figuring out all the hard stuff on my own. I need someone to talk to about this, someone who knows how hard it can be to fall for someone like Anna. I need to speak with Cynthia.

Anna won't like it, but Anna doesn't like a lot of things. I can't take them all into consideration all the time. Besides, we're not even together now.

It's easy enough to get Cynthia's number from Janet, to call her and invite her over.

When she arrives, she looks at me as though she already knows what I want to talk to her about, that this is not a simple social call of a Donovan Grove newcomer looking to connect, although it could also have been that.

"I need a sounding board," I start. "Because I don't know what to do." I explain to her what happened over the weekend.

"She told you that I was the one who coaxed her to get assessed and get an official diagnosis?" Cynthia asks.

"Yes." Cynthia's question makes me wonder if I'm recalling this correctly, but it's one of the things that stuck with me, because it didn't really make sense to me at the time.

"If I did, it was only because the not knowing for sure was driving her mad. Although, in hindsight, I wish that I hadn't pressed her to get a diagnosis." She shrugs. "I don't know. Maybe we were doomed either way."

"I do know that she feels very bad about how things ended between you. Anna knows it's her fault."

"Yeah, another thing she can blame herself for." Cynthia manages a small smile.

"She would hate it if she knew we were sitting here talking about her," I say.

"She wouldn't speak to you for days," Cynthia says. "She takes her aggrieved silences very seriously."

"You and she never lived together?" I ask.

"No. I pushed for it after we were together for about two years. To me, it just made sense. It was the next logical step. And we stayed over at each other's houses all the time. And I left more and more of my things at hers, but she always brought them back the next time she came to my house." She chuckles. "In the end, I accepted that she needed that time for herself, even though she already spends most of the day alone. I think it was more a matter of not being able to accept another person living in her house and messing things up in a way that would annoy her. She likes things just so. It gives her a sense of calm—of much-needed control. Another person's presence, even if it's her own partner, is always going to perturb her, I guess. But not living together was not a dealbreaker for me."

"Before things took a turn for the worst, you and she were happy?" This is beginning to sound as though I need Anna's ex to talk me into giving Anna another chance.

"I was. But the problem with Anna is that she thinks she's so hard to love, while she's exactly the opposite. If she's feeling good about herself, she's the most easygoing person I know. With strong opinions, of course." She smiles again. "One of the good things about not living together was actually that I could watch TV on my own. Watching TV with Anna is a special experience, I'll tell you that, and not something I was always in the mood for." She actually chuckles now. "She used to crack me up so much, though." She follows up with a sigh. "Anna's at her best when she doesn't take herself too seriously. When I met her, she didn't. But once the ASD got into her head, she started taking everything so seriously. And she hardly ever shouted at the TV again. She lost her sense of self, her perception of who she was, after she got the diagnosis. I had been hoping for the opposite effect. I truly believed it would show her who she was more, help her understand herself better, and make her see that the things she went through happened for a reason other than her thinking she was a nut case." She exhales deeply again. "I thought she was doing better with all of that now, but maybe being with someone brought it all back. Our breakup was hard for her as well, I know that much. Jamie told me once when we had a late night at Lenny's. I think she's afraid of the possible pain that opening up to someone else might cause her." She sits up a bit. "I can talk to her, you know. Make her see some sense. Tell her to not take it all so seriously. Remind her that there's fun to be had and she's just as capable of having it as the rest of us."

"She would just love that." I chuckle.

"Hey, if she can't stand it when people talk about her, she shouldn't behave the way she does." Cynthia clears her throat. "But it's one of the things that get worse when she feels like things are quickly spiraling out of her control. She believes that everyone is against her then."

I shake my head. "God, to live like that. Has she never tried to get some professional help?"

"Not really," Cynthia says. "I tried to get her some. I made an actual appointment with a counselor for her once, but she had a million excuses not to show up. We had a big row about that. I figured she'd finally get to it when she felt ready, or when things got really bad."

"But through all of that, you loved her?" I ask.

"Yes," Cynthia says emphatically. "Of course, because I saw her for who she really is. And it wasn't a case of you-can't-choose-who-you-love, because I happen to believe that we're all very capable of choosing who we love. Which is why, at the end of our relationship, I decided to leave. Because the person she had become was not someone I wanted to love anymore, even though it caused me a great deal of pain, because I knew it wasn't the real her. But I'd had enough and I had to realize that the only person who could fix Anna, was Anna."

"That's why you warned me that day that I shouldn't try to fix her."

Cynthia nods. "You should talk to Jamie, Zoe. He knows her better than anyone."

"I will." I smile warmly at Cynthia. "Thank you for sharing all of this with me."

"I'm glad to have this conversation, too. I'm over Anna now and I've moved on, but there's nothing I want more than for her to be happy. That's why I was so hopeful when you and she started dating, because I knew she wouldn't take that step if she hadn't started accepting herself more."

"Yes, well, I can be very persuasive when it comes to certain matters." I grin at Cynthia.

"I can see how Anna might have found you hard to resist."

If I didn't know any better, I would have taken that as flirting. "I think I see in Anna what you saw in her."

Cynthia nods. "Good. That does mean she's getting back to her old self." She grins at me. "If you want to test her, you should watch *The L Word* with her."

"*The L Word*? Why?" I'm intrigued.

"I can't explain it. It's something you have to experience. But if you're not crying with laughter at the end of an episode, it means she's not there yet."

"That's one of the strangest pieces of advice anyone has ever given me."

"Come talk to me after," Cynthia says.

"So what you're actually saying is that I should give Anna another chance."

"Maybe that is what I'm saying." She finds my gaze. "Maybe you should."

Maybe I will, I think.

14

ANNA

I'm not entirely sure how I ended up in the passenger seat of Jamie's car, on my way to speak with a therapist, mere days after I *mildly* suggested I might see someone. Jamie has taken my suggestion to heart—much more than I have. But if it had been left up to me, I would not be on my way to see a woman called April Jenkins right now. I'd still be googling reasons not to see a therapist, even if the thoughts inside your own head can cause such anxiety that you're barely able to function. And the scary part is that I would have found those reasons—I would have stayed up night after night, scouring the internet, to find an obscure, unvetted piece of research to support my claim, and I would have believed it.

I'm too tense to carry on a conversation in the car so we listen to the radio while I read April Jenkins' website on my phone. Even though it's too late to cancel the appointment now, my anxiety is so extreme that it will grasp onto anything. A spelling mistake on her website could be enough right now for me to demand that Jamie turn the car around and take me home. If that happened, the fact that I even made it into the car, with the actual intention of seeing a therapist, would be enough to give me back a sense of control for a while.

I would have tried. I found a reason that was valid to my mind. It didn't work out. It's an endlessly repeatable cycle that never solves anything. But I still read the text on her website again and again, even though I've already gone over it a dozen times. And I know there are no typos. And I don't even really want Jamie to turn the car around, because he had to go out of his way to set this up for me. He called April and made the appointment, and now he's driving me there. He will wait for me until I'm done, and then he will drive me back home, after which he will say, "It's no bother, coz I'm your brother." But of course it's a bother. Who wants to be driving around their autistic sister who was always afraid to learn how to drive and who can't make her own appointments and, basically, is too afraid to live? Oh fuck, I'm spiraling again, but there's no way out of it. I can try a couple of deep breaths, but the only way this anxiety spiral is going to pass is after I've seen the therapist I'm so afraid to see.

"Zoe called me yesterday," Jamie says, out of the blue.

I'm too numb to give him much reaction, even though, behind the stiff mask of my face, my brain is going into ultra-overdrive.

"She wanted to talk about you," he says.

"And did you?"

He shakes his head. "I told her to talk to you directly, but to wait until after today."

"You think one session with the shrink is going to fix me," I joke.

"God no, Anna. That will take years." He turns to grin at me. "Hell, you may never be fixable, then again, who is?"

"How did she sound? Zoe?"

"I don't know. I couldn't really pick up something like that from a phone call." The car starts slowing down. "We're here."

"Already?" Oh Christ. Is it too late to get out of this? Maybe Mrs. Jenkins has had an emergency and she'll need to cancel our session at the last minute.

"Yup." He parks the car and starts getting out, not even asking if he should come in with me, because he knows it's hard for me to say yes.

"It'll be all right, Anna. I swear to you."

I'm still clutching my phone in my hand. If I hold it any tighter, I fear I might crush it with the very force of my fear.

April Jenkins lives in a house with a lot of curb appeal. Jamie rings the bell, says our names, and we're buzzed in, just like that. My anxiety reaches peak level while we wait, and time seems to speed up and slow down all at once. And then a woman emerges from a door and she's tall and smiley and her lips are a little crooked, making her look like she's grinning at something all the time. She ushers me in and leaves Jamie outside and then I'm sitting across from what could quite possibly become my long-term therapist.

I know Jamie got her number off Cynthia, who found this therapist for me years ago, but I refused to go. I had barely recovered from the sensory overload of the Autism Spectrum Disorder assessment. Because I know the text on her website by heart by now, I know that Mrs. Jenkins specializes in helping adults with Autism, with a further specialization in Pathological Demand Avoidance.

I wanted to prepare for this—in fact, that was one of the reasons I gave Jamie for not being able to get myself together so quickly after I'd mentioned that I might want to see someone. I needed more time to prepare.

"You've prepared for this for years," he said, and that was that.

As soon as I knew I had the appointment—and Jamie was going to make me keep it—I tried to write down all the things I would say to a therapist, but I froze. A classic symptom of

Pathological Demand Avoidance if ever there was one. So it looks like I have at least come to the right place.

"I know this is hard for you, Anna," April says. "But I'm glad you made it here today."

"What did my brother tell you about me?"

"That you could benefit from talking to someone like me." She turns her crooked grin into a smile. "Would you like me to tell you a bit more about myself?"

"I've read your website," I say.

"Okay. Would you like to tell me a bit about yourself then?"

I don't know why I've always dreaded this question so much, but I do. Maybe I'm afraid I'll start talking and won't be able to shut up until all the things I've ever felt in my life have been expressed. Or maybe I'm afraid that instead of words, I will only have tears, and I'll start crying for all the times I've felt inadequate, or too different, or too unsuited for this life.

"I'm not very… verbal," I mumble. And I'm still getting over the shame of having my brother walk me in, as though he's my dad and I'm twelve. "Which is why I never thought therapy could be very helpful for me. Because I don't really express myself that way."

"How do you prefer to express yourself?" April's voice is very soft and calm. I wonder if she has to try very hard to look this composed. I mostly wonder how she listens to people like me all day long and doesn't go insane.

"I paint," I say.

"What do you paint?"

"Mostly people I like. My dog. And my house. It's all very self-centered, I'm afraid."

"They're *your* paintings, Anna. They can be whatever you like. That doesn't make them self-centered."

"Yeah." I wish I was in my painting studio, being self-centered, right now instead of here.

"May I ask you…" April leans forward a bit. "What are you

hoping to get out of this and any possible future sessions with me?"

"Well..." I briefly manage to look her in the eye. "I guess I'm sick and tired of being afraid of everything all the time."

April nods, but doesn't say anything in response.

"I guess I'm looking for some coping mechanisms for my bottomless anxiety."

"You've also been diagnosed with PDA." How does April know all this? Jamie must have told her much more than she's letting on.

"Yeah." The most fun of all neuro-strands, I think.

April nods. "How's your anxiety right now?"

I have to laugh. It's the only way I can break the tension that coils inside of me. "Through the roof," I say, after I'm done giggling nervously.

"That's okay. We'll work on that. You've come to the right place, Anna." She smiles at me again, and it's a little reassuring. At least I haven't cried yet. And she seems likable enough at first glance. "If you've read my website, you know that I have two daughters who were diagnosed with PDA when they were young adults."

I nod. Must be fun living in your house, I think.

"I'm telling you so you know that there are ways to deal with this. It doesn't have to be doom and gloom all the time. Most of the time, my girls cope well, because they know what it is they're dealing with. Knowing who you are can be a real gift." She pauses and gives me a meaningful look—although I'm not sure what it means. "Most people try to figure out why they are the way they are all their lives, and a lot of people never figure it out. To know the root cause of your behavior is a great piece of knowledge to have."

"I've known for years," I say. "And what it got me was one completely ruined relationship and one..." I don't really know how to describe my thing with Zoe.

April doesn't say anything. She must be used to people trying to find their words.

"I met this woman a few months ago. Her name's Zoe. And it feels like what happened between Cynthia and me two years ago, when we broke up because I couldn't deal with having ASD, is happening all over again, but much faster. It's like my subconscious has the need to show Zoe what I'm really like, underneath all the masking and the pretending that I'm normal, so that she knows to stay away from me." I hadn't expected to even talk about Zoe. Her walking out on me last weekend might be the direct cause for me being here today, but I have so many other issues to address.

"Tell me about Zoe," April says. "What is she like?"

I arch up my eyebrows. "What is Zoe like?"

"Yes." She gives me a therapist nod, which functions as a nudge for me to carry on talking.

"Zoe is…" I pause. "She's a force of nature. She has the kind of smile that would melt all the remaining snow in the tristate area." What am I saying? Have I well and truly lost my mind now? "Let's just say that Zoe has been the subject of many a painting since we met."

"And what happened? Are you still together?"

"No, I made sure of that."

"Do you want to give me some more details?"

I might as well. If I'd known April could help me understand how I fucked up with Zoe, I wouldn't have resisted coming here so fiercely. So I give her the broad strokes of what went down between Zoe and me, and I try to draw some parallels with the demise of my relationship with Cynthia, so she knows I'm not too stupid to realize that I'm sabotaging myself.

"And why is it so hard for you to accept yourself?" April asks.

"Because…" I shake my head. "When I see someone like Zoe, as much as I like her and want to be with her, in the back of my head, there will always be a nagging little voice telling me that someone like me shouldn't be with someone like her."

"When you say 'someone like me,' do you mean someone with your neurotype, or someone who hasn't accepted her neurotype?"

"Both." I shrug. "It's basically the same thing. Well, it is for me."

"It doesn't have to be." April puts her pen down. She hasn't used it too much yet. "It's not because you're different that you can't thrive, Anna. Or that you can't be with the woman of your dreams." She fixes her gaze on me. Her eyes are brown, like Zoe's, but not as pretty and sparkly. "I like to say that difference is a teacher."

I want to arch up my eyebrows again, but I don't. I feel like I need to give April the benefit of the doubt.

"Do you know that song, *If Everybody Looked the Same?*" She clears her throat. "We'd be tired of looking at each other." She actually sings the last bit. "It's the same for neurotype. I'm not going to lie, ASD and PDA still suffer from quite a bad rap, but that will change over time."

"It will always be a disability, as in not having the same abilities as neurotypical people."

"Maybe, but that doesn't mean you don't have other qualities and skills that neurotypical people can only dream of."

"That may be the case for some people with ASD, but I'm not one of the savants. I'm just plain old disabled."

April cocks her head. "Do you have your phone on you?"

I nod.

"Do you have any pictures of your paintings on it?"

"Some."

"Can I see?"

"Sure, but being able to paint is not a special skill. You can learn how to do it." I unlock my phone and scroll to the folder with some of my paintings, then I hand it to her.

"Who taught you how to paint like that?" April asks.

"Nobody. I taught myself."

"And you think that's not a special skill—a gift, even?"

"If it is, I can't really use it as a currency in society-at-large."

She keeps looking at my phone. "Jesus, Anna. These are stunning. Your dog in particular is utterly adorable. What's his name?"

"Hemingway," I say, my chest glowing a little, as though I'm solely responsible for my dog's cuteness, while all I ever did was adopt him.

"Is this Zoe?" She turns the phone screen toward me.

The glow in my chest changes into something else. Pangs of regret and guilt. I nod.

"She looks like a lovely person. Or at least you painted her as such." She hands me back the phone.

"Oh, no, she is that gorgeous. The painting doesn't even really do her justice."

"I'm sure it does, Anna." April straightens her back. "Right. I know what my mission is. Will you help me accomplish it?"

"Um, depends what it is," I mumble while I put my phone back.

"My mission is to get you to accept yourself."

"You sound just like Zoe now."

"Good. Nothing like a gorgeous woman to get you where you want to be."

I chuckle. "What?" April is not as therapist-y as I had expected her to be—far from it, actually. I kind of like it. I had expected a form of solemnness that reminds me of funerals, not this kind of playful energy.

"Your anxiety is hardwired, Anna. We both know that. But that doesn't mean you can't have a life in which you're not afraid all the time, in which you're not afraid to be with Zoe—even though she might scare you because she makes you face some uncomfortable things about yourself."

If you say so, I think, because I'm not entirely convinced yet.

"If you decide to come back, and I really hope you will, because I think we can do great work together, then I would like to give you an assignment. Homework, if you will."

"I was always really bad at homework, what with the demand avoidance and all that," I joke.

"I want you to go and see Zoe." April ignores my joke, which is probably the best way to respond to it in this situation. "And I want you to tell her that you've taken the huge step of starting to work on your self-acceptance. And then I want you to see what happens and report back to me next week."

"But… I haven't even decided I want to come back yet." Is the session over already?

"I know and that's up to you. I know I can't make you come back, but if you do, that's your homework assignment."

"You're challenging me." I purse my lips and look at April.

She nods. "I never said it would be easy. If it were, you wouldn't be here." She reaches behind her for something on her desk. "I'm going to write you down for an appointment at the same time next week. If you want to cancel it, email me three days in advance. My email address is on here." She gives me an appointment card. "No pressure." She throws in a smile.

"Wait… has an hour gone by already?" I check my watch.

"No, but I rarely have hour-long appointments with people with ASD. The sensory overload is too much, especially in the beginning. We need to work our way up to longer sessions."

Smart, I think. Maybe April knows what she's doing. I tap the card against the palm of my hand. "Okay."

"I hope to see you next week, Anna," she says.

15

ZOE

I WONDER why Jamie asked me to wait to see Anna until today. Ever since he said it, I've been curious to the point of distraction. To the point that not going to see Anna is no longer an option, because I need to find out what Jamie meant. What did she do yesterday?

All week, I haven't been able to get Anna off my mind. Yet, I've not even responded to her text message. It seems the time for that has passed, anyway.

By closing time on Thursday, I can no longer contain myself. No matter what Anna got up to yesterday, it didn't entice her to walk Hemingway past Bookends today, unless I missed them, but that seems highly unlikely.

I'm just glad it's not Friday, because if it were, I'd have to go find Anna at Lenny's, and that's not where I want to have a conversation with her.

I tell Brooklyn there's soup in the fridge and that I might be back in either half an hour or in a few hours.

"Why so vague?" she asks.

"Why so many questions?" I retort.

"It's only one question," she says, "And because I'm your daughter." I can't really be snarky when she says that.

"I'm going to see Anna."

That at least makes her pause whatever she's watching on her phone.

"Have you made up?" she says in an accusatory tone—as in, why is the daughter always the last to know?

"No, but I'd like to."

"Okay." She nods. "Okay." The second 'okay' sounds a touch more excited than the first.

"I don't know how it's going to go, hence the vague time frame." I'm more nervous than excited.

"She'd be a fool to not give you another chance, Mom." Brooklyn flutters her lashes.

"Are you making fun of me now? You? The only daughter I'll ever have?" I want to give her an impromptu hug, so I walk over to the sofa. "How about you wish me luck instead."

"You don't need it. Anna might be difficult, but anyone can see she's completely smitten with you."

"Really?" I hold Brooklyn at arm's length. "You can see that?"

"Of course I can. I'm not blind, Mom. And she looked miserable when I ran into her the other day. And you're my mom and therefore a huge catch."

"Thanks, sweetie." I give her a quick kiss on the top of her head. "Do something other than be glued to your phone all night, please."

"Sure," she says, even though she might as well have said 'yeah, right.'

I've barely made it out of the door, when I spot a familiar dog walking in my direction. Hemingway sees me and sprints toward me as though I hold the key to all the dog biscuits in the universe. Anna can't be far behind.

I keep one gloved hand in Hemingway's fur and look ahead.

There she is—she's made it onto my street. Anna's not wearing a hat and her hair is sticking out in all directions again.

Hemingway and I walk toward her and as we approach, I see that slightly surprised look on her face again. It's always there, but tonight, as twilight descends around us, I like to think she's just happily surprised to see me.

"I found this dog roaming the streets," I say, hooking a finger under Hemingway's collar.

"We can't have that," Anna says. "But he seemed very keen to see you."

"He was." The corners of my mouth are turning upward already. "I was actually on my way to see you."

"And I was on my way to see you," she says, smiling back at me.

"Here we are, meeting halfway." I feel something settle deep inside of me—as though my body knows more than I do. "Should we go to your place to talk?"

She slants her head. "Someone's not going to be happy that his walk has been cut short." She ruffles Hemingway's fur.

"Let's just walk then," I say.

Anna nods but we don't start walking yet.

"Why were you coming to see me?" I ask.

"Because..." She scratches her cheek. "It would appear, I might very well be in love with you and, um, I missed you. And also because I made an ass of myself, and, um..." She stops and turns to me. "Why were you coming to see me?"

"Please, just finish what you were saying." Did she just say that she's in love with me?

Hemingway whines and raises a paw.

"Let's walk," Anna says. "Not that my dog is the boss of me." She sends me a smile.

We walk slowly, side by side. Hemingway's a few feet in front of us.

"I—" Anna starts to say. She looks straight ahead now, a

little cloud of steam coming from her mouth when she opens it to speak. "I went to see someone yesterday. A therapist. Only briefly, but it helped." She takes a deep breath. "It helped me get out of my head a little, which is where I spend most of my time… predicting my life and all the ways it can go wrong, especially when someone new comes along." She glances at me now, but only furtively. "Someone like you."

Ah. That's what Jamie meant. I let Anna continue.

"I don't even know what I was so afraid of. Honestly, it sounds so ludicrous now," she says. "But that's what happens when you're stuck in a loop inside your own head." She looks fully at me now. "If I hadn't met you, I might never have gone to see the therapist. Jamie had to talk me into it. He practically had to drag me there, but it happened because I lost you. In many ways, even though I tried to convince myself otherwise, not being with you seemed much more unbearable than just moving on with my life."

Hemingway stops to thoroughly inspect a bush with his nose. So I stop as well. "It wasn't all you, Anna." I turn toward her and find her gaze. Darkness is falling quickly around us but I can still make out her face. "I pushed you too hard. I do that sometimes."

She shakes her head. "You have every right to push."

"I'm glad you found someone to talk to so that you don't have to go through everything on your own."

"I'm not on my own." Anna surprises me by reaching for my hand.

"You're not," I reassure her. "I really was on my way to see you." I take a step closer to her. "Apparently, we need to watch *The L Word* together."

"What?"

"I'll explain later."

Anna knits her eyebrows together. "Does that mean you'll give me another chance?"

"If you'll let me." Even though it's almost dark, I can see her eyes sparkle. Or maybe I'm just imagining that. But I'm sure I'm not imagining how she pulls me toward her, slants her head, and moves in to kiss me. And when her lips touch mine, I know what I've missed. I know why I was on my way to see her tonight.

I'm falling in love with her too.

The Two Hearts Trilogy
BOOK THREE

Two Hearts FOREVER

1

ANNA

"I HAVE THE MOST AUTISTIC FAMILY," April says, "and none of us would change a thing about it."

It's my third session with her, and April has opened up to me in a way that makes me wonder if she does this with every client—and if so, how does she possibly cope?

In our second session she disclosed her own Autism in such a casual way, I almost missed it.

"It's a process, Anna," she says. "You'll get there in the end."

I'm not there yet, but I've come a long way already, even though this is only my third session with April. Talking about my Autism Spectrum Disorder with her, just simply admitting it, and being open about it without feeling the crushing weight of shame I've always felt before, has snapped me out of the anxiety loop I've been stuck in for a very long time.

"What was it like when you came out of the closet?" April asks.

I shrug. I came out so long ago, I barely remember. "It was fine."

"What was it like for you to discover that you liked women?"

"In a weird way, it was a bit of a shock. Because, deep down, I guess I'd known forever, yet it took someone explicitly asking me if I might be a lesbian for the penny to finally drop."

"Sometimes the things that are most obvious about us are the hardest to see." She curves her naturally crooked grin into a smile again. "Who was it that asked you?"

"A friend I had in high school. Natasha."

"Are you still friends with Natasha?"

I shake my head. "I've had a lot of friends over the course of my life and lost almost all of them."

April nods. "It's funny that you use the verb 'lost.' Would you like to have kept them?"

"I don't know. I'm not very good at keeping up my end of the friendship bargain."

"And what would that be?"

I have to think about this. I can't immediately put it into words. April gives me the time I need, but this is a tough one for me.

When I don't reply after a few minutes, she asks, "Do you feel like you want to have more friends?"

"Not really. But I do sometimes feel as though it's expected of me."

"Expected by whom? You or someone else?"

"By… society, I guess. Connection is supposed to be this big thing. Spending quality time with your friends and all that. Friday nights with Sean and Jamie are enough for me, but it sometimes feels like I should want more than that."

"Why?" What I have also learned in our three sessions is that 'why' is April's favorite word ever.

"Because that's how it's supposed to be." I'm skirting the limits of my verbal acuity again. It feels as though the thought is waiting in my brain to be further developed by the words that come out of my mouth and when they don't, the thought stalls as well, leaving me with nothing much to say at all.

"Maybe for neurotypical people, and even then..." April says.

"But how do you stop comparing yourself to neurotypical people?"

"Why would you even *start*?" April asks matter-of-factly. "Do you compare yourself to straight people just because there are so many of them?"

"No. I mean, maybe. Sometimes, I guess I do. When I see a straight couple walking hand in hand, I can get envious of the ease with which they can do that, without ever having to worry about anything."

"You don't feel like you and Zoe could walk around Donovan Grove hand in hand?"

"Not always. Not with the same effortlessness as straight people would."

"And that doesn't seem fair to you?"

"I'm used to things being that way by now. What I'm not used to are the feelings of inferiority when it comes to neurotypical people. It's great for you and your family to embrace your Autism like that, but I would most certainly change it if I could."

"That's okay, Anna. I've been where you are. We'll work on that."

Saying things like this has, so far, been the most important thing that April has done for me. She makes me feel heard in a way I haven't allowed myself to be heard before. Cynthia tried and tried, but it was hard to accept that kind of help from her because I was jealous of her neurotypical brain and I was convinced she could never understand. What April does is make me feel one of many. Most of all, she makes me feel as though what I've been going through is completely and utterly normal, which is something I haven't felt about myself in a very long time—perhaps ever.

"I guess," I say, "what pisses me off the most is that I have to sit here and actively work on accepting myself, whereas for most people, self-acceptance isn't even something they have to give much thought to."

"I would disagree with you there," April says. "Because you have the key, Anna. You don't know how to use it yet, but you already have the key to unlocking your self-acceptance. So many people, whether they are neurotypical or neurodiverse, don't. You're the one with the huge advantage in this scenario."

April has a way of twisting my words so that I'm forced to see things differently, which is not easy for me to do.

"Let me ask you this..." A dimple appears in her cheek, so I brace myself, because I know she's going to slap me around the face with something I haven't thought of before. "You wouldn't hold it against Zoe that she's neurotypical, would you?"

"I don't hold it against anyone."

"You don't hold it against her that she doesn't have to be in therapy to feel good about herself," April says.

"No, of course not."

"And does she? Feel good about herself?"

"I think so. I hope so, at least." Maybe I haven't asked her enough. What I have done is given her plenty of opportunity to walk away from me, but I've been too focused on myself to inquire much about her own well-being. "I should make a point of asking her. But she seems fine. She always appears so confident and at ease with herself."

"Ask her," April says. "The answer may surprise you." She rests her gaze on me. "My point is, Anna, that every single one of us has stuff to deal with and work through, no matter our neurotype. Everyone has a story. Everyone suffers." For a split second there, I feel like she might burst into song again, this time the April Jenkins rendition of "*Everybody Hurts*", but she doesn't. She just looks at me.

"I'll ask her tonight." I'll have no choice. Now that April has planted the idea in my head that Zoe might be suffering, despite all evidence to the contrary, I need to make sure that she's fine.

"Good, but don't you go thinking that's your only homework assignment this week." A wide smile appears on her face.

"Trust me, I wasn't that hopeful."

"I'm glad we understand each other," she says. "Try to find the words you couldn't find earlier, when I asked you about friendship. And next time, try to tell me what it is you value about your friendship with Sean."

I make a mental note, even though I have also learned that homework from my therapist is not the same as homework you're given in school. Maybe because this homework is about myself and, deep down, I already know all the answers.

2

ZOE

ANNA ROLLS her eyes and adds a sigh.

"What?" I ask.

"I can't believe this woman has won two Oscars. She clearly can't act to save her life."

"Those three Oscars and The Academy would disagree with you."

She sighs again. "The Academy is bullshit." She shakes her head as though she has a very important point to make. "I never agree with them. Except when they give an Oscar to Meryl Streep. That's the only time I ever agree. She should get all the Oscars."

I'm well aware of Anna's schedule with her therapist—she goes once a week on Wednesdays—and I'm learning to anticipate the difference in her energy when I see her after a session.

"Sounds like *you* should be a member of The Academy." She's sitting in an armchair and I slip in next to her, even though there's no room for me. She accepts my intrusion by wrapping her arms around my waist.

"I so should, except that I couldn't bear it, you know."

"Maybe you could make it so that some Latinas get an

Oscar instead of giving three to the same white woman." I nod at the TV screen. I don't even know who Anna's talking about, although I'm sure that, whoever it is, she's white.

"I could list many a Latina who would be more deserving than—" She stops talking. "Was I ranting?"

"Nah. You were being very amusing."

A sound comes from the hallway and Anna stiffens.

"When is Brooklyn coming home?"

"In time for dinner, otherwise she's in trouble," I repeat for the umpteenth time. I lean over and kiss her on the cheek. "That wasn't the sound of Brooklyn coming home. Believe me, that is a much noisier affair."

"I should probably go before she gets here."

"You can stay, Anna. This is not a secret tryst." I smile down at her again.

"I know, but... maybe next time, okay?"

"How about tomorrow?"

I can feel her muscles tense even more. How foolish of me. Tomorrow would be nowhere near long enough notice for Anna. "Or sometime next week? Next Wednesday, after your session with April, when your anxiety is low?" I ask.

"Can I confirm later this week?" she asks.

"Of course." I kiss her on the cheek again. "My daughter is a lot like me, you know. She doesn't bite."

"I know," Anna says. "She's lovely, but I don't have much experience with kids."

"You have two nephews."

"That's very different than the daughter of the woman I'm dating. Jaden and Jeremy are my family. Brooklyn is..." She holds up her hand. "I mean, yes, she's your daughter, and therefore automatically lovely, but, well, there's a lot of pressure for her to like me. What if she doesn't? I wouldn't want you to ever feel like you'd have to choose."

While I appreciate Anna's openness, I can hardly believe

what I'm hearing. "What are you talking about? Where do you even get this stuff about me having to choose?"

"I think it's a valid concern," Anna says drily.

"Look, I get that you're a little nervous about spending time with Brooklyn, what with her being a teenager and all that. And of course I'm super biased, but she is just such a great girl. There's nothing to worry about."

"Put yourself in my shoes, Zoe. What if I had a daughter you had to get along with."

"I would be extremely excited by that prospect."

"Well, yeah, of course *you* would." Anna puts her head on my chest. "What time are you expecting her again?"

"Any minute now."

"I should probably go then."

I chuckle. "Don't go yet." I run my fingers through her hair. "I wish you would just stay and eat with us. What are you going to eat at home?"

Anna just shrugs, then looks up at me. "I promise I will have dinner with you and Brooklyn next week."

"Okay." I bend toward her and kiss her on the lips this time. It's a hell of a kiss because when our lips break apart Brooklyn is standing in the living room, only a few feet away from us. Anna as good as shoves me off her—as though Brooklyn seeing us kiss is the worst thing my daughter has ever seen.

"Hi sweetie," I say, trying to sound very casual.

Anna's rubbing her palms on her jeans as though kissing me has made them very dirty. "Hey," she says. Her body language has instantly transformed—like she's the teenager who's just got caught making out with her girlfriend. "I was just leaving," she says.

"Didn't look like you were leaving." Brooklyn smiles at her. "Aren't you staying for dinner?" She plops down on the couch and instantly reaches for the remote. "What are you watching? Ugh. Stacy Weston is awful in this movie."

I can't help but snicker. I try to find Anna's gaze, but it's glued to a spot on the wall opposite her.

"How about you lay the table, *mija*," I say to Brooklyn. I walk over to Anna, while my daughter utters the biggest sigh. When it comes to chores, she's not as lovely as I just made her out to be to Anna. "For two." Brooklyn pushes herself out of the couch as though she's hauling a bag of cement on her frail, teenage shoulders.

"I have to feed Hemingway," Anna says. "Bye, Brooklyn. See you soon."

"See ya," Brooklyn shouts without looking at us.

I walk Anna out, but she doesn't linger.

When I go back inside, I find myself almost apologizing to Brooklyn for what she walked in on, while there's absolutely nothing to be sorry for. I was just kissing my girlfriend.

"Is it okay if I have dinner at Jaden's tomorrow night?" Brooklyn asks. "His dad wants to play Risk with us."

If all they're doing is playing board games, Brooklyn can have dinner at her boyfriend's house as often as she likes.

"Sure."

"He said to say that Janet asked if you wanted to come along too, but I said you'd probably be on a date." She has finished setting the table and sits down.

"What does that mean?" It seems like I spend my days deciphering coded messages from my teenager as well as the woman I'm dating. "That you don't want me to join you?"

"I just don't want it to turn into a big thing, Mom. If you want to spend time with Janet, just go for a drink with her." There's no code to decrypt there.

"Maybe I will," I say, and start serving dinner.

3

ANNA

I OPEN the door to Bookends and let Hemingway walk in first. When I hear Zoe cooing over him, I follow him inside.

"Sorry for not staying last night," I say. "I have a few deadlines today and I didn't want to go into sensory overload." I feel a bit foolish about it now, but it's how it is.

"It's absolutely fine." Zoe doesn't kiss me hello, which is very unlike her.

Only then do I notice that we're not alone in the store, although that would usually only stop *me* from kissing Zoe, not the other way around.

"Who's this handsome fella?" A tall, blond woman walks up to us and pets Hemingway at arm's length, as though she really wants to come across as someone who likes dogs, but is actually afraid of them. I've gotten so used to ushering Hemingway into the store with me, I sometimes forget that not everyone is a dog person.

"This is Hemingway," I say, while nudging him toward me.

"You must be Anna." The woman looks me straight in the eye, then stretches out her hand.

"Um. Yes."

"This is my ex-wife, Eve," Zoe says, while Eve almost crushes my hand in her grip.

"Oh," is all I can say. Eve must be a fucking model or something.

"She just turned up," Zoe says, her voice dripping with annoyance. "Without any word of warning."

"What can I say?" Eve says. "I live for spontaneity." She has this wholesome glow about her that I truly believed only existed on television, but Eve has managed to recreate it in real life. Shanghai must be agreeing with her.

"Tell that to your daughter," Zoe says. I've never seen her like this before—I've never met this more venomous side.

"It's my daughter I came to see," Eve says.

"She's in school," Zoe says. "As children her age are this time of day."

"I thought it best if you and I talked first," Eve says.

"I think I'll go," I say. This is not a conversation—or a drama—I want to be part of.

"Hold on," Zoe says. "Can I talk to you in private?" She ushers me out of the store, without casting a further glance at Eve.

"She just turned up. Just like that. As if it's nothing. As if she still lives in New York and sees Brooklyn every other weekend." Her words come fast. "It's so fucking typical."

"Hey." I put my hands on her arms. "It will be all right."

Zoe takes a deep breath and we both watch the long cloud that forms as she exhales.

"Do you want me to stay?" I ask.

"I don't want to put you through an afternoon of Eve and I bickering. Didn't you have a bunch of deadlines today?"

"I do, but I always set my deadlines way ahead. In truth, I have plenty of time." I rub her shoulder. "I'm here if you need me. If you don't want me to stay, call me any time." I lean closer to her. "I can turn it on, you know. I can be the person you need me to be right now."

"I don't really know what that means, Anna," she says, her voice a little harsh, "but thanks." She looks through the store window. "Just as Brooklyn and I were finding our feet." She shakes her head. "She has no regard for what this will do to Brooklyn, or how it will be for her when she leaves again."

"Why don't you hear her out? See what she has to say?"

Zoe nods. "I have to call Brooklyn. She's going to Jaden's after school, but I think she'd rather see her other mother instead."

"Brooklyn's a tough kid. Maybe it will be good for her to see Eve."

"Yeah." Zoe wraps her arms around herself. "Fuck, it's cold."

"Go back in and deal with her. Call me later. I promise I'll pick up."

"Okay." Zoe quickly—flimsily—kisses me on the side of the mouth, then heads back inside.

"Holy smoke," I say to Hemingway, quickly realizing that a few words muttered under my breath to my dog won't do. It's another week until I see April again. "Let's go see Uncle Sean."

Because Eve returning can mean so many things. First of all, the suddenness of it has left Zoe clearly upset. Secondly, compared to me, Zoe's ex looks like a glamorous movie star on a day off. So regal and blonde and perfectly blue-eyed, with those sharp Alpine cheekbones. Exactly the kind of woman I would picture Zoe with, if she wasn't dating me. And just when I had found a way to cut through the anxiety loop in my head.

"I wasn't expecting you today," Sean says when I walk into the office, and starts making me a cup of coffee immediately.

"It's an emergency."

"Which client?" he asks.

"A personal emergency." This makes me think of the homework assignment April gave me. Before I started seeing her, I probably wouldn't have come here to talk about this.

"Say whaaat?" Sean jokes. "Who are you and what have you done to Anna?" He hands me a cup of coffee.

"Zoe's ex-wife just arrived in Donovan Grove," I say. "I just met her at Bookends. You should see her, Sean. Your eyes would pop straight out of their sockets."

"Okay." He pretends to get up. "Let me get my coat and I'll go and buy that book I've been meaning to get." He shoots me a smile.

"She… looks like the exact opposite of me." I shake my head. "If that's the kind of woman Zoe married, I have no idea what she's doing with the likes of me."

"Um." Poor Sean. He's not used to dealing with this. "Do you, um, want me to call Jamie?"

"No." I glance at him. "I'm sorry. I'm a bit taken aback by this. Zoe and I were just doing so well. It felt like we were finally on track, but now… I don't know what's going to happen. And not knowing what's going to happen is a massive anxiety trigger."

"That Eve's probably a bitch. Zoe might have married her, but she also divorced her."

"She looked like a bit of a bitch," I say, not meaning it. She looked perfectly lovely, like light was emanating from her pure and perfect soul.

"Do you want to go to Lenny's?" Sean asks.

"It's not even noon." And it's Thursday, I think. But nothing is regular about this Thursday. "We both have work to do."

"Work is just work, Anna. It's not every day your new girlfriend's ex-wife comes to town and throws you off guard." He looks at Hemingway. "What do you think, buddy?"

Hemingway just tilts his head. He's waiting for Sean to give him a biscuit.

"Oh, sorry, bud. All of this has thrown me off guard as well."

He opens the drawer where he keeps the dog treats and gives one to Hemingway. It's seeing this familiar tableau that restores a modicum of peace inside my whirring brain. It's seeing my best friend petting my dog and the everyday-ness of it that calms me down somewhat.

"Did she say something to you? This Eve?" Sean asks when he's done spoiling Hemingway.

"We only spoke briefly. She was friendly. Zoe must have told her about me because she knew who I was. Or maybe Brooklyn did. They must talk, right? She must have told her other mother about the weird woman her Mom is seeing."

"No need to assume something like that," Sean says matter-of-factly. He gets up. "Come on. Let's get one beer." He holds up one finger. "Just to calm our nerves a little."

"No, Sean. Really, it's fine." I pat him on the shoulder. "I'm going to get back to work. Get these covers done so I can be there for Zoe when she needs me."

When I say goodbye to him, I know what it is I will say to April about what I value in my best friend.

4

ZOE

"SHALL we get Brooklyn out of school early?" Eve asks. "I can't wait to see her."

I shake my head. Not only because I don't want Brooklyn to miss even an hour of school over this, but even more so because my brain still can't quite parse that Eve is sitting right in front of me, in my apartment in Donovan Grove.

"Why are you here, Eve?" I ignore her request.

"You know why. I wanted to see my daughter."

"Why are you in the States?" She has repeated the daughter line a few times and it's not one I can argue with. "What happened in Shanghai? Are you back for good or are you going back?"

"I'm on home leave. It's a thing when you take a job abroad." She narrows her eyes. "It's good to see you, Zoe. It's good to see you living your bookstore dream."

Eve used to call it my 'quaint bookstore dream', so I guess her dropping the 'quaint' is progress.

"You could have called, you know." I just keep on repeating myself, but as much as I do, I don't feel that my point is coming across. In the end, it doesn't matter. Eve's here now.

"I know. I came here on a bit of a whim. I was going to call you from New York and ask you to be in on surprising Brooklyn, but then the excitement got the better of me, and I hopped into my car and here I am."

"She's going to be beside herself."

"I sure hope so." She heaves a sigh. "I missed her so much. I didn't think it was possible."

"You could have been in touch more." I don't care about how reproachful that sounds. Eve leaving hurt Brooklyn.

"God, I know. But sometimes it was just easier to keep my distance, you know?" She shakes her head. "Also, sometimes, I really wondered what I was thinking when I took that job in Shanghai and moved so far away from our daughter." She shrugs. "Midlife crisis, I guess."

"I thought you had your midlife crisis when we divorced." I glance at Eve and when she's vulnerable like that, I can so easily remember all the reasons I fell for her. All the memories of our time together start running through my mind, like a slow trickle at first, but then they speed up, like a movie of which the climax is the day our daughter was born—the day we created another human being that would connect us forever, no matter what happened between us.

"There's nothing to say you can't have two midlife crises." Eve leans over the table. "Or even more than two." She tilts her head. "Brooklyn told me about the woman you're seeing. How's that going?"

I wonder what else Brooklyn has told Eve, on the rare occasions that they've spoken recently.

"Very well, thank you. And has Brooklyn told you about her boyfriend?"

Eve nods. "Oh, yeah. Jaden Gunn. I've seen pictures. I never thought she'd fall for a white boy like that." She chuckles.

"She must take after me in that respect," I say.

"I hope I get to meet him. And that I can give him my parental seal of approval."

"How long are you staying?"

"Through the weekend."

"And *where* are you staying?"

She tilts her head again. "I'm well aware I've sprung this on you, but I was kind of hoping to stay here with you and Brooklyn."

"This is a two-bedroom apartment, Eve."

"I'll take the couch. Or I'll sleep in Brooklyn's room. I'll not want her out of my sight for a minute if I can help it."

"She might be happy to see you, but she's still a teenager, so perhaps not *that* happy." I can't believe Eve would just rock up here and expect to stay at my place. I should make her go to a hotel. There's a small inn not far from here, where Brooklyn and I stayed when we came to inspect the bookstore. But something inside me stops me from asking her to find another place to stay—my love for my daughter, who wouldn't forgive me for making her other mother stay anywhere else but as close to her as possible.

"It's your call, Zoe," Eve says, and I'm glad she's not taking everything for granted.

"It's fine. Stay here. We'll figure it out." In the back of my mind, a little voice starts to say that this would be a perfect opportunity for me to spend the night at Anna's, but I'm not sure how that will go down with Anna. Although she did say that she'd be there for me. She has plenty of room in her house. "Maybe I'll stay with Anna," I say, even though I'm not even sure Anna will have me, and I realize I'm also saying it to taunt Eve. "Give you and Brooklyn some alone time."

"Perfect," Eve says. "While I'm here, I'd love to get to know Anna as well."

We'll see about that, I think. "I need to reopen the store. I'll be downstairs if you need anything. Make yourself at home."

"Thanks, Zoe." Before I have the chance to get up, Eve grabs my hand. "Really. I know I'm asking a lot."

No kidding. "I'm just doing it for Brooklyn," I say, while I glance at her hand on mine.

She nods. "Still, I really appreciate it." She smiles. "You haven't changed much, you know. Although life upstate seems to agree with you. You seem very relaxed." She finally lets go of my hand—it was about to get awkward.

"It's just very different here. There's space and room to breathe properly and life is about three hundred percent less hectic than in the city. At first, I wasn't sure if it would be for me, but now I know that it is. I'm glad for the time I had in the city, because if I hadn't, I might not appreciate what I have here so much."

Eve nods as though she understands, which I'm pretty sure she doesn't. "Shanghai is just as crazy as New York. Or no, actually, it's crazier in many ways." She pauses, opens her mouth, but then closes it again without continuing. I know her well enough to know that something more is going on here, something she hasn't told me yet. Or maybe I'm just being paranoid—she has that effect on me. But we have all weekend to talk, as it would appear.

5

ANNA

WHEN ZOE CALLED to ask if she could come over after the store closed, I was ready. Since we got back together, I've gotten kind of used to her upsetting my schedule and, truth be told, most of those disturbances are very welcome occasions. Because I can't get enough of seeing Zoe and spending time with her. Getting to know her always trumps whatever else it is I'd want to do with my time.

"I'm not asking to stay over tonight," Zoe says. "I want to keep an eye on Eve. Not that I don't trust her, but I want to be there for Brooklyn in case she needs me. But…" She smiles that radiant smile of hers. "It would be really nice to not have to spend the entire weekend in my small apartment with my ex."

"You're very welcome to stay here," I say, even though alarm bells are going off in my head already.

Zoe grabs my hands. "When you count it all up, we've been seeing each other for almost two months now."

"Well," I mutter. "Maybe a month, if you deduct the time that we weren't seeing each other." Shit. Zoe's been counting. And I know where this is going because there really is only one way for this to go.

"No, your calculator has got it all wrong, Anna," she says. "We went on our first date a few weeks before Valentine's Day."

"You're calling that a date? I was just welcoming you to town."

"Were you?" She arches up her eyebrows. "You did a pretty good job of hiding your welcoming vibe."

"Fine, two months. I submit to your far superior calculator."

"What I'm really trying to say"—Zoe turns her body toward me and increases her grip on my hands—"is that, perhaps, we should have a certain conversation." Her gaze is so warm when she looks at me, something inside me melts again.

"Yeah, I figured that was also what you were trying to say." I give her a smile back.

"If there's something you want to say about that, of course." She shuffles a little closer. "If you're ready."

I sink my teeth into my bottom lip while I nod. "Thank you for being so patient with me."

"Don't thank me for that. It's not a matter of being patient. It's just a matter of going with your particular flow. In a way, it's been good for me as well. To not rush into something new. To take our time. Even to have the falling-outs that we've had. It's all been very enlightening."

Goodness me. If words could ever melt my heart, those would be it. "You're so sweet, Zoe. How did I ever get so lucky that you wound up in this town?"

"I guess you have Mrs. Fincher to thank for that," Zoe says.

"Good old Mrs. Fincher…"

"Are there things I should know, before… I spend the night here?" Zoe asks.

"There are the house rules, of course," I say, only half-joking.

"Oh, I bet." Zoe chuckles. "Can we just assume that I will break them?"

"Let's also assume that it won't matter one bit if you do." I try to look her in the eye. "I want you, Zoe. I think you're so gorgeous I sometimes wonder if you're actually real." I squeeze her fingers, just to make sure again. "I think I'm ready, but it can still be unpredictable. I don't know. I haven't been with anyone since Cynthia. But I'm crazy about you. That's all I really know at this point..."

"I'm pretty crazy about you as well." She leans in and kisses me lightly on the cheek.

"But, um..." Instead of kissing her back, I need to ask her this question, otherwise my brain will go into a loop again, and I'll be spinning out of control for hours, perhaps days. "Eve... she's so beautiful. Like, um, conventionally beautiful. By all the standards. She's so tall and thin and toned... I hide it well, but I'm not really like that."

Zoe chuckles again. "By *my* standards," she says, "you are absolutely beautiful. You're brilliant and talented and kind and you're brave enough to work on yourself, and I hold that in very high regard." She cocks her head. "Besides, with all the smut you read, I expect you'll have some secret tricks up your sleeve."

I laugh with her, even though my looming anxiety has been far from quenched. "I don't." I manage to keep a smile on my face. "Please, lower your expectations now."

"I refuse to do so." She kisses me on the cheek again.

"Your bad," I mumble, and go for Zoe's lips, but she pulls them away.

"I wish I could take an eraser to your mind and blot out all the insecurities and doubts you have about yourself. Because they're all so unnecessary."

"It helps when you kiss me," I say.

"I can at least do that." Then she does kiss me on the lips and her touch is so exquisite, so soft and demanding at the same time, that I'm able to banish most of the anxiety that will inevitably come with having her stay over tomorrow.

But tonight is tonight. All I have to do is promise to try. Yet I want her to know my intentions as well, so as we kiss, I pull her as close as she can get. I press myself against her so I can feel her glorious body against mine, and I try not to think of Eve—I try not to compare myself to her. Because comparing myself to others is what I've been doing all my life.

Because of my time with April, I know that I will never be like anyone else, because I can only ever be me. And right now, I'm with Zoe, whose tongue feels so deliciously soft in my mouth, that it's making my entire body tingle. It's making parts of me come alive that have been dormant for a very long time—parts I had believed I'd leave resting for the remainder of my days. Until Zoe came along.

6

ZOE

"WHY WON'T YOU STAY?" Brooklyn asks, in the kind of whiny voice she had when she'd just learned how to talk and really wanted something.

"I'm staying for dinner," I say.

"It was just so much fun last night, when it was the three of us in the apartment. Just like before."

"Come here." Brooklyn and I are both in the store. Eve is doing God knows what upstairs. I give Brooklyn a hug she's not very keen on receiving. "As much as I wanted that for you, and I will always be sorry that I wasn't able to give you a home with two parents while you were growing up, Eve and I aren't together anymore. We haven't been for a long time, *mija*. There's no use in pretending anymore now, just because she's here." I put my hand on her neck. I'm grateful for the moment alone with her, because we haven't had any since Brooklyn came home from school yesterday. "How are you dealing with your mama turning up out of the blue like that?"

"I think it's great." She pulls away from me. "I wish she would stay longer."

"Has she said anything? About her job and her future

plans?"

"Not really."

"Look, sweetie, as wonderful as it is for you that she's here, don't, um, go expecting too much from her, okay?" I don't want to be the kind of mother who has to lower her child's expectations about her other parent, but I feel like I have to say something to curb Brooklyn's hopes about Eve.

"She came back for me. That's all that matters now," Brooklyn says.

I flinch at her comment, but make sure to hide it from Brooklyn. Because I've always been the one who has been there for her unconditionally, not Eve. Yet, this weekend, Eve gets credit for simply coming back, for turning up and, for once, being there.

"Okay. Sure. Enjoy it," I say, and I mean it, because I want Brooklyn to enjoy Eve's visit.

"Hey gang." Eve descends the stairs into the store as though she's walking a red carpet—she has always had a flair for the dramatic. She's never been anything but confident about how she looks. I wish I could take some of her easy confidence and give it to Anna, who so sorely needs it, but unfortunately, it doesn't work that way. Self-esteem is not something so easily shared. Eve looks around the store as though it's the first time she's seeing it. Her gaze lands, as it does with everyone eventually, on the painting above the door. "That's so you, Zoe."

"Well, yes, it is a painting of me," I reply. I put it back in its spot as soon as Anna and I got back together.

"I mean to hang a picture of yourself so prominently in your store. I'm surprised you didn't name it Zoe's Books or something along those lines."

That's Eve all over. Accusing me of being self-centered, while she's the one who did exactly as she pleased and then had the nerve to turn up as though none of it ever happened. As though her leaving so abruptly didn't crush Brooklyn.

"Anna painted it," Brooklyn says, no doubt trying to keep the peace. I hate that she has to do that. I'm also glad that Eve and I separated before Brooklyn really had to get in the middle of these kind of passive-aggressive comments in her home.

"A woman of many talents." The way Eve says it makes me feel she wasn't very impressed with meeting Anna. "She certainly looks the part of the distracted painter." She walks closer to the painting. "This, however, is a very good painting. Does she exhibit?" I hear my own words in Eve's remark, and for that reason her words grate on me even more.

"No," Brooklyn says. "Did you know she's Jaden's aunt?"

"I did not." Eve turns to us and I can almost see her bite back an offensive comment. "Keeping it in the family." She smiles at Brooklyn. "You really like this boy?"

Brooklyn's face changes from sullen to lovestruck in a split second. Just mentioning Jaden has that effect on her. It reminds me that I need to have another conversation with Janet. Perhaps with Eve as well.

"I can't wait to meet him then," Eve says. "Does he have any special talents, like his aunt?"

The door opens and a customer walks in. It's someone I haven't seen before. I greet him and stop following Eve and Brooklyn's conversation.

After I've helped the customer, I return my attention to my daughter and my ex-wife. They're huddled together like a couple of teenagers discussing their crushes. This reminds me that Eve hasn't uttered one single word about who she might be dating. Maybe that's why she came back so suddenly. Something ended for her in Shanghai. I should ask her when we're alone, but the truth is I'm not that interested in finding out. Besides, if there was someone, she would have told me already.

They walk over to me and Eve announces, "I'm going to go meet my future son-in-law."

"What? Now?"

"I just texted him. Janet asked us to stop by," Brooklyn says. "She's curious to meet Mama."

"I'm sure she is," I say on a sigh, and watch them exit the store under a cloud of giggles. After they've gone, I consider that, even though it hurt Brooklyn that Eve moved to the other side of the world, personally, I adjusted to it easily. I might very well prefer it when she's living far away. Then I check myself, because that's not fair on our daughter. But neither was it fair on her that Eve just upped and left before the date we all agreed on.

Then the store door opens again and I'm glad for the distraction. I'm even happier when I see it's Anna and Hemingway stopping by.

"How are you holding up?" she asks.

I beckon her behind the counter and hug her tightly. "Can't wait for tonight," I whisper in her ear. Against my expectations, Anna doesn't stiffen in my embrace.

"Where's Eve?" she asks, once we've let go of each other.

"Meeting Jaden and Janet," I say on a sigh.

"Wow. That was quick."

"I guess she's running out of time."

Anna smiles at me. "Should I invite her to Sunday lunch at my parents' tomorrow?"

"Please, no. But do tell me what Janet and Jamie have to say about her."

"I will be your spy," Anna says, then gives me a look. "Are you okay?"

"Just a bit tense because of Eve. It's like she's not just here for Brooklyn but also to pass judgment on the life we've built here."

"And? Does she approve?"

"It's hard to tell," I say. "But it doesn't matter what she thinks. She'll be gone soon enough and I love it here."

7

ANNA

WHEN ZOE ARRIVES with an overnight bag, excitement prevails over the fear of something happening that I'm not ready for. Because I may have only known her for a few months, but I do already know what kind of person she is. For that reason, I also know that nothing will happen between us that either one of us isn't ready for.

Cynthia and I never lived together, but she stayed over at my house all the time, and most of my memories of having her over are fond ones. And this is Zoe. A woman I barely need to take breaks from.

"Have you had dinner?" Zoe asks, like she often does.

"Yes." I give her a look.

"What did you eat?" she asks.

"Soup," I say. "Why? Does my choice of food have any impact on your plans for tonight?"

Zoe bursts into a laugh, then shakes her head. Maybe she's nervous, too.

"How did Eve's meeting with Jaden go?"

"I think she approves of him."

"What's not to like? He's my nephew."

Zoe exhales deeply and dramatically. "I'm happy for Brooklyn that she gets to spend time with Eve, but I can't wait for her to leave."

"Is she going back to China?"

Zoe shrugs. "I think so." She pauses. "I think I overheard her and Brooklyn talking about Brooklyn going to visit her there in the summer, but they haven't said anything to me."

"That's quite a trip for a fifteen-year-old."

"As long as I haven't been officially told, I refuse to worry about it," Zoe says, and then finally turns on her smile. "Sorry, I need to decompress a little bit. It's been a bit much."

"Wine?" I ask.

She nods and nestles herself deeper into the couch, in a spot where I can see her spending a lot of time in the future.

I fetch the wine and pour us both some.

Zoe glances at me over the rim of her glass before she takes a sip, and it's a glance that reveals all her intentions. A glance that makes a flush pass through me.

"I love your house," she says. "If I lived here, I wouldn't leave any more than was strictly necessary either."

"That's why I got Hemingway," I say. "Without him, I probably wouldn't go outside for days."

"There are only upsides to Hemingway," Zoe says.

I move a little closer toward her. I put my wine glass on the coffee table and position my head in her lap.

"See any—" Zoe begins to say.

"Have you—" We both speak at the same time.

"You first," she says, and runs a hand through my hair.

"Have you ever had any pets?" I ask.

Zoe shakes her head. "I have a daughter. That's enough."

"Brooklyn has never nagged you to get one?"

"God yes, she has. She nearly convinced Eve to get her a puppy when she was around six, I think. But when you live in an apartment in the city... I don't know. It just didn't seem very fair on the animal, because, as well as being mothers, Eve and I both had very demanding jobs."

"You could get one now," I say, remembering the newsletter from the animal shelter in the adjoining town. It said that the elderly owner of the cutest little dachshund had just died and the poor thing was now up for adoption. I even considered taking in a second dog myself, but then I started visualizing walking them, both on a leash, and them getting the better of me on the streets of Donovan Grove.

"Brooklyn will be leaving home in a couple of years," Zoe says. "And we still live in an apartment."

"Well, yes, but it's different. The dog could be with you in the store. And then, when Brooklyn does leave for college, you won't be alone in the building."

Zoe smiles down at me. "Why do I get the feeling you're trying to sell me something?"

"I'm just babbling," I say. Zoe's hand is still in my hair, her fingertips gently stroking my scalp. "But I do think you should consider it. Having a dog is such an enrichment to your life. If I'd known, I would have adopted Hemingway years ago."

At the mention of his name, Hemingway moves around on his cushion a little, making a rustling sound.

"That is one lazy dog," Zoe says. "No offense."

"Some pets take on their owner's personality," I say. "So I might be a touch offended."

"Hemingway's also extremely lovable and cuddly and adorable." Zoe bends over and kisses me on the forehead.

"We both like to take it easy after seven. We get each other that way." I smile up at her.

"He's not threatened by me being here?"

"He probably hasn't sussed out yet that you're staying," I say. "He's not that smart."

"Does he sleep in your bedroom?"

"No. He sleeps right there. I don't want to spend *all* my time with him."

"Good," Zoe says, and kisses me on the tip of the nose this time. Her face hovers close to mine and I gaze into her beautiful, dark eyes.

"You're so gorgeous, Zoe." I'm not usually one to say, let alone repeat, cheesy things like that, but with Zoe, I can't help myself.

"Right back at you," she says, and leans all the way over to kiss me on the lips.

I can't help but think that whatever she might find beautiful about me can only completely pale in comparison to what I find utterly enthralling about her—my pale skin compared to her glossy, dark one; my glassy blue-gray eyes compared to the intense stare of her brown ones; my unfit body with its clumsy limbs compared to her gracefulness.

But then I open my lips to her and I let her tongue inside and I make the thoughts in my head stop their endless spinning cycle, because I'm kissing Zoe, and that's a much better activity, on every thinkable level, than listing all the ways I don't feel like I measure up to her?

The kiss grows more intense and then it becomes more difficult to just keep my awareness in my body, to just enjoy her touch, to not let the intention behind it paralyze me. I try—oh, I try. Because for Zoe, I feel like I can try many things I wouldn't even consider trying for anyone else. Because she's still here. Because she didn't run away from me and my funny habits and my inability to express myself properly and, even more so, my insistence on taking things ever so slowly. Zoe's here and I feel her everywhere, even though it's only our lips touching, and her hand in my hair, drifting down to my neck now, finding its way inside my T-shirt.

"Are you okay?" she asks, when we break from the kiss.

I look up at her and her lipstick is smudged all over her lips and it makes her look funny and I can't help but laugh, even though perhaps the moment doesn't really call for that right now.

"A-okay," I manage to say after a while, because I'm focused on her gaze again, and it tells me so much, I can barely believe it. I'm not someone who luxuriates in prolonged eye contact with anyone, it's too intense and makes me feel uncomfortable, but with Zoe, it's different. Not only because her eyes are so mesmerizingly warm and dark, but because the person that she is, the person that I've gotten to know, is so visible in them. This makes me unable to look away from her gaze, which is a new sensation to me.

"This is not the most comfortable position for me," she says. "A woman my age."

We both chuckle and I get up and sit next to her, and then think, what the hell. I stand up from the sofa. I take the wine glass she's still holding in one hand and set it on the table, then hold out my own hand. Then I lead her up the stairs, where, now, only I ever go, into the safest space I know, my bedroom.

I tend to keep it tidy and clean, but I made an extra effort, because when we had the conversation yesterday, it was very much understood that Zoe wouldn't be staying in the guest room, which is a room that hasn't served much purpose in my house, because I never invite house guests.

I removed the weighted blanket I sleep under so it's just clean sheets and my big, wide bed. I haven't slept with anyone in this bed since Cynthia and I broke up more than two years ago.

"I knew I would love it," Zoe says, after I've switched on the bedside lights, which are muted, not just for this occasion, but always.

I let her admire the decoration of my bedroom for a while,

because it allows me to regroup, but then I think it better not to think too much, and just wrap my arms around her. She can gush over the colors of my wallpaper all day tomorrow if she likes—in fact, I think I might like it if she did.

I embrace her and her body feels so good in my arms, so right, and soft, and like something I can't get enough of. So I kiss her again, and every time a thought announces itself in the back of my brain I refocus on Zoe's lips and how her body feels in my arms. I run a hand over her shoulder or press a fingertip against her flesh, just to ground myself, to keep myself from spinning out of control in a way that would be hard to come back from. Because that happened to me several times with Cynthia and I don't want it to happen with Zoe. Maybe I should have informed Zoe about that possibility first, before we arrived in my bedroom, but I wouldn't have known where to find the words.

I haven't discussed sleeping with Zoe explicitly with April, but we have talked about using rationalizing thoughts whenever my anxiety threatens to take over, and it's not something I'm very good at yet. You can't just rationalize away a lifetime of anxiety with a few well-intentioned thoughts. It doesn't work that way. But here and now, with Zoe, I use her body to curb my anxiety, although I have also asked myself, since she brought it up yesterday: what's the worst that can happen? Maybe I won't be able to have an orgasm. But so what? So what, so what, so what? It doesn't matter, I've repeated over and over in my head. And it doesn't. As long as I'm here with Zoe, whom I have allowed into my bedroom, whom I'm kissing right next to my bed, and whom I'm about to see naked. At least I hope so. The trade-off is that I will need to get naked as well, with my milky-white winter skin and my flabby belly. But I'll just focus on her.

Then anxiety punches me hard in the flabby belly, because what if she's so repulsed by my body, by the dimply skin of my thighs and the softness of my muscles, that she doesn't want to be with me? This is one of the thoughts I've somehow managed to avoid, up until now. I shut it down as soon as it announced itself and locked it up somewhere deep in the caverns of my consciousness, but it never really went away. But Zoe's not kissing me so passionately in my bedroom right now because of my heavenly body. If that was what she valued in a person, she probably would have stayed with Eve. Oh God, no. No thoughts of Eve now, please.

"Hey." We break from the kiss. "Let's press the pause button," Zoe says. "If it's any help, I'm nervous, too."

"You have nothing to be nervous about," I whisper.

"Neither do you, Anna," she says in the softest, warmest tone possible. She says it in a way that almost makes me believe her.

"I'm—"

"Tell me," she says, and guides me to the bed. We sit on the edge and she takes my hands in hers.

"I'm scared," I say, because these are the only words I can squeeze past my throat right now.

Zoe nods. "That's completely understandable."

"Because you're so utterly dashing," I say, jokingly, because I need to break the tension that is growing inside of me.

"There's that." She smiles her dazzling smile. "I wouldn't be here if I didn't really, really want to be here with you. If I didn't want you." She brings my hand to her mouth and plants a gentle kiss on my knuckle.

"I'm afraid I'll disappoint you," I blurt out, suddenly finding some more words.

Zoe shakes her head. "How could you ever do that? When you've let me into your life this far? When you've shown me so much of who you are already?"

I swallow the self-deprecating joke that sits at the forefront of my mind. "Maybe we should stop talking now," I say, instead.

"Okay, but promise me that you will let me know if something's not to your liking, or if we're going too fast."

"You, too," I say, because I don't want this to be all about me again.

She cups my jaw with her hand, and the gesture is so tender, I lean in and kiss her again. Zoe's kisses are the best, the most sensual, the greatest anxiety-relieving remedy I've ever known. It's what lies beyond the kiss that frightens me the most, but this kiss, right now, on the edge of my bed—on the edge of what lies beyond for us—is perfect.

Sex is the ultimate act of giving up control, I think, and wonder if I might ever be able to say these words to Zoe. Not to make her understand, because I'm sure she knows, but as an act of communication, of opening up to her verbally. Although I've opened up to her considerably already, and I'm about to do so even more.

I curve my hands behind her neck and pull her close. We've shared kisses like this before, but still, this feels different. This kiss is the beginning of something new for us. It's the next chapter.

Zoe's hand drifts from my jaw to my neck, and then a little bit lower still. I'm of half a mind to pull my own T-shirt over my head and get the whole slowly undressing thing out of the way. I've always found it a nuisance, but maybe Zoe is into that and if so, then I don't want to take that away from her.

Her hand glides over my T-shirt, ever so gently, until it rests between my breasts, as if it's lying there in wait to finally touch them. When we break from our kiss, her lipstick even more smudged than before, she looks at me with her mouth slightly open, and for an instant, I can actually believe that I might not disappoint her. It's a glimpse of glorious possibility that sparks something in me and I try to hold on to it. But then I don't have to try anymore because Zoe's hand slips over my breast and we both look at it, as though a miracle is taking place between us, and then we look each other in the eye again, and I know that she knows that this is okay—that I'm okay with this. That I can move past the threshold that demanded this kind of patience from her.

8

ZOE

My hand is on Anna's breast and I can feel her heart beating furiously. I watch as my hand goes up and down with her breath and I try to pace myself, but her breath is coming quickly, and her heart is pounding and pounding, and I have many questions about what this is like for her, but they will have to wait until later.

I read the chapters on sexuality in the book about ASD and I worried when I learned that, often, it can be all or nothing when it comes to wanting to have sex for people with ASD. Of course, selfishly, I hoped that, for Anna, it wouldn't be the latter. She has never given me any indication as to how it would be, but that doesn't make me automatically assume that she's all in for this. I can sense her caution, her trepidation—her fear. And I don't want fear to be a part of this, but it's not as if I can magically wish it away. All I can do is take my time, check in, and make sure that how *she* feels becomes my absolute priority. Which isn't an easy thing to do, now that I have my hand on her breast, and she's looking at me as though, yes, she has finally reached the point where she can go all in. But maybe I'm just guessing, and projecting my own desires onto her. I should reassure her, because she obviously feels—so foolishly—that she's not good enough for me, while the opposite is true.

Because I see who Anna truly is. I've had glimpses of her beyond the anxiety and the need for control. More than glimpses—sudden, delightful insights into how her mind works. When Anna opens up to me like that, it's the most beautiful thing in the world. Not because it's so hard for her to do, but because of the connection it has forged between us.

And who's to say what really draws one person to another? Maybe it was Anna's darkness—the wall she put up—that attracted me to her in the first place. Or the light that I knew must hide behind it. Her tortured soul that she hides away behind faded jeans and T-shirts with quirky slogans. We have laughed and we have talked and we have walked and we have drunk wine together. Getting to know Anna happened so simultaneously with me finding my place here in Donovan Grove, that I now also think of her as home.

She puts her hand over mine, on her chest, and squeezes, and beneath my thumb, I can feel her hard nipple. Then I no longer stop myself. I rub my thumb over her nipple repeatedly and she leans toward me and we kiss again. I don't just kiss her mouth but let my lips slide down her jaw to her neck, until I kiss the skin above the neckline of her T-shirt, and I feel her wriggle beneath me.

I pause and watch her take off her T-shirt.

She sends me a wicked smile, one I haven't seen before, and then it hits me that she's sitting in front of me in just her bra. Her bra is navy—which is a color I know she likes—but also half-lace, and a part of her nipple peeks through the sheer fabric. It's the kind of lingerie I hadn't expected Anna to wear, but I don't want to comment on it now. I make a mental note to do so later—when we're in the mood for a joke. If I ever remember.

I smile back, because I very much like what I see, although I can't wait to take that bra off her.

"Do you prefer to take off your own clothes?" I ask.

"I don't care," she says, but then starts to unbutton her jeans. "Yes."

I stand up from the bed, take her hand to pull her toward me, and before I let her disrobe any more, I hold her close to me, so I can feel her bra-clad chest against me for a brief instant. It's not so much the sensation of having her breasts pressed against me that moves me, but the unrelenting intensity of her heartbeat, as if in this moment, it only beats for me.

"Are you okay?" I whisper.

Her chin bumps against my shoulder as she nods. "More than okay," she whispers back, and her hands tug at my blouse, pulling it from my jeans, and I might as well give her a hand now. I undo the top buttons, but then my fingers become clumsy as the frenzy between us builds and I give up, pulling my blouse over my head. I throw it somewhere in her bedroom, not caring where it lands. Not caring about anything else but getting naked with Anna. Because I want to see her. I want to see what she's been hiding under all those layers of unironed clothing she always wears.

She steps out of her jeans while trying not to fall over, and the sight brings an inadvertent smile to my lips. Anna sits on the edge of the bed and looks at me, but not for long—not long enough for me to take off my own jeans. She pulls me toward her, hooks her fingers under the waistband of my jeans, and undoes the button, then slides down the zipper. I'm still wearing my bra but my breasts are so close to her mouth, my nipples seem to reach toward her.

Then Anna slides my jeans off my hips. I can't see her face but I feel something inside her stiffen. I glance down at her.

"Should have known you were a thong girl," she says, looking up at me, the same wicked smile on her face as before.

"Now you know for sure," I say, and move into her a little closer, spreading her legs.

Her hands move to my ass, and, while I've known this all along, because I was there and a fully consenting party to it all, it's only now that I realize how chaste and buttoned-up any physical activity has been between us so far.

But Anna seems to have moved past that now because her hands are firmly planted on my ass cheeks, her fingertips digging in. When a small sigh comes from her mouth, I bend down, and kiss her. The kiss is hungrier than before—and not just on my part, of that I'm certain.

I don't know if she pulls, or I push her onto the bed. In between kissing, we tumble onto the mattress, and I find myself on top of her. And I feel as though, for the very first time, I've been fully let in. I have full access to this other side of Anna—a side she's finally willing to show me. But the fact that I've had to wait quite a few weeks for this while I was falling in love with her, my desire for her increasing with every passing day, also makes me brazen. I feel I really need to make the most of this, which is perhaps not a fair thought, or a true one, but it's how I feel. Then I shake off the thought, or I try, and I pull back a little, and glance down into her eyes, which always remind me of the ocean on a sunny day.

I no longer see someone who's afraid of intimacy. Lying beneath me is a woman who wants this is as much as I do. So I press myself a little harder against her, because I want to feel more of her, I want to wrap myself in the softness of her skin, in the heat of her desire.

She's gripping my ass again, but then she slides her hands upward, and goes for the clasp of my bra. She fumbles with it a bit—long enough for a small grimace to appear on her lips. But then she unhooks it and I move away from her so I can take it off. When she flings it to the side of the bed, she smiles at me, but that smile fades when her gaze rests on my breasts.

I've never been one to feel any qualms about my body, so I make sure she gets a good look—I relish in it. And my gaze follows her hands as she brings them to my breasts and cups them and her fingers do look ghostly pale against my brown skin, but, fuck, does it feel good to have Anna's hand on my breasts, to feel her fingertip move across my nipple.

There's definite moaning coming from her mouth and her eyes have narrowed to slits. I fold over her, while her hands remain on my breasts, and I kiss her again and again, until her moans and groans mix with my own, because she's tweaking one of my nipples, as if she has somehow found out how much that turns me on.

My clit strains against the suddenly too-tight fabric of my thong. It's a barely there piece of fabric anyway, and I want it off me so badly. But I'm also kissing Anna, and her hands are so delicious on my breasts, and her skin is so silky against mine. But then she swivels her hips a bit, and I take it as my cue to move off her and give her a chance to take off her own bra.

I watch her as she does, although she doesn't look at me. But then she's naked from the waist up and the heat inside me turns up a notch. My reaction to her nudity even surprises me. And I want to grab her, animal-like, purely on instinct, and get to know her body better—the part of her that she has so far always hidden away the most.

I try to be gentle, but before I know it, I've wrapped my lips around her nipple. I push her down onto the bed and one of her hands is in my hair—definitely not pushing me away, only spurring me on—while the other has moved back to my breast.

I kiss my way from her nipple back to her lips and our tongues dance, and her hands suddenly feel like they're everywhere. On my ass, my breasts, skating along my spine, and ruffling through my hair. The need inside me builds and builds.

"God, I love you," I whisper, in the heat of the moment. But the words get swallowed by our actions because our actions might as well be saying the exact same thing. There's much more to know about Anna and it might take me years to scale her depths, but I know for a fact that she would never do what we're doing now with someone she doesn't love and trust. This is her way of saying it to me. I don't need to hear the words. This is all I need. This, and to get out of this annoying thong.

Then, I feel her buck underneath me again and I slide off her—even though I've always had a tendency to stay on top.

"Lie down," she whispers, and puts a hand on my belly.

I do as I'm told and wait, which is not an easy thing for me.

"Zoe, I—" she starts to say, then stops. But I can tell this is not something that she desperately needs to say or something she can't find the words for. In Anna's gaze, all I see is desire and warmth and love.

I smile at her as best I can, because I feel all the love and desire as well, but most of all, I feel the need for much more of her and the only thing I feverishly hope is that she doesn't ask us to stop.

"You are so…" she says, then shakes her head slightly. She seems to give up on whatever it is she's trying to convey. I hope she realizes that she's done plenty of conveying already. That I understand and I feel the same way.

She drags her hand across my belly, down to between my legs. She lies beside me and her breath tickles my cheek, as her finger circles around my rock-hard clit—and I curse myself again for wearing this thong. I chose it because I had hoped it would turn Anna on, but now I'm hoping it doesn't turn her on so much that she wants me to keep it on for as long as possible.

"Anna," I groan, and I sound like I'm begging. But I'm not one to just sit idly by, even though this might mean robbing Anna of some pleasure. I'll be sure to make it up to her later. "Take it off. *Please.*"

Her lips are so close to me. I feel how they curve into a smile against my skin. She's enjoying this. She's loving watching me squirm. Oh, how I'll get her back for that later—if I can control myself.

She kisses my cheek and keeps circling her finger around my clit, and something inside me is already twitching in that telltale way and that is not how I want this to go. For my first time with Anna, I want so much more than a finger rubbing some fabric. I want skin on skin. I want her tongue on my clit. I want her fingers high inside me. I can't settle for anything less, so I hook my own fingers under my thong and attempt to pull it off.

"No patience whatsoever," Anna murmurs, but then complies, and helps me get the wretched thing off my legs.

"I'm never wearing that again, for your information," I say on a very exaggerated sigh.

"I appreciated the sentiment while it lasted," Anna says, then goes solemnly silent. Probably because I'm lying stark naked before her.

Something in her throat moves as she swallows hard, taking in the moment. And I can't help myself—just like Anna can't help who she is. I spread my legs for her because it turns me on to do so. I want to see the look on her face and the wild, sudden flush in her cheeks, the faint twitch in her muscles. Still, this is the toned-down version of me. I can't go fully Zoe Perez on Anna during our first time—I'll have to save that for later. But I can do this. I can coax her and tease her and make her blush.

Anna's cheeks flush, and she might be taken aback by my forwardness for a fleeting instant, but I see nothing but lusty determination in her glance. The kind of fire that only stokes my flames. There's no doubt in my mind that Anna wants me, and to see that so clearly on her face is even more of a turn-on.

As though my spread legs are the most welcome invitation she has ever received in her life, she moves between them, and brings her hands to my thighs.

She glances up at me and with a resolve I haven't seen in her before, she says, "You are the most beautiful woman I've ever seen in my life." And it might just be something she says, or it might not be, but I know she means it from the bottom of her heart. All her feelings and all the things she perhaps has wanted to say to me in the past two months are embedded in that sentence. She might as well have said she loves me more than anyone in the world, because that's what it feels like when Anna says it. Because her words don't come cheap.

Her hands are so close to the apex of my thighs, I'm starting to go a little wild. My breath stalls in my throat and I need to stop myself from egging her on again, because I want her to do this in her own time, on her own terms, with her very own actions.

She releases the strong grip of her hands and replaces her touch with a single finger that runs over the inside of my upper thigh. Then it feels as though my entire body is reaching for her, trying to hold onto that finger, wanting so much more of it. But I bite my tongue and I practice patience as Anna explores my body, marks my skin with her fingertip. Even though a voice inside me screams how much I want her, how wet I am for her, how utterly ready.

But it's also a delight to look at her face, at the focus and the wonder in her stare as she gazes down at me. And then, her finger skates in the direction of my clit again, and this time there's no fabric barrier, and just the proximity of her fingertip so close to my aching clit forces a strangled groan from my throat.

She finds my gaze and as she does, her finger circles my clit and something in me simultaneously relaxes and stands to attention because the tension just got ratcheted up another notch.

I can't believe she's looking at me while she's doing this. In all of this, it's the most surprising. It's also the most intimate gesture and all the warmth I feel for her centers around where her finger is doing its thing.

Her finger travels downward now, through the slippery wetness that has gathered there, and then she no longer looks at me. I close my eyes because I want to enjoy this moment as much as I can—the moment that her finger slides inside of me.

And oh, do I enjoy it. To feel Anna's intimate touch already feels like a moment of climax. Like something I had to earn. Like something not given freely or easily.

And it feels as though she, too, needs to take a moment to process, because, at first, her finger doesn't move. It just exists inside of me, insistent and present, but immobile. If this is a big deal to me, it's a huge deal to her. Because I know what she had to overcome to be here with me tonight, which is why I never pushed for it. All I did was ask for it, in not too many words, yesterday, and here we are. Anna has overcome the last part of resistance, the last inkling of doubt.

And then her finger moves, gently exploring at first. I reach for her because I need to feel more of her skin against mine, or her hand in my hair. I need more connection even though I'm already getting the most intimacy that is humanly possible. And it's as though my touch shifts Anna into the next gear, because she adds a finger and she pushes with more intensity. That shift moves through me as though a hot sun is moving over my skin. It flushes me and warms me to my core but this isn't just heat I'm feeling. It's my love for this peculiar, unique, beautiful woman.

As though earlier, when I was thinking it, she read my mind, Anna bends herself toward me, and brings her tongue to my clit.

I should have expected it, but it still feels like a shock when it happens—an utterly pleasant one. I dig my fingertips into the flesh of her shoulders. And then I just let go because there's no point in holding on any longer. I've waited to come for weeks.

I've held this desire, tightly coiled, for a long time. Anna has met me half-way and now here we are. And the hot sun is now a fireball that races across my skin, up and down and up and down, leaving me panting and groaning in ecstasy as I come at Anna's fingers and tongue.

9

ANNA

I'M ALREADY STARTING to go into sensory overload because Zoe coming is a true sight to behold. I had never expected her to be the kind of person who only expels a soft whimper at the point of climax, but the vocal fireworks are a lot, even for Zoe. Or maybe not. Maybe this is who she truly is. It wouldn't really surprise me. It's her exuberance I was attracted to from the get-go.

Her spasms around my fingers, her bucking up against my tongue like that, is quite possibly the best moment of my life so far. Because it's the epitome of so many things. I wasn't going to do this again. I wasn't going to fall in love again and subject another woman to my stubbornness and my singular antics. I most certainly wasn't going to let another woman make me feel better about myself. But Zoe has done so much more than that.

"*Dios mio,*" she says, while I gently, slowly, slide out of her. "Come here."

I lie down beside her and she kisses me crazily on the cheek and then the head, showering me with kisses and drawing me into a tight hug, until we both burst into chuckles.

"Thank you," she says.

"You're very welcome." I can't help but giggle.

"No, seriously. *Thank you.*"

"You're seriously welcome." I kiss her on the lips and she immediately draws me into a passionate lip-lock again.

"All I wanted was a bed for the night," she says, holding me at arm's length, after the kiss.

"Could have fooled me."

She raises her eyebrows high. "I would have waited as long as you thought necessary."

"I know," I say, because I do, and that's a key contributing factor to us being in this bed right now. "I'm glad you asked to stay."

Zoe nods as though she understands and maybe she does, but it's highly unlikely that she would get what I really mean by that, but it's okay. I've learned that it's not required for anyone, not even the woman I love, to fully grasp everything I say. Because it's not on Zoe that she doesn't understand. It's due to my garbled ways of expressing myself.

What I really mean is that once I get past that initial fear, the pang of dread when intimacy is required, I can enjoy sex as much as anyone. But it's that first hurdle, sometimes followed by a second and a third, that's always so hard to overcome. That initial resistance to change my current state of relative peace. The reluctance to temporarily remove some bricks from the wall that guards my heart—to relinquish all control. Maybe one day I'll make an effort to tell her this. Because Zoe is the kind of person I could tell things like that. Because she's also the person I'm sleeping with now.

"Did I say I'll need a place to stay tomorrow night as well?" Zoe smiles broadly at me.

"We can negotiate that later."

She nods again, then moves toward me. She kisses me deeply and warmly and, just like that, she seems to be able to just be in her body, to simply enjoy whatever actions her body is engaged in, while shutting out her brain, and that's the one thing I can never do. I'm a touch jealous of her total abandon, even though I know being jealous is utterly futile. But what I can do is enjoy her kiss. Her soft, warm skin against me. The feel of her ass in my palm—and Zoe does have a glorious ass.

So I let my hand drift toward her behind again, and my fingers dig deep into its flesh. Her breasts, equally divine, press against mine, and one thing Zoe has managed to do by being so unselfconscious is to let me be easily naked around her. When I took off my T-shirt and then my bra, there was not a single doubt that she wanted me. If there had been, I would have known—because no one can be so good an actress as to fake that kind of desire.

Zoe's complete lack of inhibition and lusciously free ways have an advantageous effect on my own self-image. While I do truly believe she's a thousand times more beautiful than me—because she just is—she has never made me feel that I'm any less than her, in any way.

She maneuvers herself so she lies half on top of me, the weight of her body a pleasant sensation on mine. I could sleep like this, I think, with Zoe's warm softness wrapped around me, her presence pushed against me, and it's a thought that surprises me, because I'm a light sleeper who needs all sorts of requirements fulfilled before I lay my head down at night. Having another person in the room would be defying a lot of my bedtime rules. Then I eagerly push the thought from my head, because sleeping is not yet on the agenda, and for this, too, I'm very glad.

I might not have Zoe's capacity for abandon, to surrender to the touch of another person easily, but being inside her has left my body in a state of great arousal, a tension building between my legs that won't go away on its own.

"Can I touch you?" she whispers in my ear. She's had her hands all over me already, but I know what she means.

"Yes," I say, my voice shooting up a bit, because I want my consent to be clear and unambiguous.

"Can I do all the things you did to me?" she continues in a whisper.

"Yes," I say, and swallow hard. The mere thought of her doing what I just did to her makes a shiver of arousal run down my spine. To be in bed with a woman like Zoe is like a very hot and audacious dream come true.

Then she doesn't say anything anymore, but briefly grazes her teeth over my earlobe and the hotness of her breath sends another shiver down my body, all the way to my pulsing clit.

Her lips find mine again and her tongue slips into my mouth. I hold her close to me and then I wonder why I've waited so long to do this, because Zoe has me in such a state of excitement, I forget who I really am. And it takes a little forgetting to even believe that I'm here, in my bed with her. Although the evidence is overwhelming. Zoe's delicious breasts press against me, and her lips move down my neck, while my nipples reach up in anticipation.

When she wraps her lips around my nipple, something inside me seems to explode. A new energy runs through me, like a bullet of lust being fired from inside my core. Her hand caresses my other breast gently, until her fingers latch on to my nipple, and while she sucks one nipple deeply into her mouth, her fingers tweak the other, and it's like she just found the button to switch off the never-ending alertness in my brain that's always on the lookout for some sort of danger—usually non-existent, but my brain doesn't seem to care about that.

Even though I can't see her face, I can still see her smile on the inside of my eyelids. The first one she ever smiled at me, so free of worry and trepidation that it almost angered me, because how could a person smile so sweetly at a perfect stranger like that? And all the smiles that came after, especially the ones that lit up her face whenever I've walked into Bookends unexpectedly, hoping to brighten up her day—hoping to be the recipient of that smile.

She lets go of my nipple and kisses her way down. My pulse picks up speed as I brace myself for what comes next. Her hands wander over my belly while her lips kiss my inner thighs and move in ever closer to my clit.

In my life, it's a rare and beautiful thing when desire beats fear, and for that alone, I'm already beside myself when her lips touch against my clit. Then I feel the warmth of her tongue there and even then, as an arrow of pleasure shoots through me, there's still a part of me that finds this hard to believe. But it's not a self-deprecating thought. It's one of pure wonder. If a woman like Zoe, so confident and self-possessed and beautiful, is doing these things to my clit with her tongue, I can't be so bad. I must be doing something right in my life. I must be projecting some sort of positive energy and brightness and I-don't-know-what-else that sits behind my anxiety, waiting patiently for moments like these. Because Zoe going down on me is not some sort of mistake that the universe made. It's a logical progression of what's been happening between us.

Her tongue is slow but relentless. She twirls it around my clit, then down and up again, and it's as though I can feel it everywhere. I can feel all the warmth of Zoe's personality in her tongue as she deftly licks me to a point of no return. And I'm surprised again, because I usually need a bit more stimulation than this. But nothing is typical about Zoe. Maybe it never has been.

"Oooh," I hear myself moan, my voice filling the room, slicing through the semi-darkness around me. "Oh, Zoe."

It seems to spur her on because her tongue keeps at it, but with a bit more intensity, that she ratchets up and up, until I can't take it anymore. Until I let go, for her, for me, for us, and the heavenly sensations of Zoe's tongue on my clit demand the kind of climax from me that leaves my entire body trembling and my eyes a little wet.

"Are you okay?" Zoe asks, worry in her voice.

I nod, because I'm fine, but I can't express how I'm feeling right now in words yet. I want to, though. I want to be able to tell her, so I make the effort, as I pull her close to me.

"Orgasms can make me quite emotional. As though…" I pause and I notice how we breathe together, how close we are in this moment, and Zoe's closeness seems to hand me the words I'm searching for. "It's like there are certain emotions that I hold in my body that can only ever be expressed when I come."

I feel her chin go up and down against my chest. "That makes perfect sense," she says, then she pushes herself away from me and smiles at me and it's not a full-wattage kind of Zoe smile, but it dazzles me nonetheless. Then something mischievous comes over her face. "I also forgot to warn you that I'm the queen of licking pussy."

I burst into a chuckle and we laugh together and it's exactly what I need right now, for Zoe and I to cement this moment in our memory as something joyful and light, despite the gravity it holds for me. But it can be all of those things at the same time.

"I'm going to put that on a T-shirt for you," I say, while I hold her in my arms, where she fits so perfectly. "I'll make you wear it in the summer."

"I'll wear it whenever I come to your house with this very purpose," she says. "So you never forget."

10

ZOE

"I NEED TO LET HEMINGWAY OUT," Anna says, because I won't let her go.

"We need to make the most of today." I press my leg onto her thighs a bit more. "Because I sure do hope Eve doesn't make a habit of turning up in Donovan Grove."

"I'll bring you up a cup of coffee," Anna says. It's not like she's pushing me off her. "How about that?"

I like the sound of that. We didn't get much sleep and I need something to kick-start my tired body. I remove my leg and let her go, but as soon as she tosses the duvet off her, I cover her with it again. "I've changed my mind. Stay."

Her body spasms with laughter in my embrace. "I had no idea you were so needy."

"There's so much you don't know about me yet," I whisper in her ear, then softly bite her earlobe like I did last night.

"I know you're the queen of many things." Anna wriggles herself around so she faces me.

I gaze into her eyes. They seem to catch the morning light. She looks so beautiful this morning, a little different even. Different to me, at least, because I could never have hoped she would give herself to me the way she did last night and then again, through most of the night, until I fell asleep, completely drained of all energy, in her arms.

"I love you," I say, and a warm sensation ripples under my skin, settles in my core, setting some parts of me ablaze again.

"I love you too," she says, and what floors me is how easily the words flow from her mouth now, as though she has gone past the barrier that kept them inside once and for all. "I also love my dog." She kisses the tip of my nose.

"Go." I free her from my embrace and let her go this time. I sit up in bed and watch her put on a robe and exit the room. Before she does, she turns around and blows me a kiss. Then I decide to follow her downstairs because I want to experience getting up with her, shuffling around in her gorgeous kitchen on a Sunday morning. Just being with her, after the night we've had. But it's also true I want to spend every moment I can with her this weekend so that I can spin Eve turning up into a positive experience. Sleepovers won't be turning into a habit, because I'm not the kind of mother to sneak off and leave her teenage daughter home alone. And I have a feeling Anna won't be staying over at my place any time soon.

I throw on my clothes and tiptoe down the stairs, marveling at the wealth of framed paintings that line the walls of Anna's stairwell. I barely noticed them last night, but I can't not notice them this morning.

Her entire family is represented and I stop at a particularly fetching portrait of Jaden which she must have painted a few years ago because it's a younger version of him.

"You're up." She's standing at the bottom of the stairs with two steaming mugs.

"Yeah, but I got distracted on my way down." I return my gaze to the painting of Jaden. "Do you have any recent ones of him?"

Anna nods. "A few."

"Brooklyn's birthday is coming up and I think it would make me mother of the year if I gave her a painting of her boyfriend. Can I buy it off you?"

"I only accept payment in kind," Anna says matter-of-factly.

"Got it." I walk down the stairs and stop at the bottom step. "What did you have in mind?"

"You'll find out soon enough." She hands me a mug of coffee and we head into the kitchen. The light streaming through the huge window is beautiful. On the lawn, Hemingway is running around as though he hasn't smelled any outside air in days.

"He's such a morning dog," I say, and lean into Anna as we watch him frolic about. "Please tell me we can spend the day together."

"I have to go to lunch at my parents," Anna says.

"You *have* to?" I want to challenge her a little bit because I want this time with her. We'll never have the day after our first night together again. "What will happen if you cancel?"

"Nothing will happen, but I've had Sunday lunch at my parents' for as long as I can remember. It's when I see my family. It's an elemental part of my Sunday and my week."

"I get that," I say, "but… I'd like to spend the day with you."

"It's only lunch. It's just a few hours." She's starting to get a bit agitated. Time to take the sting out of the conversation, although that doesn't mean I'm backing down.

"How about I call Sherry?" I bump my shoulder into hers lightly. "And explain to her why you can't make it to lunch today."

"What would you say?" Anna's at least willing to entertain my joke.

"That my presence in your house has left you indisposed." I sip from the coffee.

"You can't say that to my mother."

"I bet I can."

"Let's not put that to the test." Anna grabs my free hand

with hers. "I want to spend the day with you too, Zoe. Why don't you come with me? Mom will be ecstatic."

"As much as I like your family, I feel like I'm on a ticking clock here. The only silver lining to Eve turning up out of the blue is that I get to spend time with you without worrying about Brooklyn. That ends when Eve leaves tomorrow."

"You're asking me to change my routine for you," Anna says. "You also asked me to spy for you at Sunday lunch, remember? To find out what Jamie and Janet think about Eve."

"I don't care about that one bit right now, Anna." I give her hand a squeeze. "I just want to spend the day with you. I'll cook you lunch and dinner and whatever you want."

"You truly are the queen of many things." She follows up with a chuckle. "I'll call Mom. I'll tell her it's your fault."

"I'll apologize to her in person tomorrow." A smile breaks on my face.

"Don't ingratiate yourself with her even more. You'll be her favorite daughter in no time." Anna turns to me. "I think my mother might be as crazy about you as I am."

"Knowledge I will use to my advantage without mercy." I kiss Anna on the lips.

"Let me call her." Anna kisses me back and then goes to find her phone.

While she calls her mother, I check my own phone, to see if everything's okay with Brooklyn. I text her, and get a reply back instantly with a bunch of happy emojis. At least Eve's visit is fun for Brooklyn.

"Will Sherry survive your absence at her table?" I ask when Anna comes back into the kitchen.

"She will, but you and Brooklyn have to come to lunch next Sunday to make up for it."

"We will do so with great pleasure."

"I do have to walk Hemingway, though."

"We'll walk him together," I say. "Because he'd better get used to having me around and sharing his owner's affections."

Anna opens the sliding door and Hemingway comes bounding in, his paws wet from hopping all over the lawn. While she rubs them dry, I gaze out over her garden, toward the trees at the back, and think that I could very easily picture myself waking up in this house every morning.

11

ANNA

"I KNEW it would be like this," Zoe whispers.

It's Tuesday afternoon, and I've felt completely and utterly unable to stay away from the store ever since Zoe left my house yesterday. I'm amazed I managed this long, which is surprising in itself because I believed I would need twenty-four hours on my own at the very least to recover from having her in my space for so long. Turns out I just want more of her.

Zoe shakes her head. "I hate seeing Brooklyn so distraught."

"Maybe you should give her the painting now. To cheer her up," I offer.

"Maybe, but it's not a painting of her boyfriend she needs. It's her other mother in her life." She expels a deep sigh. "I should have talked about it with Eve, but I had my own distractions." She gives me a weak smile, nothing like the dazzling display of joy I'm used to seeing from Zoe.

"Is she going back to Shanghai?"

Zoe nods. "Yes. Her contract doesn't finish until the end of the year. If she comes back to New York then, she can at least see some more of her daughter before she leaves for college."

"Or Brooklyn could go to college in New York." I feel so out of my depth in this conversation about this child that isn't mine. I don't even know that much about her—yet.

"We'll see." We sit at the latest additions to Bookends, a small table and two easy chairs close to the window. Hemingway's sprawled out between us. "I'm just… I don't know. I had this amazing weekend with you and then I come home to find my daughter in such a funk."

"It will pass. She might miss Eve, but she has you, and her new life here. She has Jaden. And she has Hemingway." He perks his ears up briefly at the sound of his name. My dog lying there all cute and cuddly reminds me of the adoption appeal I saw for the little dachshund last week. I pull out my phone and show Zoe the picture. "How about this? Wouldn't that cheer her up?"

"Is that why you said I should consider adopting a dog this weekend?" Zoe asks, her gaze instantly glued to the screen because the animal is irresistible. He's probably been adopted already.

"Yes."

"I'm not getting my teenager a dog because her other mother leaving made her feel sad all over again." It's her staccato, firm voice, the one she uses when she's very adamant about something. I can hear the city in Zoe's tone, and I catch a glimpse of the person she was when she lived in New York.

"Pity," I say. "You could also do it for the dog. It needs a home."

"I just got myself a new girlfriend," Zoe says. "I'm quite busy with her."

"We could always go and have a look at the shelter… No pressure, of course." I know it's time to back off, but sometimes, when I get really passionate about something, and rescuing pets is definitely one of those things, it's hard for me to put a sock in it. Luckily, the door opens, and I naturally stop talking.

"Hi, *mija*." Zoe gets up and walks over to Brooklyn. "Come here." She opens her arms wide, but Brooklyn looks at her as though she'd rather turn around and walk right back out of the store than give her mom a hug. My heart aches a little for Zoe.

"Mom, come on," Brooklyn says.

Hemingway, who is very adept at spotting stress in humans, gets up and walks over to her. He gently pushes his snout against Brooklyn's leg. She responds very differently to Hemingway's affection and crouches immediately to give him an elaborate petting.

If only my glance could convey to Zoe what dogs can mean to people. I can't imagine my life without Hemingway. Without his constant presence and his goofiness and the unconditional love in his eyes. I can't imagine not taking care of him, a routine that has helped me through many an off day.

"Do you want to take him for a walk?" I ask.

"Can I?" Brooklyn eyes me suspiciously.

"Of course." I try to sound confident, because I don't like to leave Hemingway in the care of other people. But Brooklyn is Zoe's daughter. I trust Zoe. And Brooklyn's obviously besotted with Hemingway.

She looks at her mother and, as she does, I can see the little girl in her. I've been thinking of Brooklyn as a young woman already, but I see now that she's still a girl, helpless at times. A girl who needs her mothers.

"Why don't you walk him over to Jaden's?" Zoe says. "Ask him to walk you home."

"When should I be back?" Brooklyn asks me.

"Looks like I'll be here a while."

"Before closing time," Zoe says firmly.

A customer comes into the store and while Zoe focuses her attention on the woman, I take Hemingway and Brooklyn outside. I snap on his leash because I don't want her walking him without it.

"He's usually very well-behaved," I say. "But don't text and walk." I sound so silly when I say it. "Enjoy his company."

"Thanks, Anna." Brooklyn beams me a carbon copy of her mother's smile. She doesn't start walking immediately. "I—I talked about you in art class today."

I arch up my eyebrows.

"About your paintings. How they're unlike any paintings I've ever seen before. The teacher asked me which techniques you use."

"Techniques?" I say. "I just paint."

"Do, um, do you think you could show me some time?"

"Show you how I paint?"

Brooklyn nods. Hemingway starts pulling on his leash. Now that he's outside, he wants his walk to start.

"Um," I say, while my mind whirs. I have no idea how to show Brooklyn how I paint. I do it without thinking. I can't bear the thought of having someone in my studio while I work. Despite all of this, I say, "Sure." Because Brooklyn needs the kind of cheering up a walk with my dog can't provide—and it doesn't sound as though Zoe will be adopting that cute little sausage dog any time soon. "Any time." I am her mother's new girlfriend, after all.

"Thanks." She gives me a quick wave as she bounds after Hemingway.

When I head back inside, Zoe is still busy with the customer. This gives me some time to process the exchange I just had with Brooklyn. I wonder who her art teacher is. Jamie should know. I make a mental note to ask him on Friday.

Then my brain starts making up excuses to give Brooklyn as to why I won't be able to keep my promise. But then I look at Zoe, and memories of the weekend flood my brain. Zoe comes with a daughter, there's no two ways about that. A daughter that I will need to like me. Maybe this is how I can get closer with Brooklyn, because not finding a way in with her, which would be my default choice, is not an option.

"Maybe," Zoe says, after the customer has left and I've told her what Brooklyn asked me, "she'll get over Eve leaving in no time."

12

ZOE

"THEY'RE IN ANNA'S STUDIO," I say to Janet. "Right now, as we speak."

"Things are progressing swiftly." She smiles at me. "Truth be told, it was quite the shock to not see Anna at lunch last Sunday. She's always there. *Always.* Sam hardly knew what to do with himself because of her absence."

"Yes, well, we were busy."

"Hm," Janet says. "I bet you were."

"Of all the things I thought would happen to me when I moved to Donovan Grove, I never thought I'd fall in love," I say. "I don't know why. It wasn't very high on my list of priorities. I just wanted to build a new kind of life for Brooklyn and me. Integrate ourselves into the fabric of the town a little bit. Take it easy and have lots of heart-to-heart talks with my daughter." I chuckle. "That was my first mistake, of course. What with her being fifteen."

"She is such a lovely girl for a fifteen-year-old, though, Zoe. I couldn't have hoped for a better first serious girlfriend for my son."

"I just keep wondering if she asked Anna to spend time with

her for her own benefit or because of me. Because she wants to get to know Anna better for my sake." I think I'm beginning to understand what it feels like for Anna when she says something is hard for her to process. That her brain needs more time to fully absorb it.

"Maybe it's a bit of both," Janet says. "If she's truly interested in art and painting specifically, she might as well ask Anna."

"I'm not sure about that. Yes, Anna is a genius painter, but I'm not sure if she's also a good teacher."

"No one forced her to do it."

"I think Brooklyn might have forced her hand a little."

"This is good for Anna, too, you know."

"You sound very convinced."

"I'm always telling Jamie that she could benefit from a small kick in the behind at times. Meeting you has most certainly given her that."

I chuckle at the image I see appear in my mind. Then my mind gets pulled back to the sensation of Anna's hands on *my* behind. I need to organize a sleepover for Brooklyn soon, so I can spend the entire night at Anna's again. But Brooklyn hasn't mentioned many girlfriends she might want to have some girlie time with yet, and I'm sure as hell not going to let her stay over at Jamie and Janet's—and Jaden's—yet.

"It was nice to meet Eve," Janet says, when I haven't spoken for a while.

"Was it?"

"Yeah. It's good to have the full picture. She's very… sure of herself."

"That's an understatement." I offer a small smile.

"She's a beautiful woman. I could most certainly see the appeal. So could Jamie, by the way."

I roll my eyes. "I don't see Eve in that way anymore. Once you've gone through a divorce with someone, it changes your perception of them forever."

"Was it amicable?"

"As amicable as it could be, for Brooklyn's sake. She was only ten at the time. And before you ask, it was Eve who left."

"Would you have rather she'd stayed?" Janet's not shy with the questions tonight—she never is.

I huff out some air. "I understand you have questions, Janet, but I really don't feel like talking about my ex-wife any longer. She hurt me, but in the end, it was good that we separated. Eve always had this kind of frenetic, relentless city energy about her, a vibe she could never shake. Like it was impossible for her to fully relax. It took me a long time to shake it after the divorce. It was one reason why I wanted to move to a place like this, where life happens at a different speed."

Janet nods and leaves a pause. "That explains why you would fall for someone like Anna. From what I've seen, Anna and Eve couldn't be more different."

"They are very different, yet... there are some similarities, I guess. Anna can be very focused on herself, with her routines and rituals and rules. Eve's self-centered as well, but in a different way. She honestly gave me a bunch of reasons and debated with me why moving to Shanghai was not a selfish a thing to do."

"When I had her alone, when she and Brooklyn came over..." Janet leans over the table. "I tried to ask her what her motivation was to move abroad and leave her child. Not in those words, of course. I can't even imagine not seeing my boys for longer than a weekend."

"She fell in love. She won't admit it, but I'm sure she followed some woman to Shanghai and that's why she left earlier than planned."

"But still. You're in love with Anna. You wouldn't leave Brooklyn behind to move to the other side of the world with her."

"Not in a million years." It sounds a bit harsh toward Anna, but my child will always come first. "Anna's just so…" I feel like I have to say something nice about her, especially because Janet isn't Anna's biggest fan. "Gentle's not the right word. Thoughtful. Patient. Loving." When I put it like that, I'm not sure why I was worried when Brooklyn invited herself into Anna's studio. Because Anna is all these things. She and Brooklyn will be just fine.

"I'm really happy for you, Zoe. For Anna as well," Janet says. "She's my sister-in-law. I want the best for her. Jamie's practically beside himself with happiness now that you and Anna are together. And that she's seeing this therapist."

"It's made a world of difference already. I don't even know Anna that well yet, you know, in the grand scheme of things, but even I can see that. She has more confidence. She's more outgoing. Some days, I can barely get her out of the store."

"I believe that's called being in love." Janet bats her lashes at me. "Speaking of… Have you had the question from your offspring? Because I have."

"What question?" I'm trying to imagine Brooklyn and Anna in her studio together and I still can't picture it.

"Jaden has asked me if Brooklyn can spend the night."

My eyes grow wide. "You're kidding."

"He did add that she would sleep in the guest room, but I can read between the lines."

"What did you say?"

"That I had to talk about it with you."

"*Dios mio.*" I shake my head. "Brooklyn will be sixteen in a few months. It's not something we can stop. For all we know, they're already at it. Remember how we were when we were sixteen?"

"But still," Janet says on a sigh. "I want to be the kind of mother who understands this stuff and is open to her children about it, because that's how we raised them. But when push comes to shove, these decisions are hard."

"They *are* hard." I'm so grateful for Janet in that moment. Brooklyn could have fallen for another boy with a mother who would not want to discuss this so openly. Janet and I get to have this chat while we're sharing a bottle of wine. "But we can only do what we can. Tell them plenty of times that we're always available to them if they have any questions or issues."

"Just to be clear, when Brooklyn does end up staying at our house, she will be sleeping in the guest room and either I or Jamie will be keeping guard outside their doors." She chuckles.

I laugh with her to break the tension. "Should we talk about protection with them again?"

"It can't hurt to repeat ourselves, but I can imagine how Jaden's going to roll his eyes at me."

"Have you… given him condoms?"

"Jamie has."

"Good." I top up our wine glasses. "I really need to have Jaden over for dinner again. I feel like Brooklyn's always over at your place."

"We really don't mind, Zoe. It's not a quid pro quo." She smiles at me. "And I'd rather they be at our house instead of upstairs at yours, while you're downstairs in the store."

"I'd find an excuse to go upstairs every five minutes or so."

"God, we're walking mothers-of-teenagers clichés," Janet says.

I hold up my glass. "Walking, wine-drinking clichés," I say.

"But it will all be fine." She raises her glass as well.

"It will be," I say, and I believe it, because I have to.

13

ANNA

Because I don't want my dog's fur to be all colors of the rainbow, I taught Hemingway to stay out of my painting studio, but tonight, I wish he was here with me for emotional support.

"You've done another one of Mom," Brooklyn says as she gravitates toward the one painting of Zoe I've left on display. I've finished about a dozen more, but I managed to stack them in the attic. I've also hidden the one of Jaden that Zoe wants to give Brooklyn for her birthday. "Wow, Anna. It's so beautiful. How do you get the colors to pop like that?"

"I mix the paint until it's the exact color I see in my head." There's a reason I have never for one second of my life considered going into teaching.

"Has Mom seen this? She'll go apeshit over it." She smirks at me. "Surely you've noticed she loves admiring pictures of herself." She giggles.

I laugh, because it's true, and it's funny when Brooklyn says something like that about her mother.

"Ooh." Brooklyn has noticed another painting I've recently finished. "Who's this?"

"A dog I'm thinking of adopting," I say.

"Aw, he's so cute."

I'm not sure why I said that. Probably because it's true. The other day, when I tried talking Zoe into adopting the little dachshund from the shelter, maybe I was trying to talk myself into it.

"Are you going to do it?" She looks at me expectantly.

"I'd need to meet him first. See if we click."

"Can I go with you when you go see him?" Brooklyn asks.

It's my turn to giggle nervously. "I would really need to check that with your mom."

"I've always wanted a dog, but I also understand why Mom doesn't want one. I bet Hemingway would like a brother or sister, though." I haven't spent that much time with Brooklyn and now that I am, it strikes me that, from certain angles, like now, she looks just like her mother.

"Maybe the three of us could go together," I say, hoping I didn't just get myself into a world of trouble with Zoe.

"That would be amazing. Mom might have a fit, but I know she adores Hemingway, so maybe she won't." Brooklyn seems to have inherited her mother's confidence, because there's no shyness or any other hint of intimidation in the smile she shoots me—not that there should be. It seems so easy for her, and she's still so young. If I wasn't suffering from shyness and feeling a touch intimidated myself, I'd ask her where she gets such self-esteem at such a young age. But it's obvious that she gets it from her mother, and from the times she has grown up in. Or maybe it's all a front. I have no way of knowing.

"Are you okay, Anna?" she asks now.

I spaced out for a second there. It happens. "Yeah. Sure. We'll see what your mom has to say later, okay? Just… try not to get your hopes up too high." I do my very best to sound conversational although, most days, I have no idea what that would actually sound like.

"Can I ask you something personal?" Brooklyn fixes her

gaze on me. She doesn't appear to be as interested in painting as I thought she would be.

"Shoot." Oh no, I groan on the inside.

"You're just... I don't know. I don't want to sound offensive, but you're totally not what I imagine when I think of someone neurodiverse."

This is Zoe's daughter, so I have to do my very best to not go on the defensive. She's just a child with questions.

"What do you imagine?" I draw up two stools from under a nearby table so we can sit.

"Someone much more awkward, I guess. Much more difficult to be around. Not the kind of person my mom would fall in love with."

I wish I could press an alarm button that would notify Zoe that it's time to come and get her daughter.

"I don't mean that in a bad way, Anna," Brooklyn says. "I think you're great, but, if Jaden hadn't told me, I wouldn't even have known."

"You can't always see what a person is like on the inside from the outside."

Brooklyn sighs. "Tell me about it."

"Do you sometimes feel like you need to hide how you're truly feeling inside?" I always think I have no special gifts, and I really don't, but I do excel in the art of conversational deflection. Decades of practice have turned it into one of my most useful skills.

"Well, yeah. Of course. When we first moved here. And then when Mama turned up this weekend and I had to pretend like it was just one big party, while it also hurt me."

"Did you talk to your mom about that?"

"No, because she was already so pissed off that Mama turned up out of the blue. I didn't want to make that worse. I don't want them to fight. I just want them to get along."

"But they do, generally, get along?"

Brooklyn just shrugs. "I guess. It's not that hard when one of them lives ten thousand miles away."

"You do know that you don't ever have to hide your true feelings from your mom, don't you?"

"I know I don't have to, but sometimes I want to."

I nod because I understand. "I hide my true feelings all the time, but it's good to just let them all out once in a while."

"I know. I feel like I can really talk to Jaden. He's not like any of the boys at my old school in Queens."

I let her talk, or as my dad is fond of saying: I don't miss a good chance to shut up.

"Sometimes, I can't believe how sweet Jaden is," Brooklyn says.

My heart melts a little. Even though I have zero to do with Jaden's personality and upbringing, my chest swells with pride a little because he's my nephew.

"I know for a fact that he's completely nuts about you," I say.

"I think about him all the time," she says with the kind of passion only a teenager can muster. Although I seem to be suffering from my very own case of teenage lovestruck-ness, as I think about Zoe all the time—often to the point of distraction.

"How about we paint *him* then?" I smile at her.

She gets up. "Sure, but I have no idea how."

"Right." I scratch my head. It sounded so good and actionable when I said it. "How are we going to do this?"

"Can I watch you?" she asks. "While you paint him?" There's so much tender hope in her voice I can't bear to crush it.

I take a deep breath. "Okay, we can try. But you should know that I'm not used to having anyone in here while I paint."

"Just pretend I'm not here. What would you do if I wasn't here?"

"For starters, I would turn up the music really loud."

"I don't mind that," Brooklyn says. "What kind of music?"

"Cheesy ballads only. It's a requirement." I'm starting to get in the zone, feeding off Brooklyn's energy a little, because she seems to be quite into the whole thing. She seems genuinely interested. And I'm willing to cut Zoe's daughter a hell of a lot more slack than I would anyone else.

"Let's do it," I say.

I ask Alexa to shuffle my painting playlist and the room fills with the loud piano intro of a Lady Gaga song.

"I love this one," Brooklyn shouts over the music.

"You may want to cover yourself with this." I hand her a spare apron before putting on my own very paint smudged one. "You may want to stay out of this area." With my finger, I draw a circle around my easel.

"What were you working on?" she asks, when I stand before the blank canvas.

"I just finished a painting." I don't want to say it was of her mother, even though it was. "It's drying in another room."

"Of my mom?" she asks, because the girl wasn't born yesterday.

I give a quick nod. "Do you have any pictures on your phone of Jaden that could serve as inspiration?"

Without hesitation, she shows me her phone. "It's my background picture. I'm in it as well, though."

"Perfect," I say, sounding much more confident than I feel. I stare at the picture until it appears very vividly in my mind. Then, while I get my paints ready, I start seeing how I want the picture to look on my canvas once I'm done. I'm glad Brooklyn's not asking me to describe this part of my process to her, because I could never find the means—neither the actions nor the words—to show her how I get from one thing to the other.

Maybe April was right when she said that painting the way I do is a neurodiverse superpower, because I can't explain it any other way. The only explanation is that this is how my brain works. This is how it goes from picture to painting. This is my purest form of expression and, in a way, it's so fitting that I'm about to paint my nephew and the daughter of the woman I've fallen so head over heels in love with. It's not a chore whatsoever. It's a delight, really, and a small part of me revels in the audience of one that I have tonight, because another thing that April has taught me, or that I have come to realize since we've started our sessions together, is that I no longer have to hide who I am.

Some days, I can even feel a touch of pride in some of the things that I do. Of course, the sensation of being watched so intently does mess with me a bit, but when it threatens to take over, I listen to the music, and I focus on the color I'm applying in that moment, and what I want it to ultimately turn into, and this is a magic process that never seems to fail me. Where words can seldom truly express what it is I'm holding in my brain, my hand, the paint brush I'm holding, the paints that I mix purely intuitively—colors have always made sense to me—never let me down. Whenever I'm done with a painting and I feel the rush of satisfaction of having brought out something that was held captive inside, I'm never disappointed. Then again, I've never painted Brooklyn and Jaden before.

But doing so doesn't cause me any real problems. It's not the exact same cathartic experience that I come to expect from painting, but it's enough—and catharsis was not the goal tonight anyway.

I have no idea how long it takes me to finish, but somehow I'm still kind of surprised to find Brooklyn sitting in her designated space. She might have snuck out at some point. She must have, because she's holding a glass of water that I forgot to offer her when she first arrived.

"Done," I say.

"Jesus Fucking Christ," she says.

"Excuse me?" I'm pretty sure Zoe wouldn't approve of that

kind of language, although, personally, in the mood I'm in right now, I don't care one bit.

"You're a rock star, Anna."

"Hm," I say, then ask Alexa to lower the volume of the music, which is still blaring through the studio.

"I've never seen anything like it." She holds up her phone. "Check this out. I made a time-lapse video of the last fifteen minutes."

I'm still on a creative high, so it's easy to suppress the instant dismay I feel at being filmed without my consent. When I look at the video, the painting being completed blindingly fast, it does look kind of cool, although 'cool' has never been a word I've associated with myself.

"What time is it?" I ask.

"Half past ten."

"Oh, shit. Zoe will go nuts."

"It's okay. I texted her. She knows where I am." Brooklyn chuckles. "She knows I'm with you."

"Don't you have to go to bed?" I have to go to bed, I think. Hemingway probably passed out on his cushion in the living room hours ago.

"I'm not five, Anna." Brooklyn stares at the painting so I can't see her face, but it sounds very much as though she's rolling her eyes. "I feel like I've just been witness to a very unique experience." She looks at me. "I feel very privileged, Anna. Thank you."

God, the way these teenagers speak. Words like that would never come out of my mouth, even if I had Zoe and Brooklyn's eloquence. "It's yours. I'll bring it over tomorrow, when it's dry." I feel a twinge of guilt at usurping the birthday gift Zoe had planned for Brooklyn, but I have an alternative idea for that.

"Oh my God. Thanks so much." She brings a hand to her mouth. What did she think I was going to do with it?

"The only thing I ask in return is that you don't post that video you shot of me anywhere online."

"Why not? It's so badass, Anna."

"Being badass online is not one of my aspirations in life."

"That actually makes you even more badass," she says.

I shrug, like a teenager would.

14

ZOE

AFTER I'VE SENT my over-excited daughter to bed, I sit next to Anna. I've had a quick rundown of the night from Brooklyn, and I've seen the painting Anna made for her from all angles on her phone, as well as the video Brooklyn shot of Anna.

"You're going to be that kind of girlfriend, huh," I say, pressing myself against her. I've had a bit too much wine with Janet and I'm feeling pleasantly tipsy. And my buzz is enhanced by the fact that Anna and Brooklyn seemed to have had a great night together. I don't even care that much that I'll have to find another gift for Brooklyn's birthday, now she already has a painting of Jaden.

"Which kind is that?" Anna shakes her head. "You should probably wait until I tell you what Brooklyn and I talked about to make any more statements like that." Then she tells me about the painting of the dog Brooklyn spotted and her promise to take Brooklyn to the shelter with her, and follows up with what Brooklyn told her about not always wanting to tell me everything.

"What did you do to my daughter?" I ask. "Did you mix her a special potion when she arrived?"

"No." Anna's face looks solemn and sincere. "I might even have forgotten to offer her a glass of water. Luckily, Brooklyn was raised very well and can take care of herself perfectly."

"I'm glad that she likes you so much, Anna."

"Glad enough to let her come to the shelter with me? Perhaps you might even consider joining us?"

"When you say you and Brooklyn will go to the shelter together, how were you intending on getting there if it's in the next town?"

"We'd walk," Anna says, as if that was always a foregone conclusion.

"I'd like to see you try that with Brooklyn."

"How was your night?" Anna asks.

"Janet likes a glass of wine, that's for sure." I tug on Anna's sleeve. "Lie down with me for a minute, while we talk." I pull her down on the couch with me. We maneuver clumsily until we're facing each other. "Jaden asked Janet if Brooklyn could stay the night sometime."

"Wow," Anna says. "What did Janet have to say about that? And Jamie?"

"I think we all feel as though our kids are growing up way too fast, while, in fact, they're not. Jaden and Brooklyn are almost sixteen. We can be in denial all we want about what they get up to when they're alone, but we'd only be doing ourselves a disservice."

"Do you want to know what I think?" Anna asks.

"Of course I do. Why wouldn't I?"

"They're not my kids. I'm not a mother."

"I always value your opinion, Anna. And my kid had an awesome time with you tonight." The thought of Brooklyn in Anna's studio now fills with me warmth instead of the tension it caused me earlier.

"Both Jaden and Brooklyn are good kids at heart. And yes, of course, they're experimenting and having sex, or are about to. But they're also madly in love, so there's that, which is a huge plus. They might be teenagers, but they're both smart enough to be responsible. I think they'll be just fine without much parental meddling that will only make them feel awkward."

"You're probably right." I bring my hand to Anna's face. "If you were me, would you let Brooklyn spend the night at Jaden's?"

"I would." Her lips curve into a smile. "Janet will be beside herself, though."

"Janet will be just fine," I say.

"Let's stop talking about Janet," Anna says, and kisses me.

"Will you stay?" I ask, when we break from our kiss.

"I don't know. I left Hem at home. He was sound asleep already. And I didn't bring anything. I just wanted to walk Brooklyn home."

"And see me." I nuzzle my nose into her neck.

"There's that," she says, on a sigh, as if it's a nuisance that she so desperately wanted to see me.

"Please, stay. If it makes you feel awkward, you can leave before Brooklyn wakes up. Hemingway will barely notice that you're not there."

"It's been a long time since I slept in a bed other than my own."

"I bet it's also been a long time since you met someone like me." I flutter my eyelids.

Anna breaks into a chuckle. "Don't let it go to your head, although it's probably too late for that, but I've never met anyone like you in my life." She kisses me and I take that as her consent that she will stay.

I wake up in the middle of the night with Anna's hands all over my buttocks. I wonder if she's clutching at me like that in her sleep because her subconscious has taken over. Last night, after I convinced her to stay and we went to bed, she categorically refused to engage in even the slightest hanky-panky because of Brooklyn sleeping in the other room.

I countered that her reasoning was not very persuasive because, according to her logic, no parent would ever have sex again until their kids left home. I didn't win the argument, but I've learned to take my time with Anna. She just needs to get used to it.

Or maybe she's gotten used to the idea already.

"Anna," I whisper. "Are you awake?"

"Hm," she replies. "I can't sleep."

"Something wrong?" I ask, while pressing my ass deeper into her palms.

"You're too hot," she whispers. "And your ass is too bare and too close to me."

"Should I put on some underwear?" I tease.

"Yeah, maybe that thong." Her body shakes as she snickers. "I don't have my earplugs or my eye mask and it's hard for me to fall asleep in a different environment." Her breasts push against the skin of my back. "And I mean it. You're too hot to sleep next to. Even when you're snoring."

"I don't snore."

She doesn't reply, just creates a little space between our bodies, and moves her hand, between my thighs.

"Jesus," I whisper. "What are you doing?"

"Touching you," she says.

"You were feeling me up in my sleep."

"You insisted I stay over." A finger slides all the way between my thighs. I open my legs a little to give her better access. Anna's not the only one suffering from hot flashes in this bed.

"I did," I say on a sigh. "I don't regret it." Her finger slides over my pussy lips, gently, but oh so arousingly.

Anna's mouth teases my neck as her finger reaches my clit, and she circles it a few times, before it slides back down. It's still pitch-black outside, but I want to see whatever I can of her face. I want to see what's possessing her in this moment. I slide away from her and quickly turn around, grab her hand, and put it back where it was before.

Anna smirks at me. "You're so bossy."

"I just know what I want."

"We can call it that." In the faint glimmer of the light that comes in from outside, I can make out the soft smile on her lips.

"I want you to spread your legs as well," I say.

"No, Zoe," she says. "I can't... sexually multitask."

"What?" I run the back of my hand over her belly, hoping to change her mind.

"I can't focus on you and on myself at the same time. It's not a thing for me." Her hand has stopped all movement between my legs.

"Okay." To indicate that I've understood, I run my hand upward across her torso, to find her breast. I cup her breast, run my thumb across her nipple. "Is that okay?" I ask.

"More than," she says, before leaning in to kiss me and simultaneously push me onto my back. I let my legs fall open because this short exchange, in our world, is intimacy too. The mere fact that Anna was able to express to me in a few words what she wanted, shows me that she trusts me. The fact that she's here in bed with me, in my apartment, with Brooklyn sleeping in the next room, tells me everything I need to know about her intentions with me. A few weeks ago, this would have been unthinkable.

Anna's fingers slide through the wetness that has gathered between my legs. Her breath is hot against my cheek.

"You do this thing to me," she whispers, "where I can't seem to control myself very well." I can feel her lips move against my skin. "I used to be *very* big on control," she half-says and half-moans.

"You're fully in control now." I turn my face toward her and my eyes are fully used to the dark now and I can make out all her features and even a little bit of the love in her eyes.

"Yeah," she says, and pushes a finger inside of me. "Just the way I like it." She looks me in the eye as her finger starts moving, starts stealing my breath, starts coaxing me toward an unexpected midnight pleasure.

15

ANNA

I'M USUALLY A MORNING PERSON, waking on time without an alarm, but this morning I'm still fast asleep when I'm shaken awake.

"Anna," Zoe whispers. "We overslept."

I rub the sleep from my eyes. A headache pulses in the back of my skull and I already know it's going to be one of those days after a really bad night's sleep where I'm going to have to cut myself some major slack.

"What time is it?" I ask.

"Time to get up. Unless you want to wait until Brooklyn has left for school." Zoe's faces hovers over mine and despite feeling not in my element physically, I pull her toward me.

"You're such a bad influence," I say, before I kiss her.

"Excuse me." Her voice is full of mock indignation. "Who grabbed whose ass in the middle of the night?"

"That ass of yours is going to get me into trouble." I pull Zoe into a hug and we both chuckle. As if my brain only comes fully awake with Zoe's body pressed against mine, I say, "Oh no, Hemingway."

"He'll be fine, Anna. He's not a baby."

"He's my baby." I wriggle out of our embrace. "He'll be bursting. Poor thing."

"Am I going to have to turn into the kind of woman who has to fight for your affections with a dog? Because it's not a fair fight, you know. Hemingway's too cute. And you've known him for much longer."

"I've never been in a romantic relationship and had a dog at the same time," I say. "So we'll have to see how that plays out."

Zoe rolls her eyes at me, but she's still smiling. "I'll go see how Brooklyn's getting on."

I can't wait for Brooklyn to leave for school. But there's no way out of this apartment, as far as I know, other than through the living area. It's not as if Brooklyn doesn't know I was here. But perhaps she hadn't expected me to stay the night. I don't know if Zoe has talked to her about that. I don't know much about how this mother-daughter thing works. I've never dated a woman with a child before.

"Hi, Anna," Brooklyn says, as though she hadn't expected anything else of the morning than me exiting her mother's bedroom. "Have you talked to Mom about going to the dog shelter?" She lets the spoon with which she's eating cereal dangle in front of her mouth and looks from me to Zoe and back.

"We can go on Sunday," Zoe says. "After lunch at the Gunns."

"Sweet," Brooklyn says. "Maybe Jaden can come as well, then."

"We're just going to see the dog with Anna," Zoe says. "Don't get any ideas in your head, okay?"

"Of course not." Brooklyn's trying to sound innocent, even I can tell. "Thanks again for that painting, Anna." She sends me the sweetest smile. It's no wonder us Gunns, Jaden and I, are so defenseless against these Perez women. I do wonder how the battle of wills will play out between mother and daughter

Perez when we're at the dog shelter. If I don't fall madly in love with the little creature myself first.

"Maybe next time you can have a go," I say, to change the subject, because I do feel a bit guilty for putting the dog idea into Brooklyn's head.

"Awesome. Can I come over again this weekend?" Brooklyn says.

"Take it easy, *mija*." I can see a look pass between them. "Leave it to Anna to invite you."

"I'll let you know," I say to Brooklyn, while thanking Zoe inwardly. "But I'm sure we can arrange something soon."

Zoe taps her wrist. "Time for you to go, sweetheart. Come on, give your mother a kiss."

Time for me to go as well, I think, but I don't want to interrupt their moment. Being with Cynthia seemed so simple compared to this. There were no children or pets to be taken into account. The headache is moving from the back of my skull to behind my eyes. When I finally make it home, I might just crash into the couch and take a proper, undisturbed nap.

"Bye, Anna." Brooklyn gives me a quick wave and then she's off. The energy in Zoe's apartment is different instantly and I can feel myself relax a little.

"Do you want some coffee?" Zoe asks.

"I really have to go."

"Maybe next time you should bring Hemingway. Brooklyn would love it." Zoe walks toward me. "We can get him a cushion like the one he has at home and make up a nice space for him."

There's so much to unpack in what Zoe has just said, but my brain is too unrested to even start. After last night with Brooklyn, and the night and morning I had with Zoe, I'm in dire need of some urgent low-sensory input time. My inability to stay away from Zoe might actually get me into trouble. I make a mental note to discuss this with April next time, so she can help me come up with some coping strategies.

"I really have to go now, Zoe. I'll stop by the store later." I give her a quick kiss, find my shoes, and stumble down the stairs.

Once outside, I take a deep breath. As I walk home, my brain gets flooded with image after image of Zoe, Brooklyn and their inevitable new dog living in my house—Jaden hanging out there frequently as well. By the time I unlock my front door, Hemingway softly barking on the other side of it, the image of future chaos has me in such a panic, all I can do is crouch next to Hemingway and bury my face in his fur while I apologize to him profusely. Not that he understands a word of it. Once I get my bearings, he looks pretty unperturbed.

I let him into the backyard and make myself a cup of coffee and take some ibuprofen for my headache. My morning routine has been shot to pieces. I'm so tired I might fall asleep standing up. I shiver at the prospect of having other people living in my carefully decorated house, making a mess everywhere. But, strangely, the one thought piercing through all this anxiety that I know can start spinning out of control any second now, is that I'm so in love with Zoe, that I would find a way to cope. It's my willingness to find a way, if I ever had to, that makes me feel like I'm alive. I feel the spark of it glow deep inside me—a spark I didn't even know I needed, but now that I have it, I want to feel it again and again. It's the spark of aliveness and possibility and, most of all, of being okay with not knowing what exactly is going to happen next. Because whatever does happen, Zoe will be there beside me.

16

ZOE

On Sunday afternoon, I'm driving toward the animal shelter, with Anna in the passenger seat, and Brooklyn and Jaden in the back, and, as I glance in the rearview mirror, to keep an eye on my daughter and her boyfriend, I am grateful that I at least don't have any room left in my car for a dog. Not even the small one that Anna's been showing me pictures of, and that we're all about to meet.

"Have you asked Hemingway how he would feel about getting a brother?" I ask, stupidly.

"Of course," Anna says, playing along. "He would love it. Especially on the nights when I leave him home alone without telling him first."

We chuckle. On the backseat, Brooklyn and Jaden are lost in their own private conversation, huddled over one of their phones. How do teenagers even have time to take care of a dog if they're glued to their phone all the time?

"But seriously though," I implore and turn my gaze to Anna for an instant. "You *have* given this some thought?"

"Do I come across as the kind of person who doesn't give things enough thought?" Anna asks. "If so, I need to work on my image." She smiles at me and it's as though her smiles, also, have become more forward, more daring and at ease. She no longer shies away from making jokes about herself—or me. "I just want to meet him and see how that makes me, and him, feel." Anna puts a hand on my knee. "To see if we have any chemistry. Then, I will know."

"Fair enough." I remind myself that this is about Anna, not about Brooklyn getting a dog to replace the affection that she lost when Eve left. I turn into the street my GPS has guided me to. "We're here."

Brooklyn jumps out of the car, quickly followed by Jaden.

"Let's do this," Anna says, her voice suddenly a little tighter.

As though Brooklyn has developed a sixth sense for this particular dog, she finds its cage immediately. My daughter clearly has no time to exchange any niceties with the staff at the shelter. She hasn't even seen the dog in real life and already seems in love with it.

Jaden, this tall, dirty-blond boy with gangly limbs, who looks nothing like his aunt, seems to have caught the sausage-dog-loving bug already as well. They look more like children than teenagers all of a sudden—a sight that certainly appeals to me, what with Brooklyn growing up so fast. In many ways, they are still children. They still have so much to learn, so much to experience, so much joy and heartache ahead of them. Maybe a dog would be a good companion for Brooklyn on her way to adulthood, I find myself thinking, as though simply being at the shelter, with all the barking going on around me, and the few cute dog faces I've already spotted, will push me over the edge just like that.

"I'll unlock Boomer's cage," Venus, the woman who welcomed us, says.

"We might have to change his name," Anna whispers to me as we follow Venus through the narrow corridor until we reach Boomer's cage.

"Oh my God," Anna exclaims, as though, she too, has already fallen under its spell. What is it with this dog?

Boomer gets all excited when we enter his cage and tries to jump up and down on his tiny legs. It is an adorable sight to behold.

"His owner passed away quite suddenly, and no one in the family could take the dog," Venus says. "He's very well trained. Very sociable. Not the youngest, although you couldn't tell from his behavior." She scratches Boomer behind the ear.

Maybe the dog has some sort of magical power because just being near its sheer exuberance and eagerness to be loved does something to me on the inside. It melts the last part of resistance that I had about Brooklyn and I owning a dog, because, now that I'm standing next to him, feeling his soft hair for the first time, I can't imagine how it could ever be a chore to take care of this cute little thing. But I also know that I need to be the adult in this situation. Of course, my daughter is going to be smitten with this dog, and I can't expect her boyfriend to be the voice of maturity. I could perhaps, expect it from Anna, but one glance at her and I know she's more enamored than any of us.

"I think we have chemistry," Anna says.

"Boomer has a way with people," Venus says.

"How come he hasn't been adopted yet?" I ask.

"The family who wanted to adopt him didn't pass our background check," she says, matter-of-factly, as though screening for something much more serious than suitability to adopt a pet.

"I've already adopted a dog," Anna says. "I passed the test."

Boomer is getting beside himself because of all the human attention currently being bestowed upon him.

Anna and Venus get into a conversation about Hemingway while I look at Brooklyn. Whether it was hers and Anna's intention to bowl over my maternal heart or not, my defenses are sufficiently weakened to say yes to this dog right here and now. Just the thought of Boomer, with all his enthusiasm and pent-up love, having to stay in this cage for one night longer tugs at my heartstrings. But we came here for Anna.

Brooklyn looks at me and in her glance I see the girl she once was—the girl she can sometimes still be. I see how much that girl wants this dog and I know I won't be able to refuse her. I don't much feel like refusing myself either.

"Do you want to take him for a walk?" Venus asks. "See what he's like?"

Brooklyn nods ferociously.

Venus puts Boomer on a leash and we let Brooklyn and Jaden walk him around.

"What do you think?" I ask, when Anna and I are alone.

"I think that I'm about to witness what it's like to be a mother and to not be able to say no to your child, despite the many arguments against it you may have in your head." She adds, with an innocent tone, "Anyway, wouldn't he make the perfect birthday present for Brooklyn?"

"Wouldn't he just?" I give her my most skeptical look. "But we came here for you, didn't we?" I study her face. It doesn't look any different.

"I would adopt that dog in a heartbeat," Anna says. "But if you and Brooklyn want him, you should get him. I already have a dog. I already know what it's like. How amazing it is to see his face first thing in the morning. To have an animal love you like that, and to love it right back. More than adopting another dog, I want you and Brooklyn to experience that as well."

Whatever fight I was willing to put up has left me now as well.

"It's not as if I'm never going to see Boomer if you adopt him," Anna says.

"I haven't said yes yet."

"Maybe not," Anna says, "but who are you kidding?"

17

ANNA

Three Years Later

I wake, and Shadow's head is on my leg, the way it is every morning. When I stir to take off my eye mask, he opens his dark little eyes and looks at me for a few seconds, the time it takes for his dog brain to realize it's morning and he gets to enjoy another amazing day in his doggie life. Then he jumps up and walks all over me, waking Zoe in the process.

After I've taken out my ear plugs, also like I do every morning, I say, "God, you've spoiled that dog." It has become my version of, "Good Morning, Beautiful."

"It wasn't me, babe." Zoe scoots closer to me.

"It was all down to Brooklyn," we say in unison.

The familiarity of this scene warms my heart. But then I'm hit with the same bout of nerves that tensed my muscles as soon as I opened my eyes. Pets can have that effect on you, make you forget about your worries for a brief while. What they can't do is take your worries away entirely. Today, I have many things to worry about.

"Did you sleep well?" Zoe asks, and slings a leg over me.

"Lots of tossing and turning."

"I didn't notice." She kisses me on the cheek. "Are you nervous about the thing?"

"Is it too late to cancel?" Shadow knows we're not the type to jump out of bed immediately and cater to his needs. He lies down on the side of the bed to wait until one of us gets up.

"Way too late." Zoe snuggles up to me a little closer. "But I'm proud of you for doing it already."

Over the years, I've learned to cope with anxiety better, but that doesn't mean it isn't still there. This morning's flare-up is huge and all-encompassing, to the point of almost being paralyzing.

"Hey," Zoe whispers in my ear. "What's the worst that can happen?" She kisses me softly again. "It's just book club."

Zoe set up a monthly book club at Bookends a couple of years ago, but I've never attended. I like to read, but I've never felt any need to discuss what I've just read with a bunch of other people, to listen to all their opinions and their endless blah-blah. I'd rather be reading another book. I'm not one for group activities as it is. But tonight, I'm attending Zoe's book club, because she asked me to. Because the book they've been reading is, perhaps, one I *can* discuss with the group. Or not. I don't know. The point is that I promised Zoe I would be there. That I would do that for her, because I know it means a lot to her.

"Maybe to you it is just book club," I say, unable to keep the sulk out of my voice.

"You love books, babe. And you love me. You know everyone who's going to be there. It's going to be just fine."

I try to do the exercise April taught me, to be aware of my anxiety as just a thought, as opposed to something real that's actually happening, and to then cut through it with rationality. Which is not an easy thing to do. It has taken me years of practice to get the hang of it even a little bit, and this morning, it's like I never learned to do it at all.

"I can't get the better of my nerves." I turn on my side so I can look at Zoe's face, which always calms me down.

"You don't have to give a speech, babe. Just answer a few questions. Seeing as everybody there knows you, they won't expect you to have suddenly turned into the most eloquent resident of Donovan Grove."

"I blame Janet for this, you know. With all her second mountain bullshit."

"It's not bullshit. It's real life stuff. It's small acts that make a difference."

"I just don't like being the center of attention."

"I know." Zoe brings a hand to my cheek. "At least you know that you never have to worry about being that when I'm around." The thing about Zoe is that she actually means it when she says this, it's only partly a joke, and I love her even more for it. Zoe has been many things to me over the three years we've been together and one of the things she has excelled at the most is diverting all attention to herself. It's in her nature. There are still days I wish I could tap into her excess of self-esteem and steal some for myself. But most days, I do okay.

Not today, though. My fear of having to articulate certain thoughts in front of a group of people is debilitating, because I don't have a good track record of doing it, which is why I avoid it as much as I can. But love makes you do things you otherwise wouldn't.

"Is this a code orange?" Zoe whispers in my ear.

"It's a code red," I say, perhaps exaggerating a little.

"No, babe. I can't accept that. It can't be a code red. That's reserved for having to go to the E.R. or for when something happens to a family member. This is just book club. By definition, it can't be more than orange."

"How about pink, then?" I smile at her, because I can't keep on lying here, stiffly, my body taut with this cramp.

Zoe smiles back. "Pink, I can work with," she says, and runs her hand over my belly in a way I can't really misinterpret, because it's going straight for the prize. The time when Zoe was subtle about any of this has long passed. Her hand rests between my legs and my first instinct is to wriggle myself away from it.

"That's not what I meant," I say, despite the frisson of desire that runs down my spine. Because this is Zoe. *My* Zoe. A woman so gorgeous and kind and warm—a woman who is very hard to say any kind of no to.

"Maybe not," Zoe whispers in my ear. "But maybe it's what you need. Some relaxation because you're so tense. Let me take away your nerves, babe. You know I won't disappoint you."

I suck my bottom lip between my teeth, then let it slip back out. "I'm too nervous for any of that right now."

The grip of her hand intensifies. "That's just the point. You're in your head. Let me take you out of there." She kisses the side of my face, then breathes heavily into my ear. "You let me into your life," she whispers. "Into your bed and into your heart for a reason, babe." Her hand meanders back up and stops near my breast.

"Not with Shadow on the bed," I say, already giving in.

Zoe chuckles. "I'll go down and feed the dogs first. You, don't move an inch. I'll be right back. Okay?"

"Okay."

Zoe jumps out of bed and throws on a robe. "Come on, Chico," she says, because she still insists on calling him that, while Brooklyn and I have long resorted to calling him Shadow —Hemingway's tiny shadow.

I listen to them hurry down the stairs and revel in the sound of our two dogs' enthusiasm at getting their breakfast. I listen to Zoe talking to them as if they can understand what she's saying. These are the sounds of my home now, whereas I used to wake up to utter silence. But ever since Zoe and Shadow moved in, these sounds have replaced that silence. These sounds are my source of comfort now. The light pitter-patter of Shadow's paws on the stairs. Hemingway's cheerful bark when Shadow comes into the living room in the morning. Zoe addressing them as if they are her replacement children, now that Brooklyn's at Columbia, doing the arts program I was never able to complete when I was a student.

I hear Zoe climb the stairs and she winks at me before heading into the bathroom. As instructed, I haven't moved an inch. I've just been lying here, waiting for her, listening to the sounds of life in my house—sounds I never could have guessed I would adore so much.

"The kids are happy," Zoe says, as she slips out of her robe, and crawls back into bed with me. "Now, let's focus on you. Code Pink, you said." She smiles down at me and even though I'm nervous, when Zoe smiles her Zoe smile at me, in this bed in our house, I can feel the worst of my nerves melt away in the warmth of her smile. Not only because that smile always makes me feel loved, but also, because I can now fully accept that I'm a woman worth every bit of her love. I no longer need to negotiate with myself about that and list my flaws against my strengths. It's no longer a question of keeping score, of adding up something here because I subtracted something there. I love Zoe and she loves me. Most of the time, it's as simple as that. And one of these times is now, when she wants to do this for me, for us. When she just wants to express her love for me and, when I look at her in all her morning glory, it's all I want as well. Because I can switch off the endless list of complications my brain is always ready to generate. Because I've chosen to love myself more instead of always doubting myself. Because I know that what Zoe is about to give me will make me feel so good about myself, it will give me a much-needed dose of extra confidence that will carry me through the day and into the evening, when I have to face a bunch of people I wouldn't usually face. But sometimes—and nobody needs to even remind me of this anymore—a small step out of my comfort zone does me the world of good.

She kisses me and I can feel all her warmth in that kiss. She drapes her body over mine and the pressure, the weight of its softness on mine, relaxes me. I can go from the thought of wanting to have sex to actually having it so much faster these days. I know Zoe's body inside and out and she knows mine.

She slips off me and holds me close to her, while her hands roam softly across the front of my body. Her gentle touch, and all the love and patience I can recognize in it, ignites a series of tiny fireworks inside me, and with every cell that is lit by her touch, a knot of nerves uncoils.

18

ZOE

"WHO'S THAT?" Anna asks, and points at a woman I don't know either. "You said I would know everyone here."

"What can I say, babe?" I know how to keep this light. "My little old bookstore is so popular. Must be because of the owner." I smile at her, then give her a quick kiss on the cheek. "Anyway, your mother's here. You know what that means. Show time."

Sherry walks over to us, arms spread wide. Unlike her daughter, Sherry attends every single book club, even if she hasn't read the book, which is often the case because she isn't that much of a reader. She's too busy being the unofficial mayor of Donovan Grove to do much reading.

"What a beautiful book," Sherry says, surprising both Anna and me. "I devoured it." She hugs Anna first, then me. "But I'll keep my other comments for later."

"Do you know who that is?" Anna asks Sherry, discreetly pointing her chin in the direction of the woman neither of us know.

"Not yet," Sherry says, and bounds over to the woman,

much in the way Chico hurries to Hemingway's side when he first clasps eyes on him in the morning.

"We'll soon find out," I say to Anna. "Sherry's on it." Then the door of the store opens and Janet, Jamie, and Cynthia walk in together.

"I didn't know Jamie was coming. Isn't book club for women only?" Anna says.

"Of course not. What kind of club would that be, if we excluded men? Not many turn up, but they're most certainly welcome."

"Next you'll tell me Sean—" Just as Anna says his name, as if summoned, Sean opens the door. He's followed by his wife Cathy. I made an executive decision not to tell Anna that all her friends and family were coming tonight; I didn't want to stress her out more than she would already be. She might not have turned up.

"Sean has read this book?" is all she says, her eyebrows arched all the way up.

"Of course he has." I'm surprised he hasn't told Anna—or maybe he had the same thought I had, about keeping it from her. Sometimes, it's simply easier to not give her all the details of an event beforehand. "Otherwise he wouldn't be here." I pull Anna close. "He's your best friend, babe."

"I didn't think this was going to be so focused on me," she says.

"It's not," I assure her. "It's about the book."

"Yeah, right." She narrows her eyes. "The biggest surprise would be if my dad turned up."

"I think that would be one step too far, for you as well as him." We both chuckle.

"He's probably making a birdhouse," Anna says, as though, she too, would rather be in her painting studio right now. That's usually where I find her when I come back from book club.

"Shall we start?" I look her in the eye.

She nods. While I beckon everyone to the table we've set up, I notice Sherry is still in conversation with the mystery woman —Sherry seems to be doing most of the talking. They head to the table and take a seat.

Drinks are poured and I welcome everyone to tonight's book club. I hold up the book we're here to discuss: *No Stranger to the Dark* by Marion Webster-Welsh.

Anna read it first and as soon as she told me I should read it too, I understood why. Not only because it's written in the kind of language with never-ending, page-long sentences that Anna likes so much, but also because the protagonist is a woman coming to terms with a later-in-life Autism Spectrum Disorder diagnosis.

When I suggested the book for the Bookends book club, Anna thought it was a good idea, because anything that increases awareness of something that can be so invisible in women is worth supporting. She only balked when I asked her to join us for this particular book club. Nevertheless, here she is, sitting next to me. Because it's important to her. She may think she's doing this for me, but I'm actually doing this for her.

In the discussion that follows, it's difficult to keep Sherry from speaking all the time, until Jamie gives her a look that he must have given his mother many a time, and she takes it down a notch. But Sherry being so vocal about this book is her way of showing how much she loves her daughter, how proud she is of Anna, so it's not something I can hold against her.

"It was such an eye-opener," Janet says. Because of my friendship with her, she and Anna have grown closer over the years. They've both made an effort to approach each other. "Wiley goes through so much below the surface and no one ever knows."

"I don't think that's the point of the book at all," Anna says.

Despite their increased closeness, she and Janet disagree on many topics. Their taste in everything—from clothes, to wine, and movies—is vastly different and they're both, in their own way, incredibly opinionated.

"You're saying the point of this book is not to open the reader's eye to how Wiley has suffered?" Janet asks.

"Not the *main* point. The main point is the story," Anna says. I know the inflections in her voice so well. I know it will take her time to find her footing in this conversation, just as well as I know that she will never convince Janet of her point. But that's not the goal of this book club. The only goal is to have a chat about a book.

"I have to disagree with you there, Anna," Janet says, keeping her tone respectful. She and I try to make it to Cathy's Friday night Pilates class every week, while Anna's out with Sean and Jamie. Afterward, we often end up at Lenny's, much to Anna's dismay at first, but she has adapted to that, too. "Because what's the difference between what I mean by 'the book' and what you mean by 'the story'?"

This is not going to be a question that Anna will be able to answer just like that, although the reply might very well be already formed in her mind. I know from experience this is the kind of question she needs to take her time with. But I don't step in for her—I don't reply for her. I do find Janet's gaze and we exchange a glance that lingers long enough for her to get it, to give Anna the time she needs.

"If you put it like that," Anna says, "they're the same, but what I'm trying to say is that the main point of the book is not to make us feel sorry for Wiley, but to take us on the journey with her."

"I didn't say I felt sorry for her," Janet says. "But I could feel her pain."

Next to me, I hear Anna sigh. "Okay," she says, nipping in the bud what could quickly spiral into a stubborn argument on semantics—one of Anna and Janet's favorite ways of butting heads.

"I agree that the book was an eye-opener," Sean says, cutting Janet off from making a further comment. "I understand neurodiverse people better now." I see him shoot Anna a furtive glance. Anna had been in therapy for over a year before she told Sean about being on the Autism spectrum. "Which is very helpful."

Cynthia concurs, and the conversation livens up and I tune out for a few moments to lean back and get a good look at Anna, who is listening intently, trying to absorb every word that is said here tonight. Tomorrow, she'll be exhausted, but that's all right, because I'll be there for her to help her relax.

19

ANNA

I ONLY HAVE to visualize the T-shirt Zoe's wearing underneath her blouse, for moral support, a few times during the course of the evening. It's the one I had made for her when we'd just got together, that I had to keep at my house because she didn't want to get it mixed up with Brooklyn's laundry. The one that says *Queen of Licking Pussy.*

Since then, it has evolved from a private joke between us to a lucky garment that Zoe wears when I need an extra boost to do something.

"I'll wear my T-shirt," she says, and I always know which one she means, because Zoe's not a woman who owns a lot of T-shirts. I always know exactly what she means to say as well. That she's there for me—as if I didn't know that already. As if she doesn't show me a million times every single day.

"Good book club," Zoe says, now. "Thank you all for coming. Feel free to stick around for some more wine and a chat."

Chairs scrape against the floor and a buzz of murmurs starts up.

"Well done, babe," Zoe says, and kisses me on the cheek.

"I really didn't do that much."

"Of course you did," she says.

Then my mother is standing next to me, accompanied by the mystery woman. She didn't speak during the discussion about the book but I could tell she was very interested in what was being said.

"Anna, this is Jenny," Mom says.

"Hi, Jenny." I hold out my hand and Jenny shakes it briefly.

"I'll let you talk," my mother says, completely against expectations.

Then it's just me and Jenny at this side of the table, because Zoe has turned away from me to chat with Janet.

"Did you enjoy book club?" I ask.

"Yes, um, I follow Bookends on Facebook and when I saw which book was being discussed at tonight's book club, I just had to come. I mean, it was hard to make it here, to find the courage to actually come in, but I'm glad I did."

I nod my understanding. "I almost didn't make it myself." I send Jenny a smile.

"I really appreciate you speaking up," she says. "It's hard to express why exactly, but it really means a lot to me."

"I appreciate you saying that." These days, I can actually see the funny side of two neurodiverse women in a stilted conversation like this. What I can also see, however, is the energy it must have taken Jenny to come here tonight. I recognize it easily, because I know exactly how she feels.

A short silence falls, and I've learned to be okay with that. Even though I haven't been in therapy for a while, I can still hear my therapist's voice in my head at times like these. "Not every silence exists to be filled," April's voice whispers in my ear now.

"It's good to not feel so alone once in a while," Jenny says.

I nod.

"It's important, I mean," she says. "I didn't use to think that it was, but I see things differently now."

Old Anna, the person I was before I met Zoe, the woman who had resigned herself to a life of strict routines and a set number of relationships, would end the conversation there and then. But I know what opening up about having ASD has done for me, even though, I too, believed it wasn't necessary at first. I always considered myself too non-verbal for therapy, until Jamie dragged me to see April. I was always convinced I wouldn't tell anyone outside my family about my ASD. But then I told Sean and Cathy, and the relief of it was so inexplicably overwhelming, I felt like shouting it from the rooftops for a while.

"My partner, Zoe, owns Bookends," I say. "Would you like to stop by another time? When it's quieter and we can have a proper chat?"

Jenny nods. "I would love that."

"Here's my card." I fish my wallet out of my pocket and hand her a business card. "It's a bit faded. I don't use these very often. But my email address is on there. Let me know when you'd like to meet up."

"Thanks." Jenny meets my gaze for an instant.

It's in the very short moment that passes between us that I think I finally understand what Janet means when she talks about her second mountain.

"You'll hear from me soon," she says.

"Would you like a glass of wine?" I give Jenny my widest smile.

"I'd better get back. I'm driving."

We say our goodbyes and as I stand there basking in the dim glow of having met another woman with ASD, Zoe walks up to me.

"Were you chatting up another woman?" she asks. The smile in her eyes tells me that she's joking.

"I most certainly was." I look at her fully buttoned up blouse. "You must be so warm in that."

"No hot flashes today, babe," she says.

"Maybe you should let your blouse hang loose," I offer.

"If you want your mother to have a heart attack." Zoe grins.

Janet joins us, followed by Cynthia, who's holding a bottle of wine and refills our glasses. The three of them do their conversation thing. I've talked enough for one evening.

As Cynthia tilts her glass to her lips, I spot the diamond ring she wears these days. She and John are getting married in a few months' time. After I apologized to her for being the impossible person I was at the end of our relationship, and took full responsibility for its break down, she has become as close to a female friend as I'll ever have.

I have more of a love-hate relationship with Janet, who quickly assumed the role of Zoe's best friend in Donovan Grove. After Brooklyn left for college, and I asked Zoe to move in with me, Janet had the most annoying habit of coming to our house unannounced for a chat with Zoe. It might very well have been what she used to do when Zoe still lived above Bookends, but Zoe isn't living there anymore. Zoe lives with me, in my house—our house now—and unannounced guests are the stuff my nightmares are made of. This caused a bit of friction between us, until Zoe sorted it, the way she does. She explained it to Janet in a short, matter-of-fact conversation, and that was that.

"I do understand what you were trying to say, Anna," Janet says to me now. "Earlier, during the discussion."

I don't doubt that she does. She's married to my brother, after all. Jamie knows better than anyone that all I want is to be treated like everyone else and that the very last thing I want from anyone is pity. "I know that you do, Janet." My phone buzzes in my back pocket. I take it out, half-expecting it to be

Jenny, saying something via text that she couldn't express earlier. But it's a message from Brooklyn.

Good luck tonight! it says, accompanied by a picture of her and Jaden. I show Janet the picture of her son and Zoe's daughter.

"Excellent timing." Janet smiles at me.

"They're on college time, I guess."

"Is that Brooklyn?" Zoe asks.

I show her the picture and the message and I see her gaze go all gooey at the sight of her daughter. Even though I always thought I'd never share a house with another person, I asked Zoe to move in with me after Brooklyn left for college. The thought of her sitting in an empty apartment late at night was more appalling to me than having her take over part of my house.

"It's the thought that counts." Zoe curls an arm around my waist and draws me near.

20

ZOE

On Sunday afternoon, after lunch at Anna's parents, we open the sliding kitchen doors, and sit outside, in the red Adirondack chairs that have been in Anna's backyard for as long as I can remember.

Chico chases after Hemingway, his short legs no match for the speed Hemingway can achieve when he puts his mind to it —or just wants Chico to leave him alone.

We sit in silence for a while. Being with Anna has taught me to appreciate silence. Living in this house with her has brought me a kind of peacefulness I've never previously experienced. I've gotten used to following the slower rhythm of Anna's days, to taking the time to process emotions like she does, to relish in the kind of routine which I always believed could only end in a rut. Or maybe I'm just getting older and I want different things from my life these days.

"Eve texted me," I say, after a while. As much as I've learned to enjoy silence, I will always enjoy a conversation more. "She has asked us and Brooklyn and Jaden to dinner."

"Hm," Anna grunts, pauses, then asks, "When?"

"Whenever suits us."

"I'll have to check my calendar," Anna says, as though her weekends are always jam-packed with social activities and it might be hard to find a day that she's free.

"Let me know and I'll set it up." I reach over to her and put my hand on her arm.

"When you and mom were in the kitchen," Anna says, "Jeremy asked if I could teach him how to paint."

"Really?" Jeremy reminds me of Anna, and her father, so much. "What did you say?"

"I said yes because I don't think he'll need much teaching." She looks at me. "You've seen his drawings. The kid is crazy talented."

"He comes from a talented family." I give her arm a squeeze.

Anna, still utterly unable to take a compliment, shrugs off my comment. "It'll be different than with Brooklyn. She's also talented, but in another way. She needs more guidance. All Jeremy really needs is some supplies and a space to paint."

"He can use Brooklyn's studio."

Anna shakes her head vehemently. "No way. I can't let him invade Brooklyn's space."

"She really won't mind." I wish she were here to mind, though.

"Jeremy will mind. He needs his own space in his own home. I'll help him set it up."

Hemingway and Chico run toward us. Hemingway, forever loyal to Anna, puts his head in her lap immediately, waiting for Anna's hand in his fur.

Chico tries to jump into my lap, but no matter how hard he tries—and he does, every single day—his legs are too short to bridge the distance. I pick him up so he can sit in my lap.

"Hello, my Chico baby," I say, in the voice I used when Brooklyn was little.

"You should really stick with one name," Anna says. "He only has a tiny sausage dog brain. It's confusing for him."

"I'll have you know that sausage dogs are highly intelligent. Aren't you, my little darling?" Chico perks up his ears as though he knows we're talking about him. I give him a good scratch behind his ears. "Who loves you the most?" I ask him, because this question he can reply to—in a way that is most pleasing to his human.

He tilts his head and gives me the most adorable look, his eyes moist with love for me.

"You and that dog," Anna says.

"You're no better with Hemingway," I argue.

"Of course I am. I don't tell Hemingway how much I love him every time I see him."

"Maybe not in words." Hemingway still has his head in her lap and Anna rubs him softly between the ears. "I'm just more verbal."

"Tell me about it." Anna turns to me and smiles.

"You don't regret inviting us to move in with you?" I wouldn't ask her on this lovely Sunday afternoon if I wasn't sure of the answer. It's just nice to hear her—to *make* her—say it once in a while.

"Sometimes," Anna says, which is not what she usually says. "When I so obviously have to fight with Shadow for your love." Her smile turns into a broad grin.

"I have plenty of love for the both of you." I smile back at her. I pick up Chico, get up, and put him down in my chair. I stand in front of Anna's chair, my hands on the armrests. "Would you like me to prove that to you?"

"Not in front of the children, babe." Anna shifts forward and grabs me by the collar of my blouse.

Before I kiss her, I pause, and look her in the eye. "I love you."

"Do you love me the most, though?" The skin around her eyes crinkles with mischief.

"I'm feeling suddenly less verbal." I lean in and kiss her on the lips. Hemingway scurries off. I lower myself into Anna's lap and kiss her again and again.

"It's good to leave some words unspoken between us," Anna says, with the small amount of breath she can manage. "We have forever to say them."

AUTHOR'S NOTE

Dear Reader,

Throughout writing this book, I debated whether I should ever disclose that I have Autism Spectrum Disorder. At first, I thought I should never tell anyone at all (apart from my wife). But because this book took me so many months to write and my own process of acceptance has gone through various stages at a pretty swift speed, I *have* decided to disclose that I have Autism. Not just for the sake of doing so, but because of representation.

Being a lesbian, I already knew how vitally important representation is. I know it even more now for the very simple reason that if another woman hadn't been open about *her* Autism, I would maybe never have known about my own.

Until recently, I had no idea. Not the slightest inkling. It never occurred to me that I might be on the spectrum. Even though, these days, after the proverbial penny finally dropped, it couldn't be more clear to me that I am. All because another woman talked about it. She didn't talk about it because she was brave or courageous or anything like that. She talked about it because that's simply who she is. But in doing so, she changed my life.

As Anna's therapist says in the book, "Knowing who you are is a great gift." It has been a great gift to me to learn this about myself because it has explained so many things about me and my behaviour that were previously utterly inexplicable.

Even though it's not about the same characters at all, for me, this book is the 'spiritual sequel' to *At the Water's Edge*. The writing process of the two books was very similar because I had to dig deep and push away a lot of shame and guilt in order to get the words out.

At times, it was so hard that I wondered whether I was doing the right thing, but then it dawned on me that it might just be so difficult *because* it was the right thing to do.

I will always be an author who puts a lot of herself in her work. It's how I roll, because writing—and writing alone—allows me a vulnerability I can't reach in any other aspect of my life. It's the closest to truly expressing myself that I can ever come, therefore my fiction will always contain a little piece of my soul, even though it remains fiction. But fiction is quite magical like that.

Writing this book has changed me. I might have known that I was on the spectrum when I started writing it, but I was by no means accepting it. In some sort of meta turn of events, I wrote the scene where Anna visits her therapist for the first time to convince myself to do the same. I basically wrote myself into seeking out my own therapist. And it worked. But I'm not sure I could have done it without having Anna go through it first.

I'm also not claiming that writing *Two Hearts* has magically made me accept myself—fiction might be a touch magical, but it does have its limits. But I now realise much more than before that writing is my refuge. It's where I make sense of a world that is often quite hard for me to comprehend. It's *my thing,* to put it quite simply. My saving grace. Some days, it's my superpower; other days, I never want to do it again, although I always do. But what I've come to realise is how incredibly lucky I am that I get to do this. For me, writing is the most perfect job to suit my neurodiverse brain. Thanks to you, I get to do it for a living.

Not every neurodiverse woman is as fortunate as I am—quite the opposite, in fact. I've read so many books written by women with Autism and some of them I just couldn't finish because they were too depressing. There's so much doom and gloom about the subject, which I do understand, but I wanted to create a different voice. I wanted to inject humour and hope into my book. Because it is possible to find happiness, no matter how your brain is wired.

I've had a lot of emotional hardship in my life. I've never fitted in anywhere. I've always felt like the odd one out. I've always struggled to make and keep friends. I've always been half-paralysed by anxiety. But throughout all of that, I've also managed to have a good life, meet so many lovely people, and experience some truly amazing stuff. One does not have to exclude the other.

The one thing that has always helped is knowing and sharing (and having a few laughs along the way).

Now that I know, I had to share.

Thank you for reading. It means so much more than I can ever say.

Harper xo

ABOUT THE AUTHOR

Harper Bliss is a best-selling lesbian romance author. Among her most-loved books are the highly dramatic French Kissing and the often thought-provoking Pink Bean series.

Harper lived in Hong Kong for 7 years, travelled the world for a bit, and has now settled in Brussels (Belgium) with her wife and photogenic cat, Dolly Purrton.

Together with her wife, she hosts a weekly podcast called Harper Bliss & Her Mrs.

Harper loves hearing from readers and you can reach her at the email address below.

www.harperbliss.com
harper@harperbliss.com

Printed in Great Britain
by Amazon

43752988R10212